About the author

Clive Maddison is married to Samantha and has two adult children, Leanne and Joe. Serving an apprenticeship with a business in the East Midlands from 1980-84, he worked for the company for sixteen years. In 1996 the family relocated to South Devon, where Clive became self-employed. Writing has become one of many pastimes that he has enjoyed over the years, ranging from walking and cycling to musical instrument and model making.

CAUGHT

Clive Maddison

CAUGHT

Vanguard Press

VANGUARD PAPERBACK

© Copyright 2010
Clive Maddison

A CIP catalogue record for this title is
available from the British Library.

ISBN 978 1 843866 367

*Vanguard Press is an imprint of
Pegasus Elliot MacKenzie Publishers Ltd.*
www.pegasuspublishers.com

First Published in 2010

**Vanguard Press
Sheraton House Castle Park
Cambridge England**

Printed & Bound in Great Britain

Dedicated to my two wonderful children, Leanne and Joe. I love you and I'm very proud of you both.

Acknowledgements

Elizabeth Adamson for generously giving her time and help in shaping the first draft of this book.

Cherrill Evans for her skilful observation and professional approach. With honest assessment, encouragement and the willingness to help this project succeed, she has demonstrated the support of a true friend and helped turn a first attempt into a better work than it would otherwise have been.

Michaĺ Kogut for his time, comments and encouragement whilst reading the final draft.

My darling wife Samantha, the love of my life.

PROLOGUE

There are times when a life can present situations that during, and even after the event, you cannot exactly remember where they began or why they occurred. Some situations seem to be connected to a deliberate choice and others appear to happen purely by chance, or some bewildering mixture of the two. Some circumstances parade themselves like a predetermined path a person was always destined to follow. Others are a total mystery. Why you and why that path? Whatever the reasons, the events that unfold have connected consequences attached to every move, a little like a game of chess in which we are all pieces. A valued piece is lost because a decision was made without knowing the full facts, or by what seems to be nothing more than a chance mistake. Your piece was in the wrong place at the wrong time. These consequences can trigger other events, in a snowball effect, gradually taking on a life of their own until you wonder if it is ever possible to stop, or reverse them, or even if you have any control at all.

The tale I am about to tell is written with the help of those immediately involved. It contains both the best and the worst events of my life so far. The worst, as my relationship with those who really cared about me suffered and I suffered at the hands of those who simply didn't care. The best, as the relationships with those who cared were shown for the resilience and strength they contained. The profound love that was displayed by people who could easily have given up on me has had a lasting impact on my life.

I am ashamed of the path I decided to take and the cost it exacted on me, but also on many others around me. If I could erase the whole series of events I would do so without hesitation for the sake of the pain it caused. However, hindsight is a wonderful thing and is frequently possessed, in copious amounts, by those who think they have great insight, usually when it no longer serves any purpose. Having said that I would erase what happened, I am also aware of what now exists. I struggle to think of how rewriting the past might change the present. Would we each be the person we are if it were not for the good and bad experiences that we have lived through? Would removing some of those experiences change our view of life as a whole? It is easy to say, 'If I had only known then what I know now,' but you didn't and cannot know what you need in advance of the experience that will teach you. The reason you know now is often because of then.

When we are warned about things that we have not experienced the information is theoretical, carrying no emotional check in our consciousness. Having lived through an experience it becomes part of the essence of our being, having impact thereafter, if we will allow it.

Although this is a journey I wish I had never taken, I am glad I survived. My regret is that I was not the only one who suffered from these events and that my pride and arrogance prolonged their existence beyond any necessary span of time.

You will see that while the majority of this story is from my perspective, it begins with the view through my father's eyes, along with a contribution from my brother, who I wounded so very deeply.

CHAPTER 1

PETER

"What exactly do you mean by that?" he shouted as he entered the room. He pushed the study door with such raging force it was as if he was attempting to tear it from its hinges. There was a loud bang as the handle partly embedded in the wall, bringing the door to an abrupt, jolting stop. "I said, what exactly do you mean by that?" he repeated his demand for an answer. The threatening tone of his voice was deadly serious and more hostile than I had ever heard before.

"What are you talking about, Andy?" I asked, hoping to move him to reason and away from confrontation. I had always been a confident, often forceful, person. Having built a substantial business, I was used to dealing with all kinds of situations. However, this was out of the blue and I didn't quite know how to respond to the aggressive verbal challenge from my youngest son.

He held up a piece of paper which immediately familiar to me. I braced myself for what was in store.

It was the letter I'd written to him about his recent behaviour, suggesting that it would be appreciated if he were to show some respect while he remained in my house. It was obvious that the comments I had made caused this ferocious reaction from Andy. I wasn't willing to back down in my own house though, not in the face of such a provocative challenge. It wasn't unreasonable to demand a certain level of behaviour which considered everyone else. The atmosphere was completely changed when he was in a mood. Everyone had to taste some of his displeasure and I didn't know how to react, or approach him anymore. I spent much of my time at home walking on eggshells, as though something was always simmering, waiting to boil over. The constant feeling of being on edge, with the pervading mood that would permeate through the whole building, was wearing. He prowled around the house as though it was his domain and watch out anyone who dared to question what he was doing. For too long his elder brother and I had been tiptoeing around, trying not to wake the sleeping volcano in case it erupted, but now it had.

He stood defiantly, filling the doorway with his muscular frame. At that particular moment he looked menacing, masking his handsome face as he scowled at me. He took after his mother in looks much more than he did after me. His eyes reminded me of her features; a beautiful blue-grey colour that almost looked metallic. Standing two inches taller than me, at six feet, with an athletic frame, he looked quite impressive, but in the mood that enveloped him, what was impressive became intimidating.

As he waited in the doorway, like a guard commanding all freedoms, his posture demanded an answer to the abrupt question he had posed, no longer with words, but with a look that was close to hatred etched on his face. The beautiful reminders of my wife's countenance were lost in the mist of his seething anger. I didn't know how to respond to him in a way that would reduce the hostility, rather than inflame the situation even further.

I remembered when he was a little boy, what a joy he was, full of fun and laughter. Always there wanting to play or spend time with me. How sweet those memories of fatherhood are, but how they can momentarily fade in the face of constant friction.

I tried to pinpoint the time when things began to change, but couldn't bring to mind a clear moment when Andy moved from being the charming boy he once was to the angry man that now ruled his life. There was certainly no doubt a change had taken place. The friction that existed in the house was testament to the fact. Was it possible that I was the cause of such hostility? That question had frequently crossed my mind, causing me to examine the decisions and actions that I'd taken over the years. If I did provoke this rage that had been growing in him, I was unaware of the reason why. He sometimes seemed like a chained animal waiting for the slightest opportunity to lunge at anyone who came within its domain. That opportunity appeared to have arisen and now I would have to deal with the consequences.

"Young man, I don't..."

"Don't you 'young man' me!" he exclaimed, as he took a few steps forward. "I'm twenty-one years old and quite capable of choosing the life I want to live, without reference to you or anyone else! You can be so patronising, the way you talk down to me. I'm a grown man. An adult!" His manner was threatening. The gauntlet was being thrown down.

I was going to get up from my desk and go to him, but looking at the threatening expression on his face, I was thankful for the barrier the desk created between us.

The temptation to raise my voice and make comment about his behaviour over the past few years was immense. I knew I needed to resist as I sensed that there was something much more unpredictable in him than I had ever seen before.

"What do you mean by writing this rubbish?" he demanded, throwing down the letter in front of me.

The friction in our relationship had reached a climax and I found it impossible to talk to him without the difficulty of emotions getting in the way, so I decided to write the letter. I left it in his room, thinking he might mull over what it contained. I hoped it would open the way for us to take some time to talk.

The handwritten note now lay on the desk in front of me with Andy looming over to get the answers he wanted.

I had started the letter as softly as I knew how, 'From your father, who loves you very much,' but those sentiments had been shrugged off for a long time by the young man that stood before me. I simply thought it might be easier, for both of us, to try and express my feelings in writing, rather than risk another confrontation that ended without resolution. It appeared I was wrong.

"The father who loves me!" he sneered. "Loves me? When? When it suits *you*, that's when! What about what I want? What about my choices? My life?"

Andy thumped his fist on the desktop, to emphasise each of his abrupt questions, causing all that decorated its surface to rattle at the shock. I had never, in the twenty-one years since he was born, known him to be so absolute in his rejection of my sentiments. He dismissed them as though they were something to be cast into a rubbish bin. What could I say to him that would defuse the situation?

I had pondered over that letter for days and nights on end, trying to make sure that it would express my love, whilst still getting my point across about his behaviour. It appeared that the soul-searching work I had done was in vain. I couldn't help thinking that someone must have re-written it in order to destroy what was left of our strained relationship, but I could see the familiar curling handwriting betraying the fact that what had been read, I had written. What had I said that was so bad; bad enough to cause a reaction like this?

"I've worked for you for years. For what? You treat me like some kind of servant!" he shouted. Grabbing the letter in his fist, as though he was about to screw it into a ball to throw at me, he turned on his heel and walked over to the window. "I shouldn't be here," he said quietly, as though there was no one but him in the room.

I watched him standing only feet away from me, but seeming like it was miles, and I was lost about what to do while he stood motionless, looking out along the driveway. I was grasping at the memories of the good times we had shared together, the birthday celebrations and family gatherings, trying to convince myself that they did happen and that they would again.

When people face a life-threatening situation they will say that their life flashed before their eyes, but in this case, it was his life that flashed before mine. Perhaps this is a death-like experience to a parent; not the risk of losing one's life, but the relationship with a child. The hurt was overpowering, crushing. It felt as though years were being added to my frame as I watched him, not knowing how to re-establish a bond that had now eroded away.

The initial explosion was gone, but there was no mistaking the atmosphere of hostility, like an impenetrable barrier holding us apart. How to break through the wall that divided us was beyond my understanding at that moment.

I had worked hard for years to build something good for my family, the long hours through the hard times until the business was established enough to provide a good living. A very good living indeed. Perhaps I had neglected my sons through that period, sowing the seed that was beginning to bear fruit.

Andy continued to stare through the window, observing something happening out in the courtyard. My thoughts were moving wildly, from past to present, until Andy quietly interrupted them.

"I always tried, but I never could measure up to him, could I?"

It took me a moment to comprehend the question as his tone of resignation distracted me. It was as if it had been spoken way off in the distance, taking time to travel to me before I could hear properly what had been said. At first I was not sure whether

Andy actually wanted me to give an answer, but the silence was painful, so I queried, "What do you mean, Andy? Who... Who could you never live up to?" He had been standing motionless at the window for what seemed a long time, but my question brought him immediately back to life and he whirled around to glare at me.

"Him," he said, as he tossed his head back toward the window, "the eldest. That's how you always introduce him when we have guests, 'and here is my eldest.' It's like you're exceptionally proud of him. You want to show everyone that you are, even me. It comes out in your body language and the tone of your voice. *My eldest.*" He mocked the way he saw me behave. "Well I exist too you know. I've achieved things too. Not that you ever take any notice, being far too busy with your eldest!"

"Andy, of course I am proud of..." I started to explain.

"Yeah, yeah, whatever! How did you put it in your letter? 'I just want the best for you and for you to be the best you can be, *LIKE YOUR BROTHER!*'"

He spat the last few words out with such venom it shocked me. I felt my anger rising and struggled to keep my composure.

"I didn't mean to give the impression that I'm comparing you to your brother."

"Comparing!" he exclaimed. "How can I compare to him? Mr Perfect!"

There were sounds coming from the hallway that announced the presence of someone coming into the house as the front door closed. The voice of Carl, Andy's brother, could be heard faintly drifting toward the study, followed by a rhythmic click tapped out by heels on the wooden floor as he approached. There was a sharp knock on the door as Carl immediately stepped into the room.

"Hi Dad, do you have a minute? I wanted to... oh, Andy, sorry, I didn't realise you were here."

"Well that's quite appropriate isn't it," Andy snapped, throwing a knowing look of disgust in my direction. He turned on his heel to head out the door.

"Please, Andy. Wait a minute!" I tried to prevent him leaving and jumped up from behind my desk to go after him. It was no use. He was into the hallway and gave no indication that he had any intention of stopping. I followed to the study door, getting there just in time to see him disappear through the archway to the kitchen area. I turned back to give a word of explanation to Carl, but the noise of a door slamming stopped me before I could speak. It gave an abrupt reminder of the anger that had been expressed seconds earlier.

The silence was exaggerated all the more by the raised voices that preceded it. I hoped in vain the silent world would not be broken, almost willing Carl not to say anything, but I knew he wouldn't stay quiet for long.

"Dad," Carl said, "what's happening now?"

It was a simple and fair question, but answering it was not such an easy task. I didn't really understand what was going on myself. I went back to my desk and sat down as I tried to think of what to say. In truth I didn't want to say anything, not at that moment anyway, but it was not as though I could dismiss the situation as trivial, Carl had more about him than to believe that.

"Dad?" Carl gently pressed.

"Carl, I have always tried to do my best for both you and Andy. I love you both... but I don't know how to connect with Andy anymore. He's so distant. I'm afraid that he blames me for many things..."

"What do you mean, blames you for many things?" Carl interrupted, a little irritated that Andy could have left me with that impression. "What could *he* have to blame *you* for?"

I stared at Carl for what seemed to be a long time and could see the little boy who had grown into a fine young man, with so much promise for his future still hidden in his adult features. He was actively involved in the family business. He held a senior position with much responsibility. At twenty-six he was five years older than his brother and I wondered if that had made my treatment of the two boys seem so different to Andy. Perhaps I had treated Carl like a man, while continuing to treat Andy like he was still a boy. It was a dilemma that I faced as a parent, probably common to all parents; wanting the eldest to achieve their ambitions and become successful, but when the youngest reached the age of adulthood, not wanting to lose the children they were.

I realised that Carl was still looking at me, waiting for his question to be answered, but I wondered what I should say to him that wouldn't cause even more difficulty than already existed. The last thing I wanted to do was create a wider division between my sons than was already beginning to surface. If Carl took sides with me against Andy it would only make matters worse. I had to be truthful though or Carl would see straight through it.

"For comparing him to you," I said hesitantly.

Carl's questioning expression turned to one of incredulity, but he resisted the temptation to speak his mind. I couldn't mistake what he thought as it was displayed quite plainly in his expression.

The quiet was suddenly shattered by another loud bang as the front door slammed shut. I jumped up from my desk and went to the same window Andy had been standing at only minutes before watching Carl as he arrived. Andy threw a travel bag into the boot of his car, but before I could do anything he was in the vehicle, reversing out of the old stable parking bay at speed. The mood of the driver was clearly visible in the behaviour of the car as it accelerated across the courtyard and down the gravel driveway, spitting stones from the tyres. Since I bought him that car, for his eighteenth birthday, he had never allowed anyone else to drive it in case they didn't look after it like he did, but he took off at such a pace it was obvious that he was still simmering with anger.

I watched as he reached the end of the driveway, turning right onto the main road toward the town. I followed the progress of his car through the leafless trees until it disappeared from view. The quietness in my study hid the fact that the room was still occupied. I turned a little to glance back over my shoulder as I sensed the closeness of Carl, who had moved to stand right behind me.

"Don't worry Dad. You know he has a temper. It seems he has developed a habit of exercising it lately. He usually goes moody and quiet and locks himself away somewhere until he's got it off his chest. I'm sure he'll come back when he's cooled off a bit."

I turned to look directly at Carl to voice what was concerning me. "Will he? Will he come back?"

I went to my desk and sat down in the large leather chair that creaked in such a familiar way.

"I remember when we first moved into this house," I looked around the study as if going back in time to the cherished memory. "I bought this desk and chair on the very first day. You must have been three or four years old..."

"Four," Carl corrected.

"Four? Yes, four years old." I momentarily pondered the memories of that time, until I noticed Carl waiting for me to continue. "When Andy was a toddler, he loved to climb into this chair and pretend to be working at my desk. I suppose to him it was working – colouring. If he wasn't sitting on me while I was in the chair, he was in it the moment I moved. How time moves quickly on, like a breath of wind it passes and then suddenly you're faced with the unpleasantness of conflict that never seemed to exist with young children. It did, of course, but in a different way. Letting children grow into independent adults is not as simple as it might seem. Knowing when to intervene and

23

when not to is a skill that comes only with experience. At this precise moment I'm not sure that I have done such a great job."

"Dad," Carl said trying to break into the little world I was occupying as I searched the insecurities of parenthood through the shadows of distant memories. I wasn't really talking to him so much as to myself.

"Dad, you did a great job of raising us. Don't doubt yourself now just because of a little disagreement." I re-focused on Carl to see him pause for a few moments as he appeared to weigh-up the wisdom of continuing, then added, "Mum would have been proud of you."

He fixed his stare with mine.

I glanced down at the beautifully framed picture that took pride of place on the large oak desk. The image of a pretty young lady with beautiful blue-grey eyes and chestnut-brown hair smiled back at me. She stood looking carefree, surrounded by the autumn colours of the trees of Blandswick Park. I didn't know what she would think of me. As time passed, the memories that I once held so dear seemed to be slipping from my grasp. What did she like? What would she say, or do, if she had been here? Carl left me drifting in my thoughts for a little while, aware that I was on an internal journey to some destination he could not imagine, but, as with all silences, the first interruption seemed awkward.

"What did you mean when you said Andy blames you for comparing him to me?" he asked

"Oh, Carl, I'm sorry. I wasn't thinking..." I said apologetically.

"No, Dad, it's okay. What did you mean?"

Carl caught my eye, holding his stare purposefully. He was intent on getting an answer to his question, but not willing to be forceful as he noticed my vulnerability. He was a gentleman, but had a determination that helped him achieve his purpose, without the need to crush someone else in the process.

Andy outgrew Carl in height while he was still a teenager and in most sport, or physical activities, was much better. That never seemed to faze Carl, always sure of the outcome before they even began a match. Carl had an inner confidence that made him aware of his place in life and didn't need to put someone else down in order to better himself. 'At ease' is the way I would describe him. He had the ability to grow, as nature causes a tree to grow little by little, almost unnoticed, until one day you look and there before you is the mature article.

This became evident when he had only just turned twenty-three. A situation arose at the company that required delicate negotiation to resolve.

On the day in question I had stayed at home due to an ongoing illness, but was confident that Carl could handle the normal 'run of the mill' business. However, an unforeseen situation arose which required delicate, diplomatic handling. He refused to allow senior staff to disturb me at home and dealt with the whole situation, standing up to the challenge admirably. When I returned to the office the following week, I had no idea what had happened until one of my colleagues filled me in. Carl had not uttered a single word about the incident. When I broached the subject with him, he simply said that he had been put in a place of responsibility and that all he had done was exercise his judgement as he believed I would have wanted him to. From that moment on, Carl had gained the respect of my most senior staff and began having a greater involvement in the running of the company. I was more than happy to allow it. It's easy to throw authority around and force the conclusion of a matter based on what the person with the most power wants, but that often leaves buried issues that simmer under the surface long after the resolution. The touch that respects people is a rare one indeed, but is to be much admired.

Perhaps it was in the relaying of that kind of incident to Andy that caused him to believe that I was always comparing him to Carl. That was not my intention at all. I simply wanted Andy to share in the family success. I knew Andy had a competitive streak, but I never thought that it was so strong as to initiate jealousy in the face of the success of his brother. After all, we had celebrated Andy's achievements in the sporting arena together. The day he broke the school record for the one hundred metre sprint was one of those moments that stay in my memory like an image etched in glass.

Carl was still waiting patiently for me to clarify what had happened between me and Andy. I had left him too long while I worked through the muddled thoughts that plagued me.

"I wrote Andy a letter about a number of issues," I began. "I felt it might be better than trying to talk directly to him because I would have time to think about what to say...and how to say it. I mentioned you at one point, nothing very specific, but he took exception to my comment. Just before you arrived, he stormed in here demanding to know what I meant. He thought I was simply comparing him to you, which was never my intention. I have always loved you both equally. It's true that our relationship has been a little strained recently, but I fear it may be deeper than even I suspected. I don't know what to do to try to heal the breach. I thought a letter could be a gentle way forward, but I am not sure whether he actually read all of it."

"Look, Dad," Carl began, as he came around the desk and crouched at the side of me, "I will go to see if I can find Andy and talk to him. Maybe I can help calm the situation so that we can talk again like we did a little while ago. He has been unusually difficult lately, but I'm sure there is nothing to worry about."

Carl stood up and put his hand on my shoulder as a sign of assurance, then turned and headed for the office door. He paused in the doorway for a moment and looked back as if he were about to say something else, but hesitated as if thinking better of it.

"I'll be back later, Dad."

I listened to the click of his heels along the hallway, followed by the closing of the front door. The house was suddenly very quiet, very empty. I was alone.

CHAPTER 2

Although my mind was filled with all that had happened recently, I'd got work that required my attention. I could hardly concentrate properly, frequently finding myself staring at a piece of paper with my mind engaged elsewhere. Eventually I gave up and went to the kitchen to take a coffee break. I picked up the kettle and was about to fill it when I spotted an envelope on the table opposite. Instantly recognising the familiar handwriting as Andy's, I almost dropped what I was holding. I went across the room to the table, grabbed the envelope and tore it open. Reading quickly through the swirling lines of ink that covered the page, a number of words jumped out. I tried to read more quickly than I could make reasonable sense of what the contents conveyed. 'Unfair treatment,' 'leave your house,' 'make a new start,' 'a place to be myself.'

I felt bombarded by the words as they leapt from the page, pounding me like punches being thrown, each blow adding to the weight of the last. I dragged a chair out from the table and it screeched across the flagstone floor, the noise fighting to drown my comprehension of what was written. Then, sitting down, I began to read again more slowly, desperately hoping the meaning would be different from my initial impression.

The letter began with what seemed to be a very curt salutation and first line. *'Dad,'* it said. *'I have become more and more annoyed by the unjustified comparisons you continually make between me and my brother. Having tried to overlook this unfair treatment for some considerable time, I find I can no longer ignore the pain that it causes me. I realise that our relationship has been strained so, in order to alleviate some of the tension, I have decided I have to leave your house permanently. I think it is a good time for me to take control of my life and make a new start. Please do not try to contact me. I will be in touch at some point in the near future, but be assured I will be okay. I have substantial means at my disposal, from the fund released to me when I became twenty-one, and I have decided it is time to find a place to be myself, where I can find my feet.'* It ended as abruptly as it started, *'Andy.'*

How long I sat at that table with the letter laid out in front of me, I'm not sure. For most of the time I was there I wasn't directly conscious of the letter, or even the words on the page, it was more like looking through a window into memories of the past experiences of our family, some good, some bad. In circumstances like these a parent can feel angry that they are treated so dismissively after years of bringing up children and, at the same time, concerned about the wellbeing of their offspring. At that moment I experienced a terrible feeling of loss. Only once before in my life had I felt a similar, albeit a more pronounced, kind of emotion. Material loss never had that kind of impact on me. You can always work to buy another car or possession, but the feeling was connected to the severing of a relationship. It smothered me when I lost my darling wife twenty-one years earlier and now here it was back to visit me in a different guise, like an unwanted guest that comes unannounced and you know they will outstay their welcome, without regard for anyone else. Images passed over the screen of my mind as I continued to stare through this 'paper window' into the world that had gone before. Days out with picnics, birthdays, visits to amusement parks, Christmases… happier times.

It wasn't the passing of time itself that made me come to my senses, but the creeping darkness that steadily invaded the room, shrouding the objects it contained, blurring form and colour. I glanced up at the clock that was now barely visible in the dim light. Six-thirty. The late October dusk had chased away the daylight and then had been chased away itself by the dark.

I was probably sat there for at least two hours, but the time had skipped by in a moment. How quickly time goes when the mind is occupied. My occupation had taken me through a review of my words and actions over the previous years, particularly concerning Andy. I could have allowed myself to get angry at the way Andy behaved, I too felt an injustice about many things that I had lived through and now his words seemed so unfair. I knew that my anger could not resolve the situation and had to fight to control its influence. I was not self-righteous enough to believe that I could not behave in a similar manner, given the right circumstances. Whether one should behave that way was a different matter. I decide that I would focus on what was important. That meant finding a way to re-build the shattered bridge of our relationship, preventing further isolation.

I fetched my mobile phone from the study, where it had lain neglected on the desk, to find that I had a number of missed calls. I hadn't even heard it ring, despite the quietness of the house.

Finding Andy's number, I tried to connect, but it immediately went to his voicemail. At first I thought he might be in a 'no signal' area, but after a couple of further attempts, I concluded that it was more likely he'd switched it off deliberately to avoid being contacted. I sent a text asking him to ring home as soon as he got the message and hoped that he would respond later that evening.

I sat in the kitchen holding on to my phone as if willing it to ring, keeping it nearby for the rest of the evening so that I wouldn't miss it if it did.

While making coffee, I heard a key go in the front door. My first thought was that it was Andy coming home, having realised that he had been a bit rash and changed his mind about leaving. I went out to the hallway to see. I got there to find Carl leaning, back against the door. As it clicked shut, he stayed there looking at me and shrugged his shoulders as a sign of resignation.

My heart sank as I realised that Carl was alone and I launched into my inquisition routine. "Carl, what's happening? Did you find Andy?"

"No, Dad, I didn't find him. I went to all the places I thought he might be, but nothing I'm afraid." He shrugged again, this time holding his shoulders up longer, almost as an apology. "I'm sure he'll turn up when he's cooled off."

"He left a note... He must have put it on the kitchen table before he went out this afternoon."

"What does it say?"

"It's in here, you can read it yourself. I was just making coffee, do you want one?" Carl shook his head in reply.

I left him in the hallway hanging up his coat and went back to the kitchen to finish making the drink, then sat at the table where I'd been earlier. Carl followed me and as he pulled out a seat at the table, I passed him the note. Taking it from me he didn't look at it immediately, but kept his eyes firmly fixed on mine as if trying to weigh-up the contents from some telltale sign in my expression. Breaking his stare, he began to quickly scan the lines on the paper. For me, it was one of those times when a minute seems to last for an hour. An 'endless span' until Carl had finished absorbing the contents of the letter. He continued looking at it as if trying to formulate his response.

"Andy wrote this before he left in a hurry earlier," he stated the fact. "He's written this in anger, in haste. There's time yet for him to come to his senses. I mean, what does he think he's going to do? He can't live forever on the money he's got. What about his job? He's hardly going to throw away everything... working for the company, home comforts. He's old enough to take care of himself for sure, but just let him have a little time to work things through. I guarantee he will see that he was wrong. Again." Carl rolled his eyes to emphasise the last word and convey his opinion of Andy's wild behaviour of late. "We're the only family he's got. Just allow him some time. He'll reason it out eventually. You'll probably get up in the morning to find him back in his room," he hastily added.

It all sounded sensible, but that didn't dispel the uncomfortable feeling I had about the whole situation. I had to face the fact that there was nothing more I could do for the time being, other than try to contact him again later.

"I've got to get ready to go out this evening, Dad. The presentation over at the club...?"

"Oh... Oh yes, I remember, Carl. That's fine you go ahead and do what you have to do."

"Do you want to come with me? People would love to see you... It's been a while since you came, perhaps it would help take your mind off things."

"No, no I can't, Carl. I just want to be home in case Andy does decide to come back. Besides, if we went together without him there would be the inevitable questions about his absence. I don't think I can bluff my way through that tonight. Thanks anyhow."

I walked with Carl back into the hallway.

"Okay, Dad, but I still think it'll work out." Carl started to climb the stairs then turned back and handed me the note he still had in his hand. "I expect you'll want to hang on to this." He smiled one of those 'don't worry' encouragements that people use when words are at an end.

Andy had always been one of those people who are like a mobile noise. They have the ability to rattle around a house giving it a kind of music that lets everyone know that the place is occupied. Sure, everyone makes noise, but some people bring life with that noise, that was Andy. A constant hum in the background that, although sometimes annoying, was quite comforting as well. It gave the house soul; spirit. I could pinpoint the significant times through the past when it was missing. One occasion was when he went away on a school adventure week when he was fourteen. I believe the whole building sighed with relief and welcomed the rest from the constant reverberation created by him, his music and his sport.

It was okay for a few days, the silence was very much welcomed by me and Carl, but I soon missed the normal undercurrent of sound around the place. Of course, I knew then that the days of quiet contemplation would come to an end, very abruptly, but this time I didn't know how long the lapse of the unique 'Andy sound' would continue.

Carl was very different in character, much preferring things that didn't produce noise. He was frequently driven to distraction by the sound of Andy's guitar seeping through every open, and sometimes closed, door. It would permeate the whole house like a flood of water investigating every gap it could go through. If Carl was trying to read, he would shout up the stairs, "How many times do I have to read the same page over? You can't hear yourself think down here!" The music would stop and Andy would grace us with his presence on the landing, leaning over the long curved banister, asking if someone had called. Carl would patiently explain how loud the music was and ask if Andy could turn the guitar down. Andy would listen for a moment and announce with a puzzled expression, "It doesn't sound too loud to me," then promptly return to what he was doing at precisely the same volume as before. This would drive Carl mad, but he would mostly take it with good humour. In fact, Andy bought Carl a large pair of pink earmuffs for one of his birthdays as a joke.

I once asked Carl why he was so tolerant of the noise. He shrugged and said, "Well, he's my kid brother. He'll grow out of it," then added with a smile, "I hope."

I spent the rest of the evening with some vivid recollections of the two of them together, the images resurrecting themselves in my memory, playing like favourite films. Things that I would normally not bring to mind surfaced freely as snapshots of time from our lives together. Some of them were painful memories. Not of Andy, but the tragedy that he never knew his mother. At just a few months old she was gone from his life, before he was fully aware of who she was, or what he meant to her.

For Carl it was a much more difficult time. At almost six years old he was well aware of his mother, being 'glued' to her wherever she went. For many months after we lost her he would ask me when mummy was coming back home. I frequently had to hold my emotion in check so that he didn't get the impression that it was not good to talk about this special person we had both loved so much. Those memories can be packed away in the travel chest of secrets stored in the remote places of our minds, then a situation arises that causes us to rummage through looking for comfort, all too often finding there is still pain despite the passage of time. This was just such an occasion.

I turned on the TV in an attempt to distract myself, but scarcely took notice as the blur of images tried in vain to entertain an indifferent audience wrapped in memories.

At midnight I made a move for bed, having seen no sign of Andy. I knew that Carl would be very late, possible one-thirty or two o'clock, so there was no point waiting up for him to return. Anyway Carl could be right; it wasn't the first time that Andy had been gone all night, perhaps he would surface again the following day.

I got ready for bed and, after turning out the light, I lay in the dark for a while listening to the noises of the night. I couldn't resist getting up again to look out of the window over the courtyard that had a view along the driveway. The house had so many memories attached to it for my family. It seemed bereft with one missing, my wife, and I didn't want to lose another, even though the circumstances were different.

I gazed at the outline of the old stables that had been converted into parking places, almost hoping to see the shape of Andy's car in its usual place. It always stood in the third section of four. It was a routine that we fell into by accident. I had the first bay, Carl the second and Andy the third.

Although that was the way our ages ran, a thought crossed my mind that maybe even this had more significance to Andy than I had realised. It could have just been my overactive imagination checking everything that I had done in the past to see if in some way it pointed to a greater acceptance of Carl than Andy. Even if Andy had seen it like that I am sure, until this day, no such thing ever entered my consciousness.

It was something that began when we first moved into the house. I instinctively parked in the first bay that I came to and after a time Carl started to tell me that when he was old enough he would have the bay next to mine, then, when Andy was born, he was allocated the one after that. Carl insisted on parking his toys and subsequently bicycles, in the second bay. It was just one of those things that happened and became a family tradition.

I looked at the night sky which was heavy with cloud, blocking out the moonlight and making the dark of the night like liquid covering everything. The driveway lights had turned off earlier in the evening, leaving only the decorative light in the centre of the courtyard to defend against the whole place being immersed in the inky blackness of Durlwood's remote location. I didn't often think about how far from other houses Durlwood was, but nights like this one had a habit, on occasion, of reminding me.

I got back into bed knowing that the night would not allow rest to come easily, my mind too active to shut down properly and my thoughts on parade for inspection, my actions under judgement. Had I been a good father to them both, or was Andy right about the different way he thought I treated them? No doubt time would bring to light what the truth was, but I was ready to concede that there may be more than a grain of truth in what he had said. Whether he was right to deal with the situation as he did was another matter, but he was young and, at times, quite reckless in his dealings with others.

I woke very early the following morning after a very disturbed night. I must have eventually dropped off to sleep after tossing and turning for a long time, but I didn't remember hearing Carl come home. As I looked out of the window into the gloomy morning light I could see Carl's car and my own, but a telling space remained in the bay next to them.

After visiting the bathroom I headed downstairs to the kitchen for coffee. As I followed the curve of the banister around the balcony landing that faced out to the front of the house, I noticed the door to Andy's room was slightly ajar. Going over to it, I gently pushed it open and caught sight of the bed. The quilt was ruffled up and looked like someone was under it. I tiptoed across the room assuming that Andy must have come home with Carl early that morning and gone to bed without me hearing. In the darkness of the room I leant across to see whether he was there and okay, but as I drew closer my heart sank as I realised that the covers must have been left the way he had tossed them aside the previous morning. He wasn't there. I retreated back to the landing and quietly went down the stairs to the kitchen, conscious that Carl may want to sleep late.

The daylight was gradually increasing in intensity, throwing an orange glow into the room. I had neglected to close the blinds the night before and could see across the fields to the back of the house. The sun was attempting to make an appearance, but the day looked like it had already subdued any possibility of that and had set a course for dreariness. The scene outside matched, rather than lifted, my mood, but I made a coffee and sat in the reading chair facing the large patio window.

The flurry of wildlife was already embracing the new morning with enthusiasm, although I didn't feel inclined to join them in a hurry, the day was beginning and there were things that had to be done.

The early hours of the morning I spent in the study trying to do the work that I had neglected the day before. The scene from the previous day still hung in the atmosphere, pressing for me to give it my attention as I kept finding myself once again mulling over the events while trying to do paperwork that could not be neglected.

It took discipline to hold my concentration, as I actually wanted to go and wake Carl to see if he'd had any contact with Andy. That would not have been fair on him after the late finish that must have accompanied the previous evening's occasion.

The event he'd attended was in a good cause and I'm sure he must have returned later than I thought. I was still awake at two in the morning but hadn't heard him come home. The urge to try to find out what happened was very strong, so I kept myself as busy as I could, with an ear constantly listening for signs of movement.

It must have been ten-thirty before Carl finally surfaced. I heard him coming down the stairs, then the clash of cups in the kitchen, but I resisted an immediate interview and left him for a few minutes to gather himself.

Having waited a little while, I stood up to go and find him, but as I did there was a knock on the study door. Carl entered the room, red-eyed and yawning. He sat himself down in one of the chairs in front of my desk.

"Morning," he said wearily. "That was quite a night. Quite a *long* night, but we did very well. Steven reckons we will have raised about fifteen thousand pounds for the hospital. Not bad for an evening, though we had to prise it out of some of the guests. It can be like getting blood from a stone. You'd think it was for me!" he added with a laugh. He must have sensed that I was not really interested in the event, important though it was. "I take it he's not home then?"

"No. I was hoping that you would know something."

"Sorry, no. Have you tried his mobile again?"

"Yes. Several times this morning and twice last night, but it's either turned off, or he's where there's no signal, although I don't think that's likely."

I sat down and leant back into my chair to be greeted with the familiar creaking of the leather that was usually a comfort, but not on that morning.

"I should do something I suppose, but what? I can let this continue for a little while, but I would just like to know where he is. That he's not done anything stupid."

CHAPTER 3

ANDY

"Hey, Andy, long time no see, man. What are you doin' in this neck of the woods?" I looked up from my second pint of Guinness to see the scruffy frame of a tall man looming into view, his speech obscured by the cigarette dangling from his mouth. He looked just how he sounded, hair unkempt and stubble growth of a few days shading his face like it had not been washed in a while.

"Hi, Jake. I figured you'd be somewhere nearby. I was at a bit of a loose end..."

"So you thought you'd come to see your old pal Jake," he interrupted. "Not last on the list again I hope?"

"No, Jake. Of course not. I know we haven't kept in touch since..." I paused as I was finding it difficult to phrase what I wanted to say. "You know what I mean... I just..." I knew that my decision, if it was actually mine, to go to work for Dad had been hard on Jake. The reality of my life was that I had grown up with a certain expectation about a career path. Even when I had discussions with the school careers officer there appeared to be an undercurrent of assumption about what I was destined to do. When you're the son of a successful man it can offer the freedom to choose a direction, or impose a path that is predetermined by someone else, overruling your own wishes.

On my eighteenth birthday, Dad bought me a stunning Mercedes cabriolet. He knew I loved that particular model; I had made him aware of it when I accompanied him to buy his own car. I did everything I could to sway him toward getting one, but he didn't think it a practical choice. I noticed that Carl had disappeared from the family gathering for my birthday, but simply assumed he had gone to the bathroom or something. As Dad called those present to order to make his traditional 'mark the occasion' speech, Carl came into the living room and passed Dad a small wrapped box. It was clear that its final destination was me, but I had to endure the usual anecdotes and leg pulling before being presented with the item. I unwrapped it without a clue about its contents and found a key inside. The questioning look was greeted by Dad and Carl's beaming smiles as they duly led me to the front door. I caught sight of the car through the window before the door was even opened and was stunned by the generosity of the gift. It was the most magnificent silver blue Mercedes cabriolet taking pride of place out in the courtyard. It looked like an image from the manufacturer's brochure. To say that I was bowled over would be a monumental understatement as the gathering moved as one to check out the car.

"Well, son? Are you going to unlock it or not?" Dad slapped me on the back with glee. As the indicators flashed, accompanying the clunk of the door locks opening, Dad called the chatter to order, wished me a happy birthday and skewered my bubble with his final comment. "I thought you should have a reliable car to get you to work when you start at the company in two weeks' time."

I was thrilled with the car, but the thought of working in the environment that Dad and Carl seemed to thrive in was not a happy one. I had a tendency to buckle under the influence of people in authority, even when I absolutely disagreed with what was happening. I always seemed to be 'talked around' to their way of seeing things. Jake was quite the opposite. His inclination was to stand his ground against authority. He would take position like a bull posturing in an arena when confronted by the Matador. He would have his way, or cause as much damage as possible before being subdued.

More than my own aspirations were squashed the day I started work. Jake's lifestyle suddenly ran to a different clock than mine. I moved from the freedom to be part of the band he was gradually assembling, that met during the late evening and early hours of the morning, to a regimented life revolving around paperwork and an office. I resented the change, but rather than challenge it, I submitted to the fait accompli. Jake always told me that he was born a night owl and no amount of pressure could make him change. He didn't, but I did. I thought that I could work around the situation, but a few times late into work produced a meeting with Dad that emphasised my responsibilities to myself, the company and to him.

The drift in my relationship with Jake had begun and was mirrored by a drift in the relationship with my father.

'Tea boy', Jake took to calling me when I started work, not a joke that I appreciated and the longer the nickname continued, the greater my resentment at being in the job grew.

"Cool down man, I'm just ribbing you, but if you buy me a drink we'll talk about old times and catch up with the latest news." Jake pulled me out from my reminiscence.

He took a stool next to me at the bar and as he sat down he played out a quick rhythm, slapping his hands on the wooden surface. It made me smile as I watched him. That was the way Jake had always been for as long as I had known him. If he didn't have a musical instrument on which to create a sound, he would invariably be tapping on a chair, a table or some other object close to hand.

The old pub where we sat looked even more run down than when we used to visit it years before. I remembered the first drink I ordered had been in that very place, far enough from home for Dad not to find out, especially since I was not legally old enough, but near enough to get home without any problem. The place still hinted back to a decade long past, a time when it had seen better days and more customers. To say that it needed a total refurbishment to move it into the modern age was certainly an understatement. It had one redeeming feature and this was that it appeared to attract a lot of local musicians. One could only guess why, but perhaps it was the fact that the proprietor was willing to let them use the facilities to practise and test their abilities on the other people present, all for the price of buying rounds of drinks. It was an uneasy match, each dependent to some degree on the other. The place hardly attracted people because of its condition, so the musicians supported it by their custom. In return they had the use of it as a rehearsal venue, at a price they couldn't afford to turn down.

I ordered a couple of drinks for us and waited for the barman to move away before engaging with Jake. He was a friendly, sociable guy to those he included in his circle. He cared little about his appearance, but was passionate about music, any music.

I was fourteen the first time we spoke to each other. I remember it so clearly. It was one of those moments in life which are permanently embedded into the memory and can be recalled with such clarity that it's like watching a video. We both attended the boys' grammar school. I always felt that I got in due to parental aspiration, but Jake was a smart kid. I'd seen him at a distance on the campus, but he was a bit of a mystery. He was able to command a large group of his peers at will, but was often to be found with a small circle of constant companions. There were rumours among the students about him, but I was a loner at school and didn't engage much in the gossip. Truth is, I hated the place and the day I left was only marred by the fact that I would be moving to a place that seemed very much like another school; the family business.

One thing I had understood from those who knew; under no circumstances should any student call him by his real name, George. George Clarke. He flatly refused to answer to it, saying it made him sound like an accountant. He insisted that everyone call him Jake. Jake Clarke. "It sounds more like a rock star's name. That's exactly what I'm going to be," he would say. I was told that the issue was a running battle with anyone in authority as he would fill in any documentation with his preferred, rather than his real, name.

The school had arranged a student talent contest to raise money for a local charity. Everyone who had the slightest ability was drafted in to create a show that would be in the open air quadrangle of the school building. I was on the bill with my guitar and was acutely embarrassed at the prospect of playing to an audience. I loved to play, but the idea of public performance is never high on the agenda of a shy boy. There was a mixed blessing in the fact that Dad was not able to attend. I was disappointed that it was not important enough for him to change whatever he was doing that day, but thankful I didn't have to perform in front of him.

The day was quite a blast after I'd done my set early in the proceedings and my nerves had settled, but the capstone of the event was Jake, he was amazing, playing keyboards and backed by a young drummer. The guy was so full of charisma it was flowing from the stage like theatrical smoke. The conflict of interest for the school authorities must have created a dilemma; wanting to showcase the best, but having to use an anti-establishment figure like Jake.

He received a blast of applause from the gathered crowd, particularly the students, and he milked it with an unscheduled encore that sent the teacher due to close the event scurrying from the stage, much to the amusement of the crowd.

I couldn't keep my eyes of him as he completed his set. The rest of the closing was lost to me, some waffling about those who had made it possible and presentation of flowers. I was too busy observing Jake as he wandered through the groups of people, periodically stopped by well-wishers. I was mesmerised by the whole thing, almost star-struck.

In my daydream state I failed to realise that Jake was heading directly towards me and when it finally registered, I looked behind to see where he might be going. When I turned back he was right in front of me.

"What's your name?"

I hesitated before answering the abrupt question. I'd heard the rumours and even been warned to keep clear of him because he was trouble. 'What have I done wrong?' was my first thought.

"Andy Numan," I offered almost apologetically.

"You're a bloody good guitarist. If you want to ditch that shit they're making you play and do something worth listening to, you should hook up with me."

I was blown away by the compliment from this guy who I thought was amazing and must have looked stupid as I stood with my mouth open.

"I've got to meet someone, Andy, and anyway I need a fag. You in school tomorrow?"

"Yeah."

"We'll talk then, okay?" I nodded as he began to turn away, thinking the conversation was over, but he turned back again and said, "Oh, my name's Jake Clarke." He paused as our eyes connected for a few seconds then added, "I'm serious, bloody good guitarist." Then he was gone.

I have thought about that meeting many times over the years, but on that day it occupied my mind every moment, until I caught sight of Jake the following morning as I walked into the school campus. When he saw me, he immediately left the group of lads he was standing with and came over.

"Andy!" he shouted as he trotted toward me. "Come meet the other guys." He took me over and introduced them one by one. Many of them were only loose acquaintances, but I got to know Stuart quite well, probably because he played bass guitar and had already been drafted by Jake into the developing band. I never dreamed the shy boy that I was would link up with that group of talented young men, but the connection through our music was very strong and I knew that there was something unexplained that connected me personally to Jake.

Once I'd got to know him a little, it appeared he mixed with anyone who seemed interesting to him. Often the common link was playing and performing various kinds of music. Jake was a bit of an all-rounder, playing guitar, drums and a number of other instruments, but his real talent was on the keyboard, although he could get an impressive sound out of almost anything you cared to place in his hands and he would never refuse an offer. He was 'Jack the lad' drawing laughter in almost any situation, much to the consternation of teachers who would be trying to be serious.

Over the last few years of my teens we started to spend quite a lot of time together, along with a few others, usually playing instruments, but sooner than should have been the case, drinking. He certainly surrounded himself with people who liked to laugh and have a rowdy time. Perhaps that was his influence on them, rather than the other way round. I would often end up hurting from the convulsions of laughter at the close of the evening or, when I was a little older, the early morning.

Jake never seemed to have the time restrictions placed on him that I had to adhere to. When I was concerned about getting home in time for my Dad-imposed curfew, he appeared to be out until he decided he'd had enough; any time that suited him was time to go home.

In all the years I'd known him I never actually went to his house. I don't think he was keen to be there either. He always jumped at the opportunity to come home with me, which he quite frequently did.

The first time we got together to practise was at Stuart's home. He had a huge garage that we rearranged to set up the instruments and because it was detached from the house, it allowed us to really make the building rock. I absolutely loved the experience. What was the point of all the guitar lessons that I had taken if I didn't intend to do something with the skill I'd learned? My teacher always told me that I had the passion, and, if I practised, I could make something from it. He pressed me to get together with other musicians in order to develop my technique. 'I can teach you the theory, but it will never take the place of playing with a group,' he would say.

Dad had visions of me dressed in a penguin suit playing Bach on a classical guitar. I don't think he held on to that image for too long after seeing the posters that covered my bedroom wall indicating my preference. They certainly didn't include the well-manicured image of seventeenth century musicians.

At the end of that first session, Stuart pulled out some cans of lager which he had brought from the house and slumped himself down on the floor, leaning back against the wall. He held a can out to me, but I declined the offer. It created some laughter and leg-pulling, but was in good humour.

"You won't want one of these either then." Jake held out what I thought was a cigarette as he planted himself next to his friend. Stuart completely cracked up. "Don't be stupid, pot head. He won't want to smoke your dope."

"Dope? You mean *drugs*?"

My innocence was glaring and caused a great deal of hilarity.

When the laughter subsided, Jake put the joint to his lips, lit up, took a deep drag and let a curtain of smoke drift into the air as he exhaled.

"I can see we're going to have to educate you, Andy."

"Where did you get that stuff from?" I asked.

"*Where*?" Jake emphasised my question. "My dad has his sources."

I thought Jake was kidding and let out a laugh. When I noticed their faces, I realised he was serious.

"Your *dad* got it for you?" I queried.

"Sure. He can get some for you too, if you want. He's got... let's say he's got a lot of cool connections. He's alright, so long as you don't mess with him. Anybody who does won't forget it anyway."

I was unsure of the ground I was on. Connecting the word 'dad' with an image of someone who supplies drugs, even to his own son, was totally foreign to the world I had lived in. My upbringing sounded alarm bells, but my curiosity quickly silenced them.

"Isn't it, y'know, bad for you?"

They were having a good time laughing at my expense, but I was genuinely interested. There was never any possibility of talking about that kind of stuff at home and I wanted to know why someone would want to use drugs. I felt like a child in their presence, but it was an opportunity to learn about a side of life I knew nothing about, so I ignored the banter.

Jake held out the joint to Stuart who immediately accepted it and took a long drag. He held his breath for a moment before releasing the smoke from the side of his mouth. He looked at Jake and at his indication held out the joint to me. I didn't move at first, but Stuart stretched forward pressing me to take it.

"I've never even smoked a cigarette."

They didn't laugh this time, but encouraged me to engage, so I took the joint from Stuart.

"Put it to your lips and draw the air through it. It feels like sucking air through a wet towel. Just fill your lungs and hold a second, then let it out."

I looked at Jake and he urged me to follow Stuart's instructions, so I did. It was five minutes before the tears stopped running down my face and I suspect that Jake and Stuart were the same, but theirs were from laughter. I was dizzy and felt sick. The experience was one that I've never wanted to repeat again, but I suspect that I have had my fair share over the years from the second-hand smoke that filled many of the places I would find myself in after performing.

It wasn't long before we were at Durlwood for practise sessions, but I would make them promise that they would never smoke or drink while we were there. They kept to their word, it was like a respect thing. Not respect for authority, but for me and each other; the band. Despite the conflict of backgrounds, I had a sense of belonging with them and overlooked things that should have given me cause for concern.

Dad would come home from work to find me, Jake and Stuart trying to kill off the plants and terrify the wildlife with a barrage of unrestrained sound. 'Don't stroke that guitar, thrash the life out of it!' Jake would shout. I did feel alive when I was immersed in the music and being creative.

Carl took a passing interest in the guys, perhaps he was simply looking out for his kid brother. I wasn't too happy when he tried to engage with us through the music, I think I was jealously guarding an area that I was able to do well in and didn't want to have that spoiled by my talented older brother. Quite a ridiculous thought, but at the time it seemed very real, even though Carl didn't even play an instrument.

Jake seemed to have a finger in many pies and my fascination in his 'worldly' qualities grew, rather than diminished, as I saw some of the stuff he was up to. If suspicious items appeared at school being offered for sale, Jake was usually the one selling them. Although he had been caught and cautioned over a few incidents, he appeared to have some cloaking device that allowed him to run under the radar. One person makes the slightest error and the world knows everything about it and others have the sleight of hand that would embarrass a magician. I listened wide-eyed to some of his stories of escapades that he had been involved in. One badge of honour was his near suspension from school for putting the dry-ice we were using in our chemistry class into a number of glass jars and standing them in a pool of water on the side office desk so that they froze solid to the top. His only regret was that he couldn't film the teacher's face when he returned to his office after the class was dismissed to find the mess that waited for him.

Another area Jake seemed to specialise in was the circulation of explicit pictures. It was under his tutelage that I was educated about women. To say that I was naïve was an understatement. Jake often embarrassed me until I could feel my face burning like the sun. He certainly opened my eyes to the female form, but not in a respectful way. The consequences of that may have influenced what happened later on in my life, but the blame for how I was sucked in was definitely my own. The instruction he gave me didn't teach me that women were equal in intelligence and value, but that they were to be used. To say I didn't know any better would be lying, Dad had always brought me up to respect others and even though I didn't have a mother's influence, I knew that that respect included women. However, I was so in awe of Jake and wanted so badly to impress him, I forgot my upbringing and believed everything he said, foolishly going along with the flow and ended up getting swept downstream. My view of women became disrespectful and warped, until I later learned the value of friendship and the true meaning of love.

"How's your 'old man,' Andy?" Jake inquired, interrupting my wandering thoughts. "We got on like a house on fire, if I remember correctly," then he delivered the punch line, "burnt to the ground."

He slapped me on the back and laughed out loud at his joke, as though enjoying the memory of his abrasive association with Dad.

It was unusual for Dad to dislike anyone, but over a period of time he came to dislike Jake as intensely as I liked him. I just thought Dad was being a bit of a snob at the time. Sure, Jake didn't really fit into the world I grew up in, but then he didn't seem to have a background that made you wish you could swap places with him either. I couldn't help liking him though. Truth be told, Jake's use of colourful language and unruly behaviour in front of Dad eventually became a source of a substantial amount of laughter between us, but only away from Durlwood. Whilst Dad usually restrained himself from comment, he found Jake to be very coarse and exceptionally impolite, especially as he was enjoying the comfort of our home. He saw him as a bad influence and didn't want that influence to take hold of me. He even went so far as to ban him from the house after the last infamous incident.

Although that was probably enough, there were many other small things that slowly built up until that last straw for Dad. Jake had always been someone who loved mischief. He was nearly always the perpetrator, either directly or indirectly. He would provoke others to do what he wanted and, despite the fact he frequently got away without any blame, leaving someone else to carry the rap, everybody at school seemed to love him. There was an air of mystery that surrounded him and a constant interest about what might happen next. If there were classroom pranks to play, he was the instigator.

On the particular day of the incident, me, Jake and Stuart had been in the stable block doing our 'aggressive teenagers become a famous band impression.' As we began to wind up the practise, Jake had an idea that he thought would give us a good laugh. I didn't have the sense, or the guts, to stop him. Jake had brought a couple of packets of condoms with him and had been periodically waving them around during the time he'd been there. He suggested that we go to the upstairs bathroom and fill some of them with water, then drop them from one of the top floor windows to see how they would burst on impact. It seemed harmless enough and the consequences of our actions never crossed my mind for a second. Nor did the mischievousness of Jake, it was just a laugh.

We'd thrown a few of the water bombs out onto the front courtyard, taking it in turns to aim for the centre circle, when Jake said he was just going to the toilet. I didn't think anything of it and carried on with Stuart, periodically rolling with laughter at the results of our efforts. Suddenly, I caught sight of Dad's car unexpectedly turning into the end of the driveway. I panicked a little, thinking of the debris from our activities left scattered over the drive. It obviously wasn't the water that was the problem, but the car was approaching too fast to be able to clear up before Dad got there. Stuart and I hid below the windowsill to make sure that we couldn't be seen when the vehicle came into the courtyard. It stopped at the steps to the front door below us just as Jake reappeared. We alerted him to the difficulty at hand, so Jake crossed the room to take a look. He boldly stuck his head out of the window just as we could hear the voices of people getting out of the car below. Before I had chance to realise what was going on, Jake threw a missile straight down onto his unsuspecting targets. He launched into a barrage of obscene names regarding the approaching enemy, then sent a second flying volley of ammunition. There was a shout of shock from below, followed by Jake's hysterical laughter. Dad came tearing into the house and up the stairs. He was incandescent with rage.

"What the bloody hell are you doing?"

I was terrified. I'd never heard Dad address me like that before, but Jake cracked up laughing again, his usual response to a challenge from authority.

"How dare you come into my house and behave like that George Clarke. How dare you laugh at me!"

Dad lunged forward to apprehend him, catching hold of his jacket and hoisting him up, Jake lashed out and struck Dad's arm away, narrowly missing his face and landing a blow on his shoulder. Dad reeled backwards, clearly the punch had caused some pain and his face glared at Jake with incredulity and a certain amount of shock at the violent response. I was so focused on Dad in the eerie silence that followed the scuffle that I didn't see what Jake was up to. I turned back to see he'd pulled a knife from his pocket and caught sight of it when the blade made a sharp click as it flicked open.

"You lay another finger on me 'old man' and I'll stick you!" The obscenities that Jake let fly coloured the air blue. Dad held back, not wanting to inflame the situation further, as Jake and Stuart edged out of the door. Suddenly they were off like jack rabbits down the stairs, initially with Dad in pursuit, obviously concerned about his guest. The raucous peals of laughter suggested that they had seen the result of our earlier handiwork strewn all over the drive.

The business associate that Dad had brought home with him was a little bemused and I flushed red with shame, wanting the ground to open up and swallow me, when brought face to face with the man to apologise. When Jake had said he was going to the toilet, he'd actually gone to the kitchen taking flour and eggs and mixing them up before filling his mock incendiaries, the gooey bulk of which was still embedded in his target's suit.

Dad completely flipped about what had happened and visited Jake's home to have words with his parents about his behaviour. He didn't get any satisfaction from them, so he contacted the police. I just wanted Dad to forgive and forget, but he insisted I tell the police what had happened and although I knew I had to be truthful, I felt ashamed about grassing on Jake. I felt torn between being loyal to my father and loyal to my friend and musical partner. 'Blood is thicker than water,' was what Dad had said. As far as I was concerned, Jake had done a pretty bad thing but no real harm had come from it. I knew he had a bad streak in him, but, I liked him and wanted to continue our friendship. That no longer seemed possible and I just hoped that he wouldn't find out that I had corroborated Dad's story to the police. I was grounded for a month and banned from seeing Jake ever again. In reality, it meant that he could no longer come to Durlwood, but I couldn't, and didn't really want to, avoid seeing him at school.

It was a few days before I saw him again and was surprised that he had bruising around his eye. Jake was livid about the police being involved and made it clear that he resented what he saw as Dad's interference and snobbishness.

"How did that happen, Jake?" I asked.

"My dad didn't appreciate a home call from the 'pigs.' He wanted to let me know how he felt. If you think this is bad, you should see my back." Jake pulled his shirt up a little to reveal the clear after-effects of a belt strap. "It's not the first time and I doubt it'll be the last, but these," he snarled, as I looked at the myriad of angry reddish purple welts, "are thanks to *your Dad*."

I winced at the connection he made, but was relieved that his inference of fault was aimed only at Dad. It never occurred to Jake that he had actually been the root of the cause. Not that it would justify such punishment. His eyes clearly told the story. They weren't tearful with remorse, but hardened and vengeful. It scared me at first to think that Jake was possibly planning a vendetta. It wouldn't have been the first time. I'd heard that someone had crossed him and he had bided his time before springing a nasty surprise. The difficulty with Jake was that his peers liked him, but the authorities had a completely different opinion. I was told that the guy he had an issue with was cornered by a number of Jake's friends who laid into him, causing some serious physical damage. When the police got involved, the victim was so scared that he refused to tell them what had happened. Jake's friends wouldn't say a word about the incident either, not out of fear but because they stood Jake on a pedestal.

When I heard about it, I thought that it was just groundless rumour that enhanced the tough-guy image Jake tried to cultivate. Looking at the expression on his face as he talked about Dad made me wonder if there was a deep undercurrent of violent tendency in him that I had not been introduced to before. For a while I stood back a little from his company. The difficulty was that he seemed to be very loyal to those he liked and would do anything to help them, but I was beginning to be aware that he had little patience with those he disliked.

It took a while for the dust to settle and my friendship with Jake was distant for a time, but the music connection remained strong. He seemed to get over the incident with my dad pretty quickly, simply adding it as another story to his colourful life and took great pleasure in telling it to everyone who would listen, to my deep embarrassment. He never set foot in Durlwood again. Ever after he referred to my father as your 'old man,' usually with an expression of contempt on his face.

Jake never for a moment gave me the impression that he was angry at me and wanted me out of the band because of what happened. We continued our alliance for the following year-and-a-half without Dad being aware, but the meeting venue for practise had to be changed from Durlwood back to Stuart's house, until his parents decided to move away and he was enthusiastic to go with them. We found ourselves practising in the back room of the local pub, which became the place where I bought my first pint and the final meeting place for the band. The landlord overlooked the fact that we were underage, in light of the free entertainment on offer, and we continued to meet there until my work commitments changed that.

About six months before my eighteenth birthday, I arrived at the old pub for my usual rendezvous with Jake and a few others that had become familiar faces, when Jake arrived with a bewildered look on his face.

"Jake!" I shouted to attract his attention to my presence. He came across and slumped onto the bench next to me. I had never seen him look so subdued. "What's the matter?"

Jake put his hand over his face.

"Jake?"

He took a deep breath, moved his hand and looked me in the eye. I didn't like what I saw. Anger was bubbling near the surface.

"The bastard police have arrested my dad."

"What?"

"They've charged him with the sale and distribution of drugs."

"What are you and your mum going to do?" I asked.

Jake snorted. "Mum? What bloody mum? The bitch left us. She never gave a shit about me. Neither did my dad come to that." His hand went back over his face.

"What are you going to do?"

"God knows," he mumbled. "They don't reckon he will be released. It's not the first time it's happened. Our landlord has been trying to evict us for ages and this will give him the excuse to do it while Dad's away. I suppose I'm going to have to find a flat somewhere."

He looked at me again, but what could I do? Dad had banned me from seeing Jake ever again and I had defied him by pretending I was meeting with some other people to practise. I could hardly go and ask him if Jake could stay with us. I knew he wouldn't allow it.

"I don't suppose you can help can you?" He looked at me, then answered his own question sarcastically "No, there wouldn't be room *in your mansion* for someone like me." The bitterness in his voice made me feel very uncomfortable. "You're a lucky sod, Andy."

I felt there was nothing that I could say and sat in awkward silence for a while. Suddenly Jake jumped to his feet and declared that he had to go and sort himself out. He left quite abruptly and I sat feeling like I had very badly let him down.

I met him a few days later and he told me that he had found a flat and that it didn't look good for his dad, but as usual he was focused on what he could do and music became a means of supporting himself. The band we had created under Jake's leadership was making the most of any opportunity and all the time this was taking place I had the looming prospect of an expectation from my father.

My eighteenth birthday announced the arrival of that moment. I was being pressed from different directions, but eventually found that I could not continue the commitments of the band and fulfil the path that Dad wanted me to tread. I had deliberately avoided using the new car Dad had bought for me to go to the pub to meet with Jake. I was embarrassed at the extravagance while he was struggling to make ends meet, but the pressures I felt under finally meant I had to choose a direction and I couldn't remove one of Dad's sayings from my mind. 'Blood is thicker than water.'

I couldn't think straight, but at that time believed I had no choice, so I arranged to meet with Jake and the others to let them know what I was going to do.

The meeting was not pretty. One of the other guys used my departure as an excuse to go himself, putting me even further in the frame as the villain who broke up the band. Jake was not just mad, he went into orbit, accusing me of betrayal. I had no answers for him because I felt like I *had* betrayed him. At a time when he was down and with no family to support him, I, his friend, was dumping him. They were not the happiest days of my life and the harvest of resentment at home grew from the seeds planted along the way to that point. I occasionally saw Jake over the next two-and-a-half years, but never to speak to. They were rare occasions, but while he acknowledged me, the bond that had been there was broken.

"Dad's okay," I responded, nodding.

"Bet he's glad you're out having a nice drink with your old pal Jake, what do you reckon?" He prodded me with his comment, as well as his finger, obviously trying to see if the old magic formula for laughter would still work. I couldn't help smiling, but did make an effort to restrain it.

"Jake, I don't think I need to answer that, do you? You can hardly be surprised that he chucked you out of the house after what you did. Anyway, he doesn't know where I am at the moment."

"Oh... Now that is intriguing. Do tell me," he said, as he leaned toward me, keen to get more of the story. I didn't really want to talk about it, but Jake knew I was off my beaten track and I had given part of the reason away in the tone of my previous comment.

"I've had a bit of a bust up with him to be honest. I just get a bit sick of being treated as though I don't come up to scratch. Carl's such a smart guy, involving himself in the business and everything, but I'm not like him. I never was."

"No. No, you're not. You, my friend, are like me."

I took a good look at him. As I laughed at his comment, I waited for the punch line to drop, but it didn't come.

"How on earth do you make that out, Jake. We're worlds apart. We live different lives and I'm a heartless sod who ditches his friends to go work in an office."

Jake did a double take then observed me for an uncomfortably long moment before he continued, ignoring my blurted out spontaneous apology that hijacked my conversation.

"Not so, my friend, not so," he said, as though correcting the mistake of a schoolboy. "You and me," he pointed from me to himself and back again. "You and me, we are artists... musicians. We've got talent in a different way and, if we put our minds to it, we could go places."

"What do you mean, go places, Jake?"

"Never mind about that right now, my friend. Listen, you need cheering up and I've got just the thing for it. Micky and Jez, the other two guys in the band I've been putting together, will be here in a little while to rehearse. Why don't you stay, join in the practise, see what you think. We're setting up in the back room and I know when you play with me again it will help you put things into perspective. John said we could have the room all evening if we want to, so let's have a laugh, see what happens and take things from there. Now, you refill my glass and we'll relax and talk no more about old times, just about the future."

Getting up from the bar stool he'd been perched on he said, "I've just got to see a man about a dog, you know, business. I'll be back in two ticks, Andy." He winked as he turned, then disappeared through the door at the end of the bar.

I bought two more drinks and moved over to the window where there was a table tucked into the bay. There were only three or four other people in the bar area, it was still early in the day for musicians, though I could hear the muffled voice of someone through the other section at the back. It sounded like Jake, but I couldn't be sure. After about five minutes he reappeared and seated himself opposite me at the table.

"They'll be here about nine this evening, Micky and Jez, so we've got a bit of time to kill. How about we have something to eat while we hang around? Then, when they get here I can lend you one of my guitars so that you can join in."

"I've got my guitar with me, Jake. It's been in the car boot for a long time. I don't know how long actually. I forgot to take it out when I picked it up after being repaired, but then there never seems time to play it these days anyway. In fact it's been a long, *long* time since I played properly,." I said, apologising for my upcoming performance before it even began.

"Like riding a bike, mate," he said, with great confidence. "What you need to do is spend some time with your real friends doing the stuff you enjoy. Remember how we used to play for hours on end? We were developing a great sound you know, you should never have given it up."

I knew he was right about that, but fitting what you want to do around what you are expected to do is not always as easy as it sounds and the longer you neglect something the less likely you are to go back to it.

"I've had quite a laugh playing the clubs with Micky and Jez, but we need someone else to help fatten up the sound." Leaning toward me he put his hand on my shoulder. "There's nothing wrong with having a laugh, no matter what your 'old man' says. That's just what you need now and I've decided that's what you're going to get. I bet you a shilling you tell me later that you had a great time" Turning to the bar he shouted, "Hey, John, can we get some food over here, something sort of edible?" He laughed as abuse about his musical ability was thrown back from the bar.

John sauntered over with two dog-eared scraps of paper that turned out to be the menus.

"Not got much today, so whatever you 'ave it's with chips or chips," he said as he waited to take our order. Jake pushed the papers back at him.

"Well, whatever you've got we'll have two…and with chips… please, mate!"

The next couple of hours I spent talking with Jake, just killing time until his friends arrived for the practise session. I still hadn't decided what I was going to do about accommodation later, but as I definitely wasn't going home, I needed somewhere to sleep for the night. While it played on my mind a little, I knew that I shouldn't leave it until the last possible moment, but I was happy relaxing with Jake. The drinks kept coming, the conversation was quite pleasant and then, at about nine, the two others guys joined us.

First was Micky, a motorbike enthusiast. Dressed in full leathers with helmet in hand, he came over to our table, stopping at the bar to get a drink on the way. He stood around five feet eleven and was well-built with jet-black hair tied back in a loose ponytail. A number of tattoos on his arms were proudly displayed when the leather jacket came off, each had some kind of motorbike theme. About ten minutes later, while I was chatting to Micky about his passion for drums, Jez arrived.

Jez was such a complete contrast to Micky that it was hard to picture them having anything in common. He was dressed quite smartly, clean shaven and slightly taller than Micky, with light, almost blonde, hair. He reminded me of the young accountant that Jake always said his real name, George, should belong to. One thing that became immediately apparent, through the direction of conversation, was that they were all into music with a passion. It was an infectious passion that took hold of me very quickly. Being around them began to re-ignite my own love of music that had been suffocated with duty over recent years.

The talk meandered along for a while until Jake decided it was time to go to the practise room and set up the equipment. I went out to my car to fetch my guitar while the others gathered the necessary liquid supplies.

We started to play some simple stuff at first, just jamming around getting used to each other. Suggestions about different material were made and we would have a go, but I was aware that they were more familiar with each other's way of playing and much of the material they knew quite well.

Jake's voice was pretty good, in tune, but with a raspy edge to it that created an emotion to the songs that a clean voice would have lacked. I remembered that he used to be okay, but I reckoned he must have been working hard at it to develop his talent.

It felt like I was being carried along for a while, like a surfer catching a wave and drawing from the power it held. It was apparent that they had developed a pretty good repertoire, but were holding back a little for my sake. The power that Micky on drums and Jez on bass guitar produced was forceful and impressive. I'd forgotten how much I used to enjoy this kind of thing, but as the evening wore on and the drink flowed, things loosened up and we really began to rock. The bar had filled up as the evening passed and a number of people had come through with their drinks to make the most of the free entertainment. It was great to see them expressing their appreciation at the end of each piece, but I was conscious that I was being a bit of a cheat as the others were carrying the bulk of the sound.

It was not until we began to wind up that I realised it was well after one in the morning, "My God! Where did the time go? I need to figure out where I'm going to stay tonight," I blurted out before realising that I had betrayed the fact that I was not intending to go home.

"You can stay with me," Jake immediately offered, almost as though he had anticipated what I was going to say. "Then tomorrow we'll meet together and decide whether we are serious about this music thing or not. Two o'clock tomorrow okay with you guys?" Jake shouted across to Micky and Jez, interrupting their conversation. They both indicated that they were okay with the arrangement, then shouted their farewells as they left.

Jake and I wandered out of the old pub, and I pulled out my phone to call for a taxi to take us back to his place.

"Don't tell me that's your car over there?"

I nodded.

Jake whistled and shot across the car park to take a closer look.

"I got to get me one of these," he said, looking along the car from boot to bonnet. It made me feel conscious of the fact that we each came from different walks of life, something I'd noticed when we were younger.

"Come on then, open up." He impatiently urged me to action.

"I've had too much to drink, Jake. I'll call for a taxi," I said, showing that my phone was at the ready.

"Sod that! Who's going to know? It's after one in the morning."

"But..." my protest was immediately cut short.

"Andy." Jakes irritation was clearly evident. "Don't be so lame."

Wanting to appease Jake, I relented, and, despite my uneasiness, I pressed the unlock button. He jumped into the passenger seat with enthusiasm, preparing to go home in greater style than how he arrived.

Jake's flat was on the third floor of a four storey 'semi-derelict' looking building. The stairway was grimy with paint peeling away from the walls. It was exposed to the elements with the entrance doors to the flats on one side and a guard rail, to prevent anyone from leaping, or being thrown over the side, on the other. There were lights along the landings and stairwells, but they were either switched off or out of order.

I followed Jake up the levels until we reached the entrance. He paused before opening the door. "Sorry about the mess, Andy, but I didn't expect to have a guest tonight." He put the key in the lock and pushed the door open. "I would have cleaned up if I'd known, maybe, but at least it's better than sleeping in your car somewhere. You want a drink before we turn in?"

"Nah, Jake, I'm good. Listen, thanks for offering your place anyway, I do appreciate it."

Jake had been to my family home many times over the years and he was well aware that I was used to living in extreme luxury in comparison to his flat.

I felt a little embarrassed for him at that moment, but my awkwardness was broken when he said, "Andy, it's been good to see you again, it was cool jamming together. You need to understand though that you can't just be here because there's trouble at home with your 'old man.' I would like us to try to make a go of the music, like we used to dream about, but if you're not interested, please don't lead us along and then yank us off when you're straight with Daddy again. He don't rule over you, unless you let him. You're an adult now, remember."

We were still standing in the hallway with the front door wide open and the harsh light from the un-shaded fitting spilling onto the outside balcony walkway.

"Think about it, Andy. Think about it." He turned, waving for me to follow him into the living room, but his stare lingered on me for a few moments. "You're gonna have to crash on the sofa tonight, we don't have a guest room available here I'm afraid." He laughed. "The bathroom's through there," he said, pointing his thumb over his shoulder as he disappeared through another door, which I assumed to be the bedroom, not to be seen again until the following morning.

It wasn't long before I was trying to make myself comfortable on the sofa amid the fusty smell and general chaos of the room. All of that quickly disappeared as I soon began to drift off to sleep. The unfamiliar noises of the flat, the sound of the occasional car on the road below and the orange glow of city streetlights made a bold, but unsuccessful, attempt to disrupt my slumber. I couldn't help thinking about some of the things that had been said as I sank into that twilight zone before unconsciousness. Perhaps Jake was right, maybe I had let Dad dictate too much. After all, once I'd turned twenty-one, I had gained access to a substantial amount of money that would allow me to be much more independent than most people would have the opportunity to be. Maybe it was time to take a different road and aim for a future that looked much more enjoyable than the one that appeared to have been planned for me.

I don't exactly know what time I began to stir the following morning, but it started with a vague awareness of someone else occupying the room. I didn't feel so good at first, probably due to the amount of alcohol I'd consumed the night before. The situation didn't improve when I heard the curtains screech along the metal rail as they were abruptly opened. The sudden influx of light was painful, like pins being stuck into my eyes and my head was pounding like the sound of Micky's bass drum. It was a constant thud with accompanying pain creating a symphony of discomfort.

"What time is it?" I mumbled.

"Ooo... You don't look so good this morning, sonny boy. I don't reckon you can hold your drink too well, you lightweight."

Jake poked fun at me, but I wasn't in the mood to respond. Besides, I thought he was right. It had been a long time since I had drunk so much in one night, but it didn't seem to have affected him at all.

It was quite a struggle lifting myself to an upright position and when I finally did, I came face to face with a man eating a hearty, rather greasy-looking breakfast. Food was the last thing on my agenda. In fact, holding down what was already there was more than enough of a problem without trying to eat anything else.

"You don't look fit to move at the moment, Andy. Perhaps you should take things easy this morning and get yourself together, but remember we're meeting up with Micky and Jez at two this afternoon." Jake seemed to be enjoying my suffering, or, at a minimum, found it amusing.

"I've got to pop out for a while to deal with a bit of business. You just stay here and make yourself at home. I'll be back soon, okay."

"Yeah, yeah."

That was about as communicative as I was going to get at that point in the morning. I certainly had no intention of changing my position from the horizontal plane. A few minutes later, I heard Jake laugh as he closed the front door behind him with a bang that resonated in my skull like the chime of Big Ben.

Out of necessity rather than desire, I crawled to the bathroom to spew the little that was left in my churning stomach and confined myself to the sofa for a long time. I banished the thought of actually standing upright to a time in the distant future.

CHAPTER 4

I must have fallen asleep again because I remember nothing until I was startled by the slamming of the front door when Jake returned. He'd brought coffee with him. I could tell by the smell that drifted into the room, fighting with the fustiness for domination of the atmosphere. He didn't say anything, just held out the drink for me to take.

Propping myself up a little, I sipped the black liquid with a great deal of caution, until I realised the queasiness from earlier had eased a little, then began to take larger gulps.

"Jake, what time is it... have you seen my watch anywhere?" I asked, as I looked around on the floor and at the side of the sofa.

"It's three-thirty," he said, pulling a bar of chocolate from the pocket of his coat that he was still wearing. "You want some?"

I stopped searching and looked at him holding out the chocolate, but just the thought of eating was more than enough to start my stomach lurching again.

"No, I'm okay. Have you seen my watch, Jake? I'm sure I was wearing it last night."

"I don't remember seeing you with a watch. What's it like? Don't tell me it's a *Rolex*," he said, with great emphasis on the name.

"No, of course it isn't. Never mind, I'll look again in a minute, I'm sure it must be here somewhere." I gave up on my half-hearted attempt to locate it.

"I can't believe that it's three-thirty already. Where did the morning go?"

"I don't know where your morning went," said Jake. "Or the first part of your afternoon come to that."

"Where have you been anyway?"

"I went to see Micky and Jez at two o'clock, as agreed. You didn't look up to it so I left you to sleep off your hangover. I think we need to bring you up to speed with your new lifestyle. All that posh living has softened you up. Anyway, take your time and when you're ready, I'm gonna buy you something to eat at the café across the road. Then, a bit later on, Micky and Jez will join us to run through a few ideas we've got that might be of interest to you."

By late afternoon I was feeling much better and in need of some food, so we ventured out into the fading daylight, heading for the café Jake had suggested. It wasn't exactly upmarket, looking as though it had been built to empathise with the run down surroundings, matching the flats we had come from, but the food was acceptable.

Jake had been hinting about some ideas that might be of interest to me, provoking my curiosity. He certainly seemed pleased with himself over whatever he was planning.

When he paid for the food at the counter, before we sat down, he apologised that he had let me pick up the tab the previous night, explaining that he hadn't taken much money with him. "You were the last person I expected to bump into last night and even then I didn't think you would be staying."

To be truthful, I was beginning to really enjoy his company. It was good to talk to someone who didn't have expectations of me, but saw potential that I hadn't explored. This music thing had begun to get under my skin, prompting some very happy memories. I'd forgotten how much we used to talk about trying to make a go of it, but as Jake reminded me about our mutual past, those feelings of excitement were stirring once again.

At about six-thirty the café door opened announcing a new entrant with a 'ding' of the bell. "Micky! Jez! Great to see you again," said Jake, in a flamboyant manner. "Come and join us and let me get you guys a coffee," Jake offered, loud enough for the café attendant to hear and move into action to fulfil the request. "We were just reminiscing about how we used to practise together at Andy's mansion when we were teenagers. Got a big place his 'old man' you know." He added the last line while leaning forward as though sharing a secret with Micky and Jez. "Anyway there's this games room where we would crank up the volume to try'n'blow the windows out to scare the gardener." Jake laughed. I couldn't help joining him as I remembered the expression on Henry Price's face as he worked just outside, wrestling the shrubbery into submission. He used to jokingly tell me that it was a wonder any plants wanted to grow anywhere near the place and if we continued to play that music at that volume, we would put him out of a job.

"The gardener?" Micky and Jez said together looking at each other and then me.

"Knock it off, Jake, that's enough about me. You said that you wanted to put some kind of idea to me, so what do you have in mind?" I tried to redirect the conversation elsewhere, as I felt a little embarrassed by Micky and Jez's reaction.

"Yeah, you're right. Well... Me, Micky and Jez were talking earlier, you know, when you couldn't get up 'cos you didn't feel so good." Micky snorted a laugh about my incapacity, but tried to cover it by coughing. "We thought that if we pooled our resources, we could probably make a go of forming a professional band together, with you. You fitted in great last night and we've got some gigs in the smaller pubs and clubs to help develop a bit if we want to. But, even better than that,

Micky has been in contact with a guy who reckons he can get us some larger jobs as soon as we're ready, assuming he likes us. We would need some gear and a van, but that's no big deal and we could get a place together to use as a base to live and practise. Jez knows this guy who's got an isolated place, not too far away, that he wants to let out. It's a kind of barn that's been converted, so we'd be able to live there as well as practise at whatever volume we wanted and at whatever time we wanted."

Jake paused to take a breath after downloading all this information, but his excitement was quite infectious. Deliberately slowing himself, he continued. "Now, I know it's a lot to take in, Andy, but I don't think that it was a coincidence you turned up last night. It's what should've happened a long time ago, if your 'old man' hadn't put a stop to it." He looked at me taking a moment to gauge my reaction. "Look, Andy, its fate. It's our destiny. We've got the contacts and between us we can find the resources to pull this together, making something of ourselves and having a great time doing it. As I told you before, you're an artist like me, and Micky, and Jez. We were never meant to work in ordinary jobs like other people do. Your heart's not in that kind of job anyway, you know it isn't.

"Can you remember how you used to talk to me about how your dad, God bless him, told you that you would join him at the company when the time was right? What did you use to say to me? Remember, Andy, what did you say?" Jake prompted my response, but waited for me to deliver it.

"I don't want to wear a suit to work for the next fifty years," I mumbled.

"That's right," Jake whispered. "Now's your time, boy. Stand up and be a man. Decide to do what you want to do. Don't let the 'old man' push you around anymore. It's not being disrespectful. Look at it like this: it's time to spread your wings and fly for yourself. How's that for the artist coming out?" The three of them laughed at Jake's poetic attempts. I smiled to acknowledge the joke, but it was only on the surface, my mind was preoccupied with what was being suggested.

There was something to what Jake was saying, about how I had wanted to do certain things yet had been moulded in a different direction. I didn't like his references to Dad though. I didn't think he was being malicious, but it just made me uncomfortable to hear him talk about Dad like he was my jailer. At the same time there was an element of truth about it all that I couldn't deny.

The prospect of doing something exciting appealed to me very much. The whole 'office thing' seemed so dull to me. While Carl would come home from work buzzing from the events of the day, even reading finance reports seemed to ring his bell, to me it was little more than a tedious ritual. I couldn't see it as a course for my life, even though I had tried over the last couple of years at Dad's prompting.

Jake broke through to my little world of thought. "Look Andy, there's no need to make a decision right now. We're going to spend the evening having another practise session, but this time it will actually be in the bar at the pub. You relax and enjoy the experience, then see how you feel about making it a serious gig. Imagine an audience enjoying your talent. Imagine the perks of the job," he winked. "All I'm asking is that you give it time before you turn your back on it," and with emphasis he said, "again... You can stay with me at the flat until we decide about Jez's friend's place, then, who knows what we might do."

My mind was whirling through all the things that were being suggested, but I knew, deep inside, that however long it took for me to actually say 'yes,' I did want to team up with Jake and the other guys. It was as though the decision had already been taken, it just awaited final confirmation before the ball started to roll.

I remember very clearly the day that the dreams of fame seemed to be wrenched from my grasp. It was the very day I started work at the company. Not that I have anything against people who do those jobs, but at that particular moment I knew it wasn't for me.

I travelled to work with Carl on the first morning and he introduced me to the other members of staff that I would be working with. I couldn't help feeling like I had gate-crashed someone else's party and sat down in the birthday boy's chair, much to the consternation of the rest of the family. They weren't unpleasant, but 'square peg in a round hole' was an apt description of my predicament.

Jake was offering something that appealed to me, that I wanted to do. As I sat there mulling things over, while the others continued chatting, I knew that my decision had already been made.

The practise evening at the pub was fantastic. So much so, that it passed as fast as a train skipping a station. Everybody there seemed to really enjoy themselves, but no one more than me. I was buzzing with the possibilities that had opened for me and the adrenalin from that evening simply strengthened my resolve to throw my lot in with those guys.

I don't particularly remember getting back to Jake's flat that night, or ending up on the sofa again, but one thing I did know was that I had made up my mind. It wasn't something I just wanted to do, but something I felt I had to do.

Up to that point I had kept my mobile phone turned off deliberately because I didn't want to take any calls, particularly from the most likely callers, Dad and Carl, while I was sorting myself out. It wouldn't make much difference to anyone else as I had few friends anyway. I'd always tended to be a loner, even when I was a child. Not that I was anti-social, but my circle of friends had always been very small. That's what made it hard when Dad became so set against me spending time with Jake. He had been the first friend that I had properly bonded with and to have that taken away was quite tough at the time.

The phone bleeped to indicate that a voicemail message was waiting as soon as I switched it on.

"You have two new messages," announced the computerised voice. The first was from Dad asking me to call. The second, much more abrupt, was from Carl asking what the hell I was playing at. He went on to a lecture, reminding me that I had responsibilities to think about. I had no inclination or intention of responding to either of them at that moment in time. What I needed to do was go home to collect some of the things I would need to make a break away and it had to be soon.

I decided to go back to Durlwood the following morning, as soon as I thought the house would be empty to try to avoid any contact with Dad or Carl. It would have to be late morning to have the best possible chance, as they weren't likely to miss the beginning of the working day at the company. They were both creatures of habit, both early risers and punctual arrivers, so their predictability gave me my opportunity. I was the sleep-in layabout, always the last there and the least interested. I suppose that was one of the things that made me feel alienated from them. Still, the new life I wanted fitted me perfectly. When you play late you can sleep late without feeling guilty, right? Whatever the following day was to bring, I was going to view it as the first day of a new world that I would inhabit.

The next morning I told Jake what I was up to and that I would see him later. I set off trying to time my clothing snatch to perfection. As I drove along the country roads toward Durlwood House, a route that I had travelled so many times over the years, I became increasingly aware of an anxious knot in my stomach. The feeling was a total contrast to the high I was on when I left Jake's flat, but the closer I got to Durlwood the greater my concern grew. There was still a very slight possibility that I would have to face Dad or Carl when I arrived, although I was determined to do whatever I could to avoid that. I really needed to get some of my things from my room if I was going to seriously strike out on my own. Jake's words echoed in my ears, 'Don't let him push you around, you're a man, now go act like one.' That was all very well for him to say, but he didn't have to deal with my father, at least not since their last meeting when he was unceremoniously ejected from the house. I certainly wouldn't mention Jake if I had to face Dad, that would be like a raising a red rag to a bull.

As I came around the final bend on the approach to the house, I knew that the trees in summer would have created a complete wall of privacy shielding the whole property from view, but by late October the green fortress fence had changed to the golden shades of red and orange and finally the walls collapsed, as the leaves created a crisp blanket over the fields and verges of the road. Because it was so late in the season it gave me a chance to take a glimpse at the courtyard in front of the house and, crucially, the old stables where the cars would have been parked. I slowed as the house came into view. There was no sign of any parked vehicles. I hoped the coast was clear, allowing me to do what I needed to and be able to leave before any awkward situation arose.

Reaching the stone pillars that stood sentry either side of the driveway, I turned into the entrance to pass between them. Each one stood to attention like guards at a palace; each holding a plaque proclaiming the property under their watchful eye, 'Durlwood House,' named after the forest circling the old building. I followed the few hundred yards of gravel road that aimed straight at the courtyard and imposing portico entrance. The crunching of stones beneath the wheels of the car, a familiar sound that had accompanied my leaving and arrival to my home for as many years as I could remember, loudly announced my approach. It seemed much louder than usual that morning, probably because I was trying to operate in stealth mode, rather than just returning home unconcerned about being noticed.

I came to the edge of the courtyard and passed under the black cast iron arch from which the railings ran to the stable blocks on both the left and right sides, giving balance to the front view of the house. I glanced left to the stable block that had been converted into a covered parking area for four cars in order to confirm that it was empty. Just a few days before, three cars had stood there in an order that had been maintained since Dad bought me the car I was driving for my eighteenth birthday.

The right side stable block had been a store place for most of my childhood, one of those intriguing areas that children want to explore yet are never quite sure if they should, but had subsequently been converted to a games room. It became the place where I would practise my guitar without fear of disrupting Dad and Carl with the noise.

Most of my time with Jake had been spent in that old building as we endlessly pretended that we were on stage in front of a huge adoring crowd and playing our hearts out for their enjoyment. We initially played in the house, but the conflict it caused meant that another location was needed.

Carl had been working with Dad for a few years, being five years older than me, and he would often work in the evenings, spending a lot of time reading and compiling reports. My approach to music was not conducive to this, as loud was the only way to do it, so Dad resolved the issue by having a basic conversion done to the old stable block store turning it into a games room that became a haven of retreat for me, my friends and our instruments. No doubt it caused great celebration inside the house also.

Passing the carport stable to my left, I slowly rolled the car across the courtyard, while checking for signs of life and turned to go down through the smaller gate that led to the side door of the building. That was where Henry Price, the gardener, would park his pickup truck when working in the grounds.

Dad felt that the trade vehicles made the front of the house look untidy, especially when he would, on occasion, bring business associates home. It wasn't until I went through the small gate that I saw Henry's pickup was in its usual place, indicating that he must be around somewhere. I stopped the car for a moment while I quickly scanned the area to see if the coast was clear. I couldn't see Henry anywhere, but it was possible he was working somewhere on the far side of the house.

The grounds of Durlwood were quite extensive so it was not unusual for him to be working all day without being seen. He had a small lodge off to the left of the house, in a little copse, that became his tool store and workshop once the stable block had been converted into a games room. He would spend much of his time based there in the early spring, preparing the vibrant display of colour to decorate the gardens for the year to come.

I was in a hurry to do what I had come for and felt very conspicuous as I darted from the car through the side door and up to my room. I gathered together the essentials I wanted to take and unceremoniously carted them down the stairs, as much as I could carry at a time. The Mercedes was not the most practical car for transporting gear, but I stuffed it to bursting with everything I could get in so that I would not have to make another visit.

"Hi, Andy, how are you this mornin'?"

I heard a voice call from a distance and instantly recognised it as Henry Price. That was not good, as I didn't want to be seen, but I could hardly ignore the man who had maintained the gardens of the home I'd lived in since I was a child. His son John, John's wife Sandra, and their children, Suzanna, James and Sonia, had been associated with my family for a long time. They were like members of the extended family and I couldn't be rude to Henry who was like a grandfather to me, as well as to his own family. Anyway, even if I had conflicts with Dad, Henry knew nothing of it and I didn't want to put him in an awkward position by letting on.

Taking the initiative, I walked over to greet him, not wanting him to come near enough to see the car packed to the roof with a jumble of items. That would initiate the need for some kind of explanation and I didn't fancy that.

I reckon Henry was about sixty-five years old, but he had always seemed that same age to me as I grew up. His weather-worn skin showed the signs of the many years of his life spent working outdoors. White hair protruded around the rim of the permanently fixed cloth cap that he was never seen without while in the garden. The furthest he ever seemed to part from it was during the heat of summer when he would lift it, draw his wrist across his forehead to wipe away the beads of sweat, only to immediately replace it again. One thing was true about Henry, he was the most friendly helpful man you could ever wish to meet.

In order to avoid the awkward questions that might be difficult to answer without giving away the purpose of my visit, I tried to direct the conversation.

"I'm good, Henry, thank you. You been here all day?"

"Aye, lad, there's always somethin' to do 'ere. 'Tis a big place and the older I get the bigger it seems," he said with a laugh. "Your Dad left about an hour ago. He asked me if I'd seen you today. Well I hadn't then, but I 'ave now. You off out again?"

He nodded over to the car knowing that it was unusual for anybody other than himself and Martha, the housekeeper, to park at the side of the house. I wasn't sure if he was fishing for an explanation or whether he just thought I'd been busy with something and was about to leave.

I tried to block his view of the car as much as possible without being too obvious.

"Yes, yes, just running a few errands. I had to put something in the car. I just thought it would be easier from the side door."

"Oh, I see. Do you need a hand to carry anything, lad?" I shook my head and thanked him.

"D'you see the newspaper this mornin'?" he asked, but didn't wait for a response before telling me what had caught his attention. "Your brother made a success of that charity do he arranged. Fifteen thousand 'e raised." He paused for effect and a response that was not forthcoming "How about that?" he pressed. Seeing that I was not being particularly talkative he continued, "I reckon the 'ospital's goin' to be thankful for that." Realising that my lack of response must have seemed a little odd, I agreed with him.

"Fifteen thousand, wow. That's great, really good," then I tried to make my excuses to leave. "Er... look, Henry, I have got to get going, so it was nice to see you. Perhaps we'll talk later. Okay?" I turned to go back to the car to emphasise that I was pressed for time and had to go.

"Oh, okay, Andy. I wouldn't want to hold up the busy people. I'll tell your Dad I've seen you if he comes back," he shouted after me. I waved to acknowledge that I had heard him.

He continued to look at me for a few moments, as he leant against the spade he had been using. I pretended to be busy finishing what I was doing. I was actually waiting for him to turn away so that I could get by without him seeing into the car, but he didn't seem in a hurry to go. After what seemed like an age, he put the spade into the wheelbarrow that had always accompanied him in his work and wandered away into the garden.

Within moments of the coast becoming clear, I was heading back down the driveway just hoping that I was away without any further interruptions. Turning left at the stone pillars and onto the main road, I glanced back at Durlwood House not knowing when I would be back there again.

I was still smarting at the thought that even the gardener followed Carl's career with great interest. I didn't need it rubbing in about how successful he had been. If there was anything about home that I wasn't going to miss it was the constant reminders about my own shortcomings. I was becoming even more convinced that it was the right time for me to create my own success in something that I was good at. Something *he* could't compete with.

CHAPTER 5

I was on the road for about an hour, heading back to Jake's flat and fighting my way through the heavy traffic in town. I wasn't used to being so near to the city, having lived well out beyond the suburbs all of my life, but living in a flat in the built up area that surrounded the centre was going to be interesting.

When I was younger, the remote location of Durlwood House had made the journeys to and from school quite long. The early mornings always jarred against a body clock that thought midday was a good time to get up. Those days were long gone and, as an adult, my attachment to the countryside, Durlwood in particular, had seemed to loosen considerably. I was young and wanted to find other places and opportunities. To make something out of my new association with Jake which, to say the least, was very appealing.

After another half-hour of crawling, I finally pulled into the residents' parking bay at Jake's place and began to unload everything I had brought with me. The car looked uncomfortable in the shabby surroundings, like jewellery on display in a hardware shop window, but as I carried my things up the flights of stairs, stopping to catch my breath every so often, I felt an increasing sense of freedom that was very welcome. No questions about where I was going, or when I was coming back, or who I was seeing. It was my choice and mine alone.

Jake arrived at the flat about thirty minutes later with a four-pack of lager, two of which had already gone, pulling one off he threw it to me.

"Congratulations, Andy, you are now officially the fourth member of the music group 'SQUAD4'." He held his can up for me to join him in his toast to success, which I did. "We need to contact Jez to arrange things with his friend and get ourselves out of this dive as soon as possible. Don't you reckon? He thinks we could sign the contract and be in there at the weekend, as long as we can pull together the deposit. Now, I'm a bit short at the moment and I know that Micky isn't doing so well until the band starts earning, so we might need your financial help initially. Anyhow, Micky's put a lot of time and effort into getting things set up with this new manager, so we've all got to use our skills to make this work, right? Jez can lay his hands on some money, but there's a delay – something about a penalty for getting it without notice, so that leaves you mate. About seven hundred is what we need for now, then we'll sort it out once we're in the place. Is that okay with you?"

I was a bit surprised that Jake was so forward about it, but then while I had been trying to deal with the change in my life, I suppose he had made the effort to organise everything else. The least I could do was be thankful.

"Okay, Jake. Yes. When... when do you need the money?" I hesitantly asked, trying to cover the fact that I was a little put out that he had made such an assumption.

"Oh, tomorrow should be fine," he replied, as he turned on the TV and slumped into a chair to watch.

"Tomorrow?" I blurted out a little startled.

"Yeah, that should be fine," he responded in a matter of fact way. Then he let out a laugh, at something on the TV and moved the conversation on as though he had simply asked a small favour. "Have you seen this rubbish? They make me laugh, these people who go on TV shows and talk about their lives as though they were at the shrink's office."

I laughed at his comment, but was still thinking about the sudden 'investment' I had been 'told' to make. Still, I didn't want to stay in Jake's dingy flat any longer than was absolutely necessary. It was probably worth finding the initial seven hundred pounds for the deposit just to move to somewhere decent. While I baulked at the suddenness of the demand, it was not that difficult for me to get hold of that amount. I did have the means to support myself quite comfortably, from a fund that was set aside for me from the life insurance that paid out when Mum died and that was free for me to use as I pleased now that I was twenty-one. There was also a substantial allowance that Dad had been paying into my personal account over the years, but to be honest I hardly ever needed to use it as he bought most of the things I needed, even my car.

At the time, partly because I don't remember things ever being any other way, I assumed my life was not that much different to most other people's. Being cocooned in this world of people who are like you in wealth and lifestyle, coupled with the blindness of youth and immaturity, I didn't take much notice of others. The only person that I had connected with from a different social tier than myself was Jake. I never saw where he lived, nor did I ever meet his parents. I only knew that he didn't seem to have much and was always borrowing things from me. I can't say that I gave it a great deal thought though.

We were due to meet Jez's friend the following day at the barn to pay the deposit and to sign the agreement and, because it was about three in the afternoon, I excused myself and headed into town to the bank in order to get the money for the deal. It was only about twenty minutes' walk so I knew I would be back within the hour.

By the time I had returned, Micky and Jez were there sat around the TV with Jake.

"Andy," shouted Jez, "we okay for tomorrow? Steve is going to meet us there to make everything official, if that's alright?"

"Yeah. Sure, that's okay, Jez. It should be good."

"Well then, here's to us and the adventure that is heading our way. This calls for a drink," Jake said as he passed around more cans that had appeared during my absence.

We spent the rest of the day clowning around, telling jokes and eating pizza from the nearby takeaway. Not the sort of thing that was ever on the menu at Durlwood.

Dad had employed a 'live-in' cook-come-housekeeper called Martha. She had been with Dad since I was very small, living in a specially separated part of the house that came with the position. She took the job after having had a difficult time in her marriage and when her husband finally left, she applied to an advert that Dad had placed in the job centre.

She never talked about the circumstances that surrounded the events that brought her to us, but from what I gathered, he had treated her badly and ultimately left to be with another woman who he'd met at work.

Martha certainly gave a motherly feel to the house, helping Dad in the early days dealing with young children and no partner. In fact, Martha was the only reason that I ever arrived at school on time, making it her personal responsibility to be sure that it happened, every day, without fail. If we weren't at the end of the driveway when the school bus came by, it wouldn't stop and wait. That was never a situation that occurred again once Martha had taken control of the proceedings.

She was a stickler for good home cooking and the idea of takeaway pizza would have horrified her. In her opinion, it was either cooked by her hand or it was rubbish, or at least inferior. There was no doubt that she was a great cook, but boys like chips, pizza and all manner of food that would not dare present itself on Martha's menu. So eating pizza, with the other guys, was like a schoolboy finding five pounds and buying enough sweets to bulge his pockets with.

Later that evening we spent our time playing through some of the material we were preparing to use as a band, although Micky was quite limited, as far as his drums were concerned. The complaints from the flat above somewhat dampened the practise session, but the evening did initiate some great ideas for new songs that we could use and being involved in the creative process was an exhilarating experience. To see something take shape from a blank page, like a painting on a canvas, took my breath away.

It must have been early in the morning when we finally ended that first social event by just falling asleep wherever there was space. The floor, in chairs, the sofa, they were all exploited for the purpose that night.

The place was a bit of a dump when I had arrived the previous night and it suddenly had to contain two more adults with various instruments and equipment in tow, let alone my extra baggage, but I found that the surroundings disappeared while I was involved in the music. Fortunately we were about to move out to somewhere that would give us the unrestricted ability to practise whenever we wanted, without complaint from neighbours.

The following morning was introduced rather suddenly by the clatter of movement around me. Jez, while making plenty of noise, was periodically prodding each of us.

"Wake up you lot. We've got a meeting with Steve this morning. He'll be there in just over an hour. It will take us nearly that long to get there, so you'd better shift your lazy arses. We need to get a move on!"

It was not quite the gentle awakening of sunlight creeping through the breaks in the curtains, but much more like the brass band striking up in the middle of the room. Still it did the trick and, among the moans, groans and general abuse hurled at Jez, we assembled ourselves for parade and headed off to the barn we were looking to rent.

It was a beautiful morning, making the journey to our appointment a real pleasure. The busy, bustling noise of the city gradually gave way to the crisp clear air of the countryside, making the morning that much more stunning.

The conversation was lively and seemed to be filled with the promise of what was to come, making the journey skip by quickly so that we arrived almost on time. I don't know what I'd expected, but the place was ideal. 'Langdale Barn,' announced the sign on the gatepost.

It was a large rambling building of stone set out on its own, circled by trees and in sight of a river. Admittedly it was a little tired in appearance, but I could see that the charm of the surroundings would be great for inspiring the creative forces to work their magic. So much for thinking my links with the countryside were loosening, but I didn't realise at the time that it was Langdale's similarity to Durlwood's environment that appealed to me so much.

Steve was already there waiting for us to arrive and he came out through the front door as I drew the car to a stop. They had elected me to drive that morning, presumably because the only other vehicle available to us was Jez's car, not the most elegant machine and, as Jake pointed out, to arrive in a 'Merc' wouldn't hinder our chances of impressing Steve. He was not wrong about that. As we got out of the car the first thing that Steve said was, "Nice motor, gentlemen."

"Good start for an up and coming rock band, don't you think?" Jake said. We all laughed at his humour, then Jez introduced us to Steve.

"Okay, guys, the deposit is as we agreed previously. You will be responsible for any breakages or damage that occurs. If you follow me I'll show you around. If all's well, I will simply need the money and a signature." We trailed after him as he continued talking. "The agreement is for one year, at which point we will renegotiate, if you want to continue of course. Rent is six hundred each calendar month and you will be liable for all the services. Right let's take a look around."

As I was about to step through the front door, I noticed that Jez had stayed outside leaning against the car.

"You coming Jez?" I shouted. He waved me to go on.

"No, I've already had the guided tour from Steve last week. That's why we're here in the first place. I'm going to stay out here and have a smoke. You go ahead."

There was a lady sat in Steve's car and as we went into the house she got out and walked over to Jez. They obviously knew each other fairly well, judging by their greeting.

The tour of the house began as Steve showed us through the kitchen and into the living area, which was plenty big enough to set up the practise equipment. That alone sold the place to me, but the large open fireplace at the end of the room gave it a charm of its own. The upstairs went partly into the roof, creating unusually low windows that allowed a clear view down onto the driveway, even when standing in the middle of the rooms. The stairs went up from the living area and came out midway along the landing so that it was possible to turn left or right at the top.

The landing ran like a corridor along the back of the building with the bedroom and bathroom doors opening to the rooms which all looked out to the front of the building. There were two bathrooms, which would be useful with four of us sharing the building, and four bedrooms. The bedroom at the end of the building, furthest away from the driveway entrance, had double doors which led out onto a kind of veranda; it was by far the biggest room. The place was sparsely furnished throughout, but at least there was a bed in each room.

As we toured the upstairs, I noticed through a window that Jez was deep in conversation with the lady outside. He cupped his hand around a lighter as she leant forwards to light a cigarette, then went back to the conversation that seemed, from the body language, to be a little argumentative.

Steve led us back downstairs to the kitchen and once we were assembled said, "Right, that's the easy bit, now for the money."

The eyes of the others fell on me. I obediently pulled an envelope out of my jacket pocket, handing it to Steve, who took it from my hand quite hastily, tore it open and without apology started to count it out onto the kitchen table.

"Two hundred, three hundred, four hundred," he continued, until the correct amount was announced. "Seven hundred. Very good."

Looking up, he scanned our faces and rubbing his hands together, in a 'salesman about to clinch the deal' way, he said, "Right, I just need a signature from you to complete the paperwork, then the key is yours and you're free to move in whenever you want to." Focusing on me, he held out the pen and slid a paper toward me on the table. "On the line at the bottom please."

Taking the pen, I leant over to sign on the line where he held his finger.

"You want us all to sign?" I asked, as I prepared to make my mark.

"No. Just you."

I hesitated and looked up at him for an explanation why.

"It's just a formality, but as Jez told me that you would be the one who would provide the deposit, your signature ensures that there's no dispute when I come to refund the money at the end of the rent agreement. It will be yours without any question."

I paused for a moment longer, as I looked at him, just trying to assess his character, his honesty. He nodded urging me to action, so I acquiesced, putting pen to paper and signed as required, 'Andrew Numan.'

"Thank you very much gentlemen. Here are the keys, plus a spare set in the kitchen cabinet over there. I trust you will have a good time here and hope that everything goes well for you," he said, as he quickly stuffed papers and money into his pocket. "I will send a copy of the papers to this address in due course and now I'll bid you good day."

He turned on his heels and headed out of the front door to the lady and Jez, who were still talking out on the driveway. He shook hands with Jez and appeared to pass something to him. Then he and the lady walked to their car and were on their way.

"We're in!" shouted Jake, breaking the silence and making me jump at the suddenness of his call. "And, I've got the big room," he added, as Jez came through the door.

I was still a little intrigued by the connection between Jez and the mystery lady outside.

"Did Steve leave you something, Jez?"

"What?" He seemed a little surprised by my question. "No. I'd run out of cigarettes and I asked him for one."

"Oh... my mistake."

"Well done by the way. You've helped us take the first step on a great trip," he said, as he slapped me on the back.

The others made their appreciation known as they wandered back through to the living room, opening draws and cupboards to check for contents.

"I suggest that we begin to move all our gear in today, it's still early after all, then we can spend our first night here with a celebration party," said Jake.

There seemed to be general agreement about the idea and I saw no reason to stay at Jake's flat any longer than was necessary. We locked up, got back in the car and headed to town with purpose.

It was one of those beautiful late autumn days when the sun was too low in the sky for it to be hot, but just managing to overpower the chill of the day. I dropped the roof so that we could make the most of the drive, much to the delight of the others. I felt good about our prospects and mulled over the opportunities of the coming months as we drifted along the roads that became evermore urban. As we arrived back at Jake's flat, Micky was just finishing a phone call negotiating the use of a van owned by an acquaintance. The promise of a few drinks and an 'I owe you' seemed to do the trick, concluding the deal. Jez and Micky immediately left in Jez's car to fetch the newly arranged removal transport. Jake and I started to load up my car with whatever we could get in there, but it was pretty much full when I returned from Durlwood the day before, so there was not much else we could get in, other than my own things. Jake didn't seem too concerned about the larger items in his flat, suggesting that he would be leaving most of the decrepit furniture. Langdale already had enough furniture for our needs, sparse though it was.

As we squashed the last possible bits of luggage in, after wheezing our way up and down the flights of stairs, Jez arrived, closely followed by Micky in a ramshackle van that harmoniously blended with the run down surroundings of the area. The remainder of Jake's 'stuff' was unceremoniously shoved into the van as fast as possible, then we were off to pick up what the others needed to move. As it turned out, Jez and Micky lived in the same house only about five minutes away from Jake's place, so we were not on the move long before it was back to loading up.

To say that their house was run down was to compliment its shabby appearance. There was considerable damage to the building and that left me in no doubt why they were very keen to leave their current residences and move to Langdale Barn.

There were a couple of other guys in the house who seemed totally indifferent to the coming and going of people and possessions, not that there was much to move. It was over quite quickly with four pairs of hands on the job. In fact, as was the case at Jake's, the music equipment accounted for the bulk of items and was cherished like the crown jewels.

It was gone three in the afternoon before we were on our final journey of the day, heading back to Langdale, after stopping to pick up some necessary supplies. Jake was in the car with me, Jez in his own car and Micky following at the rear in the old van.

The convoy wound its way through the gradually narrowing roads toward the final destination as dusk was making its initial attempts to overcome the daylight. The sun was still trying to hold onto the day, but disappearing fast below the horizon. The effect was exaggerated by the increasing density of trees that lined the road, even though most of their leaves had gone.

When we finally turned into the drive at Langdale Barn, to a united cheer of delight, I could tell that when darkness finally did arrive it would be black indeed. That didn't concern me, in fact, it reminded me of the way Durlwood looked at night. I had been a country boy all my life and the uninterrupted darkness of the unpopulated areas was more appealing than I cared to admit, much more than the unnatural orange glow of the city sky at night.

We immediately began to unload everything to the living room first, but Jez disappeared off to the end of the building. He came back a few minutes later with his arms laden with logs and when we caught sight of what he was up to he shouted, "A fire tonight I think!" We all cheered him on as he struggled through the doorway into the kitchen and through to the living room to prepare the show.

Each time I went into the house, carrying something else from the van, the flames were a little higher, the room a little warmer. Each return to the van, the night was a little darker and I felt a little colder, as the chill of the evening was shown to be increasingly hostile in comparison to the fire-warmed living room.

By seven we were just about organised. The fire was raging at one end of the room, while the instruments were set out, as though mimicking a stage, at the other. Micky was the last to come in from the van and was carrying a crate of drinks.

"I picked these up when I got the van," he said, with a smirk on his face. "I thought we deserved them this evening, same as every other evening really. Anyway, we agreed a party was in order so, how can we have a party without some drink to help celebrate?"

Passing a can to each of us, he took one for himself and pulled the top, then lifting it in the air shouted, "To success, money, music and girls!" We all laughed as we followed his lead parroting him word for word. The adventure had begun.

Jake flicked the switch to his keyboard and amplifier and within seconds was goading us, with his music, to join in. That evening was one that I will never forget as the anxieties of the moment slipped away and we played our hearts out, loud, long and hard.

I remember at one point being interrupted when my phone rang while we were discussing the opening bars of a new song. The screen showed that it was Dad, but, having been lost in this world without care for the previous two hours, I didn't want to take the call and bring the delusion to an end. I didn't know what I was going to say to him anyway to be truthful. I preferred not to say anything for the moment, but I knew that this state of affairs couldn't continue indefinitely.

"Do you want us to wait while you answer that?" Jake asked.

"No, its okay, it's nothing important," I said, feeling a twinge of conscience as the words left my mouth. The ringing stopped and we resumed our discussion only for it to be interrupted by the voicemail bleep. I ignored it and threw in another comment relevant to the conversation, but just as we were picking up the flow, we were interrupted again, this time it was Micky's phone.

He immediately answered it, which made me feel all the more guilty for ignoring mine, and went to the kitchen so he could talk in private.

We semi-resumed our conversation, but were all interested in what was happening in the kitchen and when Micky finally returned, with a broad grin on his face, there was no alternative but to stop and quiz him about his call.

"Okay, guys, we've got two days to get our act together before the guy I've been talking to comes here to see us. Terry Douglas wants to discuss bookings, but before he agrees to anything he wants a demonstration of what we can do. I talked us up 'big time,' so we need to get our butts in gear and be ready to blow him away on Friday."

"Friday! Micky, I don't know that I am up to that so soon. It's one thing practising in a back room at some run down old pub, but to be ready to show something professional, that's a whole different ball game." They all looked at me. "What?"

"You'll be ready, Andy. You mark my words. You'll be ready. This is the opportunity we've worked for, for a very long time. Now we'll cut you some slack 'cos your new back into it, but this is going to work no matter how hard you find it. This is not a game now. This is what we have agreed to do with our lives. Now is not the time to doubt it. You're in and that's all there is to it, so let's get our heads down and make it work."

There was a hint of something sinister in Jake's voice as he spoke and I was taken aback at how forceful he was being.

Then, as if to try to lighten the mood again, he said, "Anyway you're the best guitarist we know, so don't put yourself down. Terry's not going to want to listen to many songs, so we'll rehearse three, maybe four, until they're perfect. If we need to do more, you can bluff them, but I doubt he will want to spend the time. He's not coming here to have a personal concert, he's interested in making money. That means he needs good bands that can be ready at short notice. That's exactly what we are."

Jake said we would rehearse and rehearse we did. It was two in the morning before he allowed us to break for some sleep. He knew how to make the band work. The perfectionist in him taking charge, he made us go over and over things while he systematically picked out the faults that needed to be changed to make the biggest impact.

After being a removal man for most of the day, a long, tough rehearsal was not at the top of my agenda, but he sure knew how to whip us into shape. By the time we finished my fingers were sore, but I was beginning to think, given the remaining time, that I could pull off enough of the songs in order to help make a good impression. Four good songs were not beyond our reach, especially considering that we still had a full day to rehearse.

When I finally crawled into bed, early that morning, I wasn't searching for sleep, it had cornered me long ago and I had been fighting to keep it at bay for too long. There were creaks and groans from the old building as each of the others settled for the night. I was on the verge of losing consciousness when I remembered the voicemail Dad had left earlier. Taking my phone, I listened to the menu voice and selected 'listen.' "Andy, it's Dad. Look son, I know we have had our disagreements, but I really need to talk to you. Please ring me when you get this message. Henry told me that he had seen you and I noticed you've taken some of your things. Please just ring to say that you're alright, if nothing else. Look forward to your call."

I deleted the message, but there was a heavy feeling in my heart. Dad sounded concerned. Why does that tone often seem to come too late; when it's so difficult to go back from the positions taken. Anyway, my life was heading in a new direction that I knew he wouldn't agree with, but the choices had been made and the chances taken, now I needed time to show him that I could become successful in the things I liked to do.

Not everyone is cut out for work behind a desk, even if a father wants his sons to follow in his footsteps. One son had, but there was no reason why they both had to.

I must have drifted off to sleep, as I don't remember anything else until the creaking of floorboards out on the landing woke me. Having never found my watch, I picked up my phone to check the time, five-thirty.

I couldn't get back to sleep again, even though it was still pitch black outside, unlike Jake's flat, where the perpetual intrusion of an orange glow from the streetlights was so unnatural. There was, though I didn't really want to admit it, something quite comforting about the similarity Langdale had with home. I lay thinking about what I'd done, wondering what the future held for me. Hasty decisions can lead to paths that are not easily retraced, but at that moment I didn't want to retrace them. If I'd known what was to come, I might have thought differently.

CHAPTER 6

CARL

"Dad. Anybody home?" I shouted, stepping through the front door. There was no response, so I went through to the kitchen, getting there just as Martha, the housekeeper, came in from the rear door.

"Oh! Carl, you made me jump. When did you get here?"

"I've just come in, Martha. I was looking for Dad. His car's outside, but I couldn't get an answer when I shouted."

"I think he's in the study, but you will have to speak up to attract his attention, he's been rather distracted the last couple of days. I asked him something earlier and it was like he was made of stone, he didn't hear a word I said. Not eating very much either, Carl, and I don't know what's happened to Andy. The last couple of meals I've made for him were still in the kitchen the following morning. I don't know, you youngsters are here, there and everywhere without a care in the world."

"I'm sorry about that, Martha, but things are not so good at the moment between Dad and Andy. He left the other day in quite a rage and we haven't seen anything of him since, so go easy on Dad. I know he's tried to contact Andy, I have too, but he isn't responding to our messages. I'm hoping he'll come to his senses soon."

"I'm sorry to hear that, Carl. I hope your Dad can work it out soon."

"It's not Dad, it's Andy acting like a child that's the problem. He's twenty-one. It's time he grew up and acted like an adult. Anyway, I'm going to see Dad, Martha, I'll talk to you later."

I walked along the hallway that was lined with a gallery of pictures of me and Andy taken over the years. Each frame was a reminder of our lives together at Durlwood and a few from the rare holidays we'd had. There were also two photographs of Mum in very special ornate frames. One of her was with Dad and me and one with Andy at only a few weeks old. I stopped for a few moments to look over some of the images that I so often walked past without even noticing their presence. It's so easy to become complacent about things that seem to always be there, but the conflict with Andy was probably the catalyst that made me want to review them again.

The office door at the end hallway was closed, so out of courtesy and habit, I knocked, then paused before going in. Dad was stood with his back to me looking out of the window across the fields to the side of the house.

"Dad, are you okay?"

He half glanced over his shoulder to acknowledge my presence.

"I'm okay, Carl. I'm okay. I've been standing here for a while watching the traffic on the road over there. From time to time I think I can see Andy's car, but when I go to the other window, to watch them come closer, they never turn down the driveway. I've tried to get in touch; I even left a message on his phone last night. It rang, so I know it was turned on, but he didn't answer it."

Not wanting to interrupt Dad too soon, I didn't answer immediately. I was thankful that I hesitated because Dad hadn't really finished what he was saying. It was just a little bit more subdued than was usual for him.

"Andy came home the other day. Henry saw him. I assume he came when he did because he thought that nobody would be around."

"What was he doing here?"

"Henry seemed to think he was trying to hide what he was doing, but thought he was filling his car with clothes and things. I went up to his room to see what was gone. All the wardrobes have been emptied. I think he's serious about moving out. I just want to make sure he's alright and not in any kind of trouble. He obviously feels really hurt about things."

"He feels hurt! What about the people he's hurt and let down? I suppose you know that he hasn't even had the decency to ring in to work to say he was going to be away. It's put the other guys in the office in an awkward position with clients who keep asking to speak to him. The whole point was to give him more responsibility so that he could develop. That's what we agreed at that meeting six months ago and look where it's got us! They're lying to cover for him, saying he's ill."

Dad didn't like what I was saying, but someone had to tell him straight. Besides, I was angry about Andy's reckless behaviour and his total disregard for others. The company was important to me. If he didn't want to take the position seriously, he should have gone somewhere else to work.

"You know, Carl, I'm not sure that it was a good idea to bring Andy to work at the company."

"Too right, Dad!"

"No, Carl, you don't understand what I mean."

"Sure I understand. He's too immature to be given any serious responsibility," I snapped.

"No, Carl. What I mean is, just because I have built this business and you have displayed a flare for developing it, doesn't mean that Andy shares that enthusiasm with us. He was always more..." he paused.

"Lazy." I offered a suggestion to complete the sentence, but Dad obviously didn't approve of my approach.

"That's enough, Carl. Don't you think I'm unhappy with the whole situation? I don't want to make it worse than it is already. Just back off a bit and allow me to try to understand what has happened here before..."

"Before what, Dad?"

"I just need to get in touch with him to see that he's alright. That's all."

"Look, Dad, I've got things to do now so I'm going to leave before I say something I'm going to regret, but I'll be back later on, perhaps we should talk then."

As I headed to the door the phone began to ring and Dad went to his desk to answer it waving in acknowledgement to me. I pulled the office door closed then headed out to the car parked in the courtyard, taking off my jacket to hang in the back. As I was about to get into the car, I caught sight of Dad knocking on the window to attract my attention. He waved at me to return inside and looked as though it was something important.

When I came back into the house, he was standing in the office doorway at the end of the hall.

"That was Andy on the phone," he shouted. "He picked up my message from last night. He said that he didn't mean to hurt me but that he had to make a life for himself doing what he wanted to do and would not be coming home."

"Well, where on earth is he then?" I asked a little annoyed.

"He wouldn't say. He told me not to try to find him and not to ring him for the time being, while he sorts himself out."

"Not to ring him!" I shouted. "What does he think he's playing at? Well if you're not going to find out where he is, I am."

I took my mobile out of my pocket, preparing to give Andy a piece of my mind, when Dad came toward me and grasped my hand with the phone in it.

"No! He specifically told me to stop you from getting involved, or he said he would change his phone number and then we wouldn't be able to ring him at all."

"What the hell is that boy doing?" I said, unconsciously raising my voice again.

To be honest, it felt like a punch in the stomach. I really thought that things were generally okay between us, but then I found he was cutting me off and for what? I had no knowledge of any of the lead up to what was happening until I walked into Dad's office a few days before, just in time to see Andy storm out. Why wouldn't my own brother want to talk to me?

Dad had gone back to the window where he was standing when I first came into the office. He was clearly upset by the whole affair, but desperately trying to hide it. It was a good job that Andy was out of arms' reach because I would have knocked his block off for what he was doing. The self-centred infant was so wrapped up in his own little world he failed to see the damage he was doing. To see Dad deliberately hurt like that made me mad and there would come a day when I wouldn't be able to hold back from telling Andy exactly what I thought about him. For the time being though, to honour Dad's wishes, I would hold my tongue.

CHAPTER 7

ANDY

The intense practise on the previous day, before our scheduled audition, was paying off and we were sounding pretty good, even in the restricted room of Langdale. Whether it would be good enough to impress Terry Douglas was yet to be seen, but my confidence was growing as we worked at each song in greater detail until Jake was happy.

Micky seemed to think that this agent knew his stuff and would be able to get us into some pretty good gigs. He was obviously hoping we could step straight into a cancellation or something. Although the prospect was quite nerve-racking, I was beginning to look forward with excitement to the exhilaration of the whole experience, sure that it would beat sitting behind a desk.

The previous day had been a long, but productive, session. We tuned up ready for the audition with a feeling of excitement. There was a real buzz in the room as we were all keen to get on with the task. Terry arrived as agreed at ten-thirty and was led into the living room by Micky to meet the rest of us.

He was a rather large man, tall, broad and loud, with a personality that filled the room the moment he entered. It did give him an air of confident assurance which, I had no doubt, was a useful trait to have when dealing with clients who wanted to book the bands he managed. He didn't hesitate to take charge of the situation, quizzing us about how long we had been playing and what instruments. Then, after several minutes, he turned the conversation to a more serious note.

"Okay, gentlemen, let's get straight to business. You're looking for someone to find work for you and I'm looking to make money," he laughed and it was impossible not to join in with the infectious chuckle. "If," he stressed the word, repeating it for effect, "If you're any good, and Micky here tells me you are, then I think we can make this work to our mutual benefit, but, one thing that I will not tolerate, and you need to know this up front, is an amateurish approach to the work. Just because it's music and at times is enjoyable, doesn't mean that it can be treated lightly. It's still paid work and my clients expect their money's worth. I want professional people who will be flexible with my clients, who turn up when they agree to and who are ready and prepared to deliver the goods. If that's how you operate, then we'll get along just fine. I assume that you've got reliable transport, a van, a truck?"

"Yes that's being dealt with right now, Terry. Hopefully it will be all sorted in the next few days," Jake immediately offered.

"That's good 'cos if you sound okay this morning, I might just want to try you out for a full audition at a club in Sheffield owned by a friend of mine."

"Sheffield?" I blurted out.

There was one of those terrible silences in which you could hear the proverbial pin drop as all eyes took hold on me.

"Yeah, is there a problem with that?" Terry said, as he focused on me.

"No problem at all, Terry, whatever you want, that's fine," said Jake, throwing another glare in my direction.

"Yeah, yeah that's fine," I added. "I was just surprised that you would want to offer us such a great opportunity straight off."

I tried to cover the surprise that was in my voice when I realised that we could be travelling 120 miles to an audition. I don't suppose that I had really thought through the implications of being 'flexible,' as Terry put it.

"Good. That's great, boys. Okay, let's see what you've got then."

Micky offered Terry a drink while we got ready to play, but he waved it off, following his own rules about business coming first and being serious.

The first three songs flew by and we were just about to launch into the fourth, when Terry indicated for us to stop the proceedings.

"That's enough. How many do you think you have like that?"

"Hard to say," said Jake. "Maybe twenty-five or thirty."

I looked at Micky, but he just looked away. We had practised flat out for the last two days to get three well polished songs and one other reasonable one. Jake knew full well that we didn't have thirty.

"Right. Give me a few minutes while I make a phone call,"

Terry headed outside shutting the front door behind him, Jake whirled around and snarled at me.

"You watch your mouth, or you'll wish you had 'cos if you screw it up for the rest of us there's goin' to be trouble."

I was so taken aback that I didn't know how to reply, but before I had chance Terry was coming back into the house.

"It's set then. Next Saturday night at the 'Blow Out' on Abbey Road in Sheffield. You go on from nine-thirty to ten-thirty, before the main band and we'll see how you handle the real thing. Your contact is Kevin Stern, I'll text the number to you, Micky. They have space to park your van, but you need to be there well before five to set up and sound check. I won't be there in person, but Kevin will give me his opinion. If he's happy, then you're on my books. I take fifteen percent from the fee and I collect it. You don't take money at the gig. Any questions?" Terry didn't leave any room for response before continuing. "Oh, of course, this first one's an audition, so you won't expect to be paid, except for your fuel cost, will you?"

Terry wasn't looking for a reply to that question either, but Jake gave him one anyway.

"No problem, Terry."

He shook hands with each of us before he made his way to the door, escorted by Micky.

Once Terry had been seen on his way, I knew that I needed to ask Jake about the van, even at the risk of an unpleasant response.

"What's this van that we've got lined up, Jake?"

He stared at me for an uncomfortably long time, making me brace myself for an explosive response that would contain his displeasure from earlier.

"We bailed you out these last two days, Andy, by practising to make sure you were ready, now it's your turn to do the same for us." Jake indicated to Micky, Jez and himself.

"What do you mean?"

"We need a van, but we haven't got any money yet 'cos we haven't done any gigs. Without a van we won't be doing any gigs, so we need to get one, a good one and quick. So I was thinking, now that you are fully committed to the project," he said, as he wandered over to the window, "that motor of yours would be more useful if we traded it in for a more suitable vehicle."

"Now wait a minute, Jake, nobody said that I would have to sell my car."

Jake spun round and looked at me, as did the other two, who were on the same side of the room as Jake and I felt like I was standing in front of a jury waiting for the sentence to be passed.

"If the cost is too high for you, Andy, you've still got the opportunity to call it quits and leave, I'm sure that daddy will happily take you back while we go off and do the grown up stuff."

"There's no need for that, Jake. I just hadn't realised that's all."

I suppose it was just a car we were talking about, but there was an attachment to it because it was my first car and because Dad bought it for my eighteenth birthday. I really didn't want to have to part with it.

"Haven't we got enough money between us to buy something? I can put some in."

"I told you that Micky and I are short. Jez has got money but it's tied up in an account and he can't get at it for a while."

"It's true, Andy," Jez chipped in. "I would be able to throw in maybe three grand, but not for a while. We do need a reliable van that can do the miles so that we can get to the better paying gigs that will come from Terry. Micky will tell you. These places he can get us into are not shitholes, they're quality joints. We don't want to be stuck playing slots either side of bingo. If we are going to do this, we need to do it pro.'"

He came across and sat next to me.

"Look man, you sort us out now and we'll look after you as soon as things start moving. The only way I know that we can get our hands on a van is sitting out there on the drive. That car is no good to transport our gear and when we're gone, which will be often when things take off, it will just be sat there on the drive."

I looked at the other two as they nodded in sympathy with Jez's argument. Jez nudged me with his shoulder like an old friend encouraging me that it would be okay. I looked at him and then at the other two.

"There is another way we could do it."

They were all quiet, waiting for me to fill them in with this new information.

"I've got a credit card that has a twenty thousand limit on it. We could buy a van with that. By the time the statement comes, you could have your share ready and the others could chip in as we start to see the money come in."

"You're some kind a' bloke, Andy Numan," Jez was looking at me intently. "Top man you are."

The tension in the room subsided, but things were moving in a different direction than I initially thought they would. Still, what did Carl always say to me, 'Andy, you have to follow through. It's no good being half-hearted. See things through to their conclusion.'

Jake interrupted my thoughts.

"Well, gentlemen, the day is still young, so I suggest we go out right now to see what we can find to make sure that we are not worrying about transport at the end of the week. Then we can get some food in and hole ourselves up to prepare for show time."

We must have visited a dozen places before we settled on a vehicle and it was substantially more than I expected to have to pay, but the others were pressing me to think of the fact that we needed something comfortable to travel in, so that we would be in good shape when we arrived at our destination. They seemed to think we could be all over the country within a short space of time.

Eleven thousand pounds, that's what we paid in the end. The salesman added a percentage because I paid by credit card and I had to verify my identity to a card representative on the phone. I felt a little conspicuous as we all sat in the sales office while I talked to the operator, but eventually the transaction was agreed and within a few days we were set to be on the road.

When we got it back to Langdale, I rang to arrange for insurance with all of us as named drivers so that we wouldn't be limited when travelling. With all the equipment we needed in place, the only remaining difficulty was the intensive practise before the following weekend gig.

The week passed very quickly as we rehearsed over and over, song after song. By the end of our daytime session on Thursday we had a pretty good set that would easily last for the time required and, if pushed, we could still pull quite a few more not so perfected ones out of the bag.

It was during that week that I found out just how long Jake, Micky and Jez had been working on the material we were using; it had been for several months before I joined them. No wonder I felt out of my depth, it had seemed to come so easily to them. I began to appreciate that they had invested a lot into this venture that I had not been aware of. I felt a bit guilty at how I'd reacted to Jake's suggestion about selling my car.

The privileged background I'd had meant that as I grew up I was surrounded by luxury in comparison to the others. In fact the run down house that Micky and Jez were in, when we went to get their stuff, was actually a squat. That explained the other people who were there. It also explained the condition of the place.

They seemed genuinely grateful that I had helped them move to somewhere much better, but Jake was much harder to read. I thought I knew him from the time we spent together years earlier, but he had changed a lot since then. I suppose the tough life he'd lived had made an impact on him, but the tone in his voice sometimes seemed to carry a bitterness or hatred. He found it very difficult to be tolerant of the opinions of other people generally, but, aside from a few moments of friction, we all got on quite well.

Dad hadn't rung again since I'd last spoken to him about giving me some space and to tell Carl not to contact me. When I talked to him, I felt a twinge of conscience about what I was doing and how my decisions had affected him, but that had eased over the last couple of days and I was becoming more comfortable with the path I was on. It was what I wanted to do and it felt good. Still, at some point I would have to ring again and face the awkward silences, but, with so much time poured into the intense preparation, it slipped down my priority list.

It was decided that we would travel up to Sheffield on the Friday night before the gig in order to make sure that nothing was left to chance, especially considering the importance of the engagement. We would leave late in the evening, sleep in the van and then spend the day of the gig in Sheffield.

Late afternoon on Friday, just after we had finished our last practise session, on 'a high' as it had gone so well, we started to pack the gear ready to load into the van. Jake suggested we should have a takeaway that evening and since he had to do some things in town he offered to pick one up on the way back to Langdale.

"I will need to borrow a car though."

"It's no good looking at me," Jez replied, as though there was an assumption that his car would be commandeered for the task. "The bloody thing's on its last legs. I tried half a dozen times this morning, but it wouldn't start."

Jake looked at me and I knew that there wasn't really any choice, as we needed the van to load up the equipment.

"Here, take mine," I offered, passing him the keys.

He grinned and slapped my arm as he took the keys from my hand, then turned and headed out into the darkening evening.

"Don't worry," he shouted back, "I promise I'll look after it!"

The driveway lit up with the headlight beams as the car swung around to leave, the taillights disappearing from view along the road just as we started to load the first of the equipment into the back of the van.

There was a lot of banter as the van gradually filled with the cases of instruments, amplifiers and other equipment. We placed it so that it was possible to lay a couple of mats over the hard cases to create two makeshift beds. The unfortunate ones would have to recline the seats in the front as far as possible to get reasonably comfortable. The preparations were enjoyable, conjuring up the same feelings I had when I was young before setting out on a camping holiday, or some other special trip.

When it was all finished, I stoked up the fire in the living room and the TV became the centre of attention for the evening while we waited for Jake to return. I don't think any of us were really focused on the screen properly. For my own part, I was working through all the practising that had been done over the last few days, simply trying to make sure that I could remember all that had been worked on and the more important pieces that had been assigned to me. I really wanted to make an impression with our potential audience, but also with the other guys, especially Jake.

It was getting close to nine when headlights appeared down the drive and Jake finally came in through the door.

"Sorry for the delay guys. I got held up with a bit of last minute business, but the food's here now." Jake threw the car keys across the room for me to catch. "Thanks, Andy. That's quite a car you've got there," he said, as he pulled the food cartons from the carrier bag, while Micky fetched cutlery and some cans of lager from the kitchen.

"I suppose we need to decide who's going to drive this evening," he said, as he landed himself back on the sofa where he'd been sitting before Jake arrived. I drew the short straw for driving, but to be honest, I wasn't too concerned. I think we had consumed enough alcohol between us over the last week to keep a pub in business and it gave me an excuse to have a night off.

At about eleven-thirty we were ready to leave and all climbed into the van in a rather joyful mood. Within half-an-hour we were out of the country lanes onto the larger roads, heading north for what we hoped would be our break into something good.

The journey was quiet and uneventful. We ran through with only one stop, until we got to the outskirts of Sheffield, at about three in the morning. Finding somewhere to park for the remainder of the night, it was time for me to settle down and get some sleep.

The van was reasonably comfortable, but having driven so far I could have slept on a park bench if needed and after the previous week working on our set, I was certainly ready to shut down for as long as possible.

We were all awake fairly early, the alarm clock was the light coming in at dawn and, with Jake at the wheel, set off to find somewhere to wash and have breakfast. The talk was lively and joking, fuelled by an undercurrent of excitement as we ran through the order of events for the show. Even though I'd only had a relatively small amount of sleep, I didn't feel tired, just apprehensive, wound up like a spring with anticipation about the evening to come.

The city was entertaining and busy, but waiting around for the time to disappear, before we had to make our way to the club to set up, was tedious, seeming to drag at a snail's pace. Eventually we had to make a move, but it was only when I had to locate the club that I realised my phone must have been left back at Langdale. I was going to use the 'SatNav' but had to resort to finding it by asking local people for directions. It turned out to be reasonably easy and once the van was in the reserved parking area, Kevin Stern, the contact Terry Douglas gave us, was there to meet us and give instructions about unloading and setting up.

The next few hours flew by as we set up the equipment, rehearsed a few songs and met the main act for the evening. They were a great encouragement to us, obviously aware that it was our first big gig. The time for our set to start was almost upon us and it seemed like the last few minutes before we went on stage had slowed down just to stretch out the agony. All of us were like cats on a hot tin roof as the adrenalin worked us to a high pitch. As the master of ceremonies announced us onto the stage I felt like a coiled spring desperate to explode. The throb of noise from the crowd that was masked behind the blazing spotlights was overwhelming, but the fact that I couldn't see them was something that I was very thankful for.

Before I had time to think about what we were doing, I heard Micky count us in to the first number, 'Two, three, four…' The wall of sound that erupted was immediately echoed by an appreciative crowd that tried to drown the first bars of the music with a cheer that could have lifted the roof. I was beside myself with excitement as the response of each instrument added to the sound that had been practised relentlessly over the previous couple of weeks. It was the beginning of the fulfilment of the dreams I pretended were reality when I was younger. I loved it. The nervousness that I'd endured to that point had disappeared instantly and I found myself standing where I was convinced I was meant to be.

When we finished the first number and the crowd responded very favourably, I knew that I wanted to do this and that my move had been the right one.

CHAPTER 8

"Jake. That was brilliant! You're a genius!" I slapped Jake on the back. "The crowd absolutely loved it and..."

My sentence was cut off mid-flow as Kevin Stern came through the same backroom door where we had waited before going on stage.

"Well guys, that was pretty good. I like what I heard and the punters seemed to appreciate it. I've just been on the phone to Terry and he's agreed that I can keep you here for the rest of the week as a warm up for the other band. Terry seemed to think that you would be fine with that." He paused a second as if to check with us, but not long enough for any comment to actually be made. "I've arranged a place for you to stay nearby and you can leave all the equipment set up here, it will be quite safe. Perhaps you would like to stay for the rest of the evening and see the band that's on next?" Again he paused a moment for a response, but I think we were still processing the information he had just relayed to us and didn't realise that an answer was required. Receiving no response, Kevin just continued with the download. "The B&B is just around the corner, a few hundred yards down the road, Sandra White is the landlady. I've written it down for you... here you go. If you guys do a good week for me here, you will be in with Terry for some good work in the future, mark my words. He knows a lot of people who can help you."

"Thanks a lot, Kevin," said Jake putting out his hand. Kevin shook it and nodded to the rest of us, then turned and left the room in the same instant way he had appeared.

A second or two of silence was broken by Jake's shrill shout, "YES!" closely followed by the rest of us. What an evening that turned out to be. The party continued for a couple more hours while we watched the main act for the rest of the evening.

It must have been twelve-thirty by the time we were knocking on the door of number seventy-two Thorburn Road to be greeted by a quite disgruntled lady who didn't exactly look thrilled to see us. "You'd better come in," was about the sum total of decipherable conversation forthcoming that evening, but at least we ended up in a bed for the night.

The notice on the bedroom door declared, 'breakfast served from 8.00 a.m.,' but I didn't even want to contemplate that time in the morning for now. Sleep, lots of it was high on my agenda.

The days that followed were merged together into a single memory, same club, similar set of songs, same time to bed and getting up, all a bit of a blur. The crowds were smaller during the week, but at the weekend the club was packed and 'buzzing.' The thought of doing that for a living was, by the end of that week, a fantastic one. I was convinced that I had made the right choice joining the others to make the venture work.

It only seemed to be a few moments since we first drove into the club parking area, when suddenly we were loading the van and saying goodbye to Kevin. I got the distinct impression he thought it would not be that last time our paths would cross. We were certainly up for a re-visit in the near future.

Jake drove the whole distance without stopping on the way back to our new base at Langdale. There was something pleasant and familiar about the narrowing roads that finally led to our driveway. The barn coming into sight signalled the completion of our first serious booking and journey's end, for the time being.

As the van turned into the driveway, I immediately noticed that there was a dent on the driver's side of my car, near the rear bumper.

"Look at that!" I shouted, making the others jump at my outburst, as they followed my indication to the damaged car.

"What are we looking at?" Jake asked.

"There's a dent in the back of my car!"

I jumped out of the van to go and examine the damage almost before it had come to a complete stop. The others, a little bemused at my reaction, sauntered up behind me to see what the fuss was about.

"You can't leave your car parked anywhere these days can you?" Micky mumbled.

"What do you mean?" I shouted, turning to look at him. The smirk disappeared from his face when he saw how angry I was. "Jake, you borrowed it before we went away!" I stated, accusingly.

"Hey, what are you suggesting, Andy? That car came back here in the same condition it left. What do you take me for? Anyway, it's only a bloody car," he said in a matter of fact way as he started for the house.

"It's my 'bloody' car, Jake, and now it's damaged!"

He swung around, his eyes flashing like daggers. Grabbing my coat lapels, he shoved me onto the car boot.

"Don't you speak to me like I'm a servant at your 'old man's' house... Who the hell do you think you are, you little weasel? We're giving it everything we've got to make this band work and you're always moaning about how much you have to put into it, or how this or that isn't right. You might have more money than the rest of us, but that don't make you 'Lord of the Manor.' You'd better be more careful before you go accusing me!" His face was red and so close to mine that our noses were almost touching. "I'm gonna say this only once more, so listen good. That car came back here in the same condition it left, you scrote, if it's damaged, then it happened when we were away. Do you understand me?"

"Okay, Jake. I was just a bit upset about the car that's all," I offered, calming my voice and trying to diffuse the situation.

"Perhaps you should be more concerned about upsetting other people," he said. Shoving me in the chest and letting go of my jacket, he turned and went to unlock the house.

I stood up and brushed my jacket, while I watched him disappear from view.

"Phew! He can get a bit hot under the collar," I said, looking at Jez and Micky.

"Wouldn't you if someone made an accusation without checking first to see if you knew anything about it? How do you know that wasn't done while we were away?" Micky asked.

"How? We're in the middle of nowhere." I turned around, holding out my arms to emphasise my point.

"Did you notice the logs stacked under the cover over there, Andy? They were delivered while we were away. For all you know the delivery truck pranged your precious car," said Micky, as he pointed to the wood store.

I suddenly felt a twinge of guilt about accusing Jake so hastily.

"I'm going inside. I suggest you think about what you're going to say to Jake," added Jez. They both headed for the front door, leaving me looking at the damage to my car. That could easily be corrected, but I wondered how I was going to repair the rift I had just caused between myself and Jake.

When I finally went inside, Jake wasn't anywhere downstairs. I was in no doubt that I would have to eat humble pie at some point later on when our paths crossed again.

I went to my room to find my mobile phone. It had switched off while we were away, the battery having gone flat. I plugged it into the charger and switched it on. As soon as it picked up a signal, it bleeped to announce a waiting message. I rang the voicemail to hear Dad asking me to call home urgently.

He sounded distressed and the message was from almost a week ago. I immediately rang Dad's mobile, but got his voicemail, so I rang the home phone.

Dad answered at the first ring, but I paused a moment, feeling a bit of a knot in my stomach, before responding to his greeting.

"Dad, it's Andy."

"Andy!" he yelled. "Where on earth have you been? Are you deliberately trying to cause me grief?"

That put my hackles up and I was not in the mood for another disagreement straight after my confrontation with Jake. I almost hung up. Who does he think he is? I thought to myself.

"We have been trying to get hold of you for over a week. You need to come home, now."

"What do you mean? I'm not coming home, Dad. We went through this last time we spoke and..."

He stopped me mid-sentence.

"We've had a burglary."

"You... you've what?" I stammered.

"We've had a break-in. Whoever it was managed to get into the house, but the police are not convinced that the intruders had to force an entry. They've caused a substantial amount of damage and taken whatever they could that was valuable. Where are you, Andy?"

"I'm at my new place."

I still wasn't willing to tell Dad exactly where I was, but told him I would leave straight away.

"Okay, Andy. We'll talk when you get here."

I shot down the stairs and through the living room almost knocking Jez over.

"Sorry guys, I've got to go out urgently. Tell Jake I'll talk to him when I get back."

I was in the car, turning it around and away as fast as I could. Perhaps driving a bit recklessly through the lanes, I pushed the speed as much as I dared, but I wanted to get 'home' as soon as possible.

With my mind focused on things other than driving, the journey seemed to slip by as if on auto-pilot, like those worrying episodes when you arrive at your destination and can't remember how you got there. It took an hour and a quarter before Durlwood came into view. I rounded the sweeping bend that gave the first glimpse of the house and within moments turned right into the driveway. Accelerating along the short distance to the courtyard, I swung the car around to a stop at the foot of the steps outside of the front door.

Dad must have seen me coming from the office window and opened the door as I got out of the car.

"Hello, Dad," I said rather sheepishly, still a little embarrassed that I'd almost put the phone down on him.

He embraced me as I got to the top of the front steps. I felt a bit overwhelmed by it, but didn't resist.

"Before you come in, son, I just want you to be aware that it's not pleasant."

Walking through the front door, not knowing what to expect, I couldn't believe the sight that greeted me. The sweeping staircase that descended to the hall looked like someone had taken an axe to it with the deliberate intention of causing the maximum possible damage. The pictures that had hung along the hallway gallery wall leading to Dad's office, that framed many events of our lives, were all stood on the floor leaning back against the wall, frames broken, pictures torn and defaced.

The door to Dad's office was ajar and I could see a continuation of damage in there. The kitchen was partly visible, again graffiti and wilful destruction peppered the once pristine building. Light fittings smashed or torn from the walls and hanging like broken branches from a tree. I was completely dumbstruck.

Dad beckoned me through to the kitchen where there were signs of water damage. Spray paint had been liberally applied everywhere. The window to the back of the house, where Dad had his reading chair, had been smashed. I didn't know what to say, but finally choked out, "Is this where they got in?"

"The police are not sure, but they don't think so. They think the window was broken from the inside using one of the kitchen stools. No footprints outside."

"Well how did they get in?"

"As I said, the police are not sure. They're working on the theory that whoever it was had a key to the house and somehow disarmed the alarm system."

"What? Who would want to do damage like this? I mean steal things, yes, but this... and where would they get a key from anyhow?"

"They took much of the small valuable stuff. Easy to get rid of, I guess. All the jewellery... Including Mum's..." Dad just looked at me and smiled weakly.

I couldn't believe what I was hearing. It was heartbreaking. I'd only been there just over a week before and the place had been immaculate. It now looked like a house that had been in a war zone.

"What about upstairs, Dad?"

He shrugged again.

"It's the same, to varying degrees. We've had the plumber and electrician here and they've made sure it's safe, but they had to leave as much in place as they could for the police to do the finger-printing. They'll be back to do further repair work tomorrow... They wanted us to move out, but I didn't want to. Fortunately, Martha has been away for a few days, to visit family, so we've been living in her flat. They didn't get in there, otherwise I think that would have been treated the same. Heaven knows what she'll do when she sees this."

Dad looked at me as though he were going to ask a question, but stopped himself.

"What is it, Dad?"

"There's something I haven't told you, Andy. Henry was working here when they came... We think he might have tried to stop them. That may have been where they got the key from."

"Hasn't somebody asked him?" I demanded.

"He was hurt pretty bad, Andy. He's in hospital and hasn't regained consciousness yet. The doctors are hopeful." Dad paused a moment to make sure he had his emotions in check. "I'm just a little afraid that it might not turn out too good for him." Despite his efforts, Dad's voice cracked while he was telling me about Henry's condition, they had known each other for a long time.

I couldn't take in what I was being told. I had only seen Henry just over a week, when I came to get some of my things. I couldn't understand why someone would hurt a harmless old man like Henry.

"You don't..." Dad hesitated.

"Don't what?"

"You've no idea who could be responsible for this have you, Andy?"

I couldn't believe what I had just heard. Why would he ask me such a question? Why would I know who had done this hideous act of vandalism and assault an old man?

"I'm sorry, son, I have to ask. I'm not suggesting that you were involved, but I just need to know if you have had any contact with someone who might take advantage. I don't know where you have been, or who with and you are being very cagey about letting me know what you are doing. You didn't respond to my message for over a week."

117

"So that puts me in the frame does it?" I raised my voice out of irritation.

"Andy, that's not what I meant."

"I should've known. That's just typical. No doubt Carl, the blue-eyed boy, thinks that I had something to do with it as well."

"Did you?"

A voice came from behind us. Carl had arrived home unnoticed and had come in through the front door to hear me raising my voice in response to Dad's question. I turned to see him standing at the kitchen entrance in his business suit and long coat.

"I said. *Did* you?" he repeated.

The anger began to well up in me.

"I don't have to stay here and listen to this. If you want to point a finger at me that's fine, but you can do it when I'm gone. No doubt you two have had a great time speculating about how I did it and who I got to help me."

I started to leave, but Carl blocked my exit at the kitchen doorway.

"I said, did you?"

I couldn't restrain myself any longer and blew my top.

"I ought to bloody well swing for you, you bastard, how dare you even question whether I would do something like this!"

It had been a few years since I had outgrown Carl in both height and strength and I used the advantage to push him away, making room for me to get past. As I pushed through, he grabbed hold of the sleeve of my jacket. I turned back to look at him and, snatching my arm away, said, "For your information, *brother*, I have been out of the area."

"Can you prove that?"

"Yes, I bloody well can prove that. I've been in Sheffield since a week last Friday, with friends, who wouldn't accuse me like you and, I don't give a shit what you think of me. I never came up to your standard and I don't intend to continue trying.

118

You've always thought of me as the embarrassment of the family, so it's no wonder that you've got me in the frame for something like this!"

I just needed to get out of there immediately, so I headed out through the front door. Dad was coming after me, shouting for me to wait, but I had no intention of doing so. I was quickly in the car before he managed to reach the bottom of the steps. The wheels spun as I accelerated away down the drive and out onto the main road heading back to Langdale. I now knew what they thought of me.

I simmered with anger all the way back to Langdale, in my mind I was running through what had been said. How dare they insinuate that I could be in any way involved! I didn't know what my life had in store for me, but one thing I promised myself, it would take wild horses to drag me back to Durlwood. That part of my life was over.

CHAPTER 9

Pulling into the drive at Langdale, I had a struggle to find a place to park. There were numerous cars scattered around the property and the lights were on right through the building. It was lit up like a funfair.

I opened the car door to be greeted by a terrific volume of music oozing from every possible part of the building's ageing frame. It was worse still when I got to the front door. An assault of sound, desperate to escape the confines of the barn, poured out through the front door as I opened it. Once inside, I had to manoeuvre my way past groups of people congregating on the sofa and chairs or standing around the fireplace and in every other conceivable space.

I'm sure when the old barn was first built the architects could never have dreamed that the scene before me would become one of its uses. The place was heaving with bodies, some dancing, others talking and all drinking. There was a haze of smoke in the rooms and a fire burning fiercely in the hearth.

I squeezed through into the living room while taking off my coat. The temperature difference from outside was overwhelming. I headed up the stairs, still passing people moving in the opposite direction, as I tried to figure out how such a drastic change could occur in the short time I was gone.

At the top of the stairs I turned left to go to my room and almost ran into Jake. He was holding a bottle of lager in one hand, a cigar in the other and had a beautiful girl in tow.

"Andy," he said, drawing out my name like some American friend who hadn't seen me in years.

"Jake... Can I talk to you for a moment?"

"Sure you can."

He motioned to the girl, who had begun to descend the stairs, to keep going.

"Join you in a minute, Sasha," he shouted after her.

I couldn't help turning to take another look at her as she disappeared down to the living room. As I turned my attention back to Jake, he made it obvious that he had noticed my interest.

He beckoned me along the landing to his room. Leading the way, he said, "Nice girl that Sasha." There was a smirk on his face as he stood aside to let me enter the room. He closed the door behind us, but its attempts to filter away the hammering of the music were hopelessly inadequate as it penetrated up through the floor.

"Quite a party, Andy. Don't ya think? Just a few people we know. You should get to know them. You might actually like some of them," he said, adding volume to his voice in an attempt to overpower the sound.

"Jake, I was very unfair to you when we got back this afternoon. I insinuated some things that were not right. I just wanted to apologise. I also want to say that I have thought about what you said, that I was holding back from giving the band my full commitment and you're right. That's going to change from now on, I promise. Can we overlook earlier and start again? It's been a bit of a whirlwind for me the past couple of weeks, but I know what I want now, so can we let what happened go?"

He looked at me for a few moments.

"Where did you go to, Andy?"

I hesitated, as his question caught me off guard.

"I went to see my Dad."

"Didn't go well?"

"No!"

"Well, Andy, we're your family now. We can forget about earlier... I know you were upset about your car, but who needs a car like that anyway now that Terry has called us. We're a touring band on his books. We're going to all the clubs he deals with. So let's put that stuff behind us and celebrate the future. Here, have a drink," he held out the bottle, "and a cigar," he pulled another from his top pocket and lit it with the one he was smoking. I had never smoked in my life before, but to please him I took it. "Now," he said, leaning right into my ear, "let's go downstairs, enjoy the music and the company and see if we can behave like a touring band. What do you say?" He winked at me as he stood up.

Putting his cigar in the same hand as the one holding the bottle, he held out his hand for me to shake. As I did, he pulled me up from the chair I'd been sat in. Smiling at me, he put the cigar between his teeth and opened the door.

The living room was pulsing with a sea of people, making the room upstairs seem tranquil by comparison. Jake beckoned me to follow; sign language was probably the best option at that moment. I obediently trailed behind him until we reached his intended destination where he introduced me to the girl that I'd passed on the stairs.

"Andy, meet Sasha. Sasha, meet Andy."

Still holding the bottle and cigar, he lifted his hands to face level and pointed at both of us. "You two will like each other."

I was a bit embarrassed, especially as he winked at me in the most exaggerated way. Sasha didn't seem to mind as she jokingly slapped his face, then pushed him to move away. Jake took the hint and went to join a group of others across the room, leaving me with Sasha.

She was petite and very pretty. I guessed she was in her early twenties, with long dark straight hair and a straight cut fringe. She wore a very short cream dress that had a sixties look to it.

As she turned back to look at me, her whole face lit up with a dazzling smile that seemed to shine through every feature of her beautiful face.

"Do you find me attractive?"

I was surprised by how forward she was, but that enchanting smile drew me in as though the surrounding noise had stopped and the bustling room was empty.

"Yes... Yes I do."

"Good," she said, standing on her toes to increase her height and dropping back down on her heels like an excited child.

"I need a drink."

"Oh. Yes, of course you do. I'll go and get us one. What would you like?"

Sasha spent the evening taking me gradually around the room introducing everyone to me. It was obvious that she knew Jez and Micky very well. She seemed to want us to be together and had no problem socialising and keeping the conversation flowing. We tried to dance a number of times through the evening, but it was difficult with the amount of people present. In truth, I hadn't ever been at a party that was so relaxed. The type of gathering that I'd become accustomed to was always much more formal than this one.

I lost track of the time in the distracting atmosphere where there always seemed to be something to entertain. The remote location meant there was no difficulty about disturbing the neighbours; there just weren't any, so the volume and the time, were of no concern to us. At two in the morning the party was still in full swing. The noise had hardly begun to subside; the appetite for enjoyment was still unsatisfied.

Sasha went to get a drink and came back with one for me, but obviously had a plan as she pulled me away from a guy I had started talking to.

"Come with me, Andy, I want to show you something."

She passed the drink to me, took my hand and led me away from the fire into the kitchen.

She didn't stop there, but went straight out through the front door, closing it behind her. As we stepped away from the building and the artificial light that spilled from the windows, she turned to face me as she walked backwards still holding my hand.

"I needed to get out for a breath of fresh air. Besides, I want you all to myself for a little while."

She suddenly stopped dead in her tracks and, not expecting it, I walked straight into her. She immediately put her arms around me to prevent her falling backwards, almost spilling our drinks as she did. It was quite clearly a deliberate move, but now that she was in my arms I wasn't in a hurry to let her go.

The clear air of that late October night, occasionally sullied with the smell of wood smoke from the fire, was chilled with the promise of winter coming causing a frosty film to form over everything. Sasha pressed in to me and, as I wrapped around her like a blanket to ward off the cold, her cheek touched gently against mine so that I could hear her softly breathing. The cold air created a swirl of mist each time we breathed out. We started to sway to the dulled sound of music emanating from the house, as if we were the only couple on a dance floor while the last song was playing.

The scene was quite magical. Strange subdued shadows were cast by the gentle glow of the moon, which disappeared intermittently behind the clouds that drew a veil over the ambient light. I don't know how long we were there, but the party had drifted into the distance as we stood completely alone. The breeze through the semi-naked trees mimicked the sound of waves breaking on a beach, enhancing the picturesque view in the silvery light.

I felt Sasha shiver a little as I held her and instinctively pulled her closer to keep her warm.

"I feel sleepy," she whispered in my ear, "and cold."

"Do you want to go back inside?" I asked, almost hoping that she would choose to bear the cold and stay outside with me a little longer.

"Yes... but not to the party. Do you have somewhere we can go?"

She lowered her head onto my shoulder, turning her face into my neck. We stood for a few moments like the statue of an embracing couple displayed in the garden of a stately home. I reluctantly turned toward the house and we began to walk to the front door arm in arm.

The light from the building, coming through the kitchen window, seemed to dazzle after the soft glow of the moonlight.

I opened the door for Sasha, but she held on to my hand as we went inside. She let me lead the way through into the living area where the fire was throwing an orange glow on the faces of the people. I glanced around the room, but they were all engaged in their own little worlds, huddled in corners or groups in deep discussion.

No one took any notice as we separated ourselves from the general mass of people and went up the stairs, but at the top, I stopped and turned to look at Sasha. She smiled and, without a word, pushed gently against me urging me on. I led her to the door of my bedroom, opening it to allow her to go in first. She slowly walked over to the low-set window that almost reached the floor. I closed the door behind me, excluding the artificial light from the landing, which left the room illuminated only by the moonlight.

My eyes began to adjust to the dimly lit room and as they did, Sasha's petite frame became clear, silhouetted in the window, her back to me and her arms by her sides. I leant back against the door to take a moment to look at her slim, shapely figure. She turned slowly to face me, but the light behind didn't allow me to make out the features of her face. I must have been clearly visible to her.

"Now that you have me here, what exactly do you intend to do with me?" she asked, in a provocative whisper. The dulled music continued from below, but my mind blanked out any distraction as I focused on this beautiful girl and held my breath as I watched her. She slipped the straps of her dress from her slender shoulders, in a very deliberate way, allowing it to drop to the floor. While I was locked to her every movement, I could hear the lines of poetry that talked about drinking deeply of love until morning. Whether it was love between us that night, or simply lust, I didn't know at that moment, but, whichever it was, we certainly did drink deeply of it. What I didn't recall so readily at the time was the warning of the poet. 'Beware of the seductress who takes what she should not and leads her victim to destruction.' That didn't enter my mind on that particular night, but would do so for many nights that followed.

Morning seemed to come so quickly. The curtains remained open from the night before, allowing the daylight to intrude far too early for the day after a party. As I awoke, I was immediately conscious of Sasha next to me. She was laid on her side with her back to me. Her hair draped across the pillow and the quilt pulled high into her neck to protect against the cold. I turned toward her and lightly ran my hand over her hair. She stirred a little. Edging closer to me she mumbled, "What time is it?"

"About eight-fifteen," I whispered, willing the moment and the warm comfort of her body close to me to remain undisturbed.

After a pause she asked, in the same sleepy voice, "What day is it?"

"It's Monday," I replied, with a laugh.

There was a sudden explosion of movement as the duvet was thrown to the bottom of the bed and she jumped up still naked.

"Oh my God!" she shouted. "I'm going to be late!"

She was frantically picking up and putting on the few clothes she'd been wearing the night before. I began to laugh out loud at the sudden urgency. One minute there had been peace and tranquillity, the next the room was possessed by a Tasmanian devil.

"Get up Andy. Now! You're going to have to give me a lift into town; it'll take me too long to get the others up. Come on, quickly!" she urged, as she hurried off to the bathroom, while I tried to rush the best I could.

We were out of the house in about fifteen minutes, speedily on our way heading towards the town.

"You need to take me to my flat first so that I can quickly get changed, then you'll have to drop me at work."

I just followed the instructions, a little bemused at the assumptions she was making about my availability and willingness.

As I sped along the roads that led to the town centre, she was looking in the visor mirror, putting on make-up, quite a skill when travelling at speed through winding country lanes. At one point I deliberately swayed the car side to side to make it difficult and she burst out laughing, mockingly slapping my arm as a rebuke. Despite the urgency of the moment, she still seemed to have that same sense of humour that she'd displayed at the party.

By ten-to-nine we arrived at Sasha's flat. I waited in the car while she went inside to change. It seemed like she was in there for about two minutes before reappearing looking gorgeous. Transformed from the 'party babe' of the night before, she now looked fabulous in a smart suit.

There wasn't time to say much on the short journey to the town centre, but as I pulled up at the place instructed, she leant across and planted a glossy lipstick kiss on my lips.

"Thanks for a great evening, Andy. Give me a call later when I've recovered from the dash, perhaps you can take me out for dinner tonight."

Then she was gone from the car, disappearing from sight down a side street before I could even respond to her cheeky presumption. She had mesmerised me, but at that moment I didn't realise quite how much.

Having nothing particular to do that morning, I decided to take the car to have the dealer look at the dent and arrange for the repair. Driving through the busy streets, on the way to the garage, I watched hundreds of people passing each other on their way to serve the day's demands. It hit me that I was not doing the same thing and that I didn't have any desire to get locked back into a ritually ordered work day.

When I arrived at the garage, I parked on the forecourt and went inside to see the representative, who, after the necessary formalities, arranged to deal with the car and supply a courtesy vehicle to use during the repair.

The rest of my day was spent back at Langdale clearing up after the previous night's events. The party was great, but the aftermath was horrific. Jake told me that Terry had arranged a number of engagements for the band and that we would be away at the end of the week, from Thursday through to Monday. While I didn't mind about being away, I immediately thought of not seeing Sasha. Although it struck me as strange, considering I had only met her the night before, it was an involuntary first thought.

At about one in the afternoon I answered my phone to hear Sasha's voice.

"What time are you picking me up to take me out to dinner then, Andy?"

Her directness continued to surprise me, but it was an intriguing characteristic. She seemed to get exactly what she wanted, but in a way that made you feel like it was all your idea and she was just asking you for the details.

"Where are we going?" She asked the second question without even waiting for an answer to the first. "There's a lovely restaurant that I know in town. The place is wonderful, the atmosphere superb and the food is terrific. What do you say I ring them and make a reservation for eight-thirty?"

This time there was enough of a pause to allow me to give the expected response.

"Yes... Yes, Sasha, I guess that would be fine." Trying to regain the initiative, I asked, "Where do you want me to pick you up?"

"Can you remember the way to my flat, Andy?"

"I'm sure I can," I answered. It was actually etched on my memory, along with the party girl that I dropped off and the sophisticated business woman I then took into town.

"Pick me up there at eight-fifteen, I must go now. See you later."

She was gone as quickly as she'd unexpectedly called. I looked at my phone and smiled at the way she had just set up our first date. Some would probably be put off by her approach, but I loved it. She knew what she wanted and went for it like an arrow for the bull's-eye.

The phone rang again almost as soon as she'd hung up and, without looking who it was, thinking that Sasha must have forgotten something, I answered the call assuming that it was her, "What did you forget, Sasha?"

There was a brief pause, then the voice of a man on the end of the line said, "Am I speaking to Mr Andrew Numan?"

Feeling a bit foolish about my greeting, I quickly changed to a more serious response. "Yes, that's me. Who am I speaking to?"

"Mr Numan, my name is Detective Inspector Crewe. I wondered if I might trouble you to make some time to speak to me?"

"Oh. What's it about Inspector?"

"I'm investigating the incident at your father's house... You do know about that don't you?"

"Yes, Inspector, I was at the house with my father yesterday. How can I help you?"

"I'd rather not deal with this on the phone if you don't mind, Mr Numan. I would prefer to come and see you. I asked your father for the address, but he could only give me your mobile number."

"Yes, Inspector, that would be fine. When do you want to come?"

"Would now be a suitable time, sir?" Crewe asked. He surprised me by his wish to see me immediately.

"Er... Yes that would be okay." I paused while I gathered my thoughts.

"An address, sir?"

"Oh, of course, Inspector, I'm so sorry."

I gave the details of the house to Crewe and said goodbye, then began to worry what the police would want with me.

It was about forty-five minutes later, after all the other guys had gone out to various places that a red car pulled into the drive. Two men got out and came across to the front door, which I opened to receive them.

"Mr Numan?"

I nodded in response.

"DCI Crewe. We spoke on the phone. This is DCI Johnson," he said, pointing to his colleague. "Do you mind if we come in, sir?"

I showed them through to the living room and offered to make coffee.

Both of them wandered around the room looking out of the windows and at the instruments and things until I came in from the kitchen with the drinks.

"Please, take a seat," I said, trying to break the ice and cover my nervousness.

"Do you mind me asking why your father and brother couldn't give us an address, Mr Numan?" began DCI Crewe.

"Please call me Andy, Inspector."

"Thank you, Andy."

His body language showed that the question still stood, an answer was not going to be avoided no matter how friendly the atmosphere.

"I left home a couple of weeks ago after a bit of an argument with Dad. Things have not been too good for a while and I wanted to get away. To be honest, I didn't want them coming here because I needed some space to myself for a while."

"You quit your job at the family firm I believe?"

"Yes, probably not in a way that made my brother too happy I'm afraid. It had always been an expectation that my brother and I would work there when we were old enough. He's really good at that sort of thing, but it's not for me. I did work there from when I finished my education, but I can't say that I ever felt comfortable in that environment. Hard to get away when it's family at home and work, if you know what I mean. Anyway, I wanted to start out doing my own thing, rather than doing something because it had always been expected."

"And what exactly is 'your own thing', Andy, I presume the instruments are not all for you?" asked DCI Johnson.

"I'm a musician in a band. That's what I wanted to do years ago. As I said, it's not easy to go against expectations, especially when they live with you. We've just connected with a new manager who has arranged a number of gigs for us, so hopefully... In fact, we're away for the weekend from Thursday through to Monday."

"And the other members of the band live...?"

"They live here with me. It allows us to practise at will without disturbing anyone."

"I see," said Johnson.

They seemed satisfied with that line of conversation, so moved on to the business that they had come to discuss.

"As you know, we're investigating the break-in at your father's house and the subsequent serious assault on a Mr Henry Price, the gardener. I understand that you were not at home..."

"No!" I cut in on what was being said. "I was away from Friday through the whole week until yesterday, Sunday morning. That's when I found out what had happened. I had accidentally left my mobile phone here when we were packing the van to leave and didn't pick up Dad's message until I got back. Do you have any idea who was responsible yet?"

"Let's just say that we have our suspicions and are following a number of lines of enquiry," said Crewe. He jotted something in his open notebook before he continued.

"You say that you were away from Friday, October 17 to Sunday, October 26, is that correct?"

"Yes. I believe those are the dates. Let me just check." I looked at the calendar on my phone. "Yes, that's correct."

"Would you be able to verify that for us, Andy?" asked Johnson.

"What are you suggesting? Are you saying that I'm lying? It sounds like my brother's been talking to you."

I was annoyed at the suggestion that I was not being truthful about where I had been.

"I'm not suggesting anything, Andy. It is our job to check and verify the facts, to eliminate lines of enquiry, so that we can catch those responsible for the damage and distress caused to your family, and for the rather brutal beating of Mr Price. I know that you want that too, Andy, so we have to ask certain questions to be thorough. I would be grateful if you would just answer the questions that we need answering then we can move on."

It felt a little like I had been reprimanded by a school headmaster.

"Look, Andy, we just need to know that you can verify where you were so that we can cross the possibilities off our list of priorities. *Can you verify your whereabouts?*"

"Yes, Inspector Crewe, I can. I was in Sheffield by the early morning of Saturday, October 18 and played at a club called 'Blow Out' that evening. We, the whole band, travelled together in the van, from here, setting off at about ten or eleven o'clock."

"Ten o'clock," Johnson immediately repeated, looking directly at me.

"Yes."

"And you say that was all of you?"

"Yes."

"How many are in the band?"

The questions kept coming and I gave as accurate answers as I could. They were quite curious about how long I had known Jake, Jez and Micky, before moving into the barn, but made no comment about it, only questions. Taking it in turns, they asked and then jotted things in notebooks for about an hour before they were done. Then, excusing themselves, they were gone, rather uncomfortably assuring me that they would be in touch if they had any further questions. The whole episode played on my mind for the rest of the day, but as evening approached the questioning faded into the background as I looked forward to seeing Sasha again.

CHAPTER 10

I was on the road to town by seven, after being quizzed relentlessly by Jake about where I was going. When he finally prised out of me that I was taking Sasha out for dinner, a wry smile spread across his face. He intimated that he knew we'd slept together the night before. I felt quite embarrassed and decided to leave a little earlier than was necessary, which only provoked him to suggest that I was very keen. Although I didn't like him pulling my leg about it, he was right, I was keen.

Parking the car a little distance from Sasha's flat, I waited for about ten minutes before pulling up directly outside. I didn't want to arrive there too early, despite the temptation to spend as much time as I could with her.

I stood on the steps, lined either side by black railings, with butterflies in my stomach as I was about to see her again. When I rang the bell I heard her shout that she was coming. With the rattle of locks, the door opened slightly, just enough for her to check who it was. When she saw me she reached out and hurriedly pulled me inside by the lapel of my jacket.

Throwing her arms around my neck she planted a kiss on my lips without the slightest hesitation. She wasn't even dressed, except for a towel wrapped around her that was only just big enough to be decent. I had never met a girl so forward, or so unconcerned about flaunting her body. Pulling away, she laughed as she ran to the backroom shouting, "Make yourself at home, I'll be just a minute."

The flat was small, but very smart. Tastefully decorated and furnished. I could hear Sasha in the other room getting dressed, as I looked around the place at the ornaments and pictures. I caught sight of her once, through the open arch, running to and from the bathroom in her underwear. To be truthful, I didn't care how long she took to get ready if she was going to keep me entertained like that. It was more like fifteen minutes before she finally appeared, after I had prompted her that we would be late.

"How's this for gorgeous?" She announced her own entrance into the room.

She was wearing a long black low-cut dress and carrying a matching three-quarter length jacket. "Ready?" she asked, as I was regaining my composure to try to say something.

"You look terrific... stunning."

"Why, thank you, kind sir," she responded, flashing a smile that could melt a red-blooded male at fifty paces.

I took the jacket and held it out for her. Gracefully sliding into it, she leaned back, inviting me to slip my arms around her waist, tipping her head to one side for me to kiss her neck. I lost myself in the beautiful fragrance that surrounded her.

"I thought you said that we would be late, Andy?" she whispered huskily, bringing me reluctantly out of the spell I was beginning to fall under.

She was right, but being late had suddenly become less important to me. I checked myself and gently steered her toward the door.

On the journey to our date, I could hardly concentrate, wrestling with the need to watch the road and the desire to look at the girl. I had to do one, but was drawn to do the other.

Following the directions as she indicated, we eventually drew to a stop outside the entrance of a very classy hotel. The doorman attended Sasha as she got out of the car, signalling for someone to take the vehicle and park it. I'd never seen that happen before, except in the movies. I'd grown up in a certain amount of luxury, but very rarely had Dad ever taken us to a place anything like this. Perhaps it would have been different if Mum had been around; she might have influenced Dad away from the functional and toward the elegant.

It appeared that everyone knew Sasha, from the doorman to the floor manager, each greeting her as we went in.

"I've been here quite a lot," she said, as yet another member of staff acknowledged her.

"You must come from a wealthy family."

She laughed out loud, flicking her head back with delight at my suggestion, but gave no other response.

We were escorted to a table that was immaculately presented, positioned near a window that overlooked the hotel gardens. Sasha requested her favourite wine, without stating what it was. The waiter, to my surprise, just nodded and left to fulfil the request.

"They really do know you here, don't they?"

"As I said, I come here quite a lot," she stated, with a smile, but still without any detailed explanation.

The ambience of the room was delightful. Every detail had been meticulously attended to. The music, provided by a pianist in the corner seated at a grand piano, was warm and inviting. It never forced itself on the diners and could easily be overlooked, but was sorely missed when each piece came to an end. I could have happily got used to such a lifestyle.

The food was both artistic and delicious and Sasha certainly knew how to carry herself in conversation. There was nothing awkward or forced about her behaviour. She fitted into that environment as smoothly as the party the previous evening. Her confidence was quite astonishing and I couldn't help watching her graceful behaviour.

The whole experience was extraordinary, but however much I wished it to last, it had to finally come to an end. I signalled to the waiter that we wanted to pay the bill, which was efficiently delivered to the table. Sasha went to take it, but I put my hand on it to stop her.

"I'm taking *you* out, Sasha." She laughed, as she leant back into her chair. "I wanted to say thank you for a great evening last night and..."

"To tell me how wonderful I am?" she completed my sentence for me. "I know that already, sweetheart. I'm going to freshen up for later."

She picked up her bag, flashed that captivating smile again, and got up to leave the table. My eyes followed slavishly after the beautiful woman moving across the room.

When she had gone and my stare had been released, I looked at the bill and was quite shocked to see the total. I'd never spent so much at a restaurant in my life, but the experience of the place and the feeling of being wealthy, it was heady indeed. After all, I did have money. More than many see in years of working, but I was not used to being so extravagant with it. Nevertheless, the idea of allowing Sasha, who was obviously used to that lifestyle, to show me the good life and its pleasures, was not wholly unwelcome.

I met Sasha at the entrance as the car was brought to the front door for us. The doormen made a fuss of her and she was genuinely warm towards them. One of them held the door for her to get into the car as though she were a celebrity.

The journey back to her flat was not long. She talked almost all the way, making our time together just like the meal, very easy. As the car came to a stop outside the steps leading to the front door of her house, she said, "Coffee?"

"I thought you would never ask," I joked, pretending that I wasn't desperately hoping she would.

One thing led to another and it became quite clear that we would be breakfasting together the following morning.

The remainder of the week was similar to its beginning. I was keen to spend as much time with Sasha as possible, knowing that I would be away for a long weekend with the band. It was a case of finding time whenever we could. Jake had us rehearsing for long periods through the days before we left, adding song after song to our repertoire and perfecting the ones we knew.

In the evenings, as soon as I could get free, I went to see Sasha. We met on Tuesday and Wednesday, but couldn't see each other on Thursday evening as we would be travelling to our gig. She was not available during the day either. "Some of us have to work at real jobs you know," she would say, mischievously taking a dig at me.

The garage wanted my car on Thursday morning to begin the repair work, so I had to go into town to drop it off. As I drove through the town centre, I thought I caught sight of Sasha walking arm-linked with another man. The flow of traffic dictated the time I was able to try to get a good look, but I could have sworn it was her. I tried to pull over nearby, but couldn't do so without causing an obstruction, it was just too busy.

Once I'd delivered my car and picked up a temporary replacement, I tried to ring Sasha, but it went straight to her voicemail. I left a message for her to call me, but couldn't resist calling at her flat on the way home, just to see if she was there.

There was no answer when I knocked at the door, but I thought I could hear music playing as if someone was home. I concluded that it must have been coming from the flat above and, having no reason to hang around, I headed back to Langdale.

Later that morning when the equipment needed to be loaded into the van, all hands were called to the task. Although it was only the second time we'd done it, the preparations went like clockwork as everything seemed to have found its natural place. I hoped there would be many more times in the future and that each time would be as filled with anticipation and excitement as it was that day.

By eleven-thirty we were on our way to the second series of gigs. I didn't drive that time, but made myself comfortable in the back with a magazine to read. I kept wondering if I had been mistaken earlier when I thought I'd seen Sasha. I'd tried to ring her once more before we left, but still there was no answer. I didn't want to do it in the van at the cost of being mercilessly ribbed about it.

The weekend was very enjoyable, the two venues were great, but I was a little concerned that, having left two more messages on Sasha's phone, she hadn't responded. I was torn between wanting to enjoy the present moment and wanting to be home so I could see Sasha.

The other concern I had was about the money situation. I needed to know how much we were being paid and who had control over it. Up to that point it seemed like I was shelling out for all manner of things from food to fuel, in lieu of payment from the other guys.

Relationships were generally good and our time together, especially when we were focused on the music, was great.

Once all of our commitments had been met and having been informed by Terry about a number of upcoming dates, we set out on our way back home to Langdale Barn.

It was a bit more of a tedious trek back, but as we neared our journey's end and Langdale came into view, it gave rise to a feeling of having accomplished something. It was good to see the place again and even though we had only been based there for a few weeks, it felt like home.

Parked in the drive next to my car was a flash two-seater sports car.

"Anybody know the car?" I quizzed, but nobody responded.

As we turned into the drive the front door opened and out came Sasha to greet us. The moment the van stopped I jumped out and couldn't contain my surprise or enjoyment at seeing her.

"What are you doing here, Sasha? I've been trying to ring you all weekend. Didn't you get my messages?"

She plonked a kiss on my lips to stop the questions and putting her hands on my cheeks said, "I lost my phone. I didn't get your messages until this morning when I got a replacement."

Jez interrupted us with a wolf-whistle at her. Girl that she was she milked it, but it was all good-natured. Jake, however, came and put his arms around her waist, lifted her off the ground and whirled her around.

"S-a-s-h-a," he said, lengthening out her name.

Again that didn't faze her at all. She laughed out loud at the fun of it, but I felt like telling Jake to put her down and never do that again. I couldn't believe the reaction in myself. There was a touch of jealousy that I hadn't ever experienced before, not over a girl. The spell she cast was greater than I'd imagined.

We hadn't been back more than an hour when my phone rang.

"Mr Numan?" enquired a voice.

"Yes. Who is this?"

"Mr Numan, this is DCI Crewe, we spoke last week about the break-in at your father's house if you remember." The familiarity of the intonation was suddenly connected with a face. "I wondered if I could ask you a few more questions?"

I went upstairs, leaving the others in the living room crowding around the fire that Sasha must have made. They were talking about the weekend's events, Sasha joining the discussion.

"Yes, Inspector, I've got a few minutes. What can I answer for you?"

"I would like to talk to you in person, at the police station, if you wouldn't mind."

I hesitated for a few moments, but realised I could hardly say no, even if I wanted to. Anyway, why wouldn't I want to help? He arranged a time for me to meet him and then hung up.

When I went downstairs, Jake caught my eye.

"Everything okay, Andy? You look a bit white."

I nodded in response, still immersed in my thoughts.

"Are you sure?"

"It... That was the police. They want me to go and see them."

You could hear a pin drop in the room as they waited for further explanation.

"My Dad's place was burgled last week. They want to talk to me about it."

"Burgled... I'm sorry to hear that, Andy. Is your dad okay?" Jake sympathised.

"Yes he's fine, but the gardener evidently tried to intervene. He's in pretty bad shape. They tell me he's unconscious and has been since the attack. The whole place has been trashed. It seems it wasn't enough to take the valuables, the bastards had to make a significant mark on the place. Spray paint and smashing things."

There was a long pause before anyone said anything.

"But what would the police want with you?" Jez asked.

"I really don't know, Jez."

We talked about what had happened for a while. They seemed surprised that the police had already been to Langdale to see me. I'd deliberately not told any of them and now felt like I was saying I didn't trust them for not doing so.

Sasha stayed at Langdale for the rest of the day, but needed to get back to her flat that evening for some prior commitment that she couldn't get out of. The remainder of the time before Sasha went was very pleasant, but I would rather that we had been on our own. She was a very sociable girl, loved lively conversation and never held back on her opinions. She would enthusiastically defend her point of view, sometimes quite fiercely.

When the time came to say goodbye to Sasha, the others took a quick decision that a takeaway was the order of the evening and, rather than go in the van, I was nominated as courier. I followed Sasha in her car for a few miles before turning off to go to the nearest Chinese restaurant.

On the way back to Langdale, I stopped at a garage for petrol, but when I went to pay for it my credit card was declined. I thought it was unusual, but later completely forgot to check what was wrong, thinking it was perhaps the garage at fault. After all, I had only used it recently for the van purchase and a number of smaller items. Fortunately, I had just enough cash to pay for the fuel. The whole prospect of having to visit Inspector Crewe the following morning was uppermost in my thoughts, so the card issue was totally overlooked.

The following morning, as I went through the front doors of the town centre police station, I felt very conspicuous. I'd never been in a position that I'd ever needed to go to such a place before, so I didn't know what to expect.

It was a very simple, austere place, with a sliding hatch and frosted glass separating the entrant from whatever important work was being done behind the screen. I rang the bell and waited for someone to appear. I gave my details and reason for being there and took a seat as directed.

After waiting about five minutes, DCI Crewe came through a side door. He thanked me for coming and led the way along a fluorescent-lit corridor to a room further back in the building. The door proclaimed its function, 'Interview Room'. Once inside there was another officer there to greet us who immediately offered to get me a drink, which I declined.

"Just to check, is it okay if I call you Andy?" I nodded my agreement and took a seat as instructed. "Thank you for coming in... er... Andy. I just wanted an informal chat with you. Of course, you're free to leave whenever you wish," Crewe stated, his demeanour challenging me to take this up and give him a reason to imply my guilt. I had every intention of complying; I had no reason not to. "This shouldn't take too long, Andy. We just wanted to clarify a couple of things for the time being. I want to ask you about the evening of the October 17." Flipping through his notebook, Crewe continued, "You mentioned that you left Langdale, your place of residence, to go to Sheffield for a gig that was booked for your band. Is that correct?" I nodded in agreement.

"Could you tell me exactly what time you set off from Langdale?"

"I think it was about ten-thirty, or eleven, in the evening, probably nearer eleven."

"And where were you before that time, Andy?"

"I was at Langdale. I'd been there all day waiting for Jake, one of the other band members, to come back from town with a takeaway for us before we left for Sheffield."

"Were you on your own?"

"No, the other two guys from the band were there as well. We were busy packing all the equipment into the van while we waited for Jake to return."

"Can you remember what time Jake returned?"

"That would be about nine o'clock. He'd been out from about five to deal with some last minute business before we left that evening."

"What kind of business?"

"I don't know. I never asked."

Crewe leant back in his chair and, much to my discomfort, studied me for a few moments. I was wondering if he was waiting for me to add something more when he broke the silence.

"As I said, you're free to leave at anytime, Andy, but I would appreciate it if you could spare a little more time. Is that okay?"

"That's fine."

"Your father's house was broken into between the hours of three in the afternoon, when the resident cook, Martha, left for a few days to visit her family and eleven-thirty when your father and brother Carl, returned. I want to be delicate here, but I need to ask if you can think of any reason someone would want to do that to your father's house?"

"What do you mean?"

"Any reason," he repeated.

"I can't, Inspector. I can't understand why anyone would do such a thing, especially injuring an old man. It's just beyond belief."

"Henry Price is in a bad way I'm afraid. The doctors are not sure at the moment what will happen, but I'm sure you know that. I expect your father will have kept you informed. Let's just hope we catch the culprit soon because I don't want to see a repeat of this somewhere else." I nodded in agreement, but was still wondering why I was there. "It might help if Henry were to regain consciousness, perhaps that would answer all our questions."

After a few more questions Crewe thanked me for going to the station and said that he would keep the family informed of any developments. He also asked me to get in touch if I thought of anything that might be helpful to them. I wasn't sure what he might have in mind as I would gladly have told them if I knew anything.

I left the station feeling a bit shaken by the experience. I had every reason to want the perpetrator caught, as they did.

Crewe had asked me not to discuss the matter with anyone for the time being as he wanted to quiz a few more people and didn't want any suggestion of matching stories. I knew I'd already spoken to my friends about the burglary and told them that the police wanted to speak to me. I just hoped that I hadn't done the wrong thing, as I got the impression that Crewe was

144

intending to talk to each of them. I was now acutely conscious that my alibi, if I needed one, lay with Jake and the others.

I couldn't remember any of the drive back to Langdale, my mind surreptitiously going over everything I'd said to the police. On my return, the guys asked a few questions, but I didn't tell them much about what had happened. I just told them it was routine stuff because I was family. Nevertheless, I was a bit concerned. Surely Crewe didn't think that I, or any of my friends, were involved? Perhaps Dad and Carl really did think that I was responsible in some way and had informed Crewe of their suspicions.

Jake broke the seriousness of the conversation by throwing an empty can of lager at Jez, which hit him squarely on the side of the head. Everyone fell about laughing and that was Jake's cue for me and everyone else to stop taking life too seriously and start enjoying ourselves. So, amid the haziness that goes with smoking and drinking to excess, the day's events were soon forgotten.

CHAPTER 11

No longer being involved in regular employment meant that the routine of a day was missing from my life. On occasions, it could make time seem to drag at a snail's pace. Sasha was otherwise occupied with her own work, but had me promise to take her out again for dinner at 'her favourite restaurant.'

Other than the relentless music practise and staying over at her place one night, the week was rather dull. Dad had tried to get in touch by leaving another message on my phone. I just didn't want to speak to him at the time, especially if he believed I had been involved in the break-in at Durlwood.

Then, towards the end of the week, the garage rang to say that my car was ready. I decided to go straight after receiving the call, simply for something to do that morning.

Again the formalities took a little time, but, once complete, it was great to have my own car back. I walked around it to examine where the damage had been and was delighted with the result. They had done a fabulous job, making it look like new again and I made sure that they knew how appreciative I was.

As I was about to leave the garage, the service representative handed me a padded envelope.

"When we were doing the repairs, Mr Numan, we had to remove the trim and furnishings of the boot and back seat area. The body work guys found this." He pointed to the envelope in my hand. "I knew that you were away for a little while, so I had it put in the office safe until you returned to pick up your car. I didn't want to draw attention or take any risks with it. I hope I did the right thing."

It was a strange turn of phrase, but I immediately thought of my watch, that had never surfaced and thanked him for being considerate as I slipped the package into my pocket to look at later.

Although it was late October by then, I dropped the car roof and took an aimless drive to get a breath of fresh air. It was crisp and cold, but the sun shone through making the lanes into the country look lovely. I could have driven for hours just for the joy and freedom of it.

Remembering that I still hadn't checked with my credit card company about the problem I had making a recent payment, I ended up at the cash machine to tide me over. I didn't want to end up being embarrassed by having no means of payment, so I withdrew a few hundred pounds from my current account, making a mental note to transfer some money from my savings. I'd gone through quite a lot of money, due to the amount that I'd spent supporting the new venture we were working on, but I was ready to see some return from my investment. I knew that I would have to be patient for a little while longer. The prospect of raising the subject with Jake didn't appeal.

Presuming we'd be away again at the weekend, as previously arranged, I was preparing myself for the coming gigs. However, when I finally got back to Langdale, Jake informed me that Terry Douglas had rung to say that the venue we were supposed to be going to next had been damaged due to a small fire caused by a faulty display light. Consequently, they had cancelled our booking and closed while repairs were made.

I'd already decided not to raise the issue of money again, but as we chatted, Jake told me that the rent was due for Langdale. He had taken the liberty of giving the money from our first week at Sheffield to the landlord to cover this and some of next month's rent as well. I was okay with that, knowing that I wouldn't have to pay it, like so many of the other things lately.

With the prospect of a free weekend, we all agreed to have another party like the one when I met Sasha. When I rang her to see if she was able to come, she sounded thrilled. I was looking forward to it very much, hoping that she would stay like the last time. I wanted to try and make a go of our relationship if I could and was happy to be able to spend as much time with her as possible.

The rehearsals were still frequent and very good, but had less urgency to them. Jake suggested that having a little extra time, before we performed again, would give the opportunity to take a more relaxed approach. "Let's just enjoy ourselves while we work."

It wasn't until we had been playing for an hour or so that I realised how uptight I'd become, trying to make sure that we were the best we could be for the performances. We all began to have a laugh, each playing a bit of our favourite material, then working on it to expand it into something new. It was great to be spontaneous, inspiring the creative abilities in each other.

Later in the day, after the practise time had finished, I was sat in the living room staring into the dancing flames of the open fire, lost in my own world of thought. Jez and Micky shouted from the kitchen that they were going out to get some drink and food for the party later and were taking the van. I waved in acknowledgement, listening to the noise of people and vehicle disappearing until quiet reigned once more.

Jake came and sat with me. He was quiet for the first time in ages, staring into the flames. It seemed odd at first, but after a while, once the anticipation of what was coming had gone, I relaxed in his company.

The warmth from the fire was soothing, almost sleep inducing, as the flames danced to the accompanying crackling music made by the logs burning. We just sat in the atmosphere that seemed like the calm before the storm of the party to come. It must have been fifteen minutes before the silence was broken.

"You," Jake cleared his throat, "you should do more of that stuff," he said. "You've lived life in a regimented way following the rules set by your 'old man.' It's time that you just did some stuff."

"What do you mean?" I asked, curious about the direction the conversation might go.

"Did you pick your school? Did you choose your career?"

I didn't answer him; he didn't seem to want an answer. His intention was to provoke me to think about how much of my life had been lived to a routine that had been laid out by someone else, rather than following my own heart. We both knew what he was getting at without it needing explanation.

"Did you choose your friends?"

I turned away from the fire to look at him and found that he was staring at me, studying my reaction.

We both knew that I had chosen my friend, Jake, but Dad didn't like him, so had separated us. 'That boy is not a good influence on you', was how he put it. I looked back into the fire, mesmerised by the beauty of its ever changing appearance. Jake made no attempt to interrupt my thoughts, leaving me to decide if I gave any response.

After a period of quiet, the pressure to make comment about what he'd said grew, until the silence begged to be broken.

"No, Jake. I know what you're getting at. I didn't choose some of my friends."

"Andy, you need to live life for yourself. Enjoy what you've got. It's a damn sight more than most people will ever have. As I said, be more spontaneous. Do something outrageous. How much fun have you had since you got together with us? The gigs, the party, another party tonight, Sasha?"

"What about her?" I said, straightening up in my chair.

"Do you think that your meeting her was planned? It just happened and you went with the flow. Did you enjoy the ride?"

He sheepishly laughed at his turn of phrase and I couldn't help breaking into a smile, but felt a bit embarrassed. Jake held his hand up as if to apologise for the way he'd phrased it.

"You know what I meant. You could have been working in a stuffy office from nine 'til five, or seven, if I know your Dad. I bet that's what Carl does isn't it?"

I was looking back at the fire, but listening to him and nodded to show that he was right.

"And, in the evenings you'd be at a 'suit-and-tie' function being nice to people who you don't know and don't like. Instead you were at a party here, with some really interesting people and you met Sasha... She's quite a girl."

"I like her a lot, Jake."

"I know you do."

He nodded to show that he understood and stretching out, to put his feet nearer the warmth of the fire, he continued, "Look, Andy, I'll be straight with you. The truth is that Sasha likes you too, but she has to be who she is. She's a spontaneous girl; someone who does things for the moment, just because it seems like fun."

He leant forward, putting his elbows on his knees and stared intently at the flames. I glanced sideways at him as I waited for him to put his last comment into some sort of context. He lowered his voice, as though the house were full of people that he didn't want to overhear the secret he was about to share.

"Sasha rang me to ask something."

As he turned to look at me, I could see that he had registered the question written in my expression.

"No, Andy, it's good stuff. She really likes you. She's been her spontaneous self again, arranging something for you both. But, after she had done it she was worried that you wouldn't want to, or that you would say she's crazy." He paused a moment, then added with a laugh, "Well, she is crazy, in a nice kind of way. All I'm saying is don't miss a great opportunity just 'cos your 'old man' wouldn't do it. Be yourself and enjoy..." His voice tailed off as though he was stopping himself from saying too much. "You're a lucky guy," he said, as he got up and went to the kitchen, leaving me with the song and dance of the fire for company.

I couldn't even imagine what he was talking about, but was intrigued to see what Sasha had been planning behind my back. The party couldn't start quickly enough for me. Even then I would have to wait and see what happened. It was quite obvious, from Jake's body language and tone of voice, he was warning me so that I would be prepared, rather than shocked, at whatever Sasha had in mind. I wondered if he was taken with Sasha himself. They did seem to be very friendly, as though they had known each other for many years.

People began arriving from about seven o'clock and the house was filling quickly. There was no doubt, from the supplies being brought, that we were in for a long session and that folks had come prepared to be stuck in the countryside until the following day. Most of those who came were from the same group as before, each one greeting me as if they'd known me for years.

Sasha eventually got there at nine, having texted me to say that she would be a little late. When she came through the front door, to my eyes, she was a picture of beauty. I couldn't ever remember seeing someone look so perfect. Her greeting was very enthusiastic. In fact, it was almost as though we had been apart for months.

The party rumbled along as people danced and laughed, generally having a good time. About an hour after Sasha arrived, when I was sat in a chair talking to a guy called Roger, she came over and put her arms around my neck from behind. Interrupting the flow of our conversation she said, "I am taking him away from you, Roger. I want him to myself for a minute." Roger laughed and shrugged, resigning himself to the inevitable loss of a conversation partner. It was as if nobody ever said no to Sasha. She just melted people with charm.

Pulling me close, she whispered in my ear, "Let's go upstairs, I want to talk to you." She cheekily placed heavy emphasis on 'talk' when she said it. I obediently followed her up to my room and watched her shut the door behind us, standing with her back to it.

"What are you up to, Sasha?"

"I want you to come on a trip with me."

"A trip. Where?"

She moved closer to me and spoke as she walked her fingers up my chest until she slipped her arms around my neck.

"If you would like to come with me, I am going to..." she hesitated. Her lips were almost touching mine. "Paris," she whispered.

I tried to make it look like I had no idea that she would be asking me something, but I didn't have to fake the surprise too much.

"Paris?"

"I've booked a room in a nice hotel," she said, with deliberate slowness as though she were letting it sink in. "Have you ever been to a casino?" She didn't wait for an answer to her question. "I mean a real casino, not your backstreet affair. I'm talking about 'James Bond' style. It's the most fabulous experience. Thrilling!"

I laughed at her explanation of the type of place she was talking about and the sheer excitement she transmitted in her joy of going to such a place.

"I've paid for the trip, but you will need to bring some spending money with you. Nothing too serious though. You suggested that I must be a wealthy girl, but I'm not a high-roller. What do you say?"

I was lost for words at the generosity of her gift, but said nothing initially. She stepped back from me, a little concerned at the lack of my response.

"You don't want to go with me?"

She used a 'babyish' voice, mimicking disappointment.

"Er... well, yeah... what I mean is, I want to go, but how? When?"

She moved back closer to me, flashing that amazing smile that always seemed to get her whatever she wanted. "When? We leave on Monday afternoon. How? I will drive us there in my car. Why? You have spoilt me over the last couple of weeks, paying for everything, so this is my way of showing you that I can play that game as well."

"I don't know what to say, Sasha."

"You don't have to say anything, darling."

She purred the words like some black and white film star from the forties.

"How much do I need to take with me then? It's not something I have ever done before."

"For a good time you need two thousand. For a great time, bring five."

"Five thousand pounds?" I blurted out.

I wished Jake had warned me about that as well.

"Well, I'm taking five, but it's up to you what you do," she said indifferently, as though we were talking about pennies.

"Five thousand it is then," I stated, as though it were Monopoly money that we were talking about. I tried to regain my composure. When you're young, how it looks counts more than it should and how I wanted to impress that beautiful woman.

The rest of the party, which seemed to continue through most of Sunday, went very well. I was even happier when Sasha made it clear that she intended to stay the night. Shortly after I had spoken to her, Jake collared me to ask 'how things were going.' I told him about Sasha's plan and he seemed very enthusiastic for me.

"You lucky sod! It all just falls in your lap without even trying doesn't it? Still, good for you. You make sure you enjoy yourself. Lighten up, man. Live life and love the girl, that's my motto."

He slapped me on the back as a friend who wants the best for you would. I really began to sense that we were bonding again, the way we had been years before.

The only thing left for me to do was to arrange to get the money before we left on Monday. Although the thought of gambling with such large amounts did prick my conscience a little, I had never enjoyed myself so much as recently. My new-found friends had opened a social side to my life that I was beginning to enjoy very much. Anyway, it cuts both ways in a casino, it was always possible that I could win.

On Monday morning I was up early, keen to make the most of the day. My first task was to ring the bank and warn them that I was about to make a substantial cash withdrawal. There was no problem and I gave them a time when I would be there.

The rest of the morning drifted lazily by as I waited to meet up with Sasha. The plan was that I would take my car to the bank to pick up the money, then on to Sasha's flat to park it there, leaving it until we returned. The whole idea of spending time alone with her in the romantic city of Paris was enough to make me want to go, whether or not we went to the casino. She seemed very keen to have me enjoy that experience as well, so why not?

I was at Sasha's flat a little earlier than arranged and had to wait until she arrived back from an appointment. She seemed just as excited as I was as she opened the door to let us both in. I had clothes and things in a travel bag, enough for the few days away, which I left in the hallway while she got ready.

"You might as well leave your car keys here," she casually shouted, as she went through the bedroom door to get changed, "and anything else you don't need to take with you. There's no point taking them all the way to Paris and back only to risk losing them," she continued. "Just put them in the drawer of the hallway table."

A few minutes later she came into the room, the business suit gone, wearing jeans and casual shirt and carrying her luggage, which I immediately took from her, prompting that smile again.

"Oh," she said, as she turned her back to the front door and faced me on our way out. I stood there holding our luggage waiting for her to continue. The smiling face gave way to a deadly serious one. "Don't tell me that you've got your mobile phone with you?"

"Yes. I have actually..."

"I'm not setting foot outside this door until you've turned the damn thing off and put it in that drawer with your car keys. Being interrupted, when in Paris on a romantic weekend, is totally out of order. I won't accept it."

It was clear that there was not going to be any discussion with her about the subject. Stepping toward me she reached into my jacket pocket, pulled out the phone and car keys, which I still had with me. Holding them up she slowly shook her head to display her disapproval and opened the drawer of the hallway table, she deposited them inside, immediately sliding it shut.

"Anyway," she said, "we wouldn't want to be interrupted doing anything that shouldn't be interrupted, would we?"

The knowing wink that accompanied the smile made sure that there was no doubt about the subject of the comment. I couldn't have agreed more. I certainly didn't want to be interrupted like that either.

The car was parked a little way down the road where Sasha had left it for safe-keeping on a friend's driveway. It was a delightful little sports car that suited her completely; brightly coloured and sexy. After loading the luggage, we were quickly on our way.

The journey would take quite a few hours, via the Eurotunnel, but the moment we pulled away from the drive it was our time together, for a few days, without any other distractions. Sasha said that she would have booked the train, but liked the idea of driving through France and being able to stop along the way whenever we wanted.

Heading south-east to the channel crossing, she chatted away easily and entertainingly, making me laugh at some of the situations she had been in with business colleagues at work. The way some men were so sexist, believing she was not their equal. I didn't realise quite how smart she was until we actually found ourselves in France. It surprised me when we were about to set off from the French terminal, on the journey to Paris, that she fluently conversed with a French security officer, even making him laugh, which I thought quite impressive.

As the car pulled away, I made a remark about her linguistic skill.

"There are a lot of things you don't know about me, Andy Numan. It's not my place to tell you, it's your job to find out," she said mischievously. The mystery was charming and enticing, making her even more attractive.

It was wonderful going on that adventure. Having had nothing to do with the planning heightened the excitement as we arrived in Paris. It was simply brilliant.

The hotel that Sasha had arranged was unlike any I'd ever stayed at before. There was a similar quality to her favourite restaurant we'd visited at home. She was clearly a girl with great and expensive taste.

My family had, throughout my childhood, been on many holidays abroad, but the hotels we stayed in were more functional than they were exclusive. It made me wonder why we hadn't stayed in more places like this. Perhaps it was the influence of Dad having to work hard for what he had and not wanting to be frivolous with money. Maybe it was just the lack of feminine influence in our lives, but as we went into the hotel it made me wish I'd had more experiences like this one.

I didn't query the cost of staying there as it had been arranged by Sasha. I thought it would appear rude to ask. She obviously knew how to put on a show and preferred the quality that surrounded us to the mundane normality of life.

Sasha told me to take a seat in the lounge area while she went to the check-in desk. I didn't question her request and instead took the opportunity to get a view of the busy street outside of the front windows. They were the external walls on two sides of the lounge located on the corner of the building. The windows ran from the floor, which was raised about three feet above the pavement outside, giving the patrons a feeling of superiority over the passing masses, to the ornate ceiling high above. I relaxed into one of the leather chairs, which beckoned visitors to enjoy their comfort and luxury, as I absorbed the opulence of the sumptuous surroundings with great relish.

I was savouring the visual delights of the building with its marble floors and high ornate ceilings, when a porter appeared at my side with a keycard in hand. He bid me follow him, immediately taking the luggage from me as he showed me to our room. Sasha joined us on the journey from lobby to suite, chatting with the porter in French as we went.

Although I didn't speak French, I had the distinct impression that they were familiar with one another, but couldn't decide whether it was just Sasha's personality having its usual influence over everyone she met. However, she did seem to be greeted as if she had been there before, not unlike her favourite restaurant. The hotel porter opened the door and placed the luggage inside the entrance to the room.

I was immediately drawn to the fantastic view over the city that presented itself like a giant living painting across the whole front of the room. There before us was Paris, lit up in the darkness like jewels on display in a shop window. Sasha urged me to go ahead and take in the view, as she went outside into the corridor to talk to the porter. She was gone several minutes, but, when she finally came back, I was eager to show her around the suite like a child pointing out things in a toy shop.

"This place is absolutely fabulous, Sasha." I put my arm around her waist and pulled her near to me "And what beautiful company. What do you want to do with the rest of this evening?"

After all the driving, Sasha suggested that we stay in the hotel for the night and order room service.

"I thought I saw a bath big enough for two in there," she said suggestively.

"What are we waiting for then?" I acquiesced, no further invitation required.

CHAPTER 12

As the late autumn morning sun struggled to fight its way past the curtains to announce the arrival of the new day, I woke to find Sasha gone. I got up expecting her to be in the bathroom, but she was nowhere to be seen.

I threw back the curtains to take in the daylight version of the view I'd seen the night before. The traffic hustled past far below in the Parisian streets. The Eiffel Tower majestically presided over the events of the city, as it had done for so many years. Some of the famous landmark buildings were now clearly visible in the panoramic scene from the suite windows. Each one that was recognised prompted a further inspection to identify more. After watching for a while, and still with no sign of Sasha, I started to get dressed looking forward to the day ahead.

While I was in the bathroom shaving I heard the suite door close.

"Andy? Where are you?"

"In here, Sasha!"

I shouted to attract her attention. She crossed the room and pushed open the door that had been slightly ajar.

"How are you this morning?" she said, as she slid her hands around my waist until her arms embraced me.

"I'm great thank you. I woke up about half an hour ago to an empty bed. Have you been out somewhere special?" I asked, as casually as I could in order not to seem nosey, though she'd been gone for quite a while, with no indication where.

"I had to deal with a few things while I was here, but I'm done now and ready to go down for breakfast. How about you?"

"I think... you've stayed here before," I suggested, trying to find out if it was the case.

"You do? Well you're a 'smart Alec,' aren't you? As I told you, there are a lot of things you don't know about me."

She squeezed me around the waist tickling me on the sides. I spun around in her embrace and pressed my shaving-foamed face against hers as I picked her up. She laughed as she struggled against my grip.

"Tell me then, when did you stay here before?" I shouted, as I playfully shook her to extract the information.

"I've stayed here a number of times," she replied, putting her nose in the air to mockingly suggest that she was from a superior class of people who deserved this kind of luxury. "My mother is French, as a matter of fact, and she used to bring me here when I was younger, to this very room on occasions, actually. That was a long time ago. Some of the people who worked here then are still here now, so when I started coming back a few years ago, for business reasons, they recognised me."

"What exactly do you do, Sasha?" She hesitated as she looked at me.

"Oh...work, work, work. Bore, bore, bore. Who cares about work? We're not here for work anymore, now that I have got the few things I needed to do out of the way. The only thing we need to focus on, from now until we leave, is pleasure. I want to take you to see the casino later this morning, it won't be open until this evening, but I have a friend who works there and he said we could look around. I told him you hadn't been in one before and that you were fascinated to see it before we go for real this evening."

"That's great. You seem to know people all over the place."

"I can't help it," she purred, "I like people and they all seem to love me."

"Anyway, shall we go down to the restaurant for breakfast?"

As we stepped into the lift, I felt a million dollars. The way we were looked after, with great attention to detail, emphasised that illusion of being wealthy. I lapped up the attention and the luxury of being treated like someone special.

After we'd finished eating, we spent a little time in the relaxing atmosphere of the lounge area for coffee. That kind of temporary lifestyle, that most people tasted very infrequently, could easily become addictive as it blocked out the real world of work.

"We're due to meet Pierre at the casino at eleven this morning, until then we can wander through the city for forty-five minutes or so," she informed me.

To be honest, I didn't care where we went, it was just a beautiful place to be, but wander around we did and laughed and loved along the way.

She must have had a route planned because we were outside the casino door at exactly eleven, without seemingly making any deliberate effort to get there. Pierre was waiting, standing just inside the glass doors and his face lit up at the sight of Sasha. He threw open the door and shouted, "Bonne journée, Mon ami. Welcome." He kissed Sasha on both cheeks and proceeded to do the same to me, which can be a surprise to a traditional Englishman, especially when it is not expected.

He was about as tall as me, but with very dark hair. His slightly olive skin hinted of Mediterranean descent and he possessed a personality that competed with Sasha's for attention; on occasions it won the contest.

As he led us inside, he chatted to Sasha in French, then, realising that I couldn't understand what was being said, switched to impeccable English. The telling hint of accent, which in his case was quite musical, was used to full effect in order to charm his guests.

The guided tour was extensive, but very interesting. He obviously enjoyed showing the novice how the casino worked. As we left the building he said to me, "I hope you are intending to impress my friend here." He placed his arm around Sasha. "She's used to men who know how to impress, you know." He smiled at me, but before I could ask what he meant, bade us good-day with a jovial, "Au revoir."

Once we were out of his sight I asked Sasha, "What did he mean by that?"

"He was teasing you. He knew my mother and father. My father came here many times to show off with my mother." She linked her arm with mine and began to steer our direction back into the city centre. "You see, you were right when you hinted that I came from a fairly well off family. My father would splash money around to impress people. He would think nothing of having ten or fifteen thousand at his disposal when he came to a place like this. Sure, there were lots of people who would come with mega-money, but as I told you before, I'm not a high-roller, but I am fairly well off."

I listened to her talking about the casino and her father in rather ordinary terms, as if it was a normal part of life to risk losing such large sums of money. Truth be told, the tales of the high life made me feel inadequate.

"Sasha."

"What?"

"Is there any way that I can get my hands on some more money from my account in England?"

"I didn't mean to suggest that you should spend loads of money to impress me, Andy," she said defensively.

"Well you told me that to have a good time I needed two thousand, but to have a great time five would be better. I didn't listen to you. I only brought a thousand with me. I've never been in a place like that before, sheltered childhood I suppose, and I couldn't believe that you were being serious when you were talking about those amounts of money. I thought you were just pulling my leg. I wasn't joking when I said I hadn't done this before. I've never set foot in a place like that in all my life. My Dad would do his nut."

She laughed at me.

"Andy, it's time to do your own thing instead of letting daddy tell you how to live your life."

"Not you as well, Sasha. That's just what Jake's been telling me for weeks."

She made an exaggerated shrug of her shoulders and rolled her eyes.

"Perhaps Jake's right."

I had to admit that there was something fascinating about the casino that made me want to give it a real go at least once.

"So, is there a way to get some more money? You obviously know the French system."

I didn't let on to Sasha that I had actually brought five thousand and as it hadn't been mentioned before she would be none the wiser. I could get enough to really push the boat out.

Dad had always encouraged us to be careful with money, so the idea of being a bit reckless got my heart racing. It was an intoxicating excitement that could easily take hold of a person. I didn't intend to let that become me, but I did want to experience it at least once in my life.

She looked at me thoughtfully, as though she were trying to read whether I was being serious.

"The best way is to talk to Pierre. He always helped my father when he wanted to get hold of money from his account in England. They have some sort of transition account in the casino that clients can use to request funds to be electronically transferred to the house account. They arrange to give you the cash. If you're serious about this, you'll need to talk to him this evening when we go back there."

There was a mixture of excitement and apprehension I hadn't experienced before as we entered the casino. Unlike earlier, when the building was quiet and unassuming, the lights were dazzling in the blackness of the evening; the large open room awash with people drinking and laughing. I had always imagined these establishments as seedy backroom places on the edge of the legal world with one foot in something 'shady.' Not only did the view before me shatter that fantasy 'film-world' image, but the whole atmosphere seemed alive with possibility. A tantalising combination of risk and reward permeated the fabric of the building, and once inside, it took hold of me.

As we slowly circled the gaming tables to see what was happening, I scanned the room looking for Pierre. When I caught sight of him, across on the far side of the room, I left Sasha at one of the tables, engrossed in the bet someone had just placed, and went to speak to him.

"Ah, Andy. Good to see you again, my friend. How are you this evening?"

"I'm great, Pierre, thank you. I can hardly recognise the place after our visit this morning. It's so different when it's busy."

"It's a fantasy world of delights and entertainment for you to sample and enjoy."

The words rolled from his lips like well rehearsed poetry that was bathed in his musical accent.

"Pierre, I have a little problem and I understand you might be able to help me."

"I can't lend you any money."

"No, no..." I began to protest, but stopped, when he broke into a grin. I realised the manifestation of his humour had caught me off guard once again that day.

"What can I do for you, Andy? If I can help you, I will, my friend."

"I need to transfer some money from my account in England to change into cash for the next few days, but I don't know how..." I stopped to look at him.

"You don't know how?" he said, with a questioning tone that beckoned me to complete the interrupted sentence.

"How to move such a large amount. Can you help?"

"How large an amount are we talking about?"

I could hardly believe the words that were coming from my mouth as I heard myself ask for ten thousand pounds. It rolled from my tongue as easily as asking for a drink, as I neglected to attach the reality to what I was doing.

"Ten thousand pounds?" Pierre laughed at me, putting his arm around my shoulder. "I thought you were going to ask me to get you a large amount." He gestured with his free hand, "We see people who gamble more than a whole life's earnings of ordinary people, in a single night. Ten thousand is easy to get, as long as you have got it of course?"

He waited for my response.

"Yes, yes, Pierre. I have twenty times that in the account I want to withdraw from, it's just that I don't know how to do it at short notice."

"You want to impress the girl I think?" He smiled at me as he switched the subject. "She isn't impressed by money you know," he cautioned.

"I don't want to impress her as such. I just want to make sure that we have a good time while we're here. This is not something I will be repeating often, but if you don't make the most of it at the time..." Holding up his hand to silence me, he said, "I understand. You're absolutely right, my friend. Follow me and we'll see what we can do."

He led the way through a door at the side of the bar, along a corridor and then into an office at the back of the building. Pierre spoke to a man who was working on a computer and he left the room immediately, nodding in acknowledgement as he passed me. Pierre sat down at the desk and began to tap on the keyboard, periodically examining the screen. Then he turned to me. "First I will need to know the bank details so that I can check if we can do it." I pulled out my bank cards with my passport, thinking that that it would be necessary, and placed them on the desk. "I will enter the bank codes and check, then, I will let you enter the amount you want to transfer. If it all passes the security clearance you can have the money, in cash, by tomorrow night. Before I start, is that all okay?" I confirmed that it was fine and that I was okay for money at the moment.

He took a long look at me and then nodded to indicate that he would proceed with the transaction as requested. After a few moments he told me that everything was prepared. He got up from the seat, indicating that I should sit there and then directed me to follow his instructions detailing the amount required. Again we swapped seats and he completed the transaction.

Turning to me, he said, "Done, Andy. Now I believe there is a beautiful girl waiting for you in the games room. If you don't go and have a good time with her, then I might just take your place."

Getting up from the chair, he slapped me on the back and pointed the way back to the bar. He watched as I went down the corridor to the door that led back into the games room. As I opened it I turned to look back at him. He waved and shouted, "I will have the cash for you tomorrow evening, ready for when you arrive."

"Merci, Pierre."

He smiled at my attempt to use the only French that I knew. I stepped back into the busy gaming area to see Sasha still at the same table. By the look of her, she was enjoying herself.

When she saw me she frantically beckoned me over and pointed excitedly to the pile of chips on the roulette table in front of her. Even the vibrant colours of this plastic money invited you to touch them and create colourful patterns on the green felt of the table. They seemed designed to mask the true value of each piece. I changed some of the cash that I'd brought in order to join in the game with her and it wasn't long before her exuberance was rubbing off on me.

It was striking how emotions swung from deep lows, when a loss happened, through to real highs, when the right number came up. The suspense, as the ball ran around the spinning number disc, created the most pronounced tension as we waited for it to make its choice, after teasing at several different numbers. On that choice rested the next emotional wave, either up or down. Frequently both extremes were in evidence at the same table at the same time. The low, from those who chose the wrong number, and the high, from those who chose right. I could see how easily people could get hooked on this thrilling roller coaster ride and in the process, lose track of the cost. Without even noticing, I had started to become one of them.

Time seemed to fly past at an irrepressible rate. We were having a fantastic time in that world of pretence. Once the cash had been changed into chips, it no longer seemed real. It was like toy money and that helped cushion the losses, but also encouraged a reckless risk-taking attitude. The full consequence of the loss was hidden in the colourful discs and, regardless of the loss, you couldn't help immediately putting up more in order to try to win it back. The deception staged by this unreal world pressed me to believe that the 'house' would not be the winner in the end. If only I continued long enough, I had to win, if not that night, then the next. It was a very, very, powerful drug.

I don't know what time we finally got back to our hotel room, in fact I barely remember the journey, but it was very late. I was so tired and under the influence of the evening's drinking, that I don't even remember getting undressed and into bed. Either Sasha had helped me, or I had run on auto-pilot for the task.

It was the sudden flash of light that brought me round the next morning when Sasha, more enthusiastically than I would have preferred, threw open the curtains. She was wide awake and already dressed.

"What a beautiful morning!" she shouted.

Then, turning to face me, she ran and jumped onto the bed where I was desperately trying to fend off the new day for a few more minutes.

"Are you always this lively after such a late night?" I mumbled from my sanctuary inside the duvet.

"Yes," she hissed, as she pulled the pillow out from under my head and proceeded to hit me with it.

What happened next was quite childish, but great fun. We must have been chasing and hitting each other, with the pillows, for the next ten minutes. We periodically collapsed in laughter before one of us started another onslaught, until there was a knock at the door. We both stopped dead in our tracks while trying to contain the laughter. Sasha went to answer the door, allowing room service to bring in croissants and coffee for breakfast, which signalled the end of the play fight.

Parking ourselves at the window, in a couple of easy chairs, we watched the world go by while enjoying the food.

"I hope you are ready for another day of sightseeing, followed by a night of risk taking, Mr Numan?" asked Sasha, in a 'don't let me find out you're a party pooper' kind of voice.

"I'm ready. Last night was just a warm-up to get my bearings, but tonight the real action takes place."

"Oh really, Mr Big shot gambling man."

Sasha's mocking tone made me feel a little foolish at my bravado, but I was sure she didn't mean to put me down.

The day flew by as we visited the famous, and the romantic, landmarks. Although the sun was out, the wind was bitterly cold, cutting through to our bones as we stared across the city from the Eiffel Tower. The only guard against it was the frequent visits to any place that sold coffee, allowing us time to warm up again before heading out to the next place.

After dinner, at six-thirty, I was ready for the evening's fun at the casino. The thought of going there again made me realise that I hadn't actually taken notice of the amount of money I still had. I didn't want to be found counting it where Sasha might see, I thought it would look bad. Anyway, Pierre was due to replenish my reserves that evening so I wasn't too worried, as long as he was as good as his word. It was only once in my lifetime and, as Sasha would say, what would life be if we didn't try something reckless at least once?

Arriving at the casino, the lights as dazzling as I remembered from the previous night, we went up the steps to the entrance and into the fantasy world that, for me at least, had been the arena of film figures like James Bond.

We bought drinks at the bar, where the temptation to ask for a Martini, shaken, not stirred, was huge. We watched the action at a few different tables for a little while before engaging, but I couldn't stand outside the fun for long. I found the money was burning a hole in my pocket and the desire to regain ground from the night before was overwhelming. The battle lines were not drawn in a field somewhere, but on the green felt covered table of numbers in front of me. The outcome determined by a small white ball landing at random on an ever slowing wheel of decision. Would I win, or lose?

Pierre was as good as his word, delivering the cash as promised. I had thousands on me, more than I'd ever felt the need to carry before. I felt so 'high society.' With hindsight, I realise that the moment I believed that I could afford it, regardless of the losses, I had moved onto dangerous territory. It was the place that shipwrecked fools.

We hit the gaming tables with a vengeance, laughing at the ebb and flow of money, represented by the pile of small plastic chips that increased and decreased before our eyes.

"Just keep those drinks coming, darling," Sasha would shout from time to time, as though it were her lucky saying as the chips went down. I loved the buzzing atmosphere. I was immersed in it completely and wanted the experience to linger long.

The following evening was much the same and by the end, while I was aware that the money was dwindling, it didn't really seem to matter to me as much as it should have. All I thought about was having enough to see us through our last night of fun in Paris. The pretence of having money to burn had taken hold of me more than I would ever have liked to admit at the time. Had it not been for the fact that we were due to leave the following day, another visit to Pierre might well have been on the cards.

We must have swayed back to the hotel at the end of our last evening as our consumption of alcohol was substantial. I can only imagine the way it looked to the night staff as we returned. A young couple, barely in control of their actions, who were clumsily making their way across the hushed hotel lobby while trying to get to their room. All of my life I had looked down on people who drank until they lost control, but here I was on the verge of the very same thing.

CHAPTER 13

When I awoke the following morning, it was to the sound of somebody entering the room. My head was spinning. I could barely comprehend who it was.

"Sasha…"

I called out in a pitiful manner at the loudest volume my pounding head would tolerate, but there was no response.

After a few minutes of struggling to try and engage with the real world again, I sat up on the bed feeling much below my usual best. The room seemed to be rotating at an alarming rate, which made me feel nauseous, and I had to take my time so that I could minimise the effects.

I was so absorbed in maintaining my own conscious connection to the morning that it took a while to notice that I still hadn't had any response from Sasha. Had she gone out again? I struggled to my feet and began a futile attempt to find out where she was.

It seemed like an epic journey simply getting to the bathroom and I must have looked pathetic as I slowly crept across the room, trying to keep my equilibrium. The image that confronted me in the mirror, when I was finally able to focus properly, was dishevelled and wrapped in the same suit that I had gone out in the night before, not in the same condition, but with creases pressed deeply into the cloth from having been slept in.

As I came out of the bathroom, after trying to straighten myself up a little, I discovered the door to the room was wide open with a cleaning trolley partly obscuring the opening into the corridor.

"Sasha?" I called again. This time my call was full of question. "Sasha, what's going on? Where the hell are you?"

A lady, who was obviously a member of the hotel staff, came into view in the corridor and said something that I couldn't comprehend. I didn't respond. It was obvious to her that I was trying to process what she meant, so she repeated it again a little louder. I held up my hand in an attempt to communicate that I didn't understand French.

"Non comprehend. English? Do you speak English?"

"Time to leave, sir. Room to be cleaned."

It took a little time for her request to sink in. I was puzzled that she seemed to want me out so that the room could be prepared for the next visitors. I couldn't understand where Sasha was or why we were being thrown out of our room, so I continued in my disoriented efforts to find her, going back to the bathroom once more. She was not there, but I thought I had better wash and try to gather myself.

Looking into the mirror again the out of focus figure from a few moments ago came into sharp perspective. Shabby, unshaven, unwashed and still wearing clothes that I would normally have been ashamed to be seen in. I looked a mess.

I went to find my other clothes so that I could change, but discovered that there was nothing left in the room, except myself and the clothes I had on. I quickly felt my jacket pocket and found that my wallet, to my relief, was still there and pulled it out to check the contents. It was all there, cards, the remaining money, just three hundred Euros and my passport. It was obvious that I couldn't stay in the room any longer, so I made my best effort to straighten up and left to go to the check-in desk in search of Sasha, to the obvious relief of the orderlies. I wasn't sure that it would be to the relief of Sasha when I found her. I was a little confused and rather annoyed.

I went down to the lobby in the lift, hoping that I would find Sasha there getting ready to leave. I thought there'd maybe been a mistake over our bags and that the hotel porters had collected them sooner than they should've done.

As the lift doors opened, to reveal the ornate clock that was a feature of the entrance, I suddenly felt overwhelmingly conscious of my appearance. Having spent the last few days trying to look and behave like a wealthy visitor, I now felt like a creased and unkempt one. While I squirmed at the thought, the clock chimed at the half hour. It suddenly registered what time it was; one-thirty in the afternoon. I felt as though I had just come out of the effects of a general anaesthetic and was trying to find the missing pieces of my life. What had happened to the morning? More importantly, what had happened to Sasha?

At the check-in desk I tried to enquire about the lady that came with me, giving them the room number 702. After a little wait, while the desk clerk checked the computer screen, she said, "If you mean the lady that was in room 704, Ms Peterson, she checked out at eight-thirty this morning, sir."

"We are talking about Ms Sasha Peterson aren't we? Room 702?" I questioned, assuming that there had been mistaken about our room number.

"Room 702 is booked to you alone, Mr Numan. Ms Peterson was booked in room 704."

In my frustration and trying to correct their obvious mistake, I raised my voice a little as I responded.

"You've got that wrong. Ms Peterson and I were booked into room 702 together. For the last few days."

Although not intentional, my agitated behaviour, and probably my appearance, drew the attention of a security guard who was suddenly standing at my side as though anticipating some kind of trouble. Adjusting my attitude to account for the looming presence nearby, I asked again about our room arrangements and the whereabouts of Sasha. It was confirmed by a second clerk, who came to the desk from a rear office. She appeared to know who Sasha was and said that she had spoken to her personally that morning as she checked out.

"Did she say where she was going?"

I had difficulty restraining my frustration and realising I'd been a bit sharp I re-phrased the question more gently. The withering stare of the irritated supervisor cut me down to size before she reaffirmed the information she had been trying to give.

"She told me she was going back to England. I wished her a safe journey. That's all I can tell you, sir, we do have other customers waiting," she replied, in an attempt to conclude the conversation. I thanked her, still aware of the guard beside me, and left the hotel completely dumbfounded. What had I done wrong for Sasha to leave like that and to leave without me?

It wasn't long before I realised that I had to sort out my own journey back home. I would have to confront Sasha about her behaviour when I got back to her flat to pick up my car. She was a fun girl and liked a joke, but that was a joke too far, stretching my sense of humour to breaking point.

It took me some time, partly due to the fact that I don't speak French and that I was still very hazy, before I figured out how to get a train ticket to take me home. I was fortunate that I did have money with me otherwise it might have been a nightmare trying to find help.

After sorting out the ticket, I sat on the station platform watching the clock edge slowly toward the departure time for the train. It was tedious, giving far too much time for my imagination to run riot with possible scenes that would be acted out when I finally arrived at Sasha's flat. Each scenario played like a movie in my imagination, over and over, each time ending with her wrong doing being proven and my justification established. I was certainly preparing to give Sasha a piece of my mind and I had ample time to make those preparations on the journey back home.

The contrast between the journey to Paris and the journey back from Paris was very stark. Then it was laughter and fun, but as I travelled back, mile after mile, my anger grew in intensity. I felt dirty and dishevelled. Humiliated. What was she thinking by just disappearing like that? I'd been on the hotel bed for hours, completely dead to the world, while she would have been halfway home in the comfort of her own car.

Eventually I got back to England and then travelled on to London, before making the final leg of the journey to my home town centre. From there I walked the short distance to Sasha's flat. By the time I turned the corner to see the railing lined street and the door of her flat, I was exhausted. It didn't help that, even after so many hours, I could still feel the after effects of the last evening in Paris clouding my judgement.

It was dark when I arrived at Clarence Street to confront Sasha about what she had done and as I walked along the street toward the brewing confrontation, I realised that my car was no longer parked where I had left it. Something just snapped and I ran the remaining distance to the flat and began to pound on the door with my fist. There was no reply, so I tried again, still no response. I was now left with a choice. Either I waited in the hope that she would turn up at some point and with her some explanation about my car, and her behaviour, or, I could get a taxi back to Langdale for the night, get changed, sleep for a while and then try to find her the following morning. While I felt like throttling her at that moment, I was dead on my feet, so gave in to the weary yearnings of my body and mind for some rest.

The taxi journey to Langdale seemed as long as the rest of the journey from Paris. The driver kept asking for directions and as he turned into the drive he said, "Crikey, mate! It's pitch black out here. Are you sure you'll be alright?"

"Yeah, I'm sure."

"It doesn't look like anyone's in."

"It's okay. How much do I owe you?"

"That'll be thirty-two quid please, mate."

I gave him thirty-five and waited as he backed out of the drive. There was a chill in the air as I stood alone in the dark and the old barn that had been lit by the taxi headlamps, slipped back into the inky blackness. The stone walls looked like some foreboding fortress stranded in a remote outpost.

I checked the door, but it was locked, so I began fumbling around trying to find the key we'd kept under the plant pot nearby. I couldn't find it and tried another pot just in case it had been put in the wrong place. Nothing. I was getting pretty cold by that time and desperately needed to get some sleep. Knowing that I couldn't stay outside and also not knowing when the other guys would be back, I decided I had no option but to break a small window to allow me to get in.

I struggled to get through the glassless frame, trying to avoid the shards on the floor, but once I managed it I immediately flicked the light switch. The shock of the scene that greeted me paralysed my movements for a moment while I tried to comprehend what had happened. There was not one bit of furniture still as it had been when I had set off to Paris. Broken pieces were scattered all over the room.

My instinctive reaction was to check everywhere else, so I ran from the living room upstairs and threw open the door to my bedroom. It was the same as I left it, bed made, clothes in order. I quickly went to Jake's room and found it was as empty as the first day I'd set eyes on the place, just a bed and the curtains. I ran to the other two bedrooms throwing open the doors in turn to find the same deserted scene.

I couldn't understand what had happened and the worst thing about the situation was that I had no way to ring anybody. My mobile phone had gone into the hallway table drawer at

Sasha's flat before we set off for Paris. There was no telephone in the house and no car to go and find a public phone.

By that time I was in a rage that couldn't be contained inside and I no longer wanted to stop it spilling out.

"You bitch! You total bitch!" I shouted into the emptiness. It wasn't that I blamed Sasha for everything that was happening, but she was the focus of my anger at that moment.

I went down to the kitchen and pulled open all the drawers until I located some matches to start a fire. The cold had suddenly become quite intense and I was worried that I needed to sleep, but I also needed to be warm. Finding a key on a hook inside the kitchen cupboard I unlocked the front door and went out to the wood store to bring in enough logs to get a fire going and keep it there until morning. I set up camp by dragging a mattress down from my room, positioning it near the fireplace for the night. This absurd situation, that I could not comprehend, was all the more cruel by the fact that I was alone and isolated, with only my rage to entertain me.

When I turned out the lights the glow of the fire caused shadows of the broken furniture to dance on the walls. I had an eerie feeling they were mocking me. If they were attempting to disrupt my sleep though they were to be disappointed as the tiredness was becoming overwhelming. My anger would have beaten them into second place anyway.

It was hard to even picture the parties that had taken place in this room only days before and contrast that with the scenes my weary eyes surveyed in the firelight. The whole episode was turning into a nightmare that had run amok, like a train running out of control. The intense humiliation twisted in my soul as painfully as a steel blade turning in my flesh.

I drifted in and out of sleep throughout the night, sometimes waking totally disoriented, totally confused, until the events of the last few days ordered themselves and I figured out where I was. I wanted the next morning to come quickly one moment, so that I could deal with the situation, but feared its arrival the next. A sense of foreboding hung over me like a cloud waiting to release its contents in a deluge.

It was early when I woke the following morning. I was just able to see through the window a glimpse of the dawn light skirting the horizon. I threw another couple of logs on the embers that were still glowing from the night before, immediately resurrecting memories of the time sat around that hearth drinking and laughing. I was trying to convince myself that it did actually happen and was not just images conjured up in that semi-conscious sleep that plays tricks on your mind, like when you wake suddenly, convinced that you're falling, but then realise it's not real. That's how the parties seemed to me, like a dream I momentarily thought was real.

I still had to figure out what to do next, but I knew that it would involve a long walk to find a phone from which I could summon a taxi to take me back to Sasha's flat. I couldn't help wondering what I would do if she wasn't there. I knew that I had to go fairly early to have a chance of catching her before she set off to work. The moment that I thought about her going to work as normal, I struggled to understand how she could even do that after leaving me in France. Just go to work like it was a normal day. I began to wonder if I even knew what normal was anymore.

As I set out to walk to the nearest public telephone, my mind churned over the things I would say and do when I finally confronted Sasha. I trudged along, lost in my little world, while the muddy lanes contributed their mark to the new set of clothes I had put on. When I was finally able to get a taxi to come out and pick me up, the guy checked that I had the cash to pay the fare before he was willing to take me as far as I wanted. In fact, I only had enough left to get back to the town centre, rather than Sasha's flat, so would have to walk the rest of the distance to Clarence Street.

When the taxi ride ended and I was dropped near the bus station, I set off at a quick pace to reach my destination as soon as possible. The town was still very quiet in the early hours of the morning and the overwhelming impression I had, on that late autumn day, was one of grey landscapes like the scene of a colourless movie. I hurried through the uninviting streets and the few souls I encountered along the way, busy on their own journeys, gave no acknowledgement of my existence.

A left turn, then down to the end of the road and I had reached my destination. I hesitated at the last corner, before turning into Clarence Street, while I scanned the road for my car and any sign of life. I quickly proceeded to the steps that rose to the front door of the flat. The black door, one of many along the road, barred my way to the woman I needed to confront for the sake of my own sanity.

When I arrived the hallway light was on, showing through the glass top light over the doorway. I hammered my fist on the door to make sure that my demand for a response could not be missed. There was definitely movement inside, but no one made any attempt to answer. Again I pounded on the barrier preventing my entry, shaking the very frame in its setting.

"Open the door!" I shouted, making my claim to be heard. I saw a few people looking from the windows of houses across the road, but was incensed and uncontrollable. My experience over the last couple of days boiled in my blood. I wanted the woman responsible to know that I was mad. Again I pounded on the door, adding a few kicks, becoming more and more furious with every minute that I was being ignored. Taking a couple of steps back to the pavement I shouted, "Open-this-bloody-door-you-bitch!" then kicked and hammered the rhythm of each word out on the door in sheer frustration. Leaning over the railings to try to get a view through the windows, I was aware that the commotion I was causing had attracted the attention of some other residents in the street. It was obvious that whoever was inside was not going to allow me entry.

It seemed futile to carry on so I started to move away, thinking I could wait out of sight until someone came out. Suddenly the sound of sirens rapidly increasing in volume reached my ears. Before I knew what was happening, two police cars came tearing down the street, one from each end, as though they were playing some kind of sick game that dared each other to stop at the last possible moment. Screeching to a halt, both vehicles seemed to eject the occupants with force as three police officers practically jumped on me, throwing me forward until I was bent double over the bonnet of an adjacent car.

"Name?" one of the officers demanded. "Now! Name?" he repeated.

Bewildered at the sudden flurry of activity, I gave him my name as instructed.

"Address?" he barked, cutting off my protest at being held across the car, while two of them kept me there with enough force to make sure there was no attempt to break free. Once my interrogator had got the information he wanted, he walked to one of their cars while giving the extracted information to someone over the radio. Meanwhile, I was held in position for a few more minutes and, before he came back, I was placed in handcuffs by the officers who held me.

Once the cuffs were on they pulled me upright by my jacket. I was greeted by an audience that had quickly gathered to witness my performance. People had come out onto the street to take a look at the cause of the commotion that shattered their early morning in what was a normally quiet residential area. Front row positions were free at this event and, although I tried, I couldn't hide my embarrassment from the onlookers. I heard someone shout, "You should be ashamed of yourself, my children were terrified by the noise you were making!"

When the officer who had gone to his car returned he said, "We're taking you to the local police station, Mr Numan."

"Why? What for?"

I didn't get an answer to my questions, but instead was firmly and rather unceremoniously, pushed into the back of one of the waiting police cars. One of the officers tried to encourage the gathered people to go back to their business.

No matter how much I protested, they were as unyielding as the door that had blocked my way moments earlier. The die had been cast and they were going to fulfil their duty, regardless of my displeasure.

The car moved away cautiously as people stood aside to let it through. I resigned myself to the situation for the moment. I didn't say anything as they drove along the streets to the main police station. I knew I'd done wrong, no matter what had been done to me I should've behaved better than making a public nuisance of myself. I could just imagine Dad's face as one of the people in the crowd and wondered what he would think of my behaviour.

It's funny what can prompt you to start thinking about others. I hadn't considered what Dad or Carl thought when I was leaving the house those few weeks ago. I only thought about myself. What had I become in such a short time? How shocking that it only took as long as it did to get here.

The town was starting to get busy as we neared the centre, passing buses stopped to spew out people, all in a hurry to get to their destinations. The traffic moved slowly along as people headed to the day's business. Some days can look dreary, even if the sun is out. It's sometimes the way you see it rather than the way it is and this day was exactly that.

The police car turned into a side street then turned again coming to a stop behind an imposing stone building. The gated archway, where we waited to gain entry, added to the greyness of the day with the years of embedded grime that blackened the facade.

As we were allowed through the security barriers, one of the officers spoke for the first time since we'd left Clarence Street.

"DCI Crewe is waiting to speak to you, Mr Numan. I believe you know him."

It wasn't framed as a question, but a statement, as though the officer was well aware of the fact and didn't need me to confirm it.

CHAPTER 14

Having spent all of my life without ever setting foot inside a police station, I found myself at that particular establishment for the second time in a matter of days, visiting the same person, DCI Crewe. The familiarity of the place, the same corridor, the same interview room, the same sparse furnishings, was a little disturbing. I even noticed some of the same officers I'd seen on my previous visit. In fact, the only difference appeared to be that I was there without my voluntary consent.

One of the officers had gone elsewhere while the other two, having escorted me to this bleak destination, took the handcuffs off, indicating for me to sit, while they stood near the door like prison guards.

"DCI Crewe will be here in a few moments."

The wait for something to happen seemed endless, but it was probably only a matter of minutes. There were muted voices outside in the corridor that seemed to drone on for a long time until, finally, the door opened and Crewe came in. He was followed by DCI Johnson who had come with him to Langdale the first time we met. I could sense in the atmosphere that I was about to be involved in more than a friendly chat.

Johnson closed the door behind him and turned so that the four of them were facing me. Crewe cleared his throat, preparing to speak and to indicate that I should focus my attention on him.

"Andy Numan. I'm arresting you on suspicion of the attempted murder of Henry Price. You have the right to remain silent. Anything you say will be taken down and may be used in evidence against you. You have the right to a legal representative of your choice. If you have no representative, we can arrange for that. DCI Johnson and PC Barrett will escort you to a cell where you will be searched and held pending a medical examination. Mr Numan, do you understand?"

I was shell-shocked and stared at Crewe in disbelief. One particular sentence was ringing in my ears blocking out everything else; arrested on suspicion of the attempted murder of Henry. Surely they didn't really suspect me of such a crime? I couldn't understand how they could even consider that it might be true.

I had known Henry since I was a boy. He was the one who set up the rope swing in the trees of Durlwood's gardens, giving me hours of fun through the summers of my childhood. That man had been part of my life for so long that I couldn't ever remember him not being there. Who could believe that I would attempt to murder him? "Murder!"

It suddenly hit me that I hadn't even gone to the hospital to see how he was doing. I was too wrapped up in my world to allow it to even cross my mind. Even when Dad told me he was hurt, when I went there after the break-in, I was so mad afterwards that I just wanted to get as far away as possible. I never gave Henry, or his family, a thought. How callous of me. How could behaviour like that be excused? I ignored his situation as though he were a superfluous object in my life. But, how could it be possible that they believed I was responsible for such a wicked act?

Conscious that the four of them were looking at me, waiting for some kind of response, I tried to protest about the error they must have made. Crewe immediately stopped me.

"We'll deal with a formal interview later. Do you understand what I have said to you, Mr Numan?"

I nodded. I understood the words, but I couldn't comprehend why he was using them to address me. Johnson took hold of my arm, led me through the door and along the corridor to the back of the building where I was asked to empty my pockets and was searched.

They were courteous but firm; taking details, filling forms, photographs, prints and then a medical check. A psychological assessment, a check to see what my mental state was like. Was I sane? I felt as though I must be insane. I couldn't understand what was happening to me, but simply complied with all the requests. I felt like I was watching the sequence of events happen to someone else, like watching a movie. Finally, when they were satisfied, I was placed in a holding cell to wait for whatever was to come next.

The closing door seemed to shut out the world I had known until that moment and introduced a new world that was an almost empty box. I wondered if this was a snapshot of the life that would be mine.

After a little while the duty officer came to my cell and asked, "Can I get you a tea, coffee, something to eat?"

"Thank you, a coffee would be good. White, no sugar, please."

It seemed to be the first normal conversation, as brief as it was, since I had got back from France. The circumstances, however, were as far from normal as I cared to imagine.

They asked if I wanted to make a call to inform somebody of my whereabouts, but I really didn't want to have Dad involved at that point, if at all, and I didn't know who else to ring. I'd been there quite a while before it truly began to sink in that it was for real.

I must have been in the police station for a couple of hours, when the cell door was opened and a tall bespectacled man in a dark suit came in. He introduced himself as Harold Ball and informed me that he had been appointed as my legal counsel for the duration of the questioning, according to my request.

His manner was gentle and he seemed truly sympathetic to my plight, as he nodded continually while I tried to explain things. His small-lensed glasses, which were perched precariously on the end of his nose, seemed to serve as an authoritative divide between the good and the accused. He periodically looked over the rim at me while I talked to him about the things that had happened. He took notes in an illegible script that I could not have deciphered, even though he was writing down what I was telling him. Still, it seemed helpful to me simply to be able to talk about my predicament.

After I'd spent some time talking to him and he had finished quizzing me, he suggested calling Dad, but I wouldn't hear of it. I couldn't face the humility, even though I knew that he would have to find out sooner or later. In truth, I was as stubborn as a mule and proud to go with it. After all that I'd said about being old enough to make my own way in life, I didn't want to be looked down on by anyone. Not that I'd had this particular pathway in mind when I struck out on my own. My judgement was certainly clouded by my arrogance.

At a little after twelve o'clock, I was taken to the formal interview room and made aware of the fact that the whole thing would be videoed and would be monitored elsewhere in the building. The room was very basic, with nothing to hide behind if the questions became difficult to deal with. It was an empty space with chairs set out roughly in a circle. In the room was myself, Harold Ball, DCI Crewe, DCI Johnson and an officer at the door. Once we were all seated and after a pause as Crewe checked through a few papers, he indicated the time, date and the identity of the people present.

Then, addressing me directly, he said, "Is it okay if I call you Andy?"

It seemed to be the opening question every time I'd spoken to Crewe, but I supposed he was just being courteous. I nodded to confirm that I had no objection and with that signal began a very difficult few hours of my life.

"Now, Andy. Can you tell me what you were doing in Clarence Street this morning?"

"It's quite a long story," I replied, as though the evasive answer would satisfy the question.

Crewe continued staring at me and I realised, long story or not, he wanted me to tell it. I started to relate some of the events, but each time I began to explain one thing it became apparent that it made little sense unless I told them what had happened before it.

After a couple of minutes Crewe stopped me. "Andy, why don't you tell us what happened from the beginning, before you moved out of your father's house. Don't worry how long it takes, we've got plenty of time and I would rather that there were no misunderstandings."

He was obviously not in a rush to get something completed and crossed off his list and looked like he was in for the duration, so I felt I had nothing to lose.

Starting from when I opened the letter Dad had written, the cause of my outburst in his office at Durlwood, I told them everything that had happened. Occasionally Crewe or Johnson would stop me to clarify a point, or ask about something they thought I might not have elaborated enough, but on the whole it was approximately thirty minutes of the Andy Numan show.

When I concluded, Crewe leant back in his chair, turned to look at Johnson, then back at me.

"Andy, we have a number of things that we need to ask you about and we will require your response to each item."

I nodded to show that I understood.

"George, or Jake Clarke, Michael or Micky Layton, Jeremy or Jez Alston and Sasha Peterson; the people who you have mentioned, don't seem to see things your way, Andy. It's my job to find out the truth." I was about to interrupt, but Crewe, anticipating my attempt, held his hand up to stop me and continued. "As I said, it's my job to find out the truth. Not just because I like to do my job properly, although I do, but because there are serious issues if I don't. For instance, I have to find out who broke into your father's house; who smashed the place up; who stole a large number of very valuable items and who seriously assaulted Henry Price so badly that he has been unconscious since then."

"Could you confirm for me that the car you talked about is yours?"

"Yes, Inspector. The car is registered in my name."

It dawned on me that I'd completely overlooked the fact that I didn't even know where my car was at that moment. I explained that I had gone to Clarence Street to get the car, but it was not where it had been parked before I left for Paris.

"We've impounded your vehicle, Andy. For forensic examination," Crewe explained. Before I could ask why or how, he asked me to confirm the model and registration, which I did.

"Can you also confirm that you recently took your car to Perry's Mercedes garage for repair work?" Again I indicated that that was correct. "I am told that you never let anyone else drive that vehicle, and that has been the case since your father bought it for you as a birthday present. Is that correct?"

Harold Ball intervened before I could answer the question.

"I advise my client not to answer that question, Inspector Crewe."

Crewe didn't seem concerned and I wasn't sure what had just happened, but he proceeded to ask what date the car went in for repair, which I gave, and what damage there was, which I described.

"Could you tell us how that damage was caused?"

I hadn't mentioned the damage to my car in the account that I gave them, thinking it was not really relevant, but was a little uneasy that it suddenly seemed to be the focus of attention.

I explained that I was not sure how it happened, but that it could have been done by a delivery truck while I was away in Sheffield with the band, as the car had been left at Langdale for that period.

"What date did the damage occur?" Crewe asked.

I told him that it could have been any time from Friday, at about ten-thirty when we left for Sheffield, to Sunday morning, when we got home at about ten or eleven. Crewe hesitated before asking the next question.

"I believe that would be the same Friday that your father's house was broken into."

I was suddenly a little alarmed at the direction the questions were going, but said that I thought it was the same day.

"Could it conceivably have been damaged before you went to Sheffield? At maybe five or six o'clock?"

"I've never had an accident in my car so..."

I stopped for a moment to think, then realising that they were waiting for me to continue my response. I began telling them about letting Jake borrow my car for a while on that Friday evening and that he was gone from about five until nine.

"That definitely wasn't you out in the car at that time?"

"No!"

I explained that I lent the car to Jake on this one occasion because I'd fallen out with him and thought it would be a gesture of friendship, and because Jez's car was not working. My story didn't seem to have much impact on either officer.

"You've got to believe me. That's the truth," I emphatically stated. "Ask Jake about it." Crewe paused to observe me.

"We certainly want to find the truth," he said, as he opened a folder from which he took out a sheet of paper. Glancing up at me momentarily then back at the paper, he started to read.

"I, George Clarke confirm that the statement above is an accurate account, signed George Clarke, or Jake as you and I know him." Taking his eyes from the paper once again he gauged my reaction before continuing. "Friday, 17 October, I was at Langdale with Michael Layton, Jeremy Alston and Andy Numan all day until five in the afternoon, at which point, Andy Numan left in his car to go into town to get a takeaway before we went to Sheffield that evening. He returned at about nine, apologising for being so long due to unforeseen business he'd had to deal with."

I was totally stunned. That was not the truth at all. Jake had twisted the facts.

"He's a liar!" I shouted.

Crewe and Johnson didn't react to my outburst, but waited until calm was restored. Putting the paper back into the folder, Crewe took out another and began to read again.

"I, Michael Layton confirm that the statement above is an accurate account, signed Michael Layton."

He then read what amounted to the same thing; that I was the one who left Langdale in my car to fetch some food. Before I could comment, Crewe pulled yet another paper from the folder and began to read again, but this time it was Jeremy Alston stating the same thing. What was I supposed to make of this, other than that they had agreed to the story and fed the police a lie, but why would they do that? I was crushed and, to be honest, I was scared.

"Do you have anything to say, Andy?"

"They're not telling the truth. They must have agreed their story before talking to you."

Without pursuing my assertions about collusion, Crewe changed tack a little.

"On the evening of October 17, the day that your father's house was broken into, a car was seen leaving the property at seven o'clock, or there abouts. We received a call from a Mr

Delman, who runs a farm about three miles from Durlwood House. He gave a statement to us earlier this week. Apparently he was in a tractor travelling along the road that runs past Durlwood at seven in the evening, heading toward the town, after working in a field nearby. As he approached the driveway entrance, he realised that a car was travelling at speed down the driveway to the road. He didn't notice it initially because it had no lights on. Mr Delman had to take evasive action, applying his brakes and bringing his vehicle to a complete stop, but not before it partly obstructed the driveway entrance. The car, however, didn't significantly slow down and just managed to squeeze through the space that had been left. In doing so, it caught the balance weights that were hung on the front of the tractor. According to Mr Delman there must have been some damage to the offside rear wing and bumper of the vehicle concerned. I asked him why he didn't report it sooner and he said that the tractor fittings could not easily be damaged due to the sheer weight of them." Looking down at a paper he had produced during the explanation he quoted, "If the idiot in the car thought he could get away scot free from such a stupid manoeuvre, I hoped the dent in his car would remind him otherwise." He described the car as, 'a light-coloured Mercedes cabriolet. Possibly silver, or very light blue. He remembers the first part of the registration as AN56. We showed him some pictures of Mercedes cabriolet cars and he was quite sure it was a CLK. Can you explain the presence of a car, the same make as yours, with a possible colour match and the same first part of the registration, at Durlwood House on October 17 at about seven in the evening?"

I was lost for words. If that was my car, it meant that Jake was responsible for the incident at Durlwood. Who else could it have been? What kind of man must he have turned into to be able to do such a thing and more importantly, why? What possible motive could he have had? The officers observed while the mental gymnastics underway in my head must have shown clearly on my face. They didn't rush to interrupt my agony, but waited patiently for my response.

"I can only say what I have already. I let Jake borrow my car from five until nine on that evening. I don't know where he went."

Crewe stood to his feet.

"We'll take a break I think, Andy. Give you chance to think for a while and stretch your legs."

I didn't want to stop. I wanted to get the misunderstanding resolved so that the real culprit could be apprehended as soon as possible.

"DCI Johnson will escort you to the duty officer who will arrange for you to have a drink and something to eat, if you wish, then we'll start again in about half an hour."

I was led out of the room and along the corridor that had become the link between my cell and interrogation room. Even as the interview room door was closing, I could hear a conversation starting. Harold Ball had stayed behind with Crewe when I left.

I knew that I should eat something, but it was difficult. I certainly didn't have an appetite. I felt sick to the pit of my stomach at the events unfolding. They gave me the opportunity to go outside for a while in the secure area. Standing in the courtyard I took a few deep breaths of the chilled October air. The feeling of being trapped was overwhelming. From every view there were security features that just emphasised the fact that my freedom had been taken from me. I resolved to be as open as I could in order to find a way to convince Crewe that I was not in my car on that evening, even if it was my car that was there.

CHAPTER 15

The break slipped by like it was only a couple of minutes until suddenly we were being called back to the interview room. As I went in, I felt a knot tighten in my stomach at what was to come. Crewe, Johnson and Harold Ball were already seated. I took my place again, ready to restart my ordeal. I wanted to run, to escape. I felt like a caged animal, terrified and alone. I'd never experienced anything like this before, but I had to tell the truth, there were no other options.

Crewe straightened in his seat as he addressed me again.

"Andy, I want to talk about the car for a little while longer. You said that you thought your car might have been damaged by a delivery truck while you were away. Why?"

"When we got back from Sheffield the wood store at Langdale had been filled with logs. When I saw the damage, I initially assumed that Jake had done it when he'd borrowed the car on the Friday evening and had deliberately neglected to tell me so that he could try to avoid taking responsibility for it. After some harsh words between us, he went into the house, but Micky pointed out to me that there had been a delivery of logs while we were away and that the damage might have been caused by the delivery vehicle."

"We have been to Langdale with a search warrant this morning, Andy. The wood store is definitely empty. Are you suggesting that the whole delivery has been burnt already, or is the delivery another part of the story to cover your real activity?"

Harold intervened again, stopping me from answering. Again Crewe didn't seem at all concerned at being prevented from getting his answer, instead he launched into the next item on his agenda.

"Langdale is in quite a state, Andy. A broken window. The furniture damaged. Evidently someone has been sleeping near the fireplace in the living room and there's no sign that anyone, but you, has been living there."

I tried to make them understand that Langdale was in that state when I got there the previous evening after returning from Paris. I admitted I'd been forced to break a window to get in because the key had not been put back in the correct place. I suggested that the others must have moved out while I was in Paris, but that the damage was nothing to do with me. The more I spoke the more I appeared to be fabricating the story as I went along. Crewe let me finish what I wanted to say before telling me that they would leave that subject for later as he wanted to stay with my car for the time being. I thought he must have exhausted all the possible questions related to that subject, so I was curious what else he could want to know.

"When you went to pick up your car from the repair shop, did anything unusual happen?"

I looked directly at Crewe, but his face was blank, refusing to give anything away. I couldn't understand what they were searching for; what they wanted me to say. I could only tell what had happened, but I was beginning to question how much of what I thought was real actually was.

"The envelope!" I blurted out, suddenly remembering I'd put it in my jacket pocket without even opening it. "The guy at the garage found something when the repair was done. He put it in an envelope and kept it in the safe until I went to get the car."

"What was in the envelope, Andy?" Johnson asked the question and the change of voice threw me for a moment. It had begun to seem like there was only myself and Crewe in the room until the intrusion of another voice.

"I assumed it was my watch. It had gone missing when I moved out of Durlwood and I thought it must have been left in the car by accident."

"You opened the envelope when it was given to you then?"

"No. I put it in my jacket pocket. To be honest there were so many other things going on I forgot all about it. It must still be at Langdale in my wardrobe."

Crewe pulled a box from under his chair and lifted out an envelope. He held it out for me to take.

"Where did you get that?"

"As I said, a search warrant was issued for Langdale. We went there this morning before we started to interview you. Do you recognise it?"

"Yes. It's the envelope from the garage."

The unique Mercedes logo gave away the origin of the item.

"As you can see, it's still sealed. I would like you to open it please, Andy."

I couldn't help the sense of foreboding that engulfed me.

"Why?"

Crewe held out the package urging me to take it from him.

"I have spoken to the garage this morning and they gave a description of the contents," said Johnson.

I was beginning to be unsure who I should talk to. If Crewe and Johnson were trying to unsettle me, it was certainly working.

Taking the padded envelope that concealed the mystery object, I tore open the sealed flap and glanced inside. The contents that were revealed to me held my attention as I sat motionless, staring into the wad of paper in my hand. Finally, I looked up at Crewe not knowing what I was supposed to do next.

"Would you carefully take out the contents please?"

I put my hand into the envelope and slowly drew out a necklace. It was no ordinary necklace. The unique design immediately gave an impression of value and I recognised it the moment I saw it curled in a bundle at the bottom of the envelope. I held it out so that it could be seen by everyone in the room.

"Do you know where that item came from, Andy?"

Harold was about to say something, but I raised my hand to stop him.

"Yes, I know."

I'd seen that necklace so many times over the years of my life that I couldn't pretend, even if I had wanted to, that I didn't know. It glistened in the light as it moved in my hand. Dad would have been mortified to see the surroundings it now occupied, in a police station, in the hand of his son, who was accused of committing a terrible crime.

"Would you care to enlighten us?"

"I've never seen this in any other place but my father's bedroom. He keeps it in a special locked cabinet so that it's not on view. I've never seen it worn by anyone... At least, I've never seen anyone wear it except in a photograph. It was my mother's. Dad had it specially made for their wedding... Their wedding day."

I choked back tears as they welled up involuntarily and fought hard to restrain their advance, but my eyes could no longer contain the flow and they began to course down my cheeks. I couldn't understand how I'd got involved in this. Dad must have known on the day I went there that this precious item had been taken. He must have been hurting so much, yet he said nothing. It made me feel totally worthless that I could shout at him about a question he asked, even walk out on him, when he was in so much pain. He had treasured the necklace I was holding in my hand, not for its financial value, although that was enough, but for its sentimental value. It was a connection to his memories of Mum. To think that someone could remove it from its place, depriving its owner of the small comfort it offered, was heartbreaking. Worse still, I was accused of being the cause of that pain. It was just unbearable. I wondered how I would ever be able to face him again. I had to mentally wrestle against the evidence that made it seem like I must have been that villain, the perpetrator of the wicked act, the one who beat a harmless, defenceless old man. Knowing I hadn't done those things gave me little comfort at that moment.

I broke down in sobs. Wave after wave of convulsing sobs that I hadn't experienced since I was a boy. What made it harder to take was that the one who was hurting over the loss of that item was the one who always used to comfort me. The rising thought in me was, 'Oh what a wretched man I am.'

I began to wonder if the people watching were interpreting my behaviour as some kind of admission of guilt, rather than empathy with the man that had been so hurt by his loss. It took a little while to compose myself before I could sit up again. I couldn't look at Crewe or Johnson for a while. Shame was my companion, at the way I'd treated my father.

Crewe told me that they would have a break for a few minutes before we continued the interview. I was given a hot drink, which I cradled in my hands while I sat lost in a world of extreme loneliness.

I stared into the cup contemplating the situation that I found myself in. I was trapped deep in a well looking up at the small circle of light above that grew darker by the moment. Even if it finally became clear that Jake was the culprit, he had used my car, with my permission, to transport him to the scene of his criminal rampage.

When the interview resumed I was very subdued and distracted, thinking about what had been said previously. It took

Crewe two attempts at the next question before I even heard what he said and engaged again.

"I'm sorry. Could you repeat that I didn't..."

"Sasha Peterson. I would like to talk about Sasha Peterson for a few moments, Andy. What was your relationship to her?"

I felt like I was repeating things that had already been discussed, but simply complied with the request to explain.

"We first met at a party at Langdale, Jake introduce us. We got on very well together and were starting to get quite serious. At least, that's what I thought."

"Sasha Peterson has made a number of allegations about you and your behaviour over the last few weeks."

"She's what? What allegations?"

"She says that you organised the trip to Paris, to visit a casino. Is that true?"

"That certainly is not true!" I shouted. The rage that gripped me earlier when I was trying to get her to answer the door of her flat suddenly resurfaced with renewed vigour. "I don't know what she's told you, but she set up that trip. She told me that it was her treat because I had spoiled her over the previous weeks and that she wanted to do something for me. What has she said to you?"

I'd forgotten that the interview was being taped and suddenly became conscious about my aggression, so I quickly reined in the anger and changed my aggressive posture. Crewe waited a moment as if to allow calm to descend back into the room.

"I have a credit card statement here, Andy. The card is in your name and it details a number of small transactions, but there are a couple of very large amounts. One is to a garage for a little over eleven thousand pounds."

He looked at me with an expression that was asking for an explanation about the purchase.

"It was for a van. The band needed transportation to get to and from gigs. I agreed to pay for it on my credit card, as the others could't get access to funds as quickly. We were running out of time to get a vehicle to carry the equipment."

He looked back at the statement without questioning my explanation. It was obvious he already knew what the item was, but wanted me to confirm the fact.

"There's another large payment of seven-and-a-half thousand pounds."

"Seven-and-a-half thousand pounds?" I immediately repeated after him. "You must be mistaken. I haven't used that card except for the van and a few smaller amounts for fuel and food. I certainly have no knowledge of a transaction for that amount."

Crewe left a short silence once I'd finished speaking, as though he was trying to draw out further information. Seeing that I wasn't going to add to what I'd said, he continued.

"We made a few simple enquiries. It appears that it's payment for two rooms at a hotel in Paris."

"No, that can't be correct. Sasha paid for the hotel. How can that be on my card?" While querying Crewe about the statement something caught my attention. "You said two rooms. What do you mean two rooms?"

"Miss Peterson claims that you paid for the hotel to induce her to go to Paris with you. She claims you were infatuated with her and she only agreed to go if she had a separate room."

"She said what?"

Again I had to make an extra effort to contain the anger that was begging to be set free. Crewe straightened up in his seat ready to deliver the next line.

"I have to tell you that Miss Sasha Peterson came into this station yesterday, late in the afternoon, claiming that she had just arrived back from a trip to Paris where she had been assaulted by a Mr Andrew Numan."

"Assaulted! I have no idea what you are talking about. I have never assaulted anyone, ever."

"She told us that you had driven together to Paris and that while you were there you were behaving in a reckless manner. On the last evening she claims that, while you were drunk, you tried to force her to have sex with you and because she refused you hit her." The words were punching me like bullets from a machine gun. "Would you like to make any comment about that?"

Comment! I wanted to kill her for lying. I didn't know how to respond to such an allegation and as I tried to comprehend what I was being told, Crewe pressed a little further.

"When she came here we had to get the medical officer to take a look at her. She had a black eye and a number of bruises. If she is not telling us the truth, do you have any explanation how that happened?"

I wondered what world I had entered, whether this was my life that we were talking about. Was I being mistaken for some criminally insane brutal beast of a man who cared nothing for people or property? The man they were describing to me was not someone I recognised, but it seemed everyone else did as they looked at me. I couldn't absorb the information that was being given.

"I rang the hotel in Paris. They confirmed that Sasha Peterson left at eight-thirty in the morning yesterday," Crewe informed me.

"Did she have a black eye then?" I snapped.

"The receptionist only remembers that she was wearing a pair of large sunglasses, but she did confirm that Miss Peterson was booked into a room by herself." He paused again allowing me time to react. I was very conscious that my body language was being observed. "The hotel also told us that when you left you caused a minor disturbance at the reception desk. A security guard felt it necessary to stand nearby until you'd gone."

I was irritated at the suggestion that it was my normal behaviour, rather than the circumstances I found myself in being the cause of my anger at the reception. My irritation wove a thread through the response I gave Crewe.

"I caused a disturbance, as you call it, because she had gone home, leaving me in Paris without a word of explanation."

"Miss Peterson told us that she had to go because she feared for her own safety."

"Her safety? She's a liar. A damn liar. For all I know she could have blacked her eye deliberately!"

Crewe latched on to my insinuation and goaded me to keep going.

"Why in the world would she do that, Andy?"

"To frame me. That's what's going on here isn't it? I'm being framed. Set up."

"Why would anyone want to do that?"

"I don't know. I don't understand what's happening."

I leant forward crossing my arms over my stomach, as I desperately tried to calm the nervous churning.

"Miss Peterson told us that you tried to impress her by taking a few thousand pounds cash with you and that you were waving it around trying to portray yourself as rich."

I sat bolt upright at the new accusation that Crewe said had been levelled at me by Sasha.

"I didn't wave it around."

I suddenly felt conscious that I had been so reckless with money, but I couldn't deny it.

"Did you take any more money with you?"

"No... But, I did arrange for some more to be transferred, when I was in Paris."

A feeling of shame washed over me as I was compelled to tell them about my actions and I squirmed in my seat as I anticipated what the next question would be. As if he was following a script that I had read before, Crewe delivered the feared, but inevitable, next line, right on cue.

"How much did you transfer?"

I hung my head a little as I mumbled the amount, desperately trying to smother my reply in almost unintelligible sounds.

"Fifteen thousand."

There was a long pause before Crewe spoke again. It was so long that I had to look up to see if he was still engaged in the questioning. As I did, he locked eyes with me and prepared to deliver the next twist in the script of my life, the next act of betrayal, as I saw it.

"We have copies of your account transactions covering the last few days." Again, that terrible pause that had become the introduction to bad news was glaringly obvious. "There isn't a withdrawal for fifteen thousand pounds."

"There must be," I interrupted. "I'm not proud of it, but that's what happened. The casino gave me the money, so they must have checked the transfer first."

"Miss Peterson told us that she became scared and decided to leave you in Paris when you withdrew one-hundred-and-fifty thousand pounds."

"WHEN I DID WHAT? I would never do such a thing. You are making this up."

"The statement here shows the transaction."

I looked from Crewe to Johnson and back again, but their faces remained deadly serious.

"I arranged with a man at the casino, called Pierre, to get another *ten* thousand pounds in a pathetic attempt to impress Sasha. I'm ashamed of the fact now, but I would never take one hundred and fifty thousand pounds. You have to believe me. I would never do that."

"I have one difficulty, aside from this bank statement, about believing you, Andy. I contacted the casino. They have confirmed that the security chief, Pierre Du Mont, did authorise a transaction of one hundred and fifty thousand pounds, on your behalf, and under your instructions, despite his caution to you. They have also confirmed that you then spent the same evening, and the evening following, behaving like a multi-millionaire gambling away the bulk, if not all, of the money."

I leant forwards putting my head in my hands.

"What is happening to me?" I whispered.

Nothing made sense to me anymore. Crewe's questions continued to rain down on me, even though I was willing him to stop, to give me some peace. He suddenly switched tack as the information I could give about the money dried up. I no longer knew what to say about the incident.

"Could you tell me what you were doing in Clarence Street this morning, when you were picked up?"

I sat up, slumping heavily back into my seat and sighed with resignation.

"I was there to get the keys for my car and to find out why the hell Sasha left me in Paris."

"A rapid response unit was sent there this morning after Sasha Peterson rang 999 to ask for help. She said that she feared for her safety and that if you got into the flat, you might try to kill her."

"I was angry, alright. I wanted to give her a piece of my mind, but I wouldn't have laid a finger on her. I have never done anything to her to make her afraid of me, despite anything that she has told you. That's not what I'm like."

"You're still claiming, despite all the evidence to the contrary, that you had nothing to do with any of the issues we've been discussing. You didn't enter your father's house intending to steal valuables and damage the property. You weren't the one who assaulted Henry Price. You didn't threaten and assault Sasha Peterson... Perhaps you can explain the damage at Langdale?"

"I don't know how that happened. It was like that when I got back from Paris. I just don't know anymore. I don't know. They've framed me and made it look like I've been involved, but I haven't."

I was sobbing again, and, truth be told, I was terrified. Even I was beginning to think that I had done the things they were accusing me of. I started to wonder if I had a mental illness or something that made me forget some of the things I'd done, but how could I forget trashing my family home, assaulting Henry Price and Sasha Peterson? It just appeared that every time I protested my innocence it made me look even more guilty than before, as though I was lying as I tried to convince them that things were not as they seemed. Alienated from my family, friendless and now looking like a criminal, my mind was swamped in a murky blackness that blotted out any thought of hope.

Crewe decided that it would be a good idea to take another break and allow me to gather myself, so I was returned to the holding cell. As empty and stark as it was, I found comfort from not feeling as vulnerable as I'd been in the interview room. No more questions, at least for now. I contemplated asking to be allowed to speak to my father, but I couldn't face him. Even if Jake was behind the whole thing, I was still responsible for allowing him back into our lives. Dad had warned me about him, but I thought I knew better than my interfering father.

I must have been in that cell for quite a while rewinding the mental tapes of the weeks that had gone by. I remember someone checking on me at some point, but I didn't acknowledge my jailer's call to see if I was okay. I was lost in a blurred world of what I thought had happened and what I was being told really happened. At that moment, I could find no way of reconciling the two conflicting stories.

It was decided that I would not be interviewed again until the following morning, while a few further enquiries were made.

I'd been warned that I could be held for twenty-four hours without charge, but that an extension had been asked for and granted.

The night was not the most comfortable I'd ever had. Besides the noises of people in the other cells and the police officers doing what they have to do, I could not shake the thought of Dad coming home to the wrecked house, to Henry Price seriously injured and the precious things that reminded him of Mum all missing. Every time I closed my eyes, his face appeared. I didn't deserve to call him my father any longer after the way I had treated him and at that moment my pride influenced me to make the most stupid decision of my life, I would never see him again. What would I ever bring to his thoughts when he looked at me, other than the shame of having such a son?

The clang of a door was my wake-up call the following morning. At first I was disorientated as I tried to focus on the room, then I felt a sudden rush of fear as another day began and the nightmare I was living in continued.

I desperately wanted to bury myself in the meagre covers on the bed, hoping to shut out the world and escape to another. I grasped at the possibility that the night had revealed something that could help me to establish the truth before things went any further.

The officer that unlocked the cell checked to see that I was alright. He made it clear that it was time to get ready, as I would be required to go to the interview room at eight-thirty. The thought brought no comfort at all, the anticipated questions, the frightening accusations. I prepared myself for the day ahead and I tried not to dwell on the possible consequences if the truth didn't come to light. A day in a place where your freedom is restricted is enough, never mind the possibility of a much longer spell.

In the interview room Inspectors Crewe and Johnson were waiting with Harold Ball. That déjà vu feeling was strongly present, as though we were about to do a second take of yesterday's interview. Could it be possible that I had dreamt about this, I thought? Could this be the real interview that would find my story to be truthful?

As I went into the room the others greeted me. It appeared to me that the pleasantness seemed out of place, considering that I had been arrested for such a brutal crime. There I was, with three other men in a room, each having their suspicions about me and my despicable behaviour, yet they treated me with respect, bordering on friendliness.

"Andy, I have spoken to your father this morning. He has asked to see you." Crewe informed me.

I was horrified at the thought, especially as I'd resolved to separate myself from his life forever.

"No. No, I can't. I need to get some of these misunderstandings dealt with before I can face him. I'm being accused of things that I could never do. I won't see him. You can't make me see him."

The last thing I wanted, in the shambles of the circumstances I found myself, was to have to face my father.

PART TWO

CHAPTER 16

I walked through the huge solid security gates out onto the pavement and looked up at the clear blue sky that stretched out above me. When I'd first gone to prison, to serve the eight year sentence given to me, all I wanted was to be free, to escape, to get out. I paced the confines of the prison, like a caged wild animal desperate to be liberated. I threw myself into physical fitness to break the boredom and as an attempt to show that I was not a push over. The result that I'd achieved worked against me in the real world. I was a man marked with a criminal record for violence and with the build of someone capable of carrying it out.

Once my release date had finally arrived, I began to realise that leaving the regimented life I'd become accustomed to wasn't going to be as easy as I'd always thought it would be. I hadn't needed to think about how I should live my life or even experience the rhundane routine of independent living. Not only my liberty, but my freedom of choice had been taken away and now I had been given all of this responsibility back. Although there was help to get integrated into society, I could hardly remember what it was like to be free and to choose what to do next and this was most disconcerting to me.

The limitations with regard to work were enormous, mainly due to the status I'd acquired as a criminal. There were a few employers that didn't discriminate against ex-convicts who were taking the first step back to freedom in wider society and I did get employment as a kitchen hand, having had experience of working in the prison kitchens. However, it was the other employees that I had problems with; who would trust someone with a record like mine? Attempted murder, to an ordinary member of the law-abiding public, can suggest that the person with that record has the tendency to lose control, or is heartless enough to plan a despicable act. The change in the demeanour of people when they learned of my past was, almost without exception, significant. The possibility that I was innocent of the crime I was found guilty of, or even had become a reformed character, seemed to be nowhere in their judgement of me.

I eventually ended up in an old rundown bedsit that frequently gave accommodation to people in my position. In all the time that I was 'inside' I never admitted to having done what I was found guilty of, even though, at times, I almost convinced myself that I must have been. When everything around you points to a conclusion that is not unreasonable to make in the circumstances and everyone thinks you did it, it's not easy to stand your ground and refuse to accept the verdict of the courts, especially when you've been judged by a jury of ordinary people. My difficulty, in a prison of hundreds, was that there were others who also protested their innocence, plenty of them, so what made me any different? The other consequence of my refusal to admit that I was guilty was that I was continually refused parole and ended up having to serve the entire sentence. The penal system believes that a lack of responsibility equals a lack of reform.

Although I was thankful to be free, I found that life was hard on the outside. The disadvantages that I'd never have considered in my former life were enormous. Most of the time, they seemed insurmountable. When faced with that uphill struggle day after day, hope dwindles very quickly.

Even though I knew I was not guilty of the crimes I was convicted of, I had hung onto the hope that the truth would eventually come out. If it didn't, as was true in my case, there was still the knowledge that one day I would be released, but when that hoped for day finally arrived, there was a vacuous aimlessness that I found very difficult to deal with. The whole process was like going through some kind of re-birth; the bad that I had done in a former life led to my resurrection as a lower class of human being. The overwhelming inclination was to reject society and behave in a way that seemed fitting for someone who has breached the social requirements. Some went back to a life of crime, the kind of life that they had always known, but for me that was not an option. I hadn't been a criminal. I despaired of the place in which I found myself. Isolated, because I couldn't face people I'd known previously, and separated from my family, because I was consumed by shame.

I hadn't spoken to, or seen, either my father or brother since they came to the court hearings. I rejected any attempt by them to make contact and continued in that for the whole duration of my sentence. There were many requests for visits, but I refused them all. I couldn't face either of them and the years of incarceration had only strengthened my belief that they were better off without me.

My father had written to me every month of the whole eight years of my sentence. I didn't read, or reply to a single letter. Instead I resolved to move a long way away when I got out, without telling them where and asked the authorities for my location to remain confidential.

Over a hundred miles away from the home of my childhood, I lived in a bedsit that resembled a flat I once went to stay at for a few nights after a confrontation with my father. I began to get behind with the rent and came under threat of being thrown out onto the streets, but through all this my pride and stubbornness held fast, increasingly burying me.

After months of struggling to get by, the roof over my head would finally no longer accept me. Non-payment of rent was the beginning of my life on the streets. There were a couple of occasions, during the month that followed my eviction, that I found a squat to live in, but there was always someone else ready to push you out. Street life demands that every opportunity is taken to make the best of the limited resources available, but unfortunately there are more than a few who are competing for those resources.

I spent long days wandering around the town, or the parks, just to kill time, to find food and to secure somewhere that would offer a night's rest with any comfort that was available. The grime of the streets became embedded in the fabric of my clothing and the lines of my skin. The endless monotony of struggle-etched pain, rejection and loneliness became my expression, as is typical on the faces of the nomadic population that I had become a member of. I felt as though the work that I'd done in prison to build myself up was being undone through the worry and lack of nutrition. I noticed the changes as my clothing became baggy, hanging on me instead of fitting properly.

Then, on a certain day, while working at my usual employment, which amounted to doing nothing, I met a guy called Tim.

Tim came across as the intellectual sort that had decided to swim against the flow. He seemed very intelligent, but he was also a little weird. Having lived on the streets for a long time, he'd built up a network of people who lived 'alternative' lifestyles. The thing that attracted my attention when I first saw him was not actually the man himself, but the guitar he was playing for the entertainment of the passing public, in the hope of being financially rewarded for his efforts. He was pretty good on the battered old instrument and oozed confidence in the manner of his playing. Some passersby had thrown coins into the guitar case which had been left open to invite contributions.

I hung around for a while, just listening to the sounds being created and then dissipating as they gradually dispersed into the space around him, only to be chased by the next barrage of notes in flight. Becoming aware of my interest, he made eye contact with me and, without breaking the rhythm or flow of the sound, he nodded in acknowledgement of my appreciation of his gift.

During my time in prison I'd deliberately made no mention of my musical ability. In some way I blamed it for all that had happened to me. I suppose my reasoning was that if I hadn't been able to play the guitar, perhaps I would never have got involved with Jake and the subsequent events would not have happened. Seeing Tim that day, sat enjoying the music he was making, flicked a switch in me that re-lit my interest once more and was the reason that I stopped to talk to him.

Tim was one of those characters that made you want to engage with him, he was intriguing and very friendly. He offered me a cigarette as he took one out for himself.

"Thanks. I'm Tony by the way."

I'd not used my real name since my release from prison. I'd relinquished that right, along with any thought of returning to my old privileged life. My time inside had taught me hard, brutal lessons about my character and I was now a million miles away from that naïve boy who'd recklessly played with his birthright and suffered its crushing consequences. I no longer deserved the name of Andy Numan.

Tim introduced himself, eyeing me with the smallest air of suspicion, probably guessing that I'd given an assumed name. Many people living rough, as Tim was only too aware, had a past they'd rather not reveal and as we smoked, he carried on his discourse about life on the streets and his interests, punctuated only by his occasional performances for the passing public. He'd known the moment he saw me that I'd been living rough and badly needed respite from the relentlessness of finding a safe place to sleep, so offered to take me somewhere I could stay, at least for the time being.

A desperate situation certainly makes a luxury from a cast off and anything was better than my current circumstances, especially as the nights were beginning to turn colder. Trying not to appear too desperate, I jumped at the chance of somewhere warm to stay without even questioning where that might be.

When I was younger and wealthy, for that is what I was, I never talked to people like Tim. Nor would I have ever considered living or sleeping in some of the places I'd been during recent months, but I followed obediently behind him without the slightest hesitation, just thankful for any comfort that was offered.

Winding our way through an increasingly industrialised area of the town, we walked toward rows of terraced houses that had been barely visible from the park where we met. The long lines of tired, regimented houses loomed closer with each step, increasingly revealing the extent of the wear and tear of a long life's service.

By the time we were at the edge of the old estate, it was obvious that demolition was the intended fate of the redbrick rows of old accommodation that blatantly shouted of an era long gone.

Slipping through a security fence, in contradiction to the clearly marked 'keep out' signs that surrounded a continuous row of six houses, we went to one of the central two. At the rear of the property a tall wall created a little private courtyard that would originally have had a gate, long since gone, allowing access through the yard to the back door. Crossing the courtyard to the entrance, Tim rapped three times on the boarded-up rotting wooden panel that had taken the place of a glass pane that would have originally been part of the door. It was wonder enough that the rest of the rotten frame didn't collapse from the signal to open it, but we waited for some mysterious approval from inside to grant us access.

After a few moments the sound of bolts being slid open was followed by pulling on the door that eventually gave in to the pressure to open with a loud crack as it came unstuck from the frame. The rusted hinges squeaked like a scene from a horror movie as it opened to reveal the guard of the entrance.

The woman who had come to let us into the building was about fifty years old with long grey hair tied back in a 'half-effort' pony tail. She was dressed in clothing that drew its design from the sixties, but was more likely the original articles from that time. The deep lines in her face hinted at a life of hardship and the fixed expression didn't betray any emotion that may have been submerged beneath the hard outer shell.

Without even acknowledging Tim's arrival, she looked straight past him and fastened a glaring stare on me.

"Who the hell is that?" she shouted abruptly.

Many years before that kind of greeting would have caused a significant reaction in me, but I inhabited a world that was full of them, prompted often by people who were trying to defend the little they had.

"That's no way to treat our new guest, Mary." Tim's voice was gentle and reassuring, displaying a concern that tried not to alarm the lady who still controlled our access, as she positioned herself like a portcullis in a gateway. "He needs somewhere to sleep for a little while, so I brought him back with me."

Tim talked about bringing 'home' a guy he had never met before as if it was the most natural thing in the world to do. He made a move to go through the door. Mary gave way to him without resistance, but muttered something under her breath as he passed by. He beckoned me in and led me through the decrepit building toward the room at the front of the house.

I was conscious that Mary, having quickly slammed shut and bolted the door again, was now following very close behind me.

The house was barely habitable, with plaster coming off the walls and sections of the ceiling missing so that the remaining floorboards of the rooms above could be seen from below and through the holes in the floor the ceilings of the first floor rooms were visible.

"This way," Tim said, as though proudly showing a visitor through the house he loved. He opened a door at the foot of the stairs revealing a large room containing various pieces of furniture arranged around a fireplace. Although the room was in a poor state, it seemed to be intact, the only one in such condition. Before I'd even set foot over the threshold to enter the room, Mary pushed past me and Tim, literally jumping into an old shabby reclining chair to the side of the fireplace.

"This is *my* personal chair, for *my* personal use," she emphatically declared and, having staked her claim, she obviously had no intention of relinquishing it, especially to a stranger.

Tim cleared his throat and stated, in a public speaking manner, "This room is what we call the 'livin' room,' because it's the only room in the house that's fit to live in." He sniggered at his joke while he slightly rearranged a shabby cushion that sat on one of the threadbare chairs, "and," he continued, "that chair is Mary's particular special chair, that no one else is allowed to sit in."

I nodded in acknowledgement of the fact, which seemed to relax Mary a little as her property was formally recognised by Tim and me.

The fireplace was clearly being used as a source of heat and light, but also as the means of cooking. When I asked why there was no fire in the hearth on such a chilly day, with purely selfish motives, Mary, with obvious displeasure at my presence and at my ignorance, snapped, "Not during daylight hours, stupid. That would give us away to the authorities. We'd be back on the streets again in a flash."

She spoke of the authorities in a way that suggested they were a 'big brother' elite group of individuals that watched constantly for her presence so that they could catch and punish her for any misdemeanour. Her answer also revealed the hard penniless existence that she must have been accustomed to for many years, a life that had etched a portrait of its roughness deeply in her features.

For a split second I wondered how someone could end up in this situation, surrounded by the broken remains of better lives lived in a different era, but I knew how. My road to that wreck of a shelter was different to Mary and Tim's, but had happened little by little, until it was accepted as having always been like it. Trying to bring back memories of the life I once lived was like recalling the scenes of a movie. I could see it, but it wasn't real. The more difficult question that plagued me was how does a person get out of a place like this once here?

"I need you to give me a hand, Tony."

Tim waved for me to follow him and as he started to climb the stairs, each step produced a loud creak from the board moving under his weight. I wasn't too keen to follow him until he'd reached the top safely so that the weakened structure would only have to support one of us at a time. When I finally traced his steps to the summit, I could see that the house was being systematically pulled to pieces in order to provide fuel for the fire. Missing doors, dismantled cupboards and floor boards torn up, leaving rooms showing the joists and the ceilings of the rooms below.

"Careful where you step or you might find a quick way back downstairs," Tim cautioned, as he handed me a crowbar. "I've put my foot through in a couple of places when I lost my balance."

The next twenty minutes were spent taking anything that was burnable down to the living room and breaking it to stack it by the fire, ready for use. All the time we worked, Mary held station occupying the seat declared as hers, supervising the process with a keen eye.

Finally, having completed the necessary task, Tim called time. Once back inside the living room he shut the door and motioned for me to sit down and make myself at home.

Having done so, despite the state of the old worn-out chair that supported me and the many layers of clothing I wore, I felt overwhelmed by the comfort of the soft furniture. It emphasised how hard and uncomfortable the benches were that I'd spent much of my waking and sleeping, hours on. I must have fallen asleep within a short time, glad to leave the world that I inhabited for the duration of unconscious relief that sleep brought.

How long I was there I don't know, but when I awoke it was to the warmth and musical crack of a fire dancing in the hearth. It took time to reconnect to reality as flashes of memory from Langdale plagued my hazy mind, but I eventually remembered where I was. The only light in the room was the orange glow of the fire which created a lively shimmering shadow effect on the walls. Mary, who was sitting over on the other side of the fireplace, must have noticed that I was awake. She busied herself around some cooking utensils next to the fire. She then handed me a chipped and cracked mug that contained hot tea. It was weak, as though having been made from the multiple use of a single teabag, but could not have been more welcome at that moment.

"Thank you."

She didn't respond to me, but I was grateful for the kind gesture.

I suddenly realised that we were alone in the room and trying to connect with Mary, I asked where Tim was.

"He's out," she said, offering no more information. I didn't want to press her further in case it risked the warm comfortable position I was occupying.

Mary and I sat in our individual worlds which were uneasily linked through the mutual enjoyment of the common comfort that has largely disappeared from our modern centrally heated houses. The hypnotic display of the fire held the focus of our attention. That trance-like state of silence, peppered with the spit and crackle of the fire, remained until the same three-knock pattern was heard at the rear door, prompting an instant response from Mary.

Muted voices seeped through the broken structure of the house to the place where I sat until Tim appeared in the room.

"I think you needed to catch up with a little of that," he said, making me feel a bit embarrassed that I'd invaded their humble space and rewarding their kindness by falling asleep. He laughed, diffusing my awkwardness.

"Our speciality tonight is soup and bread."

Mary took some tins from Tim, giving no reply to his announcement and proceeded to open them, emptying their contents into a well-used saucepan and placing it on a rack over the fire. She issued Tim with his ration of tea carefully extracted from a valuable teabag which was duly set aside for future use. The quiet hypnotic state that was previously induced by the fire slowly returned, but involved three people instead of two.

Several minutes later the quiet was broken again, but only by Mary's clink of stirring in the saucepan as she attended to the meal. I was handed a bowl of hot soup, served in another piece from the ramshackle crockery set and some slices of plain bread, which seemed like the height of luxury as it was served by the roaring fire.

I responded as I had when Mary gave me the tea, but received exactly the same response in return. Tim said nothing when he was given his share, as if he knew that no comment was required for the act of service.

At first the silence was strange and uncomfortable, but I began to realise that these two people had no expectations of me, or each other. They were not looking for thanks for what they were doing and shared what little they had simply because that was the right thing to do for someone in need. I suspected they had both been well acquainted, throughout their lives, with hunger, loss, loneliness and, above all, poverty.

As I sat there in front of the fire, contemplating the relative comfort of my place for that night, a dam that held back all manner of emotions started to give way inside me. I worked hard to hold back the physical expression, though the tears were straining to be set free. These two had not asked a single question about who I was, what my past was, what I was guilty of, or how I had ended up there. They just gave me something I needed more than I could understand at that point, a little compassion and understanding, without any expectations or demand for repayment.

I thought about how I felt when I first saw Mary. The abrupt manner was like a wall of defence that surrounded her, protecting against misunderstanding and hurt, but when I fell asleep, she left me to indulge myself in her own space. When I awoke, she gave me a drink and when I was hungry, she shared what little she had with me. How often I'd judged people who didn't fit with my opinion of what a good person was, but Mary, in only a few hours, had broken through a shell that had been hardening around me for a long, long time. I don't think she even realised what she had done, or that the task had been completed with barely a syllable spoken.

CHAPTER 17

Over the next couple of months Tim and I took turns to go out on the street and play for the public, always in the hope that people would give money in response to our efforts. Mary kept house, in a manner of speaking, and we survived the best we could in the oasis of stability that we inhabited. Despite the condition of our accommodation, it was substantially better than living on the streets, especially as the colder months approached.

Throughout the time that I spent with them, I never really understood the relationship between Tim and Mary and felt it would be too intrusive to ask. I never understood my relationship with them either, except to say that over the weeks since that first meeting, they had simply demonstrated acceptance. They didn't require me to change to their view of what they thought I should be and never, at any point, tried to prise information from me about my past.

In the first week of November, as I returned 'home' from one of my musical working trips to the streets of the local town, I noticed that there was a change in the appearance of the old estate. It was not immediately obvious, but enough to know that something was different from the way it had been when I'd left that morning.

It wasn't until I got closer that a series of large machines, parked in a line behind one of the blocks, came into view. Beyond that, at the edge of the old estate, a complete row of six houses, that had been intact, relatively speaking, were now half demolished. The roof was completely gone and the shell of walls that remained reminded me of an old war film from the blitz.

I quickly ran to the familiar old backyard entry to the place that I had called home for the last few weeks. Rapping three times, the recognised signal to gain entry, I waited for the familiar response, but this time there was none. On any normal day, Mary would have been there within a matter of seconds to unbolt the door. Thinking that she couldn't have heard my knock, I tried again to raise her attention, but still no answer came. Once more I tried to raise some response, but this time I hammered my fist on the panel with much more force. The second thump on the makeshift door dislodged it, revealing that it was not bolted but just stuck on the frame. After the hesitation of my surprise, I pushed it wide open against the strained movement of the rusty hinges and quickly went through to the front room, only to find it deserted.

I knew immediately that something was wrong because in all the weeks that I'd been there, I'd only ever seen Mary venture as far as the gateway of the rear courtyard, she refused to leave the safety of the place she had adopted as home.

I quickly checked upstairs, in the one room that still had floorboards, just to be sure that no one was in the house, then, leaving the guitar in the front room, I went back outside, slamming the door shut behind me. The only course of action I could think of was to head into the town to search for Tim. I knew many of the places he often hung around, so I systematically went from one to the next looking for him. By the time I'd checked all possible options it was getting late in the afternoon, already well into the twilight of the day. Finding no trace of either Tim or Mary, I concluded that the only alternative to continuing my search was to go back to the house until I could figure out what to do next.

I'd become so accustomed to the presence of Tim and Mary at the house that it seemed to have finally gone to total ruin without them in it.

Starting a fire with the little wood that was still there, I sat watching as it grew in size and swallowed all the available fuel that I fed to it. All that was left to eat were some baked beans and a little bread left over from the day before. I was very hungry, but decided not to eat yet as I didn't want to face the music when Mary finally returned to find me occupying her domain. She had always dealt with the food and I had never questioned it.

I waited as long as I could, but by late evening my need for food overcame any etiquette that existed, although I ate sparingly so that there would be some left when they finally turned up. As the evening wore on and I had less to occupy my mind, I grew increasingly concerned by the hour.

It was about eleven o'clock when I heard a thud on the rear door as if someone had put their shoulder to it to gain entry. I quietly went through to the back room to listen, trying not to give away any clue that the building was occupied and held my breath to see if could hear any slight noise betraying the presence of someone on the other side. The quiet was suddenly broken by the familiar three knock password that seemed extraordinarily loud in the darkness. I flinched as the first of the sequence of knocks made me jump. Still unsure, I whispered, "Who is it?"

"Tony, it's me, Tim. Open the door."

I quickly pulled back the bolts, pleased that the lost crew had finally returned and yanked the door so that it swung wide open to a symphony of squeaking.

Tim stepped in and, without a word of acknowledgement or explanation, headed straight to the front room. I thought nothing of it as he could be like that, it was just his way sometimes, but continued to hold the door open as I anticipated the entry of the other occupant of this dilapidated building, but no one appeared. I took a look out into the yard to see where Mary was, but Tim was evidently alone.

I quickly closed and bolted the door behind me and traced Tim's footsteps to the front room where he was gathering things together and stuffing them into a rucksack.

"What are you doing, Tim?" I asked, trying to find a reason for the curious behaviour, his late arrival and Mary's absence.

"I am leaving, Tony."

The urgent packing was the main focus of his attention. He didn't pause or look up at me when he spoke.

"What do you mean, you're leaving? Where are you going?" Tim didn't respond to my questions. "What about Mary, Tim? Where is Mary?"

I was willing him to stop his activity and tell me what was happening.

"Mary doesn't need us anymore, Tony," he said sharply, stopping for just a second to look at me, his face was illuminated only by the firelight, but there was no mistaking the anger that it projected. I waited for a moment in the forlorn hope that more information would follow to help me understand what he meant, but he was totally occupied by what he was doing.

Realising that I would get nothing further until he finished, I let him continue without interruption until the frantic activity came to an end. It dawned on me that he was trying to occupy himself, creating time while he fought to bring his emotions in check.

Holding a mug that he was about to push into the top of his swollen rucksack, he finally stopped. Suddenly he surprised me by hurling the mug into the fireplace, where it smashed sending up a cloud of sparks that the chimney sucked away.

"Tim?"

I whispered his name in a tone that asked the question again.

"Mary's gone," he mumbled.

"Where?"

"She's gone. For good..." The finality in his tone left no doubt about what he meant. "I was here this morning with her after you left. We were just sat here in the room when..." The emotion was fighting hard to overpower him, but, refusing to surrender, he paused a moment to fight back. "We heard the machinery moving in. Before I could stop her, Mary ran outside to see what was happening. She doesn't go outside you know. She's been frightened for years about going out into the open in daylight. I had to bring her to this house from our last squat, when it was dark, with a blanket over her to stop her from losing it. When I first met her she didn't like me that much, but that's Mary... That was Mary." He quickly corrected himself and then sighed, locking his eyes on the slumbering fire.

"Tim, tell me what happened," I demanded, as forcefully as I dared, but he didn't respond immediately. He just continued to stare at the fire.

Then, in a monotone, resigned voice, he said, "She ran outside and I followed her. When she saw the demolition crew she completely freaked out. I caught up with her just as she collapsed... They phoned for an ambulance to come... Well they came, but it was too late. She's gone and now I need to leave this place too."

"No, Tim, wait. Just sit down for a minute."

He reluctantly followed my instruction, slumping heavily on the edge of one of the chairs.

We sat there for a long time before either of us said anything else. As the pathetic little fire tried to give some comfort to our wounded souls, I tried to make sense of the new upheaval in my life.

"Tim, where are you going to go tonight? It's cold and dark out there. You really should wait at least until morning and then decide what you are going to do."

He gave no indication that he'd even heard what I said, until he leant back into the chair and pulled his coat tightly around him for comfort. I threw a few more sticks onto the fire and sat waiting for the moment to say something, or listen to what Tim wanted to say, but that moment never came. In time, I drifted into a restless, uncomfortable, sleep that was disturbed by my imagination painting pictures of the moment when Mary collapsed. She was an unusual character that had seemed aloof and distant, but there was a routine that Mary created in my life that was comforting. With her gone and Tim obviously having the intention to leave, I began to wonder what would become of me now.

I was woken the following morning by the chill of the air and the very early roar of powerful engines creating a cacophony of noise outside. Shaking away the cloudiness of thought that always accompanies that first flash of consciousness, I looked around the darkened room. Without the assistance of the fire and the dingy morning light not able to make a dent in the boarded windows, the room was very dark. It felt cold and empty. It wasn't just the lack of heat and light, the room was only occupied by me and the collection of makeshift furniture. Tim must have slipped away, before I woke, taking his things with him. I guessed the real reason he was in this place originally was suddenly gone for good; Mary's departure, in one way, preceding his own, but in a different manner.

I never saw Tim again, although I did return years later to walk the streets that had been my home, only to find the run down estate was gone and new housing had been built in its place.

I was continually grateful for the compassion that was shown to me by those two unusual people who gave me, for a short time, a measure of stability that I badly needed.

With the rapid changes that were occurring around me, it was obvious that it was becoming impossible for me to stay at that location for much longer. The end of the road for the derelict buildings was clearly in sight, so I had to decide what my own course of action would be. Where to go next was not easy to answer.

I sat huddled in my chair while listening to the rumble of machinery, which was periodically interrupted by the clatter of bricks collapsing into heaps as the nearby buildings were systematically demolished. Reasoning that the progress of destruction would most likely be slow, it would allow a small amount of time for me to work out a plan. Up until that point, I hadn't considered how precarious the routine of my life was. The consistency of behaviour, over the previous couple of months, had given rise to a false sense of security about my existence, but the illusion had crumbled as it was being physically mirrored by the falling masonry around me.

I began to gather the few belongings I had and anything else that might be useful for a move that might end with me being back on the streets. If the demolition work continued to progress at the speed I'd been observing, it wouldn't be more than two or three weeks before they began on the block that had been my recent home.

While that gave me a little time, the more immediate problem was that Tim had taken his guitar with him. It had been our only source of income. Although the flow of cash was meagre, it kept the hunger pangs at bay, but without the instrument I was not going to last long. While I was able to scavenge for wood to feed the fire at night, warding off the cold, I could not as easily find money or food.

The next few weeks saw my situation gradually worsen, both mentally and physically. I had to find more and more wood to keep warm, but the root cause of the constant chill was not the weather, but the lack of nourishment. I spent a lot of my time simply begging on the street. Some people would buy food and give it to me, or give a little money out of pity, but it was inconsistent.

One day while I was out fairly late at night, driven by the need to find something to eat, I happened across an open side gate that led to the rear yard of a pizza takeaway. Before I had time to think about what I was doing, I found myself rummaging around in the bins for any scraps that had been thrown out. The need to eat pushed any pride that I had left to the side and an animal instinct to survive took control.

It wasn't long before someone came through the rear door, with cigarette in hand, presumably for a work break. I don't know who was more surprised, me being caught raiding the rubbish bin, or him coming face to face with a human 'rat' that was taking advantage of the waste. He froze like a statue as he caught sight of me, but before he could decide how to react I was off and out through the gate.

I'm ashamed to say that I visited that establishment a number of times over a period of weeks, to the point that it seemed like they would deliberately leave sections of pizza in a box on the bins, as though putting out food for the local wildlife. Whether or not it was done on purpose I was never quite sure, but it was a lifeline that I was very thankful for.

When my 'home' finally became unsafe to occupy, I moved out to the streets permanently, sleeping in all manner of places, from doorways to train stations. I even broke into a garden shed at one point, just to try to get out of the cold wind that sliced through multiple layers of clothing, chilling my frame until it was hard to remember the comforts that most people take for granted.

I had deliberately tried to stop thinking about my previous life, as I found the memories tortured my soul, like a comforting dream only to wake up to find reality was a living nightmare. A nightmare that was more real to me than my past life ever had been, even when I was living it. I never appreciated the good fortune that had been given to me, but I was about to be given a reality check from a source that I would never have expected, and initially resented.

By early December I'd been living on the streets for just over four weeks. I spent all my time looking for opportunities to exploit to ease my existence. I was dirty, constantly cold, frequently hungry and consistently lonely; a broken man without hope. I hadn't experienced despair to that degree since being sent to prison and even though I had reached some low points over the years, I no longer had the physical or mental capacity to fight my way through the circumstances I now faced. Despair had become my constant tormentor, following me like a ball and chain on a convicted criminal. I was losing the will to fight against the oppressive feeling of helplessness and began to believe that I deserved nothing more than the lousy cards life had dealt me. Pride had been a companion that I had welcomed, especially during my early adult years, but, at that point, I found the result of that pride had led me along a path of total humiliation and self-destruction. The weariness was not just on the inside, it was in every movement of my weakened body. It was evident in the tired old clothing that hung on me. It was in everything I saw and did. My life of recklessness crashed head on into a day of reckoning.

That day started as usual with aching, creaking joints from a chilly night endured in the evening's accommodation; a bus shelter. The cold night was enthusiastically joined by the noise of traffic, decreasing through the middle of the night and then increasing as the morning crept in, preventing any rest and ensuring an early waking. I'd become accustomed to ignoring the disgusted responses of the early commuters finding a tramp occupying the shelter that was put there for the fare paying customers. Occasionally some would make comment, but more often they would just ignore me and put up with the inconvenience of standing out in the weather, rather than associate too closely with me.

I was hungry, having eaten very little the previous day, so the most important task was to locate some food. I'd been visiting a number of places over the last few weeks that, often unbeknown to the proprietor of the premises, had sustained me in my pitiful existence. The ideal place, early on that morning, was a club near where I'd stayed for the night. I'd been to it a number of times in the past with reasonable success, particularly on a Monday, after the weekend's business. I set off intending to make the most of the opportunity available, expecting to have the pickings to myself, but when I got into the restricted area where the bins were located, I was surprised to find I was not alone. There was an old man in there already in full flow sifting through one of the large waste containers. Often in this kind of situation, I would back away and find somewhere else to go. It was always difficult to predict the kind of reception that would be given to any competition for the occupier's prize. On that particular day, however, the hunger overcame my reticence and the fact that I didn't know where else to go that could offer the same possibilities, I decided to be bold and gatecrash the bin raid.

The old man was already digging deep into the waste looking for something that, although worthless to the general population, was a lifeline to people in our predicament. As I approached he looked up at me, pausing to weigh-up the manner of my advance. I stopped while he took his time to size me up and make his assessment, then giving me a nod as if to signal that my presence was acceptable, he went back to trawling through his trough for anything 'good.'

I immediately started work on another bin nearby, but it yielded very little, so I moved to the one next to the old man.

"Not much worth havin' this mornin,'" he said, as he pulled out a discarded cigarette butt. Putting it in the side of his mouth, he continued to rummage through the contents of the container. I watched him for a few moments and wondered about the life he'd lived up to that point, before going back to my own industry, without even considering that he might have been having similar thoughts about me.

When he'd exhausted his chosen spot, he joined forces with me at the bin I was ransacking, as if we were a team intent on exploiting whatever was available for the common good. Grabbing at a bag deeper down among the rubbish, he lost his balance almost tipping over into the bin. I quickly took hold of his coat to stop him from being swallowed and pulled him back out to find he still had hold of a small bag of waste that had attracted his attention. It had obviously come from a kitchen and once he was safely on the ground he eagerly ripped it open, allowing the contents to spill out onto the tarmac. Catching a piece of pizza on its route to the floor, he took a big bite, releasing the cigarette butt that had been in his mouth.

"Ooo, that's good," he remarked, his mouth full of the discarded food and more being hastily added. He looked at me as he chewed, while his mouth gave a running commentary on the progress to digestion in pictures of masticated food. "You wan' a bit?" he asked, spraying bits of food from his over-full mouth. He held out the piece he still had left in his dirty hand. Beggars can't be choosers and hunger drives a man to do what is necessary. I didn't wait for a second offer that probably never would have been given.

We both stayed there, systematically processing the waste until all the available resources were exhausted. The old man stuffed various things in his pockets as he worked through the bins, food bits included, saving anything he thought might be useful for later. Eventually I went and sat on the ground, leaning back against a wall to make the most of the little warmth that was offered by the weakened rays of the December sun. I watched the old man finishing off his business. He then sauntered across and sat down next to me.

"I'm Old Bill," he said, laughing. "Old Bill Grent. Man o' the road I am."

I turned to look at him and was greeted by a smile that contained few teeth and those it did were discoloured to the point of being barely visible, well-hidden behind a mass of facial hair. He held out his grubby hand for me to shake, which I did reluctantly. I don't know why I was reticent, as I must have been a younger version and his visual equal, not a striking picture of elegance.

"There ain't nothin' better than a good breakfast." He laughed with obvious delight at the morning feast he'd enjoyed. "An' it's free, all free!" he said, as he rubbed his hands together at the bargain price. The cold air caused his breath to be visible as he cackled over his comment, but I wasn't inclined to join him in his joviality.

"I been on the road since I were a young 'un. My father, 'e were a sod. Kicked me out the 'ouse when I were fifteen. Still it weren't as bad as it sounds, at least if I weren't living there anymore, 'e couldn't use me as a punch bag." Again the laugh echoed in the shadow of the buildings surrounding us. "The bastard. I ain't never wanted to be a father 'cos they's all bastards the lot of 'em. I 'spect yours is too?"

He looked at me waiting for a reply that would confirm his suspicions about why I was sat in his company and living the way he was. He couldn't have shocked me more with his assumption if he'd unexpectedly punched me in the face. My father wasn't a bastard. That wouldn't be a word I would ever use to describe him, but the bluntness of the comment made me uncomfortable, knowing that someone had looked at my condition and assumed it was down to the bad character of my father.

"My father..."

I began to try to set the misunderstanding straight, but was not totally sure that I could explain that my father was a good man and he was not responsible for my condition.

"Well if 'e ain't a bastard, I bloody sure 'e don't care a toss about you!" Bill speculated.

"No. No, my father's a good man."

"A good man? Good man?"

Old Bill looked at me with surprise that hinted he thought I was lying because I didn't want to tell the truth about my life. I tried to explain about Dad and the experiences that I'd gone through so that this stranger wouldn't think ill of him. I don't exactly know why it mattered, as I would probably never see this man again. It just didn't seem right to leave the assumption, based on his experience, standing without challenge.

He listened to me for a while as I tried to justify my assertion that my father was a good man and as he sat there being entertained by my discourse, he rolled a cigarette butt from side to side in his mouth. We must have been there a while as I talked, but I don't think I was really talking to him, perhaps more to myself than anything else.

When I finished, he didn't say anything for quite a long time. I was too lost in my own thoughts over what I had told him to even care. Finally, Old Bill stood up and wrapped his coat more tightly around his scrawny body to ward off the cold. He looked down at me still leaning back against the wall.

"Funny in't it?"

"What is?"

I looked up at him to meet his beady black eyes staring at me, his brow deeply furrowed.

"I look like this, an' live like this, because my father was a bastard to me when I was younger, an' I never got over it. I know it an' I ain't goin' to protect 'im by telling you, or anyone else, anything but the truth about 'im and me. But you look like

231

this because you were a bastard to your father. If your father's a good man, then what kind of a shitty son are you?"

This man held back no punches and wasn't interested in, or prepared to stay to hear, any response I might have. He turned on his worn out heels and left. Disappearing around the corner of the building, he disengaged from me with a sneering glance and a dismissive wave of his hand.

CHAPTER 18

I was reeling emotionally from the dynamite that Old Bill had let loose. However I tried to justify my actions, I couldn't shake the truth that had been revealed by Bill's bluntness. I *had* been a shitty son, as he put it. I felt engulfed in shame, not because of my external appearance, but my internal appearance that had been revealed in all its ugly, twisted form by a tramp that I'd met only minutes before.

With my mind churning over the decade that had passed since I last spoke to my father and the piercing words that tore into my soul about my life, I wandered aimlessly for the whole day, as if trying to escape the turmoil that was resident in me.

I remember very little of the time immediately following the encounter with Old Bill. I did try to find him once again by going back to the place where we'd met. I waited around in the area for a few days. I don't exactly know why I wanted to see him. Perhaps I wanted to see the prophetic picture of the way my life would go unless I changed what I was doing. My mind seemed empty and numb and I found it very difficult to set Old Bill's comments to one side. They prodded my conscience, taunting me at every opportunity.

While I was in this state of mind, the last barrier of my stubbornness finally gave way. I'd been near the train station, not far from the town centre, sat in a public walkway hoping that people would take pity on me and give some loose change. After sitting there for hours, I was stiff with the cold and had amassed just a small amount of money. Taking what I had, I went to find somewhere to buy a hot drink and perhaps something to eat.

Although it was a cold day, it was bright and sunny. The beauty of the blue sky and the yellow rays of sunshine that skimmed low across the horizon helped to sooth the sadness that had descended on me days before.

As I crossed the road opposite a large department store, I suddenly caught sight of a scruffy, bedraggled tramp moving in my direction. For a split second I felt such pity at the state of the man. His appearance was appalling; torn clothing many layers thick, unkempt hair and unruly beard that was trying to disguise the humanity buried amid the whiskers and years of grime embedded in the creases of his face. At first I thought I'd accidentally come across Old Bill again, but suddenly stopped in the middle of the road as I became aware of the truth that hit me like a lightning bolt. The man that I'd pitied was not someone else, but a trick of light in the store window pane that showed my own reflection as truthfully as a mirror. How many times had I looked in the mirrors of public toilets, but not really seen my condition? Suddenly I was pictured in a street with other people busy shopping and as I walked over the road an invisible boundary that surrounded me became visible. No other human being was willing to occupy the immediate area around me; instead evasive action was being taken to avoid any close contact. What Old Bill and others had seen became visible to me, with a focus so sharp that I couldn't ignore it.

The image before me suddenly blurred, like a camera being turned out of focus, as my eyes filled with tears. I knew that I was in a state, but that revelation made it uncomfortably real to me. Sorrow wrapped around me like a cloak swirling around the shoulders.

A car horn angrily shouted displeasure at my obstruction of the traffic, breaking the emotional flood and sending me scurrying for the pavement, but once I'd seen the truth, I could no longer pretend. As I came close to the store window, I could see the full horror of my condition displayed in the reflection, with the superimposed image of a well-dressed mannequin inside for comparison.

People passed along the pavement behind me, going about their business, as I stared at the image before me and wondered how I'd come to look that way. At least Old Bill had an excuse, but I had only my pride and stubbornness to blame. I clearly saw the cost of my actions. What a fool I'd been all those years. I began to wonder if it was too late to change my lot.

I stood motionlessly staring at the tramp who stared back from the glass window, while the world around me faded into the background. I stayed that way for a long time, until I was roused from my isolation by someone bumping into me by accident. I apologised, but he swore at me for standing in his way, calling me a filthy hobo. Letting him pass, without responding to the insult, I was acutely aware of the fact that I'd been given a glimpse of the way people were seeing me. I felt overpowered by shame and embarrassment.

I stood back against the shop front, waiting until the crowded street offered an opening to escape. I started to walk away from the town centre. For the first time in as long as I could remember, I'd become very conscious about the way I looked and squirmed with embarrassment at every glance made by a passing stranger. The focus had been so much on survival in the hostile world I'd inhabited, looking at others and the possible threat they posed, that I'd neglected to take a good look at myself to see if the perceived threat was their defensive reaction to me.

Following the road out through the suburbs, I aimlessly continued until the buildings gave way to the greener surroundings of the countryside. I continued to walk on and on, watching the light fade as the early exit of the sun reminded that it was winter. It was like walking through fog that had been resident in my mind for many years. I began to see it gradually clear until the sun dominated the landscape of my thinking, lighting up that internal world with glorious colour and absolute determination to change my destiny.

I must have gone about ten miles before I stopped near a little copse in order to try to get some rest. The twilight of the day had overtaken me and I needed to find somewhere to stay for the night.

Stored out in a field, a little way from the road, but still visible in the advancing moonlight, were some cylindrical straw bales wrapped in black polythene sheeting. They looked like an inviting way to combat the cold that was penetrating the layers of clothing I wore.

I climbed over a gate that closed off a break in the hedge and made my way to the stack. It promised shelter and warmth from the winter elements that sliced through my flimsy defences. With a sharp stone that I'd found, I started working at the securing bands of a bale so that it would release some of the straw to create a bed. With the numbness of the cold chilling my fingers it took a little effort, but once the compressed straw burst loose it immediately provided a comfortable place to sleep. Once I was bedded down for the night, I threw the polythene sheeting over the top of me to serve as a guard against the possibility of rain and the relentless wind.

I'm not sure if the straw was just very comfortable, compared to the benches I'd been sleeping on, or if I was very tired, but it wasn't long before I was completely lost to the world until daylight crept into my den and woke me the following morning.

Rousing myself with determination, I reluctantly left the comfort of my lodgings and set out again, leaving behind the years of misery and discomfort, sparsely sprinkled with occasional moments of happiness, that made up my recent memories.

The time with Tim and Mary, I would always remember. My conversation with Old Bill, I could never forget. Although painful as a hammer blow at the time, it became a guiding force that urged me to do what I knew needed to be done. What I'd avoided for so long. It was time to go back to my family home and face my father. Whatever the consequence of that meeting, I knew that our lives had to cross paths at least once more before I could put to rest the nagging guilt that I'd carried, but ignored, for so many years.

With very little money at my disposal, the journey seemed so much further than it actually was. The possibility of hitch-hiking some of the distance was small, mainly due to my condition. I watched vehicle after vehicle pass by as the stony faced occupants ignored my appeals for a lift. I couldn't blame them. If I'd been in their place I doubt that I would have invited such a person into my vehicle either. That didn't stop me trying though, as I took every opportunity to get help to close the distance between myself and my ultimate goal. I estimated that it was somewhere around a hundred miles to my destination, which would take a number of days to cover if I couldn't hitch a lift and would also inevitably mean hunger.

Trudging my way through many miles over the next two days, I reduced the distance step by evermore painful step. The first night I slept under the cover of trees just outside a little village church. I tried the church doors, but they were securely locked, leaving me with little option. I didn't want to try to force an entry, even though the temptation was great. I don't think anyone would have heard if I had tried and I would have been gone as soon as it was light, but somehow it just didn't seem like the right thing to do. The following night I spent in the luxury of an old abandoned barn within sight of the road, but far enough away not to attract any attention. It was a spooky place in the darkness with eerie noises surrounding it, but my desperate need for rest away from the elements was greater than my fear of the dark, or anything else that might be enjoying my company without me knowing.

I was able to start a small fire on the earthen floor with the remains of some kind of racking that once served the owner's purpose but had long fallen into disuse. The matches I acquired from a nearby garage, along with a loaf of bread, using the few coins that I had left from my begging before I started my journey. Anything to eat that would silence the hunger pangs was very welcome.

The warmth of the fire struggled to overcome the unfair advantage of the elements through the partially covered windows and the casting of shadows that danced to the flames reminded me of my time with Tim and Mary. I wondered where Tim was and how he was doing as I sat staring at the flames while toasting some of the bread. Even though I had nothing to put on the toast, the sensation of warm food, the first I'd eaten for a few days, was a delight to the senses and to my hungry frame it tasted like the food of royalty.

I made use of anything that was at hand to shield myself from the cold through the night, periodically building the fire up to give some comfort. Sleep was constantly disturbed by the wind that moaned and groaned, intensifying and then easing, as though responding to waves of pain. My mind was also occupied with the reality of my situation. Though I'd covered about thirty or forty miles from leaving the station at the town, I still had about sixty to go. I had no food or money and although I could cover quite a distance during the short daylight hours, my pace was slowing. I lacked energy due to insufficient nourishment, and the inadequate footwear that once belonged to someone with slightly smaller feet than my own, caused a lot of pain after covering such a distance. I needed to find some way of speeding up my journey for the following day or two, but my options were very limited.

The following morning I was up at first light, having barely slept during the night. My mind had been too consumed with thoughts of the coming meeting to allow me to switch off enough to relax, but I knew I had to get back to Durlwood House, and soon.

The morning light gave me an open view that was closed to me when I'd arrived the previous evening. I could see a farmyard off in the distance that looked worth investigating. After eating the remains of the loaf which I'd saved for the morning, I set off to see if I could find anything that would help sustain me for the remainder of my journey.

As I came near to the buildings it became clear that it was an aged, abandoned farm, probably swallowed by a larger concern many years before as agriculture become more mechanised. I peered through the windows of the old farmhouse which was securely bolted and padlocked. It looked like the decor dated back to the fifties and hadn't been touched since.

In an effort to see if I could gain any advantage from the place, I went from building to building and eventually found one of the sheds was being used as a store place. Though the doors were locked, they were so rotten that it was easy to part them enough to be able to struggle through. Once inside, I found heaps of heavy brown bags piled all along the back of the building in an orderly way, as though put there deliberately rather than just being dumped. The dingy light restricted my vision, but I pulled at the fastening of one of the bags which, once opened, revealed its contents. Carrots. Bags and bags of them. I grabbed one and immediately began to eat, driven by sheer hunger. Though they were a little rubbery, it felt good to eat something that would normally be considered good for you.

Thinking that I might find some better samples in a different bag, I climbed onto the pile and pulled a sack from the top, only to be greeted with the frantic scurrying of rodents scattering in different directions. I leapt back with fright at the sudden movement, the dim light adding to the drama of the scene. Recovering my composure, I went back to the sacks, pulled one down and dragged it a little closer to the door where I could take advantage of a bit more light. Quickly undoing the top, I plunged my hand in to take hold of the contents and immediately turned away to heave at the repulsive smell that assaulted my nostrils. My hand, now several inches deep in a glue-like substance, was pulled back out covered with the rotting remains of the vegetables the bag once contained.

I wiped away as much as I could of the foul-smelling fluid and with my need overcoming my revulsion, I went back to the first bag whose contents were not so far gone that they were inedible, albeit beyond their best. Rather than risk another repulsive experience, I pulled the bag over to the door to check what I was putting my hand into and began sorting through for the best it had to offer. As I rummaged, I ate.

By the time I'd emptied the whole contents of the bag my pockets were bulging with as much as I thought I could use, or stomach. Just for good measure, I put some back into the bag to carry along the journey and hastily made my exit from the old building, while the lingering smell of rotting vegetation still hung in the air. I reasoned that if I found something more palatable I could always dump what I didn't need.

Back out in the daylight the brightness hurt my eyes after the dim light of the shed, but I quickly located an old trough that had filled with rainwater on the other side of the yard. Wanting to drink before I washed the remains of the gooey substance from my hands, I leant down and started lapping the water like an animal.

The water was cool and had a distinct taste of vegetation to it, but it did the trick, quenching my thirst. I then washed away the foul-smelling liquid that remained on my hands and washed my face the best that I could without soap.

Waving my hands around in the air to dry them, I walked slowly back and forth until it was time to move on. I bent down to pick up the folded brown sack with my supplies in it, but as I did I noticed the edge of a label hidden by the folds in the paper. Slowly opening out what had been concealed, the label proclaimed its information boldly. 'NOT FOR HUMAN CONSUMPTION. ANIMAL FEED ONLY.'

There had been few times in my life that I had lost control of my emotions to the extent that everything around me seemed to disappear. The last time I could remember was when I was in the police interview. I was asked to open an envelope where I expected to find my missing watch only to be faced with my mother's stolen necklace. That morning I was standing in a farmyard, having been living in the fields, lapping water like a dog from a trough and eating food marked specifically for animals.

During the life I'd been leading it had always been necessary to deceive myself in order to survive. The incident with Old Bill, then the store window and now the label, had ripped away all the modest survival defences I'd developed, exposing the nakedness of my life for what it was. A phrase that I'd heard in my youth involuntarily sprang to mind for the second time in recent days. It was a phrase that perfectly described the way I felt at that moment. Oh what a wretched man am I.

Needless to say, the wind had been knocked out of my sails and the emotion poured from the depth of my being until the tap ran dry.

As the weak sun skirted the horizon, disappearing once more, before preparing to be reborn the next day, I sat in total ignorance of the progress of time, frozen inside this decrepit carcass, looking out into a world that was my prison. What possible dignity could I have left, now that I'd been reduced to the status of an animal?

Eventually I was forced, by the biting cold and the dark, to make an effort to protect myself for the night. The day had been lost as I wallowed in self-pity.

Taking refuge in one of the shelters, I made a small fire and, using the light it gave, foraged for anything that would help keep me warm until morning. The only food on offer were the barely edible carrots, scavenged from the bags when I first arrived at the old farm and, despite their poor quality, I made myself eat as much as I could simply to fill my belly for the journey ahead.

Only one thing possessed my mind that night; that *maybe* my father would take pity on me. I decided that no further delay could be tolerated. I would leave as soon as I woke in the morning and would not stop until I reached the sentry guards that stood either side of the driveway to Durlwood House. I was going home.

CHAPTER 19

Dawn could not introduce itself soon enough for me that day. I set out while it was still dark, aiming for good progress. I soon achieved a modest rhythm in my pace that would allow me to cover as much distance as possible, while trying to protect my sore feet.

After about five miles and repeated attempts to hitch a lift, I finally had a turn of luck with a local farmer who allowed me to ride in the back of his trailer for several miles. He must have stopped because he could see my desperation as I held out my hand, thumbing frantically, while almost standing in the road. The fact that I was unlikely to mess his working vehicle, unlike someone's car, meant it made no difference to him how I was dressed. He pulled alongside and shouted for me to jump in the back and bang on the bulkhead when I wanted to stop. I stayed with him until he turned into the entrance of his farm, my passenger journey coming to an end sooner than I'd wanted. Nevertheless, I was grateful for the respite from walking. Before bidding me a safe journey, he kindly offered a sandwich from his packed lunch, of which I was very appreciative.

I was still walking when it started to get dark and, except for an occasional break to rest my painful feet, continued until very late that night. I figured that I still had around forty miles to cover, which would take at least two days at the pace I was able to achieve, especially as I had to walk the whole distance in footwear that tried to dissuade me from making any further movement. I decided it was better not to keep going right through the night, but rather to rest for a period and get underway again early the next morning, so I started to look for a place to stay. In the dark it was difficult to see the opportunities that were available. I was a long way from the nearest populated area, so I walked on hoping that something would materialise.

It was perhaps a mile or two further on that I came to the entrance of a wood-yard that traded in logs for fuel. Toward the back of the yard I found an old tractor. I tried the door. It was unlocked, so I climbed into the cab. Carefully removing my worn-out old boots to ease my aching feet, I made myself as comfortable as I could. Although it wasn't the height of luxury, my exhausted body took advantage of the stop. I fell asleep almost straight away. The silence offered by the cab, which blocked out the noises that had kept me awake on the previous few nights, was blissful. Even the soft cushions of the seat were, to my aching legs and back, like music to my ears.

I awoke the following morning to what seemed like the distant noise of machinery running and was initially disorientated when I found myself surrounded by the steering wheel and controls of the old vehicle. As I came to, I realised that the machinery wasn't distant, but very near. Through the tractor windscreen I could see a couple of men loading a pickup truck with logs over on the far side of the yard. Not wanting to be found trespassing, I slid down as low as possible and, as I pulled my boots on, was greeted with pain like sandpaper scrapping against raw skin. The sores from the previous day reminded me of the distance I'd covered and the distance still to go. I waited a while, hoping the pickup would leave so I could quickly make a move without being seen, but it soon became obvious that they were in no hurry.

Opening the tractor door slowly, I slipped down to the ground using the vehicle to hide my presence. Keeping as much out of view as possible, I headed in the direction of the road. I wasn't able to cross the yard without attracting attention, so I made my way around behind the various wood piles that edged the compound. Once I reached the perimeter, I checked that it was clear and jumped over the fence. As I hit the ground at an awkward angle, I lost my balance and fell over into the soft wet mud along the dirty roadside. The intense pain in my feet from the impact gradually subsided as I scrambled along the bank. I had thought that my appearance could get no worse until I was coated with wet mud up most of my right side. Once again intense misery threatened to overcome me and I was close to giving up. The heavy load of many hope-crushing moments piled one on top of another until they pressed the very life out of me, like some medieval torture. Had it not been for the fact that I didn't want to be discovered, I would have fallen prostrate and screamed at the ground to express my frustration and despair. Suppressing the urge to let off steam, I was compelled to move on and steeled myself to begin the next leg of my tortuous journey by the only means available, step by painful step.

My progress went quite well that day, considering the condition I was in, except for having to force myself to eat the carrots to fuel my weary body. My stomach heaved as I chewed them over and over, trying to time my swallow so that it didn't trigger vomiting, but I had to eat something, no matter how bad, or how little.

Although there were many changes to the infrastructure, the landmarks along the road became increasingly familiar as I drew closer to the area where I grew up. The nearer I got to Durlwood House, the more I was conscious of my appearance. Others would probably never have recognised me as Andy Numan, but I knew who I was. I'd done enough damage to my father's reputation for me to feel concerned that I was not seen to be his son.

As with many journeys, the last few miles can seem long and tedious. This was exaggerated by the slowing pace of progress, as each increasingly painful step reminded me that my feet were rubbed raw, not that the pain was going to make me stop. I'd become intrigued to see the silhouette of the old house again and the possibility of catching a glance before dusk masked some of the discomfort I felt as I pressed onward.

It was around five in the afternoon, on that dark mid-December day, when I finally caught my first glimpse of Durlwood House for over a decade. It involuntarily triggered vivid memories that had long been buried deep in the subconscious vaults of my mind, suppressed by a fear of being hurt all over again. I had a flashback of my cautious approach all those years ago. I desperately hoped no one would see me as I retrieved my belongings with a determination to leave home for good. The scene played in my mind as clear as a film on a movie screen.

The last time I came around the particular bend in the road that I was walking along, I was in the comfort of a beautiful Mercedes car. This time, there was no such luxury. The intervening years had stripped me of my vanity, my dignity and my self-respect. I approached the bricks and mortar that I had loved as a child with a mixture of relief and fear.

At a point where there was a clearer view of the building, I stopped walking in order to look at the house, which was about a half mile away in the distance. The softness of light that spilled from the windows into the encroaching darkness, cast a warm yellow glow across the courtyard and surrounding garden. The view had a hypnotic effect on me, just like staring at an open fire. The drive was illuminated, linking the gate to the house a small distance beyond, with a daisy chain of candle-like lights that revealed hints of the canopy of trees arching over the gravel road. Something that hadn't even registered with me properly, until that moment, was that it was less than two weeks to Christmas. For many years Christmas had simply been a painful time that exaggerated the loneliness of my situation. It was a cold, friendless, despairing time that had no equal throughout the calendar. I had, until that moment, managed to block out its impending arrival. I didn't frequent the places that the crowds visited with the intention of spending money. But, in the picture of my childhood home that held my attention, the coloured lights adorning the traditional Christmas tree set in its usual place, the turning circle of the front courtyard, proclaimed the festive season at hand with such elegance that I'd been trapped into acknowledging the impending event.

The significance of that moment is difficult to express, but it brought home to me the fact that I'd abandoned the celebration at the same time I had abandoned my family. The point of the whole event had gone missing when I detached myself from those who lived there. It was not that I'd never noticed or acknowledged Christmas since then, even though I always tried to blank it out, but seeing that tree in the setting that had been its place every year of my young life, jolted the realisation I'd tried to escape from. Those who loved me, when I was growing up, were now very close by.

I stood at the side of the road battling with mixed emotions. I wanted to run to reach the house in the shortest possible time, not that I was in any condition to run, but I also had a strong urge to run from the house, as far away as I could get.

Suddenly the headlights of a car, approaching from behind me, lit up the road as it headed towards the house, breaking my trance-like fixation on the scene before me. It seemed to slow down a little before reaching me, but I quickly turned away to hide my face and started to walk in the opposite direction until it had gone well past. I looked back just in time to see it indicate, then turn right into Durlwood's driveway. I watched it steadily move between the daisy-chain lights until it reached the front of the house, coming to a standstill next to the steps leading to the entrance.

It was too far away to see any detail of the events, but the Christmas tree decorated image of home was beautiful. I don't think I'd ever seen Durlwood like that before. I think I was more inclined to take it for granted. Nor would I ever have described it as beautiful before, but that was exactly the right word to express what I saw.

The lost childhood memories of snow-sprinkled fields and gardens flooded my mind as if I was thumbing through a family album. I found myself muttering reproachfully to myself for having been so complacent about the beauty and comfort that was the theatre of my young life. "Stupid, ignorant, ungrateful fool," I mumbled under my breath. The words I whispered fogged in the chill air as they landed on my own ears. They were acknowledged by a shake of my head that emphasised my own self-loathing for the life of luxury that I'd spurned on an arrogant whim. I accepted the memories that drew out the sorrow of my loss through my stupid actions in order to re-live the joy of the good memories from that time. I began to realise the blessings from those days were abundant.

Another car approached, this time with much more speed, swinging into the drive with great precision and travelling along the gravel much faster than the last one. From where I stood I could hear the crunching of stones under the wheels as the sound carried on the breeze and provoked a yearning for something of my past that had long been rejected.

As the car reached the courtyard and passed through the arched entrance, it turned hard through one-hundred-and-eighty degrees disappearing into the old stable. I stopped in my tracks and held my breath to try to magnify every sound that might offer a clue to the driver's identity. Straining to see, or hear something of the occupant, I concluded that it must have been my father or Carl, following a well-practised manoeuvre to the parking bay. The dark and the distance concealed all the clues.

Resuming the final span of my journey, I hobbled along until I neared the driveway entrance to be greeted by the large stone gateposts, each holding the identification of the building in their care, 'Durlwood House.' Again, I was interrupted by the headlights of an approaching vehicle in the distance. I darted behind one of the stone pillars to avoid being seen and waited for the vehicle to pass by.

I listened as the engine tone betrayed the fact that the vehicle was slowing down and then I realised that there was more than one. Headlight beams swept past the gateposts like spotlights in a prison camp. I huddled tightly behind the stone pillar to avoid being discovered.

As the car turned into the drive from the smooth tarmac onto the gravel, there was a sudden increase in volume. The headlights illuminated the area beyond, creating a long shadow from the pillar that stretched away from me and moved across the ground like a speeding clock-hand travelling in reverse. I peered out to catch a glimpse of the new arrivals, but pulled back immediately as two other cars followed in close convoy toward the house.

As they stopped in the courtyard, less than two hundred yards away, I could hear the passengers spilling out into the night to be greeted by a distant voice that I hadn't heard for over ten years. I couldn't help myself and, at the risk of being seen by any other arrivals, I moved quickly from tree to tree, pausing behind each one, trying to get close enough to see the party that had arrived. I moved as close as I could, but from my position the Christmas tree obscured the steps and portico of the entrance. As I tried to focus my hearing on the distant chatter of many voices, they were suddenly gone as the front door swallowed the new guests and closed out the cold winter evening, and me.

Cautiously making my way to where the cars were kept, I tried to stay behind the trees and bushes that lined the drive. I moved carefully to prevent my presence being revealed to anyone who might raise the alarm. From the side of the stable block, furthest away from the drive, I had a restricted view of my father's office at the far corner of the building, a clear view of the main entrance and what was Martha's apartment on the near corner. I could hear music and voices and, considering the number of cars that had arrived while I was in sight of the house, it was clear that a party was getting under way.

The chill was cutting deep into my wasted, bony frame, but I couldn't pull myself away from the scene before me. I slipped into the parking bay that my car used to occupy and was surprised to find a tarpaulin covered vehicle. In the dim light I could just make out a sign on the back wall and as I carefully moved closer, aware that I was a little exposed and could easily have been discovered, its letters became visible, 'Andy Numan.' I looked along at the other two cars parked in the adjacent bays to see the matching signs, 'Peter Numan,' my father, and 'Carl Numan,' my older brother. The signs hadn't been there when I was last at the old place so must have been fitted after I left. I grabbed at the tarpaulin, pulling it up from the front of the covered vehicle and was shocked to see the very same car that my father had bought me on my eighteenth birthday. The last time I'd seen it was when I parked it at Sasha's flat, before setting off to Paris; the trip that began with great happiness and ended with oppressive sorrow.

I slumped down to the ground unable to control my body which had begun to shiver quite violently. Perhaps it was more than the cold that shook me that night, but whatever it was, the movement was involuntary.

Feeling the heat from the car in Carl's bay, it must have been him I'd seen arriving, I carefully lay myself over the bonnet, putting my legs against the front grill to take full advantage of the warmth from the radiator. As I straddled the car for some relief against the cold, another vehicle arrived, swinging around the Christmas tree in the centre of the courtyard. It came to a halt near the steps to the front door. I watched from my vantage point through the windscreen and rear window of the vehicle, as though looking through a telescope.

The new arrivals seemed very near and I was alarmed that I might be discovered, but their focus was clearly on the house and the event in progress. As they went to the front door it opened, as if anticipating their approach, but this time I heard that familiar voice very clearly and saw the man that it came from.

My father walked out under the portico to the top of the steps to welcome his guests and, holding his hand out, greeted them with a phrase I'd heard him say hundreds of times as a child; a phrase that he loved and filled with his own particular warmth, 'Merry Christmas.' The temptation to run to him was almost too much to bear, only being tempered by my shame. I held fast, determined that this selfish runaway would not spoil the moment for him. I couldn't prevent spoiling Carl's car bonnet which was comforting me with its warmth. It became the resting place of my flood of tears and the grime that they carried from my dirty face, which bore witness to my lost years.

My mind flashed with the image of the father that Old Bill had described from his childhood and I sensed a deep injustice that anyone, especially me, could ever use such terms about this man, who greeted his guests with such genuine joy and warmth.

I didn't want to move from my position as I took full advantage of the warmth from the car until it was no longer effective. Even then the glimpses of the event in the house held my attention more than the chill that tried to drive me to find better shelter for the night. I could hardly risk approaching the house that evening, potentially destroying the joyful occasion with my sudden appearance.

For hours I watched, attentively and eagerly devouring each visual moment that I could glean from the meagre offering of the illuminated windows. It was like observing a stage full of actors

251

bathed in spotlights, performing for an audience lost in the darkness of the theatre. On that occasion the actors were many and the audience, one.

I had no way of telling what time it was when the front door finally opened, releasing a sudden burst of laughter-filled sound out into the courtyard. I instinctively ducked to conceal my presence, but couldn't resist moving back to an advantageous position to get a better view of the drama unfolding before me.

After various goodbyes and final comments, most of which were beyond my hearing, a couple of cars were filled with people and prepared for departure. The roar of engines starting up intruded into the quiet night air accompanied by the crunching of gravel beneath the wheels as the driveway led the vehicles to the gates at the road. The sounds faded as they disappeared into the night. The front door once more secured the remaining inhabitants of the house.

It must have been another hour before the next group came out to leave. I took up my viewing position against the car, which had long since lost its value as a source of warmth, careful to remain invisible to the jovial guests. Watching the proceedings, I strained to listen to the conversation, with each contributor looking as though a cartoon speech bubble came from their mouths as the chill air took its effect and the house lights illuminated the mist that rose.

Suddenly my father, his hands on the shoulders of two guests said, "Come now, let's get you both home." He turned to the old stable block, where I'd remained hidden until that point. A fluorescent lamp suddenly flashed like a strobe above me and came on, flooding the building with stark white light. In the panic, I froze like a rabbit caught in the headlights of an oncoming car.

CHAPTER 20

Dad caught sight of me almost immediately and reacted with a shout that alerted the other guests outside to the uninvited visitor.

"Hey you, what are you doing there?"

Without hesitation the three men present leapt forward to assist Dad in the apprehension of the trespasser. I shot around the cars and down the side of the building, but was stiff from the cold and my painful feet slowed my progress. The men followed with determination to apprehend me; two directly on my tail and another with Dad around the other side of the building to try to catch me from the opposite direction. I tripped in my haste to escape from the pursuers and fell flat out on my front long enough for the two who had followed me to take a hold. I yelled out in defence and the sheer horror of having the re-introduction to my father dictated by others in such dreadful circumstances.

"Please! No! No! Please don't!"

I protested as they pulled me up like a rag doll and shouted that the task was in hand. I knew, once they had taken hold of me, that there was no way I was going to get free from their grasp. As they brought me back to the front of the building to face my father, I physically, emotionally and mentally withered with every step that brought me closer to the impromptu meeting.

The harsh light of the stable block that so adequately illuminated the cars, and much of the adjacent courtyard, exposed my shameful appearance for all to see. I was the tramp held between the gentlemen, our differing mode of dress drawn from the extremes of the spectrum. I was later told that I had visibly shrunk into myself before their eyes as the light fell on me, and while they believed they saw it happen, I definitely felt it.

Returning from the other end of the building, my father launched a question at me about my presence before he even got close.

"What were you doing in my garage, sir?"

The abruptness of his tone was firm rather than harsh. Perhaps my pitiable state, now on full display, softened his approach, but courtesy was still present in his manner as he addressed me as 'sir.' The two men who held on to me did so almost at arm's length in order not to be soiled by the wretch they'd apprehended.

"Well?" Dad demanded, as he came closer.

Standing no more than three feet away from me, I lifted my head enough to glance at him only to be confronted by his staring eyes, as clear as ever I remembered. He'd physically aged since I last saw him and I wondered if I'd been the cause of much of it, but the same confident air surrounded him. He was always a man that was used to taking charge of a situation.

I quickly broke the gaze, feeling crushed by the exhaustion of my life, I crumpled at the knees, slipping from the grasp of the men either side of me as I slumped to the floor in front of him. He took a step back away from me, unsure what was happening. All I knew was that I had no more fight left in me. No resistance to whatever was about to happen. I'd spent all the final reserves of my energy and willpower just getting to Durlwood, and now I was done, as helpless as a car that lay abandoned by the side of the road having run out of fuel. I deserved nothing less than total rejection by this good man who now towered over me. I toppled over prostrate before him, exhausted and finished.

He reacted instantly, kneeling down beside me.

"Are you okay, son?"

If he'd only known how his turn of phrase pierced the depth of my soul, he would have walked away from me out of mercy for the wretch I'd become, but I suspect his compassion drove him on. He put his hand on my shoulder and leant in a little closer.

"Speak to me. Are you okay?"

He was unaware that I couldn't speak at that moment. Instead I began to shake as I sobbed, painfully struggling for breath against an unconscious, uncontrollable release of pent-up emotion.

Sensing the anguish of the man laid out before him, he waited for a few moments before he tried again.

"Are you okay?"

He pressed his hand to my shoulder to emphasise his concern.

"Can – you – ever – forgive – me – for – what – I've – done?" I sobbed intermittently into the ground.

"I'm sorry," he said softly, his voice tempered with concern. "I couldn't hear what you said." I repeated my question as he leant in closer to hear me.

"Look, I know that you shouldn't have been in my garage, but it's not such a terrible offence. Of course I can forgive you. Let me help you. You look like you could use some help."

He waited for my response and I was willing it to come, but the words wouldn't materialise.

"Why don't we take you inside to warm up and get you some food," he offered, as he gently encouraged me to get up from the ground. One of the ladies present knelt down next to me, adding to the encouragement to come into the house.

"I don't mean... I don't mean can you forgive me... for being in your garage."

I choked out the words against the tightness of my throat that felt like someone was trying to strangle me.

"Then, what do you mean?"

I buried my face deep into my hands, willing the ground to open up and swallow me. I felt the edge of my father's shoe against my wrist, as I sobbed into the gravel that pressed into the back of my hands.

"I mean..."

My throat was strained, making it hard to speak, as I fought to control the involuntary sobs. "I mean for being..."

I hesitated to find the right thing to say, but the only words that seemed to describe how I saw myself had been given to me by a tramp that saw straight through the self-pity. Old Bill Grent provided, what seemed to me at that moment, the only appropriate description I could summon to mind.

"For being... such a... shitty son."

The enormity of what I'd said didn't appear to invoke any response from him at first and there seemed an agonisingly long delay before anything happened. Then the woman knelt at my side said, "Andy?"

Waves of shame hit me as the revelation of who I was became clear to someone, someone who I hadn't even recognised. As she uttered my name, a name that I had so deliberately relinquished a long time ago, I felt so vulnerable. The mention of it immediately reconnected me to Durlwood, to my past, to my family.

My father shot to his feet taking a few steps back and I braced myself for what would happen next. If seconds could have turned into hours, they did at that moment. It was as if the pause button had been pressed, halting the film at a critical moment, unfairly delaying the vital next act.

Suddenly Dad grabbed me by the shoulders of the torn and battered coat that surrounded me and yanked me upright, almost lifting my scrawny frame clear off the ground, then planted me on my feet. He clasped his hands on the unkempt beard that swamped my face and forcibly turned my head directly into the light. I squinted as the brightness hurt my eyes after the dark, but didn't resist the wishes of my captor. I focused properly, for the first time in years, on the face of my father. If it were possible to weep and laugh; display joy and relief; show loss of control, but be in command of the situation, all at the same time, it was there in his face for just a second. Then he grabbed me with such force that I expected to be thrown to the ground. He threw his arms around me, totally oblivious of the state I was in, or the fact that my soiled clothing was ruining his pristine shirt. As he pulled me close to him, almost squeezing the breath from my racked body, he let out a cry of such emotion that I was shocked. He'd always been able to maintain control of himself regardless of the circumstance, but I felt as though I was supporting him as he almost collapsed to the floor. The tears were like the bursting of a dam, a decade of pain released over me like a flood. His head buried into my shoulder as he sobbed. I felt ill-equipped to handle the situation. He brought his hand up to my cheek and caressed my face with such tenderness that I began to wonder if this was the same man I had known from a decade ago.

"My boy. My boy," he repeated over and over through the sobs. I couldn't believe what I was witnessing. The shock of the acceptance was enough to floor me, but Dad's response was unexpected and overwhelming. The lady who had knelt beside me was nearby, rubbing Dad's shoulder to try to comfort him, but I couldn't see her clearly through my own blurry vision.

I thought Dad was gaining control of himself as he lifted his head and held mine in his hands, staring at me intently, but only to start sobbing again.

How long we were stood like that, I don't know, but I sensed that no one present wanted to end what was happening one second before Dad was willing for it to end. Once again, he tried to look directly at me. I could see the difficulty he was having, it mirrored my own. As he finally controlled himself enough to speak, he gave a deafening shout for everyone to hear, "A thousand times over and nothing withheld, I forgive you, I forgive you, I forgive you!"

Once he had liberated the words he wanted to say, he was once again lost to the expression of his inner feelings and we stood joined together in an embrace that had been years in the making.

Eventually he released me from his grasp, grabbed the coat he had thrown to one of the others when the chase began and threw it around me, as if symbolically cloaking my shame with his respectability. He began to laugh like a child that had received the desire of its heart. Gathering me to himself in the middle of what seemed like confusion, he barked instructions to the others that had been part of the reunion. As he marched me to the entrance of the house, I was so bombarded with the flurry of everything happening at once that my mind was confused in the blur of movement. The guests who'd witnessed the events outside stormed the hallway, creating a shield to cover my shame from the possible interest of the remaining guests in the house who knew nothing of the drama that had unfolded. As his friends stood guard over the remains of my dignity, my father whisked me immediately upstairs to the master bedroom and without a single word he sat me on the bed, went into the en-suite bathroom and set the bath running.

Coming back he threw his coat to the floor, followed by my clothing, just as quickly as he could remove it. I didn't resist his efforts, nor did I envy them. I was disgusted with myself and very conscious of my filthy appearance.

Throwing my arm over his shoulder, he helped me as I limped on bloodied swollen feet to the most luxurious experience of my entire life. Sure, I'd been in a bath before, but never in those circumstances. The fragrance of the soap bubbles overloaded my senses, having been more accustomed to the putrid, pungent odours that had accompanied me for so long. Still he didn't utter a word as he left the room swiftly. There was rustling in the bedroom, then the door closing, followed by quiet, except for the muted tones of the party that appeared to be continuing downstairs. A few minutes later the bedroom door again and my father was back with a hot drink and a plate full of food.

I watched him, unsure of the man that stood before me. Once so careful of emotional displays, he had no concern for the openness of his weeping. When he rallied himself enough to speak again he said, "I don't want to see you out of this bath until you have enjoyed every moment of the luxury that I want you to have," he instructed. "There are clothes on the bed when you are ready. You don't need to say anything, or do anything, except feel the warmth of my love and the comfort of '*your*' home."

He emphasised the word 'your' to impress upon me his belief that I was back where I was wanted and belonged. If I hadn't been in the bath at that moment, I would have been wet through from the tears that literally poured down my cheeks like rivers of grateful thanks at the compassion of my father.

He knelt beside the bath and took hold of my still grime-impregnated hand in his and squeezed it against his cheek. I could feel the gentle shaking of his whole frame and the waves of released emotion flowing out. Choking back the tears, he looked me directly in the eye, "If I never see another Christmas celebration for the rest of my life," he held for a second trying to still the emotion that choked the words from his mouth, "I will live joyfully on the memory of what this Christmas has brought me."

I had never before seen my father cry as he did then, but he did so openly in front of me that night. If ever I'd misjudged a man, it was him. He stood up, still holding onto my hand, as we both communicated without words.

I could tell that he was torn between wanting to stay with me and duty to his guests, his face filled with regret as he made his plea. "I have guests that I must attend to, Andy. Will you forgive me if I leave you, just for a while?"

I couldn't believe what I was hearing. My father was asking for forgiveness because he needed to leave me for a few moments, overlooking the fact that I'd left him for over a decade. "It's okay, Dad. Do what you need to," I nodded in response, wiping over my face with the bathwater to dilute the tears.

He squeezed my hand again and then as he let it go to turn and leave, he pierced me once more with his words. "I love you, *son*." I slid down into the warm soapy water listening to the words I thought I would never hear again echoing round and round in my mind, like a record stuck on a single phrase, only interrupted by the increase in volume of the party downstairs as the bedroom door opened and then closed behind my father as he left.

The large spacious bathroom was like a palace built for kings. The most profound pleasure was to be found in the simplest of things; warm water at hand; soap; a razor; soft towels. I scrubbed and cleaned my dirty frame then emptied the bath before running another, feeling conscious of my extravagance, but with an overwhelming desire to scrub the last ten years from my shameful body.

Shaving the mass of hair that had been my defence against the cold of outdoors and the stare of strangers, I saw my bare face for the first time almost since I had left the prison. My gaunt look was testimony to the lack of care for my physical needs. I got back into the bath, taking the shaving mirror with me and, lying there, I stared at myself for a long time, the glass occasionally misting over from the moist air rising from the hot water. What kind of man had I become? How much had the last ten years changed me? These were questions that plagued me and continued to do so for a long time after. I knew that my family and those who had been closest to me were better qualified than I was to answer those questions, if only I had the courage to ask.

I must have begun to look like a prune after the length of time I'd sat in the water and although I was reluctant for it to end, I was desperately tired and needed to catch up from months of disturbed and uncomfortable sleep. Taking the dressing gown from the hook on the door, I wrapped it around me and went to the bed that had clean clothes laid out on it. My old rags were gone. I presumed that my father had disposed of them at the first opportunity. I couldn't blame him.

I climbed into the large bed, sinking into the softness of its surface and pulled the quilt up around me like a cocoon. There was something embryonic about the experience, almost like re-visiting my early childhood and being embraced by the warmth of a past that I hadn't ever taken the time to appreciate properly. With the last minutes of my grasp on consciousness, I wondered about the other people who were outside when I was discovered, particularly the lady who first spoke my name, but that would have to wait for another day, as the world of deep slumber awaited me. The noises of the house began to fade away into the distance and I enjoyed a journey of aimless drifting, like a boat on a mill pond gently pushed by a warm breeze, until the most peaceful sleep I could remember in years transported me away from my concerns, at least for a time.

When I awoke the following morning it seemed like I was in heaven. In the first place, I was warm, a novelty that had been long forgotten and the comfort of the bed beckoned me to stay and indulge. The beautiful large bedroom was filled with the soft light of the late morning sun that partially illuminated the curtains. I glanced across at the clock on the bedside table; eleven-fifteen.

Listening to the familiar sounds of the house which I'd long forgotten, I lingered in blissful luxury for just a few moments more. I thought about the evening before and the response of my father. On this new day I would have to face him properly now that the distractions of the party had gone and the drama of my unmasking done. The time was fast approaching when the real world had to be faced.

I got up and went over to the window, parting the curtains to take a look at the gardens to the rear of the house, and was greeted with the most spectacular view. They looked stunning as they ran out to join the fields in the distance with a dusting of white frost covering the green lawns and the boughs of the trees, making the view look magical. I wondered why I hadn't valued it before the way I did at that moment and concluded that complacency was always nearby in my youth, an experience which has to be guarded against through the whole of life.

I was a little unsure what I should do next. Clearly, I had been left in peace to wake up naturally and the house was very quiet, refusing to betray any occupants who might be around. I pulled on the jeans and shirt that my father had left on the bed the night before. They looked like clothes Carl might have once used. The shirt hung from my scrawny body which had wasted through lack of nourishment and the jeans were a little too short. After checking that I was presentable, which was not difficult compared to the previous day, I made my way across the balcony landing to the stairs.

The huge open hallway that stretched out below like the stage of a theatre viewed from the dress circle, looked fabulous, beautifully adorned with the decorations for the Christmas season. The polished wood floor that swept through the building and along the corridor gave natural warmth to the house, connecting the inside to the tree-lined driveway. The large arched window that rose high above the front door with its glass side panels, reached up to the first floor ceiling, allowing in so much light that it was almost like being outside. There was a clear view from the hallway and the balcony landing to the entrance courtyard, with the real Christmas tree taking centre stage and beyond that the full length of the driveway was visible, all the way to the main road.

As I moved to begin the decent down the stairs to ground level, slowly, so that I could admire the scene before me, I felt at home and like an intruder both at the same time. Completing the last few steps I could see the stable garage with my father's car parked in it and knew immediately that he had chosen to stay home today, instead of going to the office. There was an empty space next to his car, where the car that I assumed was Carl's had been parked the previous night. I couldn't help seeing the irony that last night I was a tramp looking into the house from the garage, but this morning I was a guest looking out from the house. I stood at the bottom of the stairs for a few minutes simply mulling over the thought and the unpredictable nature of life.

Along the corridor to my father's office, I could see the photographs that I'd last seen damaged and stacked on the floor against the wall. They were all back in their place. I slowly wandered along from one to the next, as though I were visiting an art exhibition, except that all the displays were very familiar. Captured images from long ago confronted me from each frame, my own past woven into each picture.

I hadn't initially realised that there was music coming from Dad's office. Its influence had been so subtle while the pictures held my attention that it was like the sound of a breeze rustling through the trees. There, but not imposing. Once it had entered my consciousness I honed in on every note. The sweeping harmonies created by the orchestra were beautiful, lifting my spirits as I listened intently. The volume would ebb and flow. It reminded me of the way waves drift onto a beach then slide away.

It struck me that the house had always been filled with Dad's music. When I was younger I had blocked it out in favour of a more aggressive sound, but standing in the hallway I soaked up the majesty of the piece and wished that I'd been able to appreciate it years before.

When I reached the end of the corridor, I knocked apologetically at the office door and then cautiously went in. The room was empty, but remained much as it had been the last time I was in it. The impressive desk and leather chair took pride of place among the other furnishings, giving the room a judicial air. I went to the desk and ran my hand along the wooden edge as I walked around to the other side and slowly sat down in the chair. The well-worn leather creaked as I leaned back into its comfortable support, a sound that drew up so many memories of the past.

Glancing up, my eyes fixed on the photograph at the corner of the desk and I was greeted with the smiling countenance of a face that was so familiar, but of a person I don't remember; my mother. Every detail of her face intrigued me and I could see the likeness that I'd seen in the mirror that morning when I washed. I picked up the frame and went to the window that looked out over the courtyard, in order to take a closer look at the image. The last time I was in that room the picture I held never entered my consciousness, but at that moment, it seemed to be the most valuable of all possessions the house contained.

Although I had never really known her, she had known me and I recalled all the stories about her that my father had told me while I was growing up. Many of them he related while I was sitting on his lap in that same leather chair, the long-term partner of his desk.

I was so engrossed in that world of memories that I didn't hear someone come into the room and was a little startled to be interrupted by a voice.

"The last time I saw you stood at that window was the last time you slept in this house, until last night." I spun around to be greeted by my father, who held out a mug of coffee. "You look a little better this morning, my boy," he said, a wry smile crept on to his lips.

"I feel a little better, thank you." I felt awkward, unsure what I should say and floundered as I searched for the words. "I... I want to apologise for the way you found me last night I..." He held up his hand to stop me and I immediately obeyed the request, realising I was a guest in his house and in his office.

"Before either of us say anything, Andy, I want to show you something."

He went to the desk and unlocked one of the side draws. Pulling out a folder, he removed a piece of paper and held it out to me, beckoning me to take it. Crossing the room, I carefully put my mother's picture back in its place on the desk and took the creased worn paper from him. I began to read my father's handwriting; *'From your father who loves you very much.'* I felt a sudden rush of shame, as my memory brought forth unwanted pictures of the last time I had held this letter, along with the resonant echoing of my arrogant mocking of those words. I slowly looked up at him to meet his gaze, struggling for words of contrition, when I was halted at the sight of my father crying unreservedly. Any words of apology seemed pathetically inadequate at that time; nothing I could say would make up for the pain I'd caused, so I just stood there, head bowed, waiting for the agony of hearing his sobs to pass.

It took several minutes before he regained his composure, wiped his eyes and came over to me. I wasn't sure what he was going to do next and waited for some kind of confrontation, but to my surprise and bewilderment he gently took the paper from my hand and stepped over to the window saying, "I've had this letter in my desk since the day you left this house over ten years ago, Andy. I must have read it countless times and every time I wondered where you were." He paused, turned around and came to stand squarely in front of me, looking directly into my eyes, demanding I meet his gaze. I could see he wanted to make sure there could be no mistaking the meaning of what he was about to do. Lifting the paper right in front of my face he suddenly tore it in two, then again and again.

Placing his hands on both of my shoulders, he pulled me into an embrace that would have done a grizzly bear proud and said "I swear, Andy, that I will never again write a letter like that to you. I will never make comparisons between you and Carl and I will support you in whatever you want to do. More importantly, I need you to understand that I don't believe for one moment you were involved in the crime you were convicted of, whatever our disagreements of the past. I love you, son. I always have, but I was not always good at showing it."

"Neither was I, Dad."

We spent the next few hours together talking about anything that came to mind. Sometimes the conversation became too painful for that moment, so we moved on without any drama or the need to speak further on the subject. Years of estrangement could not be wiped away in a matter of hours, but there was a distinct effort to begin the process from both sides, until the gulf was bridged.

At one point, while I was standing at the window, overlooking the parking area in the stable garage, the tarpaulin that covered the car Dad had bought for me caught my eye and I raised the question of why it had never been disposed of.

"I couldn't bear to part with it. It helped me believe that one day you would return and then it would be used again..." He paused and looked at me for a moment.

"What?" I questioned.

"Would you like to go out for lunch with me?"

In the grip of our conversation I'd hardly thought about food, but once it had been mentioned I realised that I was very hungry. I was, initially, not very keen to go out so soon after returning home. I didn't want to be seen with Dad by people who might remember me from the past. I mentioned that I felt uncomfortable and without question or hesitation about the issue, he suggested we go somewhere away from any of his usual haunts.

After a search for necessary clothing and footwear, we left through the front door and walked over to the stables. As we got there it reminded me that I wanted to ask something, so I stopped and turned to look at Dad.

"What's wrong?" he quizzed.

"Dad, that lady who first spoke my name last night... Who was she?"

"She's rung me this morning, while you were still asleep, to see if she can come to see you," he said. "You will have to wait until later when I introduce her."

He broke off the conversation before I could question him further, but what came next was totally unexpected. Dad pulled back the tarpaulin that covered my car, revealing its gleaming body work.

"I had it serviced and polished every six months to make sure it was ready for this very day." The grin on Dad's face showed how he'd enjoyed removing the cover from the car that signified the momentous occasion he'd waited so long to see. I, however, took an involuntary step back, as the car was completely revealed in the daylight. I knew that it was my car, I'd already seen enough beneath the tarpaulin to confirm that, but faced with it uncovered and in full view, I was suddenly confronted with some unpleasant memories that I didn't want to deal with.

I watched, with a certain amount of alarm, as Dad got into the driver's seat and started the car. The soft purring engine, a familiar sound from my past, was accompanied by the crunching of the gravel courtyard as he drew the car out of the stable bay and stopped. I was standing a few feet away, dealing with emotions that were roller-coasting inside of me, when the passenger door window lowered and Dad called me to get in. I took another involuntary step back and shook my head at him. He greeted my response with a quizzical look.

"What's wrong, Andy?"

I turned on my heels and headed for the house, trying to block out some of the pain that I was feeling. It took Dad only a moment to realise what was happening. He immediately returned the car to its original place and quickly followed in my footsteps. By then I was at the steps in front of the portico, the initial shock having eased a little. I turned and sat down as Dad paced across the courtyard to reach me.

"I'm sorry, Dad. I can't get in that car. Not now. Not yet."

He put his arm around my shoulders as he sat down beside me.

"I'm sorry, son, that was not very thoughtful of me was it? I just got a bit carried away with the idea of you seeing your car again. I didn't stop to think that it might have some difficult memories attached to it."

"It's okay... I'm okay. I would just rather we went in a different car if you don't mind. I know it sounds silly, but it's just too soon for me to deal with at the moment."

"Well, whatever happens, that car is not as important as you, but it's still your car."

There was that emphasis again, that he had used the night before, *your* car, as he made his point. I nodded in thanks for his understanding, especially as I felt like I had thrown cold water over his parade.

"Come on let's go and get a bite to eat."

He patted my shoulder as he stood to his feet and offered a hand to pull me up.

We crossed the courtyard back to the stable block, got into his car, but as he reversed out of the parking bay he came to a stop. I looked across at him puzzled at his hesitation.

"Andy, I think I am going to have to do something."

"Oh! What's that?"

I expected, by the look on his face, to hear some serious comment about life or relationships.

"I think this driveway has been left in peace for far too long." He jammed his foot down hard on the accelerator, pressing me back into my seat and spitting gravel in all directions. "Isn't this how you used to leave home?"

We both laughed out loud together as we rapidly approached Durlwood's gateway.

CHAPTER 21

I was under no illusion about the difficulties that I, and everyone involved, would face in my trying to start a new life back at home. It was comforting that Dad had expressed his belief that I was innocent of the crime I was convicted of, but that didn't mean everybody would think like that. I'd been found guilty by a court of law, served the sentence and, as far as many would be concerned, I was a criminal. I had no doubt that there would be issues for Dad to face as well, but nothing prepared me for the events at hand, both good and bad.

The day Dad and I went out for lunch together was probably the most memorable time I had ever spent with him. We talked non-stop for hours that day. He switched off his phone and gave me his full attention, while I greedily indulged myself and it was quite obvious that he was keen to make the most of the time too.

Having literally blanked out the people who were part of my life before I went to prison, it came as a surprise to find out that my brother Carl was no longer living at Durlwood, having married seven years before my return. I hadn't even considered when or how we would meet again and the same apprehension that I felt at my first sight of the old house immediately knotted my stomach at the mention of Carl's name. Not only had I not seen my brother for over a decade, but I had no knowledge of his wife, or his children. That fact alone emphasised the span of time that I'd been absent and it hit me with a tinge of sorrow that all this had taken place while I had tried to blank the memory of my family from my consciousness. What I didn't realise was how soon that meeting between myself and Carl would come, and how unprepared I was for it.

When Dad and I returned to Durlwood late that same afternoon, it was amazing how emotional I found the experience. Turning into the driveway in the car, I found I had to pinch myself as the event seemed so momentous. I asked Dad to stop at the gateway while I took in the scene, but I had to wait a minute or two while the brimming tears in my eyes cleared and the sight before me came into proper focus.

I think Dad was aware of it. He simply went quiet to allow me deal with what I felt. I turned to him and nodded in thanks, unable to speak for fear of triggering an emotional outpouring that I thought I would never bring under control. He started to roll the car slowly forward again.

I took great delight at the turning sensation in the courtyard, as he swung the vehicle in a semi-circle to bring it back into its parking bay with such precision, something I had done many times in my own car.

As we came to a stop and Dad turned off the engine, I remarked on the car that was parked at the bottom of the steps leading to the front door. Dad acknowledged it, but gave no further clue about who its owner was. Instead he rallied me to the entrance with a purposefulness that made me feel a little uneasy about what he was up to.

As he put his key into the front door, he gave a sideward glance at me.

"Do you remember the lady that you asked me about earlier, the one who first recognised you last night?" I didn't answer his question; a little alarmed at what was coming next. "She told me that it was very important that she see you as soon as possible. She was so insistent last night that I didn't have the heart to say no."

"Why are you telling me this now, Dad?"

"I'm telling you because I'm afraid that I arranged for her to be here to meet us when we got back. I hope you don't mind."

I was quite uncomfortable at the prospect of seeing this mystery woman, especially so soon after coming home. In truth, I would have happily hidden myself away for as long as I could, but when Dad saw the concern in my face, he reassuringly put his hand on my shoulder.

"Where is she?" I said, taking a deep breath, as though preparing for action.

"She's inside, Andy," he laughed.

I was a little puzzled.

"How did she get in? There's nobody else here is there?"

"No, Andy. There's nobody else here, but she has her own key. I knew she was here because that's her car."

Anticipating my next question, Dad pushed the door open and went into the hallway overriding my attempt to find out who the person was.

I followed him through into the living area where the young lady, who was about twenty-four years old and very pretty, was seated on the sofa with a drink in hand, watching TV. Her long brown hair was tied in a cute ponytail which was draped onto the back of the leather seat. She looked as comfortable as anyone who was enjoying their own home. What's more, Dad didn't bat an eyelid at the fact she was sipping coffee she must have helped herself to.

She turned to look as we entered the room and the moment she caught sight of me she shouted, "Andy!" She leapt to her feet, crossed the room and threw her arms around my neck.

I couldn't help noticing Dad's amusement at the bewildered expression that adorned my face, but I was at a loss how to respond correctly to this welcome. Initially I felt very awkward and stood quite rigid, it must have been like hugging a lamppost, but I relaxed a little as Dad's expression seemed to urge me to reciprocate the gesture. I returned the hug, which seemed to last a little too long for strangers.

Over the preceding years I hadn't been in close contact with many people who I would have allowed to cross the 'personal space' boundaries like that. It was a defence mechanism in the life I'd led, but the overwhelming, unconditional greeting that I was being given by this lovely young woman was, although in some ways quite challenging, not wholly unwelcome. Just the aura of lovely fragrance that followed her was very agreeable indeed.

Finally, she pulled away from me a little. Putting her hand on my face, she said, "Andy, I can't tell you how glad I am to see you again."

To see me again? I was quite sure when I entered the room that I didn't know who this person was, but she seemed to know me. In fact, she had recognised me before my own father, when I was still disguised by the ruin of my life over the last decade.

"You don't know who I am, do you?" she quizzed, as her eyes lit up with delight at the mystery she was the centre of. She quickly stood to attention in front of me, still holding my hands and staring straight at my face, urging me with her body language to take a good look and then guess. I glanced at Dad, but he was no help. He seemed to be enjoying the episode almost as much as she was.

I looked back at her sensing a lack of concern at my closer inspection of her features. I tried to place the pretty face in a context that might remind me. It took a few seconds for me to realise that although she clearly knew me, I would have last seen her ten years previously when she would have been a young teenager. It was as though my mind flicked instantly through an album of pictures of people I'd known. Then in a flash it came to me.

"Suzanna?"

"Yes!" she shouted, jumping into my arms again and hugging me while laughing at the enjoyment of the game being played.

"Wait a minute. Let me look at you again," I said, prising her away from me so that I could hold her at arm's length. She threw her head back and laughed. I heard Dad join in from behind me.

"Suzanna..." I shook my head in disbelief. "Suzanna Price..."

I was suddenly taken back, as though someone had punched me in the stomach.

"Oh my God!" I shouted, as I forcefully pulled away from her. The atmosphere in the room instantly changed. One moment it was jovial, even I had been caught by it, but when I spoke her surname, guilt flooded over me. The shock of the meeting hit me as shudderingly as being deluged with ice cold water.

"How... how could you of all people, be pleased to see me after what happened to your grandfather?"

Dad had moved close behind me. I felt his arm slip around my waist as he gently guided me over to the sofa. Suzanna knelt in front of me, taking hold of my hands in hers.

"Andy, my grandfather made all of our family promise that if we ever had the chance to speak to you again, we were to tell you that he never, ever, believed that you did what they accused you of." Her eyes danced as she tried to lock onto my gaze while she spoke to me. Mine were guided by a sense of shame, desperately trying to avoid being caught.

"Granddad Price died only last year, Andy. He dearly wanted to see you again, but never thought it would happen, so he wrote a letter for you. I drove to my parents' house early this morning to fetch it so that I could give it to you. My parents moved away after granddad died, but I have been staying with Uncle Pete for a couple of weeks while I complete a training course."

The last time I heard this girl call my father 'Uncle Pete' she was about thirteen or fourteen years old and, having recognised the lively young girl in the pretty lady before me, it reminded me of the times our families had spent together enjoying the lazy summer days in the garden.

Suzanna finally managed to capture my gaze. I took in the beautiful, welcoming, countenance of the face of the girl I used to laugh and play games with. She squeezed my hands as a sign of reassurance. Then, letting go, she reached into her bag and brought out an envelope addressed to me. She placed it in my hands.

"Your Dad and I are going to leave you to read this in private, Andy, but if you want anything, we'll be around."

They both quietly left the room so that I could take my time and I was grateful for their thoughtfulness. I looked down at the envelope and the inevitable tears again pressed hard to be set free.

I spent a long time reading and re-reading that letter written by Henry. To say that he was very gracious was a monumental understatement, but his absolute insistence that he knew it hadn't been me who assaulted him was like soothing oil on a festering wound. The same kindness that I'd known in him was bountifully evident in his granddaughter and she hadn't hesitated for one second to show it.

As I was mulling things over, I heard the door open behind me and then a gentle hand on my shoulder, followed by the fragrance once again filling the room.

"I've made us something to eat, Andy. Do you think you could come and join us?"

The softness in her voice showed genuine concern for me and I was deeply touched by it. I took hold of her hand resting on my shoulder.

"Thank you, Suzanna Price."

"For what, Andy Numan?"

I laughed at her mimicking my use of her name by doing the same back to me.

"For being you."

She squeezed my hand in recognition of my compliment, then patiently waited until I was ready to follow her through to the kitchen.

As we ate together that evening, we talked about Henry. It was the first time I had allowed myself to look back to the dark days when he'd been so brutally hurt, but I was comforted by the fact that he'd recovered quite well, although it had taken many months. He even returned to part-time work in the gardens for Dad. They told me the work helped him to recuperate. He very much appreciated the opportunity to continue what he saw as a hobby that he got paid for.

Suzanna's openness convinced me that she believed I was not involved. She was not just acting according to her much loved grandfather's wishes. This family had obviously suffered in the incident and the time that followed. In prison, regardless of how much I protested my innocence, no one was willing to believe there had been a mistake. Convicted, punished; end of story. Yet those who had been hurt most in the whole affair, knowing the way that I'd behaved in the past, were willing to trust that I would never have hurt Henry. I felt very humbled to be welcomed back by them.

The extreme swing from poverty to luxury, in such a short space of time, was hard to adjust to. I frequently found myself indulging in the touch, or sound, or look, of many ordinary things that surrounded me. At least they were ordinary for many people, but for those who'd lived the way I'd been living only a few days before, even hot running water wasn't ordinary.

My strange behaviour seemed to impact Dad as he observed me taking delight in the simplest of things. He caught me closely examining the beauty of an ornament which had stood neglected in the same place in our hallway for as many years as I could remember. He later told me that he'd come to appreciate it again after years of never noticing it. How easy to become complacent with the blessings that surround us and how sad that they are often only considered valuable once they've gone.

It was a delight to have the company of Suzanna at Durlwood. She never once tried to disguise her fascination about the homeless life I'd lived. At times I felt like a patient on a psychiatrist's couch, but I couldn't deny that there was something therapeutic about the time we spent together over the following day. I don't know if Dad deliberately kept out of the way, allowing us time to talk, but he would occasionally pass the living area and, without actually intruding, would check that we were okay.

It was late in the evening, after I first met Suzanna again, when I finally confided in her that my greatest fear was meeting Carl again. I told her about how hostile he'd been the last time we had spoken. I was worried that he wouldn't be as welcoming as my father had been. She didn't respond to my concerns, but instead appeared to avoid discussing the subject, which made me wonder what I was yet to find out. It wasn't long before I did.

Dad apologised that he needed to return to work the following day, but said that Suzanna would be around for some of the time so that I would have some company. I sensed that he had a question he wanted to ask, but he seemed unsure about whether he should.

"Dad!" I called out, as he started to climb the stairs to go to bed.

"Yes?" He turned back to look at me.

"What are you avoiding asking me?"

He paused for a moment as he looked away to run his eyes up the stairs, as though contemplating his escape from my question.

"Is it that obvious?"

"You are... were not... a man who tended to hesitate, so it's noticeable when you do. If you need to say something I would like to hear it."

He laughed.

"No, I suppose I can be a bit forward." He hesitated before continuing, "Andy, you're home for good aren't you? No matter what?"

"If you will have me, I am."

I caught sight of Suzanna, with a cup clasped in her hands, leaning against the kitchen door frame. She smiled as Dad slapped his hand on the stair banister like an auction room gavel completing a transaction.

"Good, then we shall talk no more about it."

I watched as he mounted the stairs and disappeared across the landing, wishing us both a goodnight. I turned back to Suzanna who was still staring at me. She smiled again and turned on her heel to go back into the kitchen.

"You want another coffee?"

She didn't wait for any answer and I knew it was an invitation to chat a little longer, an offer that I was not going to refuse.

The following morning was heavily overcast, almost dark. It had an ominous feel to it. Those sort of days are the worst kind when living without proper shelter. The cold digs deep into your bones and the greyness has an impact on you mentally.

I got dressed and headed down the stairs to the kitchen for a coffee. As I got to the hallway, I could see out on the courtyard that both Dad and Suzanna's cars were gone. The overcast day was trying to obscure the view to the distant gates at the end of the drive. Even the Christmas tree was struggling to bring some cheer on that sorry morning. I stopped to look at the scene for a while and noticed the silence in the house; no traffic or people-sounds.

In the living area, I settled myself in a reading chair facing out to the gardens and began to flick through a magazine that had been left on the coffee table. I couldn't relax properly. I didn't really notice any of the pages before me as I turned them systematically one after the other. My mind was too occupied with the future, for the first time in a long time. Not the immediate future, like where to stay for the night, or how to find food and money. These things had been the only future that had existed for me over the last few years, but now I was concerned about the future of my life. What would I do?

CHAPTER 22

CARL

"Hi, darling, we're home!" Jane called out as she breezed in through the side door. I could hear Andrew and Alice squabbling as they grappled with tugging their boots and coats off.

"I'm in the kitchen, sweetheart. I'm just about to make Dad a tea. Do you want one?"

Jane put her head around the boot-room door.

"Peter. How lovely to see you. Grandpa's here!" she shouted back to the children. She was always able to excite the kids just with the tone of her voice. She made even Grandpa's visit sound like the most amazing thing that could ever happen. The squeals of delight were a joy to hear as the kerfuffle gave an indication that boots were being removed at high speed. Dad had always been the storybook granddad from the moment they were born. I think he softened visibly the day he lifted our first baby from his crib in the hospital, and when Jane and I told him that we were going to call him Andrew it was the first time I recall seeing him shed a tear.

"Where are my two little angels?" he shouted to beckon them in. There was a race between them to be the first to jump on his knee and he pretended that they were too heavy for him to hold. "What do you think there is in my jacket pocket?"

Jane shook her head at his familiar routine, but she had long given up the possibility of reforming Dad's behaviour. He just couldn't help himself. Without fail there would be something for them both every time he came to the house. Jane had managed to steer him away from bringing sweets too often, but the children absolutely adored him coming and the generosity that followed him. I always pulled his leg about how he bribed them to love him. I told him that's why Daddy came second for hugs when Grandpa was around.

As peace began to descend once more, Andrew came bounding up to me and leapt into my arms to show me what had been in Grandpa's pocket. While we were looking at it together, in a matter of fact voice that dragged out the word, he said, "D-a-d-d-y."

"Y-e-s." I mimicked his intonation which made him laugh, so I copied him again.

"Why do Mummy and Grandpa call me 'Andy' when they talk about me."

"What do you mean?" I quizzed.

"Didn't you mummy?" Andrew patted her on the back to get her attention. Jane turned from her conversation with Dad to respond to Andrew's beckoning.

"What's that, darling?"

Andrew shrugged his shoulders with a measure of exasperation at the need to repeat himself.

"I s-a-i-d, why did you and Grandpa call me 'Andy' when you were talking yesterday?"

I caught the change in Jane's expression, even though she tried to cover it. Panic flashed across her eyes, but Andrew hadn't finished. "You said Andy can live with Grandpa."

Andrew looked at me as he completed his sentence, but my eyes were fixed on Jane and she knew it.

"Andrew. Alice. Go put the TV on, it's your favourite cartoon." The tone of Jane's voice caused Dad to turn his attention from Alice to see what the matter was. She quickly ushered the children to the lounge, giving Andrew instructions.

Jane was the most open person that I'd ever met. She was terrible at hiding things. The thing that I found most attractive now betrayed her and I knew that something was being concealed. The concern on Dad's face confirmed my suspicion and I was not going to let go.

"What's going on, Jane?"

She glanced at Dad.

"*Jane?*"

"Carl…" She apologetically said my name, but whatever she said next was drowned by the sound of blood rushing in my head and the echoing of a name that did not refer to my son. It was my brother's name and I knew it.

I looked from Jane to Dad and back again, demanding an explanation. Suddenly Andrew was back at the kitchen door and Jane spoke quite firmly to him which was not at all like her.

"Oh, Andrew, stop… just run along and play with your sister for a while. I need to talk to your father."

Andrew sloped off, crestfallen that his appeal seemed to have fallen on deaf ears.

"What's Andrew talking about Jane? What does he mean, 'Andy can live with Grandpa'? I don't understand."

"Oh, Carl I didn't want you to find out like this, I'm so sorry…"

Dad stood to his feet and made a move toward me, but I stepped aside so that I could respond to Jane.

"Sorry, for what, Jane?" I caught the glisten of tears in her eyes and so did Dad. The playful expression gone, he turned to face me directly.

"Andy's back, Carl," he said. The expression on my face must have stopped him for a moment before he resumed his explanation. "He came back a couple of days ago… I thought I would leave it a little while before I told you. He was in an absolutely awful state. Carl, I'm sorry, I should have told you sooner, but I thought it best to wait, that's why I came to speak with Jane yesterday."

"TO DECIDE WHETHER TO KEEP IT A SECRET FROM ME?" I yelled.

I could feel the blood rising in me. All the pent up anger I'd felt, which I'd managed to suppress these last ten years, came flooding back, coursing through me until I thought I would burst.

"Are you *sure* it's him?"

"Yes, Carl. It's Andy."

"No, I don't believe it."

"Yes, it's true Carl. He's back at Durlwood."

"I can't believe he's got the gall to show his face after what he's put us through. I thought he must be dead. Why would my own brother treat me like he has if he wasn't dead? Dad? After what he's put *you* through! No, I'm not having him come breezing back into our lives, setting us up for a fall again." I was furious and any rational thinking had gone out of the window. My normally cool façade collapsed like a house of cards.

Dad had been so vulnerable when Andy left. He cut us out of his life completely. How many times had we tried to get in touch with him? He never even looked at us when we went to the court trial. It was as if we didn't exist. That broke Dad and I'd worked too hard for Andy to think he could come back and mess it all up.

"I just can't believe he's done this! I'm going to Durlwood." I pushed past Dad, but Jane stepped in front of me.

"Please, Carl, don't go! Just stay here and let's talk about …" Jane's words hung in mid-air. I knew she was trying to placate me, but I was having none of it. I turned to look at Dad.

"Please, Carl," he echoed Jane.

I hesitated a moment while the past ten years seemed to fast rewind through my mind and every hurting moment cranked up my anger. Jane sat down at the kitchen table, encouraging me to do the same, as she sensed the turmoil she had been witness to most of the last decade spilling over the brim. Then Dad sat next to her, but I couldn't shake off the urge to bolt out through the door.

"Carl. Please." Dad's voice carried the same pain that I had heard so many times over those early years of Andy's absence and I flipped. I ran out to my car, throwing myself into the driver's seat and tore off out into the road heading for Durlwood. My head was consumed with racing thoughts. Where had he been all this time? Why no contact? Why didn't he let us know where he was? Why did he cut us off like that? Why would he even let us think he might be dead? Why come back now? Didn't he know what he'd done to us?

I struggled, trying to make sense of what was happening; just a moment ago, everything had been peaceful and now it felt like a bomb had exploded. I didn't want to have to deal with the carnage, or put Dad back together again. Not a second time. I didn't want to have to be the one shouldering the burden of trying to make things better, trying to be strong. Trying to be everything to Dad to make up for what he'd lost. He'd grieved so long and so hard for a son he thought was lost forever. We all feared the very worst. I'd had to protect Dad; he was so vulnerable. No contact, no messages, nothing. Absolutely nothing for ten long years.

I'd grieved too. I'd loved him. I even thought it was my fault he'd gone; that I'd driven a wedge between him and Dad. I couldn't see what was happening then. I just thought Andy was being arrogant and selfish, wanting more and more. I realise now I was fed up with him getting away with doing what he wanted; I was the one who was fulfilling expectations. I'd done everything Dad had requested. I'd done my duty; fulfilled the role. I worked damn hard. I helped build up the family business. Andy just wanted to play around with his music and enjoy himself. He wanted to spend life partying, having fun. Didn't he understand that I wanted some of that too?

I was the one who had to pick up the pieces when he pissed off to enjoy himself, acting like a playboy. I wanted him to go; end the nightmare we were living through with his endless arguments and 'it's not fair' attitude. I'd had enough of trying to be the peacemaker in the house. I thought it would be so much easier with him out of the way. Sure, I tried to find out where he had gone when he walked out, for Dad's sake. I never thought he'd go for good.

My God did we pay a heavy price, but I thought things had reached equilibrium. I even named my son after him, trying to dull the ache that had constantly been there. I thought it would please Dad too, but neither of us could bring ourselves to shorten his name from Andrew, it prompted too painful a memory. My little boy even looked like Andy when he was younger. I so desperately missed him, but I was not ready to forgive him for what had taken place.

I don't remember any of the journey to Durlwood, but the things that ran through my mind are as vivid as ever. The only time that I could see past the pain that blinded me was when I turned into the driveway and raced toward the house, intending to vent the pent up anger of the decade gone by.

I swung the car around the courtyard and scraped to a halt, spitting gravel from the locked wheels that ploughed a furrow. Pushing the door open, I jumped out and ran up the steps to the sound of the car warning that the keys had been left in the ignition and had to return to get the house key. Adrenaline pumped as I neared a confrontation that had been waiting to happen for a whole decade.

ANDY

It was eleven o'clock and the day still seemed to be waiting for the sun to rise properly and gave no indication that it would change. As I looked out over the fields that joined the rear gardens, I heard a vehicle on the gravel outside. I braced myself for the silence I was enjoying to be disrupted by the return of Suzanna. Not that she was an unwelcome companion. I smiled at the thought of her coming back through the door, full of the joys of spring in the middle of winter.

I listened until the front door opened and then slammed again with a loud bang.

"Wow, Suzanna, that's what I call an entrance!"

There was no reply, so I got up to go out to the hallway and almost walked straight into Carl. I jumped back in surprise. At first I didn't realise it was him.

"Carl!" I exclaimed, "I didn't know you were coming!"

He didn't wait for introductions or niceties, but launched into what he had obviously come to say.

"What the hell are you doing coming back here, you little shit!" he shouted as he pushed me in the chest, so that I lost my balance. Tripping on the chair that was behind me, I fell to the floor.

"I... I..."

As I stammered to start a sentence, I found I was so shocked I couldn't even begin to get the words out as I lay flat on my back. I lifted myself to my elbows, trying to regain some composure, but Carl hadn't finished yet. He quickly knelt down, putting one knee on my stomach and grabbed hold of my shirt.

"Why don't you just bugger off back to the slime pit you came from and leave us all in peace. God knows you've caused more than your fair share of damage to this family."

The venom in his expression was frightening as he spat the words out at me. I was in no doubt that he meant every word.

Suddenly the front door slammed again, followed by rapid footsteps, then Dad burst through the lounge door. Carl looked round at him and then back at me.

"You shouldn't have followed me, Dad," he said angrily. "Why didn't you tell me before now that he'd come back?"

Carl looked back at Dad. His thunderous expression displaying exactly what he was feeling.

"Why? Why, Carl? This is why! You left home like a madman intent on killing somebody. Jane was terrified that you would have an accident. Heaven knows how you made it back here in one piece driving like that. You want to know why I didn't tell you? Look at you! Look at what you're doing!"

Carl was still pressing down on me, intent on making a point. I could have fought back I suppose, but the fight wasn't in me anymore. I'd seen enough quarrelling to last me forever and the last person I wanted to fight with was my own brother. Anyway, he was right. I'd caused a lot of damage to the family, but I wasn't going to make it even worse by swinging punches around. If he wanted to hit me, then I was going to let him. I owed him that for what I'd done. In fact, Carl's response to me seemed much more appropriate than every other response I'd encountered to that point.

Dad leant back against the wall, staring at the two of us sprawled out in front of him. He sank down until he was sat on his heels and, putting his elbows on his knees, cupped his face in his hands.

"I have just got my missing boy back. Must I now endure the loss of the other one?"

I could see the tears on his cheeks as he looked at us. Carl looked back at me. With a thrust of his fists he let go of my shirt and stood up to tower over me as I lay on the floor.

"You might have won over some of this family, but don't you ever set foot in my home, or come near my family. Do you hear me? Never!"

Carl turned on his heel and headed out through the front door. He had swept in and out like a passing thunderstorm. I couldn't ever remember him being so forceful in the past. I had always found his character very passive, but there was nothing passive about what had just happened.

As I lay there considering what had taken place, the front door slammed again and Suzanna ran across the hallway to find me sprawled out and Dad slumped down leaning back against the wall.

"I just passed Carl in his car tearing down the driveway."

"Yes, he came to say hello," I replied sarcastically.

"It didn't go too well then?"

I think my withering look was enough to answer the question.

"No, Suzanna, I'm afraid it went almost exactly as I thought it would," said Dad.

The sigh that followed his comment betrayed a tiredness that seemed to sum up the years of my absence. With that single response, the weight of what I'd done, by cutting myself off from them, became crystal clear to me.

I'd been given warning that there was a rough road ahead if I was to ever reconcile myself with Carl. I'd thought that it might have been even more so with Dad, but I counted my blessings with a grateful heart over that outcome. That sigh Dad breathed made me vow to make whatever effort I needed to try to repair the breech, but how to begin that process, when Carl was so resolute, was beyond me. I certainly could not have a situation where Dad was forced to choose between his two sons.

The three of us were quiet over dinner that evening. I was lost in my thoughts over how to deal with my relationship with Carl. Dad seemed very subdued in comparison to the previous few days and Suzanna was stuck in the middle. Once the meal was finished, I excused myself and went to find a hideaway where I could be on my own for a while.

I went to Carl's old bedroom, knowing that there was a little study area tucked away around a corner where he used to do his college work. The desk and chair were still there, positioned under the window, which had a view to the side of the house looking out to the garden store shed; Henry's old haunt. It was too dark to see much more than a vague outline of things. I was reminded of the last time I'd seen Henry, standing with his wheelbarrow on this same side of the house. He had disturbed me while loading my car with my things. That was the last time I had seen Durlwood, except for the visit after the break-in, until my recent return.

I spent some time thinking about the old man and his kindly ways. He had been as much a grandfather figure to me and Carl as he had been to Suzanna. In a strange sort of way, I almost felt like I was hoping he would give me some advice from the after-life about what to do next; how to reach out to Carl in a way that would not provoke him further.

The next thing I knew, I was waking up with my head on my arms, leant forward onto the desk. I was a little disoriented at first, not knowing why I had woken, but then I heard Suzanna shout my name.

I went out onto the landing to find her looking into each of the bedrooms in search of me.

"Oh, Andy, are you okay? Your Dad was worried that we hadn't seen you since dinner. I think he's quite concerned that Carl upset you and was worried that you might..."

"Might what?"

She briefly smiled and finished the sentence, "Change your mind about leaving again?"

I put my arm around her shoulder to guide her back down the stairs and as we descended I told her that I had no intention of leaving again, especially now I understood the damage I had caused already by following that course of action.

"In truth, Suzanna, I need to try to find a way to reconcile with Carl. For Dad's sake, if nothing else."

I stepped down the last stair to the hallway. Suzanna didn't. Instead she turned me to face her. Standing on that first step she was at my eye level and there in front of me was that warmth again as she smiled at me.

"Andy, I know you have made some mistakes, well, so have all of us, and I know that you want to put things right, but it is going to take some time. You weren't here to see what Carl went through when you refused to see anyone while you were... while you were in prison. I know that you had a tough time in there, but it was like Carl was in another kind of prison out here. He changed a lot in that time. It took him a long, long time to get on with his life again. It was almost as though he had to train his mind to accept that he didn't have a brother. You had died to him. You would have no contact with him and he could get no access to you, even though he wrote to you. That was a painful process for him. Your Dad told me that he went as white as a sheet when he told him that you had come home. What you saw was the pent up anger he has hidden from all of us for years. You need to give him time."

She saw the pain of her words in my face, but it was the truth that I needed to hear. I was thankful that she could give it in such a disarming way. She put her arm around my neck and pressed her forehead against mine.

"Don't worry, Andy. It'll all work out in the end."

I pulled away a little to focus on the face of this remarkable lady and the light coming in from the windows behind me lit the warm features that had been so welcoming from the first moment. With a quizzical expression, she tipped her head slightly to one side.

"What? Andy, what's wrong?"

"Nothing. Nothing's wrong."

I smiled as I pulled away from her and as I did, I asked if she would like a coffee, simply for something to say to break that moment. I was becoming concerned and a little embarrassed that each time I spent time talking with Suzanna I inevitably found myself wondering what it would be like to kiss her, even to the point that I'd occasionally had to ask her to repeat what she'd just said because I'd missed it. Only just back from a squalid life on the streets and meeting this girl again and all I could think about was what it would be like to take her in my arms. I couldn't think of anything that could be more inappropriate. I had to face it, she had really got under my skin and I was beginning to experience a feeling I hadn't had since I'd made my last mistake of falling in love.

CHAPTER 23

To say that the first few days back at home, except for the incident with Carl, were fabulous, would have been the biggest understatement ever. I was extremely grateful for the circumstances I found myself in, but, unlike my younger days in that house, I was not going to take anything for granted again. I savoured every comfort with gratitude.

I felt strange about using my car and had to spend some time talking to Dad, trying to explain why. On my first trip to the town, I had walked to the nearest bus stop to use public transport, just to avoid using the car. I sat in the driver's seat contemplating the trip, when I took a sideways glance to the passenger seat, it immediately gave me a flashback of Sasha sitting there beside me. It disturbed me so much that I jumped out, slamming the door shut as if to lock away the memory. It was as though I couldn't just step back into the things from my younger life, like nothing had happened. A lot had happened and my car was one of the most poignant reminders of the times that had passed.

The journey into town was a slideshow of childhood memories as I took in the view from the bus window and every moment of the trip fascinated me. All the buildings and roads were familiar. There were so many things which I'd seen so often as a child that stopped being registered when I got older. It was as though they didn't exist anymore, but everything I passed that morning, the trees in the park, the monuments, the majestic buildings, were all new to me again and I found every feature fascinating.

When I arrived at the town centre, without any plan for the day, I aimlessly wandered through the precinct, window shopping, until the smell of coffee drew me into a small café. The pleasure of the comfortable leather chairs, positioned to give an advantageous view of the street, kept me there for a long time that Wednesday morning. I watched people go by and wondered who they were and what they were doing. My daydreaming was interrupted by the bleep of the phone I was carrying, at Dad's insistence. I checked the message and was delighted to see that it was from Suzanna, asking if I was up for having lunch with her at one-thirty. I rang to let her know I was in town and that it would be very nice to meet up, but, in truth, I couldn't wait to see her.

It was just after twelve and I'd been sat in the café for at least an hour at that point, so I decided to go for a walk to while away the time. Suzanna was to drive into town, meet me for lunch and then take me home. She laughed when I told her that I still felt uncomfortable taking my car and had come by bus instead. I felt a little embarrassed, but didn't for one moment think she was laughing at me. I told her I would explain over lunch and hung up feeling good about how my day was going.

It was as I left the café that one of those improbable events that you sometimes hear about, happened to me. Everyone I tell the story to seems to conclude that I must have arranged the incident before hand, as it was so unlikely to happen by accident, but I swear to them that it was pure coincidence.

I pushed the door open to leave the café, but turned back in response to one of the staff shouting after me that I had accidentally left my scarf over the back of the chair. After retrieving my scarf, I expressed my thanks as I reversed out of the door, not properly watching where I was going. With a final wave of thanks, I spun around and immediately stumbled over a little boy who was enjoying his day out on his toy scooter. I went headlong onto the pavement in an attempt to avoid knocking him over, but my efforts were in vain as we both crashed to the floor. He didn't make any big deal about it, but jumped to his feet brushing his hands and proceeded to pick his scooter up, as I watched from my embarrassing position, sat in the middle of the walkway. It was funny that I was conscious of people around me looking, even though I had lived on the streets completely ignoring the opinion of others for years.

About to get up, I hesitated as I realised the little boy, rather than continuing on his journey, was standing looking at me as he hung on to his precious toy. It was as though he knew that one of us should say something before we each continued on our way, but he was waiting for me to make the first move. All I could do was smile at him.

"Andrew, are you okay?"

The concerned tones of a parent invaded the situation as the lady, who I presumed to be his mother, descended upon us. She crouched down by the little boy and after a quick check that all was well, looked at me. With a hint of blush in her cheeks she said, "I am so sorry, sir. He gets a little carried away I'm afraid. He just loves that scooter. I'm so sorry."

I waved my hand to protest that there was no need to worry and that I was okay. She straightened up and held out her hand to offer to help me from my seated position and I thought it impolite to refuse. Once vertical I came face to face with her. Her dark, shoulder-length hair spilled from beneath a Russian fur hat onto the shoulders of her cream-coloured coat. She had a confident air in her manner and didn't hesitate to lock eyes with me as she pressed again, "Are you sure you're okay?"

"Yes, yes. I'm perfectly okay thank you." I bent down to address the little boy, "How about you young man, do you think we had great big crash?" He laughed at my impression of what had just happened, sound effects and all. I couldn't help responding to his infectious giggle. So enthusiastic was his enjoyment of the moment that it made his mum's concerned face break into a warm smile. I looked up and smiled at her and then addressed the little boy again.

"Now then, after our little trick I think it's time for me to give you some room to carry on with your scooter. What do you think?" He nodded in response, but his answer was totally unrelated to my question, as a child's answer often can be.

"What's your name?" he asked.

I looked at his mum, conscious that I might be holding them up and shrugged as an apology for the delay. She just smiled, as if it was a normal event for her. Crouching down to his level I held out my hand to introduce myself to him.

"It seems that you and I have the same first name, although I shorten mine to Andy. My name's Andy Numan."

He looked at me with a puzzled expression before turning to his mum and saying excitedly, "Mummy, he's got exactly the same name as me!"

I turned to look up at his mother, unsure of what the little boy was talking about. Our eyes met and she hesitated for a moment before speaking.

"I'm sorry. What did you say your name was?"

I stood to my feet, to face her properly, and as I did I noticed a little girl hiding behind her mother's legs, but still taking a keen interest in the proceedings. I took a quick glance back at the little boy as I answered her question.

"Andy Numan. My name is Andy... Nu... man," I stuttered, noticing her surprised expression as I was speaking, which made me feel very awkward. "Do I know you?" I asked, puzzled at her reaction.

"No, Andy. You don't know me. Not at all," she said, as her gaze was a little uncomfortably fixed on me. She took a breath and enthusiastically said, "Well, let me introduce myself and the children properly. This is my eldest, Andrew, whom you have already become acquainted with." She said it as if everybody became acquainted with Andrew in a similar manner to my first encounter, ruffling his hair as she spoke, only for us to be greeted again with that wonderful giggle. "And this..." She turned to bring the little girl around her legs until she was facing me, with her mother's hands on her shoulders. "This is Alice." The little girl coyly smiled at me, then turned away as if embarrassed, as her mother planted a kiss on her forehead. Then, standing up to look directly at me, she said, "And my name is Jane." She hesitated in her sentence as she pulled her glove from her hand and held it out for me to shake in greeting. Slightly bemused at the formality of the introductions, I took the offered hand and as I did she completed her sentence, "Jane Numan... I'm Carl's wife... and these are our children."

I didn't need an explanation of the relationship between her and the children, that had become abundantly clear, but I did need the extra few seconds it gave me to try to comprehend the situation. I still had hold of her hand, but tried to pull away out of concern about what Carl had said when I met him, but she gripped tighter to stop me.

"Andrew, Alice," she addressed the children, while holding her stare at me and my hand in hers. "Say hello to your Uncle Andy."

The children dutifully responded to their mother's instruction and almost sang the greeting in unison without the slightest hesitation. It sounded like a class of two children addressing teacher in morning assembly. I was a little lost for words, but Jane didn't skip a beat.

"Your father is so pleased that you're home, Andy. I can't tell you how good it is to see him so happy." She stooped down to address the children and gathering them together into her arms, she continued, "Isn't that right you two? We like to see Grandpa happy, don't we?" They squealed as she playfully shook them.

"Your..." I found I had to clear my throat to speak properly. "Your children are lovely..."

I hesitated, unsure whether I should address her as Jane, or Mrs. Numan. One seemed too familiar, for people who had only just met, and the other too distant, for people so closely related. Noticing my dilemma, she completed my sentence with a nod of reassurance.

"Please call me Jane." Then, in a mixture of addressing me and the children, at the same time, she said, "They are lovely aren't they? Uncle Andy will like you even more when he gets to know you better, won't he children?" As my eyes met with hers again, she smiled.

"I know that Carl is struggling a little, Andy, but you must allow for the fact that he has felt very protective towards your father for a very long time. Give him some space, and some time, and it'll work out. It has to..." A beaming smile punctuated her explanation. "I promised Dad that it would work out and I always keep my promise. He is such a sweet man, your father."

"Thank you for your understanding, Jane. I'm sure I don't deserve it, but thank you anyway." She smiled again at my response and deliberately making sure I was not left feeling awkward about what to say next, she took control of the conversation.

"So, what are you doing in town today?" She turned to start walking along the street and putting her hand on my arm, encouraged me to fall in step with her. That simple gesture carried more weight than a thousand words could ever have done.

"I'm meeting a friend for lunch in a little while."

Jane gave me a look that bid me continue with more information.

"Oh, I'm sorry. Suzanna, Suzanna Price." I said, almost apologetically. I had no idea who knew who in my estranged family world.

"Oh, Suzanna is a darling, Andy, but you know that don't you?"

I wasn't sure if she was being presumptuous or perceptive, but concluded that she must have been kept informed about the latest happenings at home, presumably by Dad, and she was right, I did know that Suzanna was a darling.

"Well, we must get a move on because we have to meet Daddy, don't we children?" she said, half talking to the children, as well as informing me of their schedule. As we reached the next junction, she stopped, then turned to face me.

"We have to go this way, so we must say goodbye for now, but it was a pleasure to finally meet you, Andy, after all the time I've spent talking to your father about you. He missed you very much while you were gone. Don't ever believe he stopped loving you and hoping for you to return. When I spoke to him yesterday he seemed like a changed man. Over the years, he's been much more of a father to me than my own father ever was. I'm just so happy that he is happy."

Her words were a mixed blessing, reminding me of the lost time while I was away, but also that my father found great joy in his family.

Leaning forward, she kissed my cheek as if we were old friends parting for the thousandth time and encouraged the children to wave and shout goodbye. Then, as quickly as we had been introduced, she was gone.

As I stood watching them head down the road, all doubt about the sincerity of her greeting and the warmth of her words was laid to rest when, twenty yards along the street, the whole group of them turned to wave again before they were lost in the crowd of shoppers. The image of their goodbye has been etched in my mind ever since and will always be a treasured memory that reminds me of the meaning of acceptance.

That meeting with Jane and the children was the most extraordinary coincidence of my life. It left me standing on the pavement wondering about how things would turn out as I looked at the place where I'd watched them, members of my family, disappear into the crowd. The hustle and bustle of the busy street didn't interfere with my thoughts, as I wondered how that meeting would affect Carl.

The chime of the town hall clock made me re-engage with my immediate surroundings, reminding me that I needed to make a move to the arranged meeting place for lunch with Suzanna.

At twenty-five-past-one, Suzanna breezed into the little restaurant where I had been seated at a table for fifteen minutes or so, waiting for her arrival. Casually dressed in jeans and shirt with a quilted white jacket and colourful scarf, she looked a picture of loveliness. Even though I'd been having a good day to that point, it suddenly seemed so much better. She walked across the room, unzipping her jacket and unravelling the scarf as I stood up to greet her.

"Hi, Andy," she said, as she placed her jacket on the chair, then kissed me on the cheek, her familiar fragrance delighting my senses as much as seeing her enter the restaurant had done.

"It's my lucky day today, Suzanna," I said, displaying a 'cat that got the cream' grin.

"What do you mean?"

She playfully slapped me on the arm.

"You're the second pretty lady to kiss me on the cheek today and it's only half-past-one."

She amusingly furrowed her brow, as if jokingly suggesting disapproval.

"Not that I'm jealous, but who was the other woman?"

I loved the way that she phrased her question with such theatrical delivery.

"Oh yes," I said, playing along as though we were on stage in a play. "She was a dark-haired beauty."

Not wanting to miss any opportunity for some fun, Suzanna picked up the rhythm.

"Dark-haired beauty was she, pray tell me who, sir?"

"Yes... wearing a Russian fur hat."

I didn't realise that I had been rumbled.

"You've met Jane. When? How did that happen?" I was quite surprised that Suzanna knew straight away who I was talking about.

"I bumped into them. To be exact, I bumped into Andrew and his scooter."

"Oh, you met the children as well. They are little angels, aren't they? I'm so pleased, so pleased."

Suzanna couldn't contain her delight about the meeting and it never seemed to cross her mind that it might not have gone well. I couldn't believe that somehow the pair of them hadn't orchestrated the events, but they both later assured me that it was a complete coincidence, and that neither of them could have planned it so well, despite their great skill at such things, they would add.

I wasn't in a hurry to get back home too soon that afternoon and it didn't appear that Suzanna was either. The busy shopping area was filled with the typical Christmas decorations and music and, in the company of Suzanna, it was like I was experiencing it again for the first time in years. As it grew dusky the Christmas lights came on, adding a charming ambience to the town, making us resolve to stay until it was properly dark so that we could see the full effect. It was so beautiful and so was Suzanna.

We eventually arrived back at Durlwood at about six o'clock, coming from the same direction that I had walked on that first evening, the distant lights of the house reminding me vividly of that night. Suzanna turned into the driveway and at the end looped around the courtyard decorated with tree and coloured lights, coming to a stop behind another car.

"Look we've got visitors," she shouted gleefully, obviously not realising that I was not quite as enthusiastic at meeting new people as she was.

Feeling a little apprehensive about the next stage of my rehabilitation, I asked who the visitor was.

"Don't worry, Andy. You know them already." She jumped out of the car before I could get anything else out of her and was already at the steps to the house door before I'd closed the car door behind me. She spun round to face me when she reached the top steps and shouted, "Come on, slowcoach, what's taking you so long?" The playfulness was charming as she goaded me further. "Bet you can't catch me, lazy bones."

It didn't take another invitation, I ran up the steps to try to reach her before she could get her key in the lock, but by the time I made the distance the front door was ajar and she laughed as I pulled at her arm while we spilled into the hallway.

One thing that I appreciated very much was the gaiety that seemed to surround Suzanna wherever she went. It was a delight to be in her presence simply to be able to enjoy her cheerfulness. That had been something that was missing from far too many years of my life and I indulgently entered into the sheer fun of it.

As we stood looking at each other, catching our breath and laughing at the situation, having nearly run into the hallway table which supported the festive decorations that greeted visitors to the house, I became aware that we were being watched. Standing in the entrance to the kitchen were Dad and Jane. I immediately checked myself. Suzanna spun around to see what had taken hold of my attention.

"Well, I must say that you two are getting along fine," said Jane, as though she were pretending to be a disapproving aunt. Dad laughed at the scene before him and I had the distinct impression that he was pleased that Durlwood was echoing with the sound of family fun.

Suzanna had no hesitation greeting Jane, they might well have been sisters with the warmth that each of them displayed and as I watched them, I had trouble reconciling the choices I had made to separate myself from these people who knew what it was to be loved and were more than willing to love in return. The depth of the emotions that hit me at that moment were not related to my past, but were connected only to that very second in time. So powerful was the sensation, that it was too much for me to retain my composure in front of them, so I quickly excused myself, feigning the need to visit the bathroom.

I had cried a number of times in my life, usually from remorse or sorrow, from guilt or despair, but the tears that I washed away that evening were actually an entirely new experience to me. In more than thirty years I had never cried without there being some negative emotion or feeling attached to the expression. That evening was different. My overwhelming sense was one of genuine thankfulness for the circumstances in which I found myself. My dilemma was understanding why, or how, I could simultaneously laugh and cry, but that is what I did.

Having gathered myself enough so that I wouldn't feel embarrassed, I returned downstairs to the others, a little concerned that my face might betray what I'd really been doing.

"Andy. I was just asking Jane..." Dad started to tell me something as I entered the room, but stopped when he looked at me a second time. "Are you alright, son?"

The cat was out of the bag and the three of them were looking at me as if not wanting to say anything inappropriate, but each waiting to see who would break the silence first.

"I just wanted to say..."

I knew, after the first couple of words, that the composure I thought I had steeled inside me was no more than a flimsy paper holding back a flood. My resolve gave way against the pressure of my emotion as soon as I opened my mouth.

"Thank you."

I choked out the completing words for my sentence. Feeling rather silly, I dropped my head to look at the floor, partly in an attempt to conceal some of my embarrassment, but also to disconnect from their gaze as I tried to contain myself while I clarified what I meant.

"These last few days... they have been the happiest of my life and... and I'm... I've been a little overwhelmed at your kindness. Today..." I gasped to try to hold on to the last of my composure in order to finish the sentence, "Today has been a very special day for me... Thank you."

I thought I was finding it difficult, but as I wiped my eyes and looked up at them, I was greeted with three other adults who had about as much control of their emotions as I had of mine. There wasn't a dry eye in the house. As my eyes met theirs, I laughed and they didn't hesitate to join me. The release was as palpable as the air released from a balloon burst with a pin. I was swamped by the hugs of three very dear people.

Jane left Durlwood at seven. Having seen her interaction with Dad, I realised when Jane had told me that Dad had treated her better than her own father had, she was being honest about the bond of their relationship. Dad had raised two sons on his own without the family female influence of mother or daughter. We had a wonderful housekeeper when I was a child through to when I left home, Martha Breen, but she was not the same as family. Martha had left several years before to go and live with elderly relatives, but that female influence seemed now to come from an even closer connection between Dad and Jane. They truly behaved like father and daughter. It was a joy to behold.

All through that evening, I couldn't help having my suspicions that they were up to something. It wasn't anything that I'd seen, their relationship and behaviour were new to me so I had no pattern to judge them by, but there was something that I detected, perhaps with a sixth sense, about a scheme that was being hatched.

We spent most of the rest of the evening watching a movie, Dad, Suzanna and I. I was enjoying their company, especially when Suzanna sat herself right next to me on the sofa, but I was slightly distracted by an answer to a question I'd asked Suzanna earlier in the evening, before we started the film.

In the general chat, I asked Suzanna, "What's this training course you're doing?"

"The training course? Oh, it's related to my university degree in psychology. I needed to spend some time with a group that operates in this area, so your dad let me stay here as long as I needed to."

The information she gave was interesting, but very sparse, so I pressed a little further.

"When does the course finish?" I casually asked, trying not to add too much weight to my query.

"Last week," she said. "Do you want tea?"

She got up from where she was sitting and in doing so terminated my line of questioning. I couldn't help thinking it was deliberate. While watching the film I was wondering why, if she'd finished her course the previous week, was she still at Durlwood?

CHAPTER 24

With Christmas Eve only a few days away, I was revelling in the atmosphere and taking every opportunity to keep busy by helping out where I could. Much to my great pleasure, Suzanna was still at Durlwood. Jane came to visit a couple more times, once while Dad was there, although it was a little obvious that she was using his presence as an excuse to call with the children. The second time, it was quite clear that she came to see me, again with the children. After chatting with her and Suzanna for a while, I excused myself, Andrew and Alice, so that we could go out into the garden to the swing that I'd used as a child, which they obviously wanted to play on. When I asked if it was okay, Jane waved me off shouting that the children were only using me to power the swing.

It was a bright day, but cold in the shade. Where the sun was out, the warmth was very welcome, even if it was only weak and passing, but the landscape looked beautiful as the naked trees allowed a more distant view across the undulating farming landscape. The children laughed and played, while their conversation was predominantly about what Santa Claus would bring, only punctuated by calls for another push to go even higher on the swing. We finally returned to the house, about three-quarters-of-an-hour later, at the call of Suzanna indicating that lunch was ready.

I goaded the children into a race to see who could get to the door first and deliberately let them both beat me, as I pretended to keep tripping up. They knew that I was pretending and enjoyed the fun and I knew that they knew I was pretending and enjoyed their delight in the fact. They were such lovely children that I was happy to spend time with them; children can be so accepting and I felt that lump in my throat when they so naturally called me Uncle Andy, at the obvious instruction of their mother.

When Andrew and Alice were otherwise occupied for a few minutes, I asked Jane whether Carl knew that they had all met me.

"He knows," she said, in a quite matter of fact way, accompanied with a smile that said, 'leave it to me, I have it all in hand.' Who was I to doubt this lady who had shown me such generosity. Her confidence was more than a comfort and I was very willing to trust her.

It was on that day that I had my second encounter with Carl. Although it was brief and not in person, nevertheless I was left in no doubt that I was not very welcome.

While I was sat talking to Jane over lunch, the telephone rang. Up to that point I'd meticulously avoided answering it, but Suzanna was dealing with the food and asked me to pick up the call. Instinctively following her instruction I reached for the receiver and said hello before realising what I'd done. The stony silence at the other end was not what I expected, until I realised that it was Carl. He possibly didn't expect to hear me answer either. He was very direct; quite abrupt in his manner.

"Could I speak to my wife please?"

"Yes, certainly," I answered, flustered at the awkwardness of the situation and the apparent coldness in his voice. I handed the receiver to Jane, simply informing her that it was Carl. She was obviously not going to let his conflict with me be allowed to spill over to her, or anyone else, for that matter. Chatting away to Carl with total ease, regardless of the fact that I was within hearing distance, made me see she was unfazed by the whole affair.

When Jane ended the call she looked at me and smiled, reached across the table and patted my forearm.

"Don't give up kiddo, all will be well."

Suzanna gave me a knowing look that I knew should not be questioned, so I let it go. It was unsettling. I didn't expect to run into open arms when I returned home, but having come so far and having found such a reception from people, I just hoped that I could come to some understanding with Carl that would at least give Dad and Jane some comfort.

A couple of days later both Dad and I were at home, Suzanna having gone out to some appointment. Feeling at a loose end, I decided to wash Dad's car. Through the winter months the vehicles seemed to need washing every couple of days from the muddy country roads that led from the town out to Durlwood. Dad usually went to the car wash, but I wanted to make myself useful, so I put my hand to the plough. I moved his car out of the stable block parking bay and set to with the sponge and bucket. I had just finished lathering it over when I heard a car coming along the driveway, the gravel was always an early warning system that was used to great effect when I was a mischievous youngster. I thought it was Suzanna coming back. I quickly took hold of the hose pipe and waited for the approaching vehicle to emerge between the courtyard gates on its way to loop around the Christmas tree in the centre. At just the right moment I shot a jet of water toward the oncoming vehicle, in order to douse the windscreen, but to my horror it wasn't Suzanna. I clearly saw Carl's face flinch at the oncoming jet before the water obscured the view and then the wipers immediately dealt with the splash. I felt such a fool and spun around to rinse Dad's car, pretending that my surprise attack was a total accident.

Carl stopped at the entrance, got out and headed straight up the steps to the front door without looking back. Meanwhile, I tried to put the courtyard Christmas tree between myself and him to avoid any unnecessary contact.

He was obviously aware that I was outside, which possibly made his visit more comfortable. I deliberately prolonged the job of car washing, so that I wouldn't have to go inside to meet him. Dad's car was spotless by the time Carl emerged from the house. I was cold, very cold.

I pretended not to notice at first, but couldn't resist a glance across. Carl was walking around the back of his car to get to the driver's side ready to leave. He caught my glance as I looked across. He stopped for a moment, nodded in acknowledgement, which I returned, then continued on his way.

I followed his car as he completed the turn around the courtyard and disappeared down the driveway. Looking back to the house, I saw Dad taking note of the whole event. He raised his hand and waved to me.

"I think that car is clean enough. Any more and you'll wear through the paintwork, unless you freeze over first."

I smiled and waved back at him, knowing that the only person I was fooling was myself, so I packed away the gear and went back indoors to warm up.

On the Thursday evening, the day before Christmas Eve, I was enjoying the company of Suzanna. We were sat playing a game of chess in the lounge when Dad arrived home from work. He announced that we were going out to eat and he'd booked a table at his favourite restaurant. Under his instruction, we were jokingly ordered to put on our glad rags and prepare to leave at nineteen hundred hours precisely.

Suzanna, always displaying a good sense of humour asked, "Exactly what time is that?"

As quick as a flash Dad said, "That's on time for the men and typically late for the ladies." I found it rather funny. Suzanna threw a cushion at him in mock disgust declaring that, "men were generally uglier and needed less time to get ready, having given up hope of improvement."

The chess game was immediately terminated by Suzanna's deliberate sabotage as she tipped the board, pieces and all, into my lap. She was gone, leaving Dad laughing at me trying to gather the pieces and restore them to their rightful place.

I'd collected a few items of clothing since first returning home, but found my desire to own mountains of such insignificant things was gone. It had been replaced with gratefulness for the few things I had. Still, I made the effort for the evening by raiding Dad's wardrobe for a tie.

At seven, Dad and I were waiting in the hallway for Suzanna. Dad shouted up to encourage her to get a move on and I joined in, much to his amusement, by reminding her that the ladies are usually last. The wait was well worth it. When she walked out onto the landing and paused at the balcony rail, interrupting my flow of conversation with Dad, she looked a picture. We both watched as Suzanna elegantly swept across the landing in her long gown and then started to descend the stairs. She looked stunning, in an elegant strapless black evening dress that perfectly showed off her slim frame. If my mouth didn't drop open it was simply because my father was there to restrain such a display. When she reached the hallway she twirled around.

"Just a little something I threw on. Will I do?"

"You look..."

I started, but stopped, feeling conscious of Dad behind me, close at my shoulder.

"Gorgeous, Suzanna."

He finished my compliment for me.

"Why thank you, kind sirs," she said, as she flamboyantly curtsied.

I felt Dad nudge me from behind and glanced back to see what he wanted, only to be greeted with raised eyebrows that informed me that I was missing something.

"A lady needs the arm of a gentleman to escort her," he whispered.

"Oh! Please allow me," I spluttered. Moving to Suzanna's side, I offered my arm as I led her out through the door, held open by Dad, to the waiting taxi.

The conversation on the journey to the restaurant was light and I was still mesmerised by Suzanna's beauty. No matter how I tried to distract myself, I couldn't help feeling like I was staring at her all the time, not that she seemed to mind.

The taxi finally drew up at the entrance to a lovely building. The windows along the front looked out over to the cathedral grounds and diners could eat while taking in the view across the park to the magnificent building. As we disembarked from the vehicle, Dad paid the fare. Suzanna didn't hesitate to take my arm again and I was not going to object for a moment.

When Dad was done, we turned to go in through the main entrance where we were greeted in the lobby by the house manager.

"Good evening, Mr Numan. Welcome to you and your guests. Everything is ready and your other guests are already here and seated at the table, sir."

Dad quickly glanced back, catching Suzanna's eye and then mine. That was the moment that alarm bells began to ring in my head, just as clearly as the bells hung in the cathedral tower opposite. I hadn't even questioned whether we were going out alone that evening, but suddenly the sixth sense that had told me that Dad and Jane had something up their sleeves, put the pieces of the jigsaw together. I was suddenly more than a little concerned.

I hesitated and Suzanna noticed the hiccup in my step. She hung on to my arm as if to make sure I didn't try to turn and leave. She squeezed tighter and, leaning very close to my ear, whispered, "Smile, look happy and trust me. Oh and by the way, you look fabulous too."

I quickly turned to look at her, but she hadn't turned away and our cheeks brushed together. There was something so innocent, yet so intimate, at that second. That single connection confirmed in my mind that I was more deeply involved with this delightful lady than I'd ever dared imagine possible. I was falling for her, head over heels. She smiled at the accidental touch, but I realised from her comment that it was not just Dad and Jane who were orchestrating events that evening, it was Suzanna too.

I was suddenly presented with a choice that I had to make there and then. As a young man I took a chance and it worked out badly, but this time I decided to make a choice. I chose to trust the three people who had so accepted me that I couldn't believe that they were intent on causing any harm. I returned Suzanna's smile and nodded that I was with her and trusted her.

Dad turned again to look at us both, smiled, and followed the house manager through into the restaurant, with Suzanna and I following close behind.

It was with a certain amount of relief that I saw that the children, Andrew and Alice, were present at the table. Being in a public place with the children there, my nervousness eased and I took comfort from the fact that most of those present had been very good to me. Nevertheless, I was apprehensive about Carl. The last time we met, at close quarters, he had knocked me to the floor and I didn't fancy a repeat of that in the middle of a restaurant. Neither of our subsequent encounters had set me any more at ease.

Carl was seated at the furthest end of the table with Jane on one side and the children on the other. To my great relief the most charming thing happened before we had a chance to greet each other. Little Alice leapt from her chair shouting at full volume, "Uncle Andy, I brought Tigger to see you!" I crouched down to meet her as she ran straight into my arms without any apology for her open gesture of affection. Waving the stuffed toy above her head, she had instantly stolen the hearts of the whole restaurant, and will, forevermore, have my profound thanks for her timely and wonderful breaking of the ice.

"Wow, what a fabulous Tigger, Alice!"

"Yes and I've got Winnie the Pooh and Eeyore at home," she added, so that everybody in the room could hear and enjoy. Noticing the laughs of approval from tables surrounding us, I looked up to see all my family surveying the scene with delight and caught the gaze of Carl. He acknowledged me with a nod then broke the look to greet Dad and Suzanna. That nod was enough at that moment, it caused me to hope.

I was seated at the end of the table, opposite Carl, with Suzanna between myself and Jane. Dad sat between me and the children. Leaning across Suzanna, Jane smiled at me and mischievously said, "Andy, how lovely to see you again." I pulled a face at her that said I knew she was up to something. She jokingly stuck out her tongue, which the children saw, causing them to laugh beneath the conversation between Carl and Dad. Jane put her hand up to her face to hide her gesture from Carl, but not from Suzanna and myself, and stuck her tongue out again at the children, which caused even more laughter. Carl smiled and glanced across at Jane, momentarily stopping at me en route. Jane displayed the most innocent look that denied any knowledge of what was happening. I laughed at her attempt to disguise the cause of the laughter and when she looked back at me I silently mouthed the words, 'Thank you', Her gaze was held long enough and her smile was warm enough, to indicate she understood my meaning.

I was suddenly aware that Suzanna was taking note of the whole thing. As I took the napkin from the table to place over my lap, she took hold of my hand, out of sight of the others and squeezed it. She didn't let go, as you would in a momentary gesture. I was in no hurry to let go either, so we remained hand in hand until interrupted by the waiter who came to take our order.

Jane and Suzanna gave their requests and satisfied the children's requirements. Carl indicated for Dad to go next. During this time I was studying the menu, partly using it as a reason to keep from prolonged eye contact with Carl. I presumed that once Dad had given his order, I would be next, but before I could make my choice, Carl got there first.

"Andy."

I looked up and connected with his stare, slightly startled that he was addressing me so directly. Apparently everyone else was taken unawares as well and had all turned to focus on Carl to see what was coming next.

"I can particularly recommend the smoked venison starter and for the main course, the Devon lamb is very good."

I closed my menu, quickly glancing around at the others who had all turned their attention to me. They looked like a crowd watching slow motion play at a tennis match.

"Thank you, Carl." I looked at the waiter, who was anticipating my instruction. "In that case, I would like to take my brother's recommendation please."

"Very good, sir."

The waiter was totally unaware of the magnitude, in my eyes, of what had just happened, but it didn't escape the notice of everyone except the children at our table.

The attention returned to Carl, I locked eyes with him again, as the waiter asked for his choice. He didn't break away from my stare to look at the waiter, who was standing at the ready with pen in hand.

"I would like to have the same as my brother, please." He smiled and nodded at me, then immediately broke his gaze to turn his attention to the children. Meanwhile the waiter glanced

313

back and forth trying to understand what the big deal was with the 'brother' thing. The rest of us just looked at one another and, if they were thinking what I was thinking, all of us breathed a sigh of relief as some of the tension left the table.

I enjoyed the meal very much and the children added a lot of focus to the proceedings, their excitement at the proximity of Christmas greatly influencing the atmosphere.

Part way through the evening, I started to become conscious that every time someone addressed me, I was breaking my gaze away from Suzanna in order to respond. Whether it was noticeable to anyone else, I couldn't tell at the time, but they all made sure, a few months later, that I understood how obvious I had been about my affection for her. In truth, I had never been in the company of someone that I considered to be so beautiful, both inside and out. To my eyes she seemed perfect.

When the meal was over, we all retired to the lounge for coffee. As we were seated I noticed, whether by design or not, that Carl ended up sitting next to me. We didn't speak directly for the rest of the hour or so that we were in the restaurant, but it was comforting to know that he hadn't knocked me to the floor and didn't appear inclined to do so.

Finally the house manager gave notice that our taxis had arrived and the slow procession made its way to the entrance. Various goodbyes and embraces were enacted until the only move left was for Carl and me to part company. I stood up after saying goodbye to Andrew, Alice and Tigger and was greeted with Carl's outstretched hand. After a moment's hesitation, because the gesture was unexpected, I reciprocated. His handshake was firm, business like, but certainly not hostile. I smiled at him, but refrained from saying anything, partly because I could feel the emotion welling up again. It was not the time for such a display. It was more than I could have asked for, simply acknowledging each other.

There followed one of those moments when all has been said and done and no one is sure of the next move, but Jane, beautifully, and delicately, came to the rescue again. Linking arms with Carl, she pulled in very close to him, displaying the emotion that flows between two people who are deeply in love with each other.

"I love you, Mr Numan, but I'm tired, our children are tired and we want you to take us home." He kissed her in response and smiled.

"Come on, children; let's take mummy home, shall we?"

We filed out to the waiting taxis parked at the curb, one behind the other and separated into the two groups in which we'd arrived. Carl and I were the last to get into our respective vehicles, both of us paused a moment as we did. I waved at him. He responded likewise. I thought I noticed a hesitation in him, as though he wanted to say something, but he looked away, got into the waiting vehicle, and was gone.

EPILOGUE

It would be wrong to assume that my story, our story, ends very neatly, so that we all lived happily ever after. Rebuilding relationships is not an easy task. The past has an ugly habit of raising itself at the most inappropriate times.

That handshake with Carl, on the day before Christmas Eve, was, without any doubt in my mind, the beginning of something new between us. It still took a long time before we were truly comfortable in each other's presence, without others around to create a distraction. The role played by Jane and the children was pivotal in the beginning of our reconciliation. It might have taken much longer without the gentle, subtle, determination of that remarkable woman. Her work didn't end at the handshake either. She has tirelessly helped to resolve ongoing difficulties, to the point that Carl and I actually enjoy each other's company once again, at least for limited lengths of time. I'm sure that our relationship will continue to strengthen over the time to come, but I will never be able to repay the kindness that Jane has unconditionally shown.

Suzanna? We took our time working through our relationship, what it meant, how deep it was and whether the emotion of my homecoming was clouding our rational decision making. In fact, most of the time was really about me adapting back to a life at home, re-engaging with some of the people who I had known earlier in my life. However, after due consideration, I came to the conclusion that she was the most perfect woman I had ever, or was ever, likely to meet. So, I asked her to marry me. I was blown away when she so enthusiastically said 'yes.' It was she who first spoke my name when I returned home and it was she who was, and continues to be, the patient listening ear that has helped me to find my place in the world again. I love her with all my heart and treasure the love she gives in return.

As for the villains of my story, I don't know what's become of them, nor do I care to find out. It wouldn't have been my choice to follow the path that I trod, much of that road was travelled simply by chance rather than deliberate choice, but if that was the cost I had to pay to gain the immense treasure I've found in my family, then, as hard as it was, it has been paid. I don't ever wish to go back to a single moment of my past. What has happened, has gone, only the future still remains.

Without doubt, the biggest hero in my story, by a mile, has to be Dad. Despite the pain and anguish I caused him, he has always remained true to himself and faithful to me, his son. It would have been, in the eyes of some, a far easier option to cut me off as a man without hope, but not for him. He gave me all that I had and when I rejected it, and him, he refused to reject me. From being caught in feelings of inadequacy, caught in pride and arrogance, I was caught by my Father who desperately wanted the opportunity to rescue the son he thought he had lost forever. He is, and always will be, my Father, whom I most profoundly love, and thank.